CHARBONNEAU'S GOLD

CHARBONNEAU'S GOLD

A Lewis & Clark Story

RITA CLEARY

SAGEBRUSH
Large Print Westerns

First published in Great Britain by ISIS Publishing Ltd.
First published in the United States by Five Star

Published in Large Print 2010 by ISIS Publishing Ltd.,
7 Centremead, Osney Mead, Oxford OX2 0ES
by arrangement with
Golden West Literary Agency

British Library Cataloguing in Publication Data
Cleary, Rita, 1941–
    Charbonneau's gold. - - (A Lewis & Clark story)
    1. Lewis & Clark Expedition (1804–1806) - -
    Fiction.
    2. Explorers - - West (U.S.) - - Fiction.
    3. Frontier and pioneer life - - West (U.S.) - -
    Fiction.
    4. West (U.S.) - - Discovery and exploration - -
    Fiction.
    5. Western stories.
    6. Large type books.
    I. Title II. Series
    813.5'4–dc22

ISBN 978–0–7531–8520–9 (hb)

Printed and bound in Great Britain by
T. J. International Ltd., Padstow, Cornwall

Introduction

In *Charbonneau's Gold*, the Lewis and Clark Expedition of 1804–1806 pursues the most dangerous leg of the expedition. The perils were many: geographic, cultural, and political. Danger lurked in the expanse of the plains, the absence of natives, the waterfalls and enervating portage, the misleading river, the height and reach of the mountains, and the untamed Columbia River. These same difficulties must have evoked shock and fear, especially for the less educated members of the Corps of Discovery.

The appearance and culture of the Columbia River tribes were totally alien. Think of snatching a tough, headstrong, illiterate teen or a hard-bitten pirate smuggler out of the familiar and shoving him into a world of creatures that modern science fiction might produce. In today's terms, that is what happened to John Collins, François Labiche, and the other members of the corps. What would their reactions have been? Wonder? Violence? Disgust? Fear?

The political climate, too, was alien. Spanish records show British forts in the northern Missouri River Basin, i.e. the present states of Minnesota, North and South Dakota. The present states of Utah, Nevada, and California were Spanish. Arizona, New Mexico, and Texas were part of Mexico, i.e. also Spanish. The northwest states of Idaho, Oregon, and Washington beyond the Rocky Mountains were contended by Britain and Russia and were never part of Louisiana.

Both Spain and Britain restricted the fur trade by license or political charter. They opened it only to those in political favor, and used their influence with the tribes to exclude all competition. They resisted any American incursion. So the perils for Lewis and Clark were political as well as cultural and geographic. The expedition was venturing outside the proper bounds of the purchased territory, extending the influence of the infant United States and of free trade, making possible our country as we know it today. The European colonial powers did not want Lewis and Clark to succeed.

Add to this brew Toussaint Charbonneau. He was distinct from any other member of the expedition. He was from Montreal, French on both his father's and mother's side, not part Indian like all other members with French names. Charbonneau was employed by the British North West Company. What kind of persuasions would have convinced him to defect to the American cause? That is not recorded in the expedition journals. The historical record has many blanks that leave space for the fiction writer to fill. As luck would have it, Charbonneau brought his wife, Sacagawea, and their newborn child, certainly a cause for jealousy. He was accorded special privileges and he joined the expedition one year late, after friendships and loyalties had matured. Finally, Charbonneau had to earn his living. In 1805, employment with Lewis and Clark was risky, but it promised greater gain for his labor than the tightly controlled Spanish or British systems of trade.

The captains certainly would have dismissed any personal thought of monetary gain resulting from their discoveries, but other members of the expedition, especially those free agents like Charbonneau, and the enlistees, too, would not have overlooked opportunity. Nor would they have entered their more questionable dealings into the official record. In 1805, as today, the profit motive was alive and well. Thus, *Charbonneau's Gold*.

Rita Cleary
Oyster Bay, New York

CHAPTER
ONE

John Collins bristled with annoyance. For the last month, since Toussaint Charbonneau had come to live at Fort Mandan, he'd made a pest of himself. He was living with three wives in the shelter he'd built outside the stockade at Fort Mandan, not ten feet from the sleeping quarters of Sergeant Pryor's mess, where Collins and his bunkmates slept. Three wives did not make for a peaceful household. Loud public arguments, constant bickering, and the creaks of the conjugal bed interrupted Collins's sleep. During the day, when Charbonneau was absent, two of his wives tried to peddle their dubious charms to the lustier members of the expedition. A knife, a lick of whiskey, would buy a quick lay in the buffalo robes. The tall wife flirted constantly with any man with yellow hair. She was vulgar and open even within sight of her husband and Captains Lewis and Clark. She liked Collins. He was tall and blond. But Collins had a faithful wife with long, silken, ebony tresses in the Mandan village, and rejected her advances. She chased him harder, and for this Charbonneau did not love him.

Now one wife had disappeared, and Charbonneau drove a scruffy horse and the other two before him with a willow switch no less gently than he drove his horses. They scrambled down from the hills on the steep switchback trail. Charbonneau was singing loudly. He was a square man, and his voice reverberated from out of a massive black beard and massive chest that dominated his boxy torso. He bounced along on stubby legs and flapping feet. His arms, too, were short but attached by muscled biceps to powerful shoulders. He was a trapper, used to hauling heavy hides and the iron tools of his trade, used to chopping through ice and wood.

Collins and Georges Drouillard were coming home from hunting, nearer the fort, below Charbonneau on the narrow trail, when a shower of rocks tumbled down from above. Collins stopped his horse, and bellowed: "You, there, you're not alone on the trail! I've a heavily loaded animal." There was no response and the tumult above advanced without a pause. Collins's blue eyes contracted to menacing points, his mouth to a concave frown. At the next switchback, he stopped, lifted his rifle, and blasted: "There's folks here, on the trail below you! Slow your pace." He spread his long legs athwart the trail, cocked his rifle, and then yelled: "Halt or I shoot!"

With his two women and two horses, Charbonneau rounded the switchback and came into view. He stopped abruptly when he saw Collins, shoved a dirty clay pipe between yellow teeth, and responded in fluid French: "*Fe n'ai rien fait, m'sieur.*"

"Damn you, speak English." Collins put up his rifle. "If you come with furs for the trader, you're on the

2

wrong trail. He's at the village, not the fort." The village was Matootonha, trading center of the Mandan nation. The fort was several miles from the village. It was a tight triangular structure, shelter to the Corps of Discovery, winter home to Captains Lewis and Clark, the scout, Georges Drouillard, Private John Collins, and about thirty other members of the American expedition to the Pacific. They were preparing to leave as soon as the ice broke in the river. Some would return downriver to St. Louis while others would proceed west to the Pacific Ocean.

Collins's grimace hardened. "Heney's already acquired his allotment of pelts. You're too late." Alexander Heney was the British trader at Matootonha village.

Charbonneau tamped tobacco into the bowl of his pipe. "Not Heney. I come to see American traders. If they do not buy, then I take my pelts to the trader who will arrive at Awatixa from the northern villages tomorrow or the next. He is rich." Charbonneau spoke French, ignored Collins, and addressed Georges Drouillard.

Drouillard had a French father and a Shawnee mother. He was tall, dark, with perceptive, fiery black eyes. He lifted his chin and fired back in perfect French. "We Americans are explorers, not traders. We don't want your furs."

"You are wrong, *m'sieur*. The *patron* will buy everything I bring in." Charbonneau meant Deschamps, leader of the hired boatmen who had accompanied Lewis and Clark to the Mandan village and would return to St. Louis with the spring flood. William Clark

3

had just paid Deschamps for the services of the boatmen.

"So Deschamps is the gainer," Collins said, snickering, knowing Deschamps had a nose for profit. He sniffed the Frenchman's intentions with the acuity of a bloodhound. Deschamps would not pay his boatmen, not yet. He would use the money to buy furs and use his boatmen to transport the furs to St. Louis. There he would reap a healthy profit — if they did not drown, if they escaped the clutches of the thieving Sioux, if they still possessed the precious furs when they arrived at the post downriver. Only after selling the furs would Deschamps pay his men and pocket the difference.

Collins grinned. He had an appealing smile that accentuated laughing, mischievous, Irish blue eyes and youthful enthusiasm. He would have done the same in the Frenchman's place, like others, like his mentor and friend, the scout, Drouillard. It was the Yankee way — scratch a profit from a dung heap if you can and turn it to advantage. It meant a better life for the common man but it meant competition for the Hudson's Bay and the North West Companies that dominated the lucrative fur trade on the upper Missouri. It meant strained relations with British factors who controlled the trading posts. It meant luring the Indians away from their accustomed markets with better guns, better whiskey, and better prices. Just one year after the Americans had acquired Louisiana Territory, they were on the scene. They were free agents — Drouillard, Corporal Warfington, and this *Patron* Deschamps who the Indians called the spider because his devious schemes resembled a greedy web-weaver. Collins and others had made the dangerous journey with Lewis and Clark because they sniffed a profit. Soon news of new buyers would race like a prairie fire through every tribe that inhabited the rivers and each would send a delegation to the Mandans to trade.

Collins blocked the trail while Drouillard inquired: "This new trader who comes, what's he called?"

Charbonneau exhaled a stream of black smoke before answering. "Bunch. He comes to Matootonha from Fort Assiniboin in the north, but he has not yet arrived. Me, I will deal with Deschamps who works for the man, Lewis, who bears the name of my sainted king." He snapped oily syllables with rapid-fire precision. Charbonneau was trying to ingratiate himself, to insure the good will of the Americans.

Drouillard snickered. Lewis was not a French name. It was Welsh, no more French than Shawnee or Delaware. But Toussaint Charbonneau, the stubborn, French hunter and trapper, preferred to deal with Deschamps because Deschamps had been paid in gold. Collins had glimpsed the guineas one evening when he served Captain Lewis his dinner. The room had been dark, illuminated by a single candle and a crackling fire. The sun did not linger long in the winter in the northern latitudes and the guineas reflected the soft light like tiny stars. They were unmistakable. Lewis had swept them swiftly into a leather purse as soon as he saw Collins enter, but Collins had recognized the tempting glint and *clink* of the metal. They were gold. He had no doubt.

He had told the scout, Georges Drouillard, and the gambler, François Labiche, what he had seen. Labiche had taken out his dice, blown on them, and wiped them clean with his kerchief. "We wait, Johnny, for the day of reckoning when they grow heavy in the man's pockets."

Now Charbonneau waited to pass. He was disagreeable and stubborn. He had a reputation for greed, but he was well known for the quality of his pelts. He kept his word and, for this, the Indians respected him.

Collins flattened himself against his tired horse's shoulder to make space on the narrow trail for the Frenchman, his horse, and two women to pass. The first swayed her hips, brazenly brushing against Collins. Instantly Charbonneau's face ignited with anger, and he smacked her hard across the buttocks with the willow switch. The second was shorter and carried a baby in a cradleboard on her back, and Charbonneau cracked his whip a second time. She tripped innocently and started to fall. Collins dropped his rifle and, with a stroke of his arm, broke her fall. He lifted her with her baby easily and set her down gently on solid ground. The baby awakened and started to cry, and she removed the cradleboard and began to unlace the child gently from his bindings. Charbonneau would have none of it and he shouted angrily and raised the switch a third time. The mother turned defiantly to shield the child.

Collins did not think. He whirled on the Frenchman as the switch descended, caught it in the palm of his hand, wrenched it free, and, with a vicious swipe, laced Charbonneau across his black-bearded cheeks. The blow split hair and drew blood.

Charbonneau's bull's head withdrew instantly into his massive shoulders. Every muscle of his frame contracted. Suddenly he flicked a hand.

The motion was slight, but Collins saw the tomahawk. He raised the switch and swung again. It struck the tomahawk and broke.

"Stop it both of you." Georges Drouillard slammed the stock of his rifle into Collins's arm, then cocked his rifle and leveled the weapon at Charbonneau. Charbonneau froze, letting his tomahawk fall. Drouillard tossed the broken switch far into the trees, picked up the tomahawk, and gushed a torrent of rapid-fire French that Collins did not understand.

Charbonneau spat, bit down on his pipe, cursed through a veil of exhaled smoke, and followed his women who had fled in fear down the steep trail.

When they had disappeared from sight, Drouillard put up his rifle.

"What did you tell him?" Collins asked. His disgust had condensed to white-hot anger.

"That we will return his tomahawk at Fort Mandan and that he should manage his women and babe with greater care than he gives his horse. But you, *mon ami*, why do you act the fool always for a woman? That one is ugly. Word has it he won her in a game of dice because your friend, Labiche, would not raise the bid."

Collins protested: "She's a mother. She deserves respect."

"Foolish Irish talk. She's a second wife. He cannot treat the second better than the first or there would be war in the household. The tall one is a tramp, a *putin* we say in French, not worth the pebble under your foot. She would couple with a rattlesnake if he didn't herd her with the whip. I don't envy him the conduct of his wives." Drouillard turned a piercing gaze on Collins. "You're handsome and women admire you. Be careful. Be prudent. There walks a lecherous woman and a jealous man." He handed the tomahawk to Collins, and added with a backward glance: "Don't forget. Return it or wait for retribution."

They straggled down to the fort, delivered the meat to the cooks, and set the animal out with the pony herd to graze. As they returned, by the gates of the fort, they came upon Charbonneau's wives huddled outside the lodge of *Patron* Baptiste Deschamps. It had begun to snow. The feathery flakes settled softly on the dark fur of the women's clothing. Sounds of prolonged haggling echoed from inside the lodge.

Collins stopped and stared at the second wife who sheltered her infant under her own fur cape. "How long have you been here?" He said it in English.

Drouillard stepped up behind him and squeezed his arm. "She speaks Hidatsa. Leave them. This is the Indian way. The men kill and fight and hunt. The women obey and work and wait, except for the tall one. He would do well to cast her out and save himself the tools and beads he brings to keep her happy." He

8

flicked a sidelong glance at Collins. "It's why Indian women love white men . . . for the baubles they bring."

Collins protested vehemently: "Laughing Water loves me more than my presents." Laughing Water was Collins's Mandan wife.

"Does she? Does her brother love you because you bring powder and lead for the buffalo hunt? Does her grandmother? Be reasonable, *mon bon ami*. Today she loves you. And tomorrow . . . when you are old and poor and have nothing to offer?" He let the question hang, shrugged, and pulled Collins away. "You embarrass the mother with your glaring. Give her the tomahawk you took from her husband."

Collins drew Charbonneau's weapon from his belt and gave it to the mother. Her soft brown eyes glanced up at him from a round, smiling face. For one so small, a midget to his towering six feet, she was not afraid.

Drouillard drew him aside. "Come. It's better you don't see Charbonneau and he does not see you. You would have to defend yourself, and Charbonneau is fierce with the 'hawk." He added casually: "The woman will say she found it."

They walked away, but thoughts of the tiny mother and her bully man pursued John Collins. She seemed fragile as an eggshell and at the same time dense and hard as quartz.

Days passed. Toussaint Charbonneau spent increasing time away from his wives with *Patron* Deschamps and the French-speaking boatmen. They were men much like himself: strong-willed, stubborn, of tough sinew and thick bone. They spoke a hybrid French, spiced with colorful phrases of Indian and English. Their French was better than the hackneyed croak of the North West and Hudson's Bay traders and more exact than the Americans' slur. The boatmen came from St. Louis and St. Charles, places whose names rang with music of the old Gallic songs Charbonneau had heard as a boy at his French mother's knee in Montreal, songs he still sang during lonely hours trapping. They were stories of knights and ladies, jousts and battles, and the saintly and powerful kings of France. They kept him company along with his pipe, his tobacco, and a medicine pouch that he kept tucked under his shirt, beneath the wide red sash that circled his waist. He never parted with the pouch even when he coupled with a wife. It contained what he called his treasure.

CHAPTER
TWO

It was Drouillard, the half-Shawnee scout, who discovered the contents of Charbonneau's pouch and the background of his second wife, the short one and mother of his baby. "She's Shoshone, from a tribe that lives far to the west in the shadow of the Shining Mountains. She's very young. She was a captive slave and speaks Shoshone. Maybe she's worth a small price to the captains," he said to Collins with a lick of tongue and wink of eye, and left to go hunting.

Collins, an illiterate private, mentioned the woman to his sergeant, Nathaniel Pryor, as an afterthought.

Pryor snorted: "The Frenchman is a pimp. Sells the services of the mother of his child!" But he sniffed a possibility. "Who are the Shoshones? Do they live on our route?"

"I don't know, sir. I didn't think it important."

Pryor consulted *Patron* Deschamps who communicated with Toussaint Charbonneau. Deschamps was not one to forego a profit. He feared the dissolution of his business with Charbonneau, patted his paunch smugly, and replied: "I ask Charbonneau and tell the captain myself."

It was true. The woman was Shoshone, and the Shoshones lived in the western mountains where the expedition had to pass. Deschamps, the tough *patron* of the boatmen, approached William Clark and Meriwether Lewis with hat in hand. Firelight outlined the silhouettes of three men in the dark officers' quarters: a stone-faced Clark, an irritable Lewis, and the officious New Englander, Sergeant John Ordway. Lewis leaned intently over a parchment map at a rough table in front of a blazing hearth. Clark stood behind him, and Sergeant John Ordway stood rigidly to one side. Two candles dripped oily wax and barely illuminated the shadowy map. The captains' expressions remained darkened, but they stiffened abruptly at the interruption and listened closely to what Deschamps had to say.

"The woman speaks Shoshone, *mes capitaines*. I tell you because I want to insure the success of your exploration, just as you desire the safe homecoming of me and my men. I have credited you, sirs, your fairness and your generosity, and so I have permitted my men some added recompense." He stopped, eyed the captains apprehensively, arched his fat neck, and drummed his fingers on his ample girth. His choice of words carefully omitted his own self-interest but not his self-importance. He spoke pompously, like a haughty aristocrat. "My men have traded for a few pelts with this man, Charbonneau. He is difficult, fickle as a handsome woman. He does not associate with English or easily befriend his own countrymen. I have explained to him that you are no English, that your country is the enemy of England that banished France and our beloved General Montcalm . . . God rest his soul . . . from our Plains of Abraham at *la grande ville de Quebec.* You, *mon capitaine* Lewis, you speak his language, like me. Speak to him in French and he will help you. His wife will help you, too . . . the little one. I can persuade him to offer her services to aid in your grand voyage."

It seemed an endless harangue. Meriwether Lewis lost his patience. "Are you telling me, Deschamps, that we should take a woman with us to the Pacific?" He answered his own question. "One woman with thirty men spells disaster." He paused, shaking his shaggy head — President Jefferson would have been appalled. He stated flatly: "We don't need the woman's services."

"Not the services you think, *mon capitaine.*" Deschamps was quick to correct the false impression. "I do not recommend his tall wife, the tramp. But the woman with the babe is worthy. She is short and dumpy. She will not be the object of men's lust. She can translate and interpret Shoshone. There is no other here, man or woman, who can do the same. She will communicate with the natives of the Shining Mountains. She will tell them that you come in peace."

"And how will she do that?" Meriwether Lewis rolled up the map and tapped a fingernail restlessly on the splintered surface of the table. His sharp blue eyes nailed Deschamps. "How much will you gain, Deschamps, in your dealings with Charbonneau? What consideration has he allowed you for delivering this message?"

Deschamps never blinked. He sucked in his paunch and raised his eyes to meet Lewis's flinty glare. "I tell you true, *mon capitaine*. He pays me only a sum that will feed my family for one winter. I am a family man. If I . . . if *we* . . . return safely, I must repay my wife and children the cost of my absence. God has blessed me with many children, *mon capitaine*, little ones, three fine boys and five girls. They are many mouths. I confess to you that I have traded with this Charbonneau for a small profit, but then there is this *affaire de* Collins . . ."

There was a sharp snort from Meriwether Lewis who blurted: "What *affaire de* Collins?"

"On the trail, when they were coming to the fort, Collins struck Charbonneau across the face."

Silence. Lewis's frown etched angry lines in the contours of his patrician face. Collins was Clark's and Drouillard's man, not his.

Clark interrupted: "Hearsay . . . camp gossip . . . are you sure?" Collins's behavior had been exemplary all winter.

"Charbonneau will return with his wives to the Hidatsa village at Awatixa, *mon capitaine*. He vows he will never speak to Collins again." Deschamps did not add that Charbonneau would take the coveted beaver plews with him.

Silence loomed. Clark glared past Deschamps, out the door at the fog that blanketed the river bottoms like thick paste. Gradually he retrieved his thought and nodded. "Thank you, *patron*. You have been of help." Deschamps bowed and began to back away. When he was out of earshot, Clark snapped sarcastically: "And good luck, *patron*, in your commercial endeavors." He turned immediately to Ordway. "Get me Collins, Sergeant. Bring him here."

Collins answered the summons moments later, and William Clark launched his inquiry. "Private Collins, you have angered Toussaint Charbonneau. What has transpired and why?"

Collins shrank from Clark's grizzly frown, as Lewis demanded: "Speak, Collins. Do not trust rumor to assign you justice."

Collins blinked. He shifted nervously from one foot to another and cast a sheepish glance at his toes. Cold, calculating eyes stared back. He'd seen them before, the day he was whipped. He turned a foot inward, scraped the mud from the edge, and began hesitantly: "I was coming down the trail, sir, with Drouillard, at the steepest part. We led a horse with a heavy load of meat. Charbonneau was behind us. He whipped his horse and loosened the gravel that tumbled down on us and knocked the wife with the babe into me. He struck her with his whip. He was angry, sir, going to hit her a second time for no reason. I was angry, too. I grabbed his whip and used it . . . on him." The recitation gave him confidence. He was not sorry.

That Collins was impetuous, Clark already knew. He prodded: "Did you draw your knife?"

"He drew his tomahawk, sir."

There was a pause, then Meriwether Lewis added: "I trust you speak the truth, Private. Any indication to the contrary will cost you dearly. This man Charbonneau may be important to our enterprise. Treat him with deference and respect."

"Yes, sir." Collins bit his lip. The implication was clear to the young private. Discipline, in some corporal form, was a distinct possibility. He waited and proffered a slight self-defense before he left. He said: "Sir, Drouillard saw it all."

Lewis folded his hands and turned back to his map. The interview was over. Then Sergeant Ordway poked his hawk nose through the doorway and interrupted: "Charbonneau waits outside, sirs."

"Thank you, Sergeant. Bring a new candle and send Mister Charbonneau in. That is all, Collins."

The Frenchman shuffled disdainfully past the departing Collins and stood quietly before the captains. Meriwether Lewis pushed away from the table and scrutinized the stubby trader for a long moment through narrow slits of eyes. Finally he motioned. "*Assied-toi, monsieur.*" Charbonneau sat, croaked terse syllables, and chewed his pipe while Lewis fired questions in a rapid volley of imperfect French. He stopped occasionally to mutter the translation in the ear of William Clark.

It was a revealing interview. Charbonneau had been west. He knew of the Shining Mountains, but he stalled and obfuscated. He did not speak any native tongues of the mountain tribes, but his second wife, Sacagawea, the mother of his baby, had been born a Shoshone and spoke the language. She had forgotten some, not much.

16

The captains muttered between themselves, then Lewis turned and outlined possible terms of employment. "We need an interpreter to the western tribes, Mister Charbonneau. We are a military expedition. We enforce military discipline according to the Articles of War, both in the conduct of our daily lives and in our dealings with outsiders. If you choose to come with us, we must treat you no differently than the regular members of this corps. We expect good conduct." Lewis squinted and added: "We could tolerate one wife . . . the one who speaks Shoshone . . . but not two, and you must keep her strictly off limits to the men, both officers and enlisted men."

Charbonneau listened impassively. He muttered two words — "*On verra*." — pivoted abruptly, and left.

Clark looked inquisitively to Lewis who repeated: "He says we'll see." Lewis continued: "These young scoundrels don't learn discretion easily, Will. One year has passed, and still we cannot fully control their youthful impulses." He was referring to Collins.

"We chose them like we'd choose a 'coon hound, Meri," Clark responded, "for toughness and endurance. We didn't care if they growled. They'll wrestle each other, but they'll fight for us. And they all chase women like mice in a granary, even Ordway, and he's of straight-laced New England stock. Collins thinks himself some sort of knight to Charbonneau's woman. We cannot take a woman with us, Meri, and Collins and Charbonneau in the same unit is setting a fuse to the powder." William Clark pinched the bridge of his nose, rubbed his weary eyes, and blinked at the candle's flame that sputtered in the dim interior of the room.

"We could send Collins back to Saint Louis in the keelboat with Deschamps?"

"And do what with twenty-nine others? Collins didn't draw his knife. He actually showed restraint."

Lewis chewed his lip thoughtfully. He leaned forward into the candlelight and drummed his fingers on the table. "I want the woman with us, Will."

"Why? For what possible good?"

"She speaks the language of the mountains. That alone could spell our salvation."

Clark's head shook violently, but Lewis was captain as signed and sealed by the Secretary of War of the fledgling United States. William Clark's official promotion had never arrived. He was a mere lieutenant, although he and Lewis had never revealed the rank to the men of the corps. Clark mumbled in reply: "Then hire Charbonneau, but separate him and the woman from the rest of the men. They can sleep with us under a close eye. Or assign old Cruzatte, who speaks French and has the morals of a celibate priest, to look after them." He rubbed his red eyes. "You're the diplomat, Meri. I'm tired. I can hardly see. I'm going to sleep."

"Will, before you go." Lewis held the candle high. Soft golden light illuminated the flat surfaces of his features and reflected in his soulful eyes. "What if Charbonneau wants to bring both wives?"

Clark snapped angrily: "Absolutely not. It's against all laws of Christian propriety. The men would mutiny.

18

Shields has a wife. Bratton, too. And Sergeant Ordway, Privates Gibson, Hall, and McNeal, all have women in the Indian camp. This Collins even bought and paid for his. Thinks he's married to the woman." He smiled wistfully. "I hear she's very beautiful."

Lewis nodded. "Her family is powerful within the Mandan tribe. If we come back this way, if Jefferson's ship does not meet us, she may be useful. So may Collins. How badly do we need Charbonneau? How badly do we need Collins? How badly do we need the woman? We have to decide, Will, who comes and who returns to Saint Louis. All is ready. We wait only for open water on the river."

Clark's cheek throbbed nervously. It was a problem that had developed over the winter when food supplies had run low and negotiations had faltered. Now he warned: "I don't want any women, Meri. The Shoshones are nomadic. We may never find them."

"Are we sure to find a Northwest Passage, Welsh Indians, silver and gold? The Spanish and English have tried and failed. Mackay and Evans came back empty-handed. How do we know the ship President Jefferson has sent to resupply us will not sink rounding Cape Horn or founder in the California currents? How do we know it will be waiting at the mouth of the Columbia River when we arrive. We don't, Will. We prepare. We pray. We hope."

"Then state our terms to Charbonneau and see how he reacts. We can decide about Collins tomorrow."

Lewis rubbed his knuckles and glared at the changing shapes of coals in the fire. He had an artist's hands with long, tapering fingers. They rapped the table irritably now. "Charbonneau won't like it, Will. We may be blowing our chances up the chimney with the smoke."

Lewis followed Clark to bed but could not sleep. He lay back on the curly-haired buffalo robe and stared into the darkness. Strange shapes loomed gray and black and threatening, like the crumbling ashes left from the cook fire. They glowed like ghosts before his eyes, then burst and disintegrated to nothingness. He thought of Charbonneau. He thought of Collins. He thought of deserter Moses Reed and mutineer John Newman. Was John Collins also one of the dishonorable? Should he be sent back with the offenders? Collins was popular with his peers and with the Indian maidens, and he was a good hunter and cook.

Meriwether Lewis rose in the tar-pitch night, wrapped himself in the buffalo robe, and walked out under the stars. They gleamed brightly but there was only a slim moon. The fort was quiet. The smell of burning wood and charred meat rose from the fire pit. Lewis moved toward it for warmth and lifted his eyes to the glittering stars. The North Star shone like a distant god, immovable and constant. Lewis was not a religious man, but he muttered a wish and a prayer. "Lead me like you led the Magi to the Christ." With an involuntary shudder, he turned his sights to earth again. "God, light my path like you light your heavens. Show me how and where." He went back inside and lay awake and cold on the hard pallet that was his bed.

In the morning, he summoned Charbonneau a second time. This time William Clark was absent, and Lewis motioned the square little man to a stool. The Frenchman trotted in, humming to himself, sat, lit his clay pipe, clamped it between his teeth, and puffed away impassively with arms folded tightly across his chest. Lewis tempted and cajoled, but his words crashed like waves on rock. Charbonneau's demands were immutable as the stars. He could not leave one wife behind and take the other. One would be envious, the other overworked. His family unit would disintegrate. If he chose to leave a wife behind, it would be his second wife, the small one who spoke Shoshone, the mother of the baby who could be better cared for in a village. He did not trust his tall wife away from him. But he gave Meriwether Lewis a reason for including both women on the journey, and Lewis repeated it word for word to William Clark. "The presence of women will convince the tribes we come in peace. No native takes women on a war party." Lewis added grimly: "He is right, Will."

Clark was not convinced. "Two women, one woman, any woman will distract and divide. And how can thirty tough men nurse and care for an infant?"

"The men already love the babe like they love my dog." Lewis's Chesapeake retriever followed him everywhere. "The babe could be a civilizing, soothing influence."

"What will he eat?"

"She'll nurse him."

Clark pondered. His cheek pulsed. "He'll have to guard her well." He added: "I'll speak to Collins."

He went for Collins before muster. Collins was not in his bunk. The sergeant of his mess, Nathaniel Pryor, explained: "He was two days hunting and butchering, sir. Only came in yesterday. I gave him permission to visit his wife. He left immediately for Matootonha, but I can fetch him if you need him, sir."

"No, Sergeant, I'll go myself. Conduct the muster without me."

Clark set out over the track that led along the banks of the Missouri River to Matootonha. A dusting of snow had fallen during the night. It blew off the wide prairie and collected in the narrow track. Passage had been easier when the ice was thick and the river a solid highway between fort and village, before the spring thaw was under way. Now the ice was cracking and the river dangerous. Cold penetrated his soft moccasins and crept up the long length of his legs. The slant rays of morning sun glanced off the wet, brilliant surface of snow. The glare pained his eyes, and he lowered his sights and half closed his lids. He heard the scuffle before he spotted the man coming toward him. The figure stopped only a few yards away. Wide, shocked eyes bulged from deep sockets above a hawk nose in a face that blanched whiter than the surrounding snow. Sharp, staccato words squawked defensively: "Captain, sir, good morning."

Clark nodded. "Sergeant, you're up early. I hope you had a good night's rest." Sergeant Ordway had obviously spent the night in the village, probably in the arms of an alluring siren. One year ago, Ordway would have berated another man for such slovenly conduct. Now Clark smiled while Ordway squirmed.

"I was hurrying back, sir, so as not to miss muster."

Clark sucked in his cheeks to mask his mirth. "Then I shall not delay you further, Sergeant." Ordway turned briskly to make his escape while a chuckling William Clark launched an irresistible salvo at his back: "Was her bed warm?"

Ordway stopped in his tracks and stammered: "She was . . . satisfactory, sir." His jaw hung open. His breath hovered like smoke. "There's something you should know, sir."

"Another fight? Who was it this time?" Fights over women were common.

"It's the Indians, sir. The chief and Mister Heney, the Hudson's Bay man, are expecting a visitor who arrived at Awatixa last night and will come on to Matootonha later today, sir. He holds a powerful position in the Hudson's Bay Company at Fort Assiniboin." Fort Assiniboin was the British collection point for trade goods destined for shipment south to the Mandans.

Clark frowned and questioned: "More powerful than our friend Heney?"

"His superior, sir. The new man is bringing great quantities of guns and beads and mirrors to trade, competition for the North Westers. And they say he's bringing whiskey, although the company denies it, sir. The natives are in a dither, rummaging and collecting every tradable item they can lay hands on."

Clark mumbled audibly: "Another greedy Brit who likes to see them grovel." He dismissed Ordway, and Ordway hurried on. But William Clark stood anchored to the spot, the tick in his cheek as regular as a clock, his keen eyes squinting at a spot where the sun's rays glittered like diamonds on the wet snow. He rubbed his burning eyes and muttered to himself: "Should meet the Hudson's Bay man. So should Meri."

CHAPTER
THREE

Clark entered the village near a grove of trees where the Indians cut wood. Sight of the fur-wrapped forms of women, chopping, soothed his sore eyes. He nodded as he passed the sacred cedar post that stood alone in the central square. The humped, round, earth dwellings were scattered haphazardly about, but he knew where to find Collins — third lodge, second tier.

It was the large dwelling of a respected family, the owners of the sacred Snowy Owl Bundle. Two snarling, yellow mongrels dashed out to block the entry. An old wrinkled crone followed, smacked one dog across the nose, and turned to face Clark. Her keen old eyes measured his length as if she were choosing an animal for slaughter. She turned on her heel and went back inside. He waited. She came out again and ushered him in.

Collins was sitting cross-legged at the far edge of the fire pit, melting lead in a crucible. The dogs bounded up to him and planted themselves at his feet. Startled, Collins jumped up. "Captain, sir! Sergeant Pryor gave me leave, sir." When Clark nodded, he set down the crucible and stammered: "The Indians have only cheap weapons that they pay the Brits dearly for. I'm making extra balls for the hunt." He was melting expedition lead and tensed uncomfortably. But William Clark grinned as if he approved, and Collins spread a robe for him in the place of honor. "Please sir, there's hot broth. It'll warm you." Clark's bloodshot eyes watered. Collins continued agreeably: "Don't look at the fire, sir, if it pains." He led his captain to the space he had prepared in front of the windbreak that blocked the entry, where the heat of the flames reflected off the flat partition and the cold draft did not penetrate. The old woman shuffled past and lifted a small skin bag from a rear beam.

Clark followed her movement with interest. "That's not your woman, Private."

"No sir." Collins smiled and felt his chest swell with pride as he spoke of his spouse. "My wife, sir, has gone to sort the pony herd with her brother. You remember, sir, I paid for her hand in marriage with many horses. They will trade horses for guns to the Hudson's Bay trader who is expected. Pitiful, defective weapons Heney and the British traders sell them, not as accurate as a bow in the hands of a good archer." He stopped, uncertain how to continue, handed the captain a cup of broth, then stammered: "They pay dearly, sir, for the cheapest of British wares. I took the liberty of showing them my Harpers. We had a shooting match. I never missed. They think me some kind of god. They would trade many horses, sir, for one Harpers rifle."

Clark sipped slowly, cast a sidelong glance at his young subordinate, and commented: "The Harpers are not for sale, Private, at any price, not even for the

26

friendship of God himself." It was a conclusion Collins would not admit. The captain scrutinized the younger man more thoroughly. "They have domesticated you . . . I almost said civilized you, Private Collins." It was not often that Clark observed one of his men in other than military surroundings.

An uncertain grin spread over John Collins's face. "Yes, sir, a good woman, family, even the dogs love me." The old crone had come around with a platter of boiled meat, and Collins quipped: "Except for my mother-in-law who thinks me unworthy."

Now it was William Clark who was uncertain how to proceed. He said: "Finish what you were doing, Private. Then we talk."

Collins poured the remaining molten lead into the molds. He had only enough for five more balls, which cooled quickly. He snipped off the excess, filed them smooth, placed them in his pouch, and set the crucible carefully aside. He leaned back when he was finished. A dog shoved his head into his lap. In silence he scratched the scruffy ears, then rose to offer Clark more broth and fetch a cup for himself.

The silence was awkward. Clark drained his cup while he studied the interior of the lodge. He noted the neat bedding of thick buffalo robes, the Hudson's Bay blankets, baskets of grain, a tidy storage pit dug down into the hard-baked floor, cooking vessels stacked carefully under the eaves of the outside walls, the sacred bundle that hung suspended on the windbreak over his head. Finally he broached his reason for coming. "Your antics have every man in the fort buzzing, Private. Captain Lewis is considering sending you back."

"Back where, sir?" Collins's innocence was disarming.

"Downriver, to Saint Louis."

"Why, sir?" Collins reacted like a snapped whip.

"Charbonneau." The name was accusation enough. "What have you to say for yourself, Private? Speak honestly. It was not I who issued you one hundred lashes."

Collins winced. He'd forgotten contesting Charbonneau, but memory of the whipping still rankled like acid on a blister, even after a year. A jury of his fellows had sentenced him to one hundred lashes on his naked back for drunkenness while on watch. He had felt their rejection cruelly. "I don't want to go back, sir. Not now."

"Because of your Indian woman?"

"Yes, sir." He hung his head. "I love her and I was not welcome in Saint Louis."

The whole corps knew the story. Clark let seconds slip by. He had a kind face with soft, blue eyes and lips that turned naturally upward at the corners. When Collins did not volunteer details, he probed deeper. "Charbonneau has lived too long alone. He thinks only of his own self-interest, but he's not malicious." He stopped, inhaled deeply, and let the last words softly settle like leaves on the surface of a pond. Still Collins did not speak, so Clark continued: "The natives are our hosts. We must tread softly and come like guests to their table. We mean to befriend, to placate even those who work for our most recent enemy, Britain, like this man, Charbonneau. Don't assign great weight to his thoughtlessness."

"He's a brute, sir. She could have died."

"The woman carrying the babe?"

"If she'd fallen, yes, sir." For a man who had trouble finding words in his own defense, Collins was quick, almost passionate in the woman's defense. Marriage had made him more considerate and aware of a woman's plight.

William Clark rubbed his eyes and reflected. She was a slave, like his own York, purchased for a price, like a pony or a buffalo hide. Collins had helped the woman at some expense to himself. He had offended the husband and owner, Charbonneau, who probably deserved it. Clark rose abruptly, placed a strong palm on the young man's shoulder, and squeezed gently. He liked Collins. He was impetuous. He preferred action to thought and restraint like most of the crusty young men he'd hired. Through it all, the insubordination, the drinking and womanizing and fighting, there was an honesty in the youth. Collins was quick to take offense, but he was infallibly loyal to his friends and faithful to his woman. Clark had been young once in a cabin that overflowed with brothers and sisters. He understood. And Collins was an excellent hunter and responsible keeper of Sergeant Pryor's commissary. Clark's hand was firm and warm. "Private, do a favor for me and a good turn for the corps. Apologize to Charbonneau."

Collins neck stiffened. Words stuck like indigestible bones in his throat, but he croaked: "Yes, sir."

"You'll see, Private, that apology will not diminish you in the eyes of your peers. Neither will it threaten your manhood."

Clark turned, then stopped again before making his final exit. His eyes lit on a trade gun that rested upright in the shadows against a post near the entry. "These guns that your wife's brother will purchase, who is the trader who brings them in winter when travel is difficult?"

"The Indians call him Bunch, a Brit of the Hudson's Bay, sir. He prefers to travel before the thaw, when he can walk upon the rivers and slide heavier loads across the ice. Heney comes in the fall and trades for pelts through the winter. This trader, Bunch, arrives every year at this time, before the buffalo return, when the braves are still in camp. He brings muskets. Bunch is chief factor at Fort Assiniboin and stays here only until the trails dry out so that he can return by horse with new animals he has acquired. And he comes for the buffalo-calling ceremony that the Indians conduct every year. This year he's late. They were worried that he would stay away, that they would not have guns and powder enough to defend the village and feed themselves."

Clark nodded and pursed his lips. He weighed in his mind what he should reveal to young Collins, how much the young private would convey carelessly to the salty chatter of enlisted men. An Indian wife seemed to have stabilized the young man. Collins had not been drunk all winter. During the entire stay at Fort Mandan, there had not been one black mark against him — until now, until Charbonneau. But Charbonneau was not a formal member of the corps. He was foreign, his allegiance suspect. Charbonneau had separate dealings with Deschamps and admitted he sought profit for himself. His services would be guaranteed only if they advanced his own aims. William Clark waved a cheery good bye to John Collins and decided to forget Toussaint Charbonneau.

Shouts rang out from the direction of the river as William Clark exited the village. He stood for a moment, every sense fine-tuned. Dogs bounded by him, barking furiously at a long-legged runner who was coursing between the lodges, crying in a shrill, penetrating voice. Men and women, old and young, rushed from their lodges, clapped, gestured, laughed, greeted each other boisterously and shouted to friends. The din was deafening, the chaos complete. They surged in a crowd toward the central square. William Clark tried to resist the onslaught and escape the village. It was impossible. Suddenly a familiar voice sounded above the commotion.

Collins was waving and shouting to him: "Sir, the Hudson's Bay trader has arrived!"

They followed the surging crowd to the central square where Rupert Bunch and his retinue appeared from behind a long curve of lodges. He led a motley column of men and sleds from the villages upriver. Bunch was mounted on a white horse that he had snatched from the pony herd to make his grand entry into the village. He rode now past the sacred cedar post toward the lodge of Sheheke, chief of Matootonha. On first glance, he seemed taller than William Clark and taller than lanky John Collins, grander than the chief himself. His horse's long winter's coat had been brushed, combed, and the stains washed out so that it glowed the color of snow. Bright ribbons and beads festooned the braids of its mane and tail. But any vestige of dignity ended there. The horse was short at the withers and sway-backed, and Bunch was tall, so that his feet reached below the animal's knees and slush spattered his moccasins and soiled his leggings. A voluminous, white woolen capote enveloped him. It was a tremendous garment that collected in folds above his knees and expanded the top of his narrow frame. He had belted it tightly at the waist with a wide red sash so that his appearance was of a gigantic sack tied round with a ribbon. His knobbed head poked out through the hole at the top, on a long, arched, goose's neck. A knitted, red stocking cap covered his head and wrapped like a feathered ruff around his neck. His face was clean-shaven and raw-boned, his skin chapped and red. He glanced from side to side at the throng of people, nodding, smiling obsequiously and gesturing like a potentate on parade or a priest granting absolution. The Indians obviously regarded him as some sort of sainted, mystic power. They shouted and hailed as he passed and climbed atop the round surfaces of the lodges and straddled the tunneled entries. They stretched to the limit of their height, craning necks, clapping, pushing, peering, shouting.

John Collins laughed. To a white man, Bunch was ludicrous. But Clark watched in silence, appalled at the gaudy display, acutely aware that no American had received such a welcome, amazed that these intelligent, stately Indians could be so duped by pomp and show. He narrowed his steel blue eyes and noted every pack and every crate, tallying in his mind the total of guns, powder, lead, and trinkets that this man brought. By comparison, the Americans had only paltry items to trade. Clark's unerring gaze summed it up, and he muttered: "Six crates, twelve canisters of powder, and that is only what is in plain view. How much is there lashed down beneath the hides? How much that we cannot see?"

Collins wondered aloud: "And how much whiskey, sir?"

"The Brits don't trade whiskey, Private." That was the official line.

Collins struck his thigh with a fist. "Sir, it's like he was returning with a coup stick and fifty enemy scalps." He could not take his eyes off the casks of black powder and the numerous muskets of the henchmen of Rupert Bunch. "It's a bloody bribe, sir. Guns for friendship. And there's whiskey, sir. I know."

"Guns and whiskey for Mandan ponies and grain." Clark shook his head ruefully. "No talk of whiskey, Private, or we may alienate those who we call friend."

Silently the procession came to a halt at the lodge of the chief. Bunch dismounted and entered while his men fanned out to either side, spread their blankets, cracked open crates, and pulled tarps from their wares.

There were not only quantities of trade guns, but also crates of knives, tomahawks, pots, mirrors, blankets, colorful beads, and the inevitable, forbidden kegs of whiskey. The Indians descended like maggots to the smell of blood. They stroked cool musket barrels, unfurled bolts of bright cloth, ogled mirrored reflections, and squinted at the glint of sun on steel. They shot off the muskets, and the explosions echoed like near claps of thunder. They brought trade goods of their own: baskets of hulled corn, strings of squash, pemmican and preserved meat, furs and buffalo robes, and, on the prairie and scattered down the alleyways of the village, the coveted ponies. Men and women alike pushed and elbowed and maneuvered for advantage.

John Collins had seen such haggling only twice before, once on the docks of Baltimore when his older brother, Robert Collins, had taken him to see the city and a sloop had anchored with a hold of Barbados rum. And in Kaskaskia — he was there when the inhabitants of the Ohio and Mississippi brought their year's produce to sell. Neither could match the bargaining of the Mandans at Matootonha for British exports. British stores diminished quickly to be restocked continually. British prices climbed. The Indians' stock diminished, too, especially the ponies, and these were not replenished.

"They'll not have any horses left for us, sir," Collins observed. The Indians seemed to be trading away their very livelihood.

"We'll not need horses where we're going, Private."

"Not even to hunt, not even in the mountains, sir?"

William Clark did not explain further. The tic in his cheek was pumping and he clenched his teeth to mask the tension. "Get your friend, Private Labiche. Let's see if the gambler can earn us credit." Labiche, the ugly former pirate who had jumped ship, had a nose for a bargain, a quick eye, and persuasive tongue, and he knew how to live by his wits. Clark continued: "And bring Captain Lewis. He'll want to record the manner of their commerce." He added urgently: "Take a horse, Private. Borrow, buy, steal, if you have to. And gallop. Bring them fast."

Collins chose a long-legged dun, leaped aboard in a bound, and splashed down the trail through melting slush and mud. He arrived at the fort in minutes.

Labiche was on guard at the gate when Collins skidded to a halt. "Captain wants you and Captain Lewis at the village. I'm to replace you."

"Do I get a horse?" Labiche drew back the heavy log gate as Collins trotted through.

"Not this horse. He's winded."

"Captain's at the warehouse, packing."

Charbonneau was behind the gate, waiting with his furs for *Patron* Deschamps, and Collins almost ran him down. The surly Frenchman swore and raised a fist. Collins dismounted, drew himself to his full six feet. "Captain Clark said I should apologize to you." A passive stare was the only response. Collins drew saliva to the tip of his tongue and spat.

Charbonneau's eyes narrowed and retracted. He puffed like a chimney on his clay pipe. Smoke and air belched from nose and mouth like the hot breath of a pawing bull.

Labiche stepped between them. He placed his rifle across Collins's chest and pushed him back. "Johnny, you chatter like a magpie."

Collins did not resist. Captain Lewis had appeared behind the surly Frenchman.

Lewis began mildly as if the two men opposed each other over a friendly game: "Mister Charbonneau, Private Collins, gentlemen" — he chose the word deliberately and let it linger on his tongue — "the welfare of this corps cannot benefit from your continued enmity." To Collins, the words were feathery, without substance. Lewis repeated himself for Charbonneau in French. Collins drew his lips to a bloodless line, tucked his hands in his sleeves, and glared into empty space. Charbonneau pivoted disdainfully on his heel and stalked away. Collins followed him with his eyes. "Damn, miserable pig!"

"I didn't hear that, Private. Now tell me why you come. Is Captain Clark in danger?"

Collins bottled his rage. "There're goings on in the village, sir. Captain Clark asks that you join him promptly, you and Labiche. A Hudson's Bay trader has arrived. The Indians are trading away their souls."

Lewis turned to Labiche. "Get your pack. Tell Whitehouse to replace you here. And fetch mine. Sergeant Pryor can assume command. See that Charbonneau remains outside the walls until I return. Collins, cool that horse, then come after us." He added: "Come slowly Collins. Don't kill the horse."

★   ★   ★

The trading had not slowed when Lewis reached Matootonha and joined Clark. Nor had it stopped when Collins rode up later. Now the three stood watching Labiche who hawked his games like a fishmonger on a wharf. His hideous face skewed itself into incredible shapes, but a glint of sheer glee shone from his eyes. Labiche loved to match his wits against swindlers and cheats, especially English cheats. He shuffled nutshells on a flat board with practiced dexterity in front of two sniffling Englishmen and one Indian. One Englishman held a jug. The other carried a silver flask. Both were drinking freely. The Indian held strings of bright beads and a powder flask and he was losing. Labiche's agile fingers flicked from shell to shell like brief flashes of light. From time to time, he looked to his captains for approval and grinned from ear to ear.

Meriwether Lewis remarked to William Clark: "We won't confess to Tom Jefferson, Will, how games of chance have enhanced our fortunes. We'll say the good Lord has blessed us. Who can fathom the ways of the Lord?"

Labiche gained valuable buffalo robes, quantities of powder, lead, glass beads, and the horse Collins had ridden. It was a fast horse. They were profitable hours.

At the end of the day, they loaded Labiche's winnings on the pony and took them to the lodge of Laughing Water for safekeeping. Labiche boasted of his prowess in the privacy of the lodge. "Milked them like stupid cows, Johnny. Watch me ride like Prince Bunch back to the fort."

Collins laughed. "You'll fall off if the horse stumbles."

"And they'll think I'm a proud cavalier with the scars to prove it. I'll come again tomorrow and drain them dry. Now we eat."

When Labiche returned to trading the next morning, activity had slowed. He folded the cards and pocketed his nutshells. "Time to go. Look, Johnny, the flat-footed man comes to share our good fortune." He shook his head and lifted a skinny arm. Charbonneau padded steadily up the path between the lodges on his stubby legs and flapping feet, herding his two wives who tugged his scruffy horses after them. Labiche uttered a curse. "The scavenger cannot resist the smell of meat. See that sash, Johnny? See how thickly it folds around his waist?"

Collins nodded, and Labiche winked and rubbed his hairy chin. "Do you wonder what's in it, Johnny?"

Collins snapped: "Medicine, bones, a sack of venom for all I care."

"It might surprise you."

Charbonneau had come to see if he could strike a more lucrative bargain with the English traders than with Deschamps. But Heney, the Hudson's Bay trader, had eyes and ears among the tribes. That Charbonneau had been to Fort Mandan and dealt with the Americans had been duly noted. Heney had purposefully not informed Charbonneau of the arrival of Rupert Bunch. But Charbonneau had overheard it from Collins's own lips when he summoned Meriwether

Lewis to the Indian village. It had taken Charbonneau most of the day to round up his wayward wife and pack his wares. Now he was late. Heney, Bunch, and the earlier arrivals had spread their goods prominently in the thick of activity. With their henchmen and Mandan customers, they filled every available space in Matootonha's central square and relegated the Frenchman to a back alley on the fringe, behind Labiche and several of their Indian friends.

CHAPTER
FOUR

Trade was not the only reason for the arrival of Rupert Bunch. It was spring. The earth was moist and fertile. Soon shoots of green would emerge from the slumbering soil. The Indians celebrated the earth's warming joyfully by calling the buffalo. As trading filled the days, festivities and rituals filled the nights. Chief Sheheke invited all to observe, but only the most prestigious of the white men to participate. This included Bunch and Heney, the two captains, Georges Drouillard who the Indians respected as a superior hunter, and Private Labiche who they honored because of his trading skill and because his facial scars proved he was a great warrior. However, Charbonneau was excluded.

As the trading waned and the crowd of customers diminished, preparations for the spring ceremonies began. The Mandans swept out the medicine lodge and erected the sacred cedar post in its center. They stoked a blazing fire; its smoke rose evenly through the central hole and mingled with the godly clouds above. In the evening, when the red sunset ignited the horizon, before the purple cold of evening settled over the frozen ground, the people of the village gathered in the ceremonial lodge. It was a huge, round structure, fully fifty feet in diameter. The old men of the tribe gathered first and sat in a wide circle around the fire.

They motioned the two captains with Drouillard and Labiche to take places among them, but young Collins and his wife remained standing on the perimeter looking on, with the younger braves and women. The children sat to one side, still as stones. Old women sat to the other side, chattering like magpies. The younger women moved among the crowd, passing food and drink.

Chief Sheheke lit the sacred pipe, hailed the four directions and the earth and sky, and signaled the ceremony to begin. A hush fell over the onlookers as drums struck up a lively rhythm. The dancing began slowly and increased in tempo as feet stomped and breechcloths flapped like wings in flight. Heavy headdresses swayed. Bells and rattles dangled from waistbands, wrists, and ankles and jangled to the *thump* of the drums. Brightly beaded moccasins caught the light of the roaring flames and flashed colorful prisms of light. Sweat poured from bare shoulders and dripped down spines. Manly exertion and hot breath permeated the air, and the drone of singing rose with the billowing smoke through the central hole to the heavens above.

The couplings began near midnight when the dancing ebbed. Collins watched with increasing unease. It was dark where he stood in the shadow behind a supporting post, under the eaves of the concave lodge. Only parts of the rite were visible. The burning fire leaped upward in great orange flares and masked still more of the ceremony. It was cold where he stood, and he pulled Laughing Water close against him for warmth. He paid little attention to the events evolving around him because the feel of her body was soft and reassuring.

Collins sensed movement behind him. A young Mandan was marching forward with his wife in tow. Slowly they elbowed their way through the pressing crowd to a place just behind an ancient elder of the tribe. He was a decrepit old man, arthritic, scarred, and deformed, but he had been a powerful war chief long ago. The husband stood meekly to one side. The woman, lithe and beautiful like Laughing Water, with rounded breasts and hips that lent soft curves to the drapery of her tunic, stepped confidently forward. She tapped the old man once lightly on the shoulder and helped him to his feet. He hobbled after her as the crowd opened a pathway to the door. Collins paid no attention. He was contemplating the pleasures of his bed after the frenetic ceremony was over. Another couple moved forward. Another wizened old man followed another young beauty out into the cold. The next man chosen was the Hudson's Bay man, Rupert Bunch. He stalked off like a preening rooster. Yet another young woman moved up behind Georges Drouillard, and he rose and followed. The firelight cut a brilliant swath across his dark face as he turned toward Collins. His eyes were hooded but the turn of lip, almost a smile, surprised John Collins. When another young couple approached Captain Lewis, he flushed with embarrassment, hesitated, but went.

Minutes ticked by. The pairing continued. When the first couple returned, Collins's suspicion awakened. Grunting with beastly satisfaction, the old man stumbled back and nearly fell into his place. But the young woman held her head high as she resumed her place beside her husband not far from Collins.

It was not until Georges Drouillard returned and winked suggestively that full comprehension finally dawned. Collins knew Drouillard. He knew that wink. He knew the smirk that spelled physical satisfaction. The knowledge hit him like a crashing wave: the old men were coupling sexually with the young women. For Collins, it was an objectionable act, but the Mandans had raised it to the level of holy practice. Intercourse of young women with proven leaders assured that tribal virtues — bravery in battle, wisdom in council, prowess in the hunt — would pass to the next generation. Intercourse with white men would acquire for the tribe resistance to disease, ability to fashion metal, and the mysteries of the written word.

Meriwether Lewis returned. His lips were flushed. He flashed a pasty smile at the chief, then bowed his head.

Collins felt his resistance build like a storm rising when crystal flakes swirl and thicken, drift and deepen over the cold, hard ground. Great piles of emotion were amassing and freezing in his soul. Finally he grasped Laughing Water firmly by the wrist and pulled her after him along the dark perimeter of the lodge, around the windbreak, out through the tunneled entry, past the hide curtain that blocked the wind, and out into the black, biting cold. The wind hit him in the face like a thousand icy needles, but he exhaled and felt a vise release his heart from its grip. He gulped the frigid air like a man half drowned and let the cold invade his lungs. It choked off any explanation he might have offered Laughing Water.

She had not come willingly. He could feel her backward tug, but he stopped only for a moment in front of the medicine lodge to clear his head, then continued on, dragging her after him, to their own empty lodge.

The interior was dark and cold, the fire low. Even the dogs had found their beds elsewhere. But the old woman was there. She sat in the place of honor under the sacred bundle like an ugly sorceress. Collins leveled a withering glance at her and she retreated into the darkness under the eaves.

He sat Laughing Water in her place near the fire, wrapped her in a warm robe, went for wood to stoke the flames, and then sat down beside her. She sat with head bowed. He could not see her face. He could not speak, so strong was the passion that tore at his breast. Jealousy, anger, disgust congealed like powerful winds in a giant vortex. He refused to share his lovely wife with a withered old man. This was tonight, now, present time, not some bloody battlefield of yesterday. He spoke to her finally, narrowly measuring events by the only standard he knew, the Christian code of white man's law. He whispered: "You are my wife, not the woman of another man." But she would not look at him.

44

When the lodge had warmed, he removed the buffalo robe from her shoulders and folded it carefully away. He began to stroke her silken hair and fumble with the lacings of her tunic. She did not resist, but neither did she respond. She placed a staying hand upon his knee. Gradually his breathing eased, his tension ebbed. He stared at the fire, his jaw clamped tightly, his lips sealed in awe. Words formed like chimeras and melted as quickly. He scrambled for meaning and finally spoke the sweet nothings that in English flowed like water, but in Hidatsa were broken and harsh.

She answered softly, eyes down. "You have shared yourself with me, granted me all the wonders that make you a man." She stopped, hesitating to meet his gaze. "This ceremony is the lifeblood of my people. It is not for me or for you. It is for those who will be born after us, that they may share the powers that make us great."

He struggled to comprehend her rapid speech, so many words that he had not heard before, that fell like gentle raindrops from her lips and were as alien to him as the Celtic runes of his Gaelic ancestors. He lifted her chin and saw the dry streaks of tears. For the first time in his life, he wished he had learned to read and write and interpret sounds and signs. He stared into the brilliant flames until his own eyes wept. He had embarrassed the woman he loved in front of the whole village. Finally he raised his eyes to hers, but his words emerged in English. "In my life, in my home, it is not so."

He felt her hands kneading the flesh of his shoulders, running down his long length of spine, sweeping, tingling down his arms and across his chest. Her touch brushed like a petal on his cheek. He pulled her to him with terrifying force, and they rolled together passionately into the soft robes that lay on the hard clay floor of the lodge.

Much later, after the fire had died, the lodge was dark again, and their coupling had drained, he awakened holding her tightly in his arms. Dawn rained its shadowy mist down through the smoke hole. Others had returned and were sleeping soundly. The covering of robe had slipped, and he rolled away and lay for a moment admiring the smooth, female outline of her sleeping form. She shivered suddenly, and he pulled the robe back up and over them both. Laughing Water slept on. The old woman snored. The parents and children lay on their pallets under the low eaves.

Collins got up, went outside to relieve himself, returned, and gazed down on the slumbering form of his wife. He reached his arm to within inches of her face, but he did not touch. She appeared distant as a disturbing dream, and he asked himself what he was doing here. It was he who was the weed in the meadow. He had married into an alien culture. Would he ever comprehend it? Drouillard did. Captain Lewis, too. But they could read books, write journals, record and interpret the words and customs of strange peoples. John Collins was not sure that he could ever understand. He was not an educated man. No one had ever described to him the wide reaches of human behavior and custom. He acted and reacted on instinct tempered by the discipline of his officers, the opinion of his fellows, and the perception of Georges Drouillard. He did not comprehend political necessity or social expediency. He was quick to incite, he was jealous, and he was in love.

It was day. The village slept after the exertion of the night. Even the dogs did not stir, but John Collins went outside to escape what he could not fathom and could not fully accept, and he felt better. A light snow had fallen and the sun was high and Drouillard was walking toward him across the square.

"Johnny, *mon ami*, I go back to the fort. Come with me. Bring your wife. Here she will only be the object of curious gossip."

Collins reacted instantly. He ran out to the pony herd and caught the spotted horse that was his wife's and prayed she had not traded it to the English. He loaded his pack and enough food to keep her for a week, and went to awaken her. The slanting rays of the morning sun illuminated the contours of her face. He smiled at the vision, traced her cheek bone, her nose, her eyes, so lightly she did not even stir. He lifted her as she slept, and set her gently onto the horse. The young woman awakened then, trusting to the good will of her husband, unaware of where he was taking her. They walked lazily after Georges Drouillard, away from her village, down the narrow trail to the dreary white world of Fort Mandan. She went because it was a wife's duty to follow her husband.

But for her, Fort Mandan was a dark, forbidding structure, sealed off behind a high stockade from the natural world she knew. The men lived in dirty, dank, cramped barracks, warmed by stone hearths that hurled most of a fire's heat up the tall chimneys to the open sky. The buildings were log, strictly utilitarian, without adornment of any kind. They smelled of whiskey, tobacco, and manly sweat.

Collins led her past the boatmen who were preparing the vessels for imminent departure. The ice was breaking up quickly, and the river had begun to rise. Drouillard shouted a hail, and Deschamps, who was on guard, cracked open the heavy timbered gate.

Drouillard, Collins, and Laughing Water passed through the tall gates, entered the muddy yard, and came to a halt as Deschamps slammed down the bar that secured them. Drouillard left them there. Collins stood dumbly, uncertain where to take his wife. He had never made a shelter for her near the fort. The earth lodges were warmer, more spacious, cleaner. It had always been easier to walk to her lodge in the village where he had always been welcome. Now Charbonneau's wives occupied the place for the shelter he might have built. But, since most of his bunkmates were absent in the Indian village, he decided, temporarily, to place her in his own bunk, and escorted her to the tiny room that served as sleeping quarters for him and the seven rough-hewn men of his mess.

She recoiled in disgust when she saw the drafty doorway, hardwood bunks, and stone hearth that lined the dark perimeter of the room. "I would not ask an animal to live so caged and dirty."

Joe Whitehouse was lying on his bunk when she and Collins entered. He sat up abruptly when he saw the visitors. His form moved forward in a halo of firelight, a black figure against the orange glow of the fire. To Laughing Water, he appeared like a devil rising. She gasped in horror, turned, and fled to the fort's closed gates and beat upon them with her fists. Collins ran after, with Whitehouse close on his heels. Appalled, Deschamps lifted the heavy bar that held them shut. Laughing Water ran out.

Collins came up as Deschamps pushed the heavy gates shut. "Let her go. You will reap no good by keeping her here. You would only kill the beauty that is her soul." Deschamps stood, shaking his head, shrugging his shoulders. He gripped Collins firmly by the arm.

Collins shook loose, protesting: "She is my wife."

"She could not be happy here. We are leaving soon." And to Whitehouse: "Take him back. Feed him. Calm him."

Only then did Collins begin to comprehend the futility of his actions. The horse was waiting, still loaded with the provisions he had brought. He grabbed the lead, shoved Deschamps aside, and went after his wife. He caught up, and she stopped. He began to speak any sweet Mandan nothing that pricked his tortured brain: apology, explanation, endearment. She stood still, listening, then put her hand to his brow. He saw a tear form, escape, and drip down her smooth cheek. They stood for a long moment facing each other until she stretched up on her toes to kiss him lightly, then turned, picked up the horse's lead, and led the animal slowly away.

John Collins watched in shocked disbelief. He stood immobile and cold, like a statue carved in ice. Finally he called after her: "Wait for me there! I will come!" But she was too far away to hear.

CHAPTER
FIVE

Toussaint Charbonneau sat with his second wife in a back alley under a makeshift shelter, thumbs tucked into the wide sash that spanned his middle. His first wife was drunk. In spite of the cold, she slept soundly under a thin blanket. She had neglected to build a fire, and Charbonneau prodded her awake. She got up, wobbled unsteadily, propped herself against a crate, and proceeded to bat her eyes at Alexander Heney.

Heney ignored her. He was busy. He was a superb salesman, with winning blue eyes and light tenor voice that emanated melodiously from the groomed, pomaded hairs of his beard. He displayed his wares on brightly colored blankets. Tin cups, kettles, brass buttons, needles, knives, beads, and mirrors lay glittering like precious gems in the direct rays of the sun. Brightly colored cloth and satin ribbon drew every maid's appreciative eye. Trade guns and tomahawks lay in open crates within reach of men's eager hands to weigh and stroke and lift or press a sturdy stock into a soft tuck of shoulder. Heney sold the cloth and guns cheaply but kept powder, lead, and flints locked securely away. For these, the Indians received half or less the true worth of their furs and ponies.

Charbonneau watched the proceedings from beneath hooded lids, behind a veil of pipe smoke. By contrast, his goods lay in deep shadow, in a muddy, narrow space between lodges where few takers cared to walk. All day long, Charbonneau glared at Heney's broad back and Rupert Bunch's bony neck. All day long, he listened to the broad, sugary vowels of the Englishmen. All day long, he watched the Englishmen rake in profits that would stuff the coffers of distant London investors, the same investors who had financed General Wolfe and seized French Canada for England. Charbonneau's father had fought with General Montcalm to defend the city of Quebec on the high cliff overlooking the River St. Lawrence. As a family, after the defeat, the Charbonneaus had worn black mourning for one year.

Now Charbonneau sucked his pipe in ever more rapid puffs while resentment rose like ferment with every breath. He hit his unfaithful wife, but it did not stop her flirting. He finally protested to Heney.

The Englishman smiled, waved, and shouted a reply. "You put too much faith in the virtue of the fair sex, my man! The woman is weak as the mother of Cain. But you should have no fear of me. I could take no pleasure from an insatiable drunk." Heney waved a bottle of French brandy over his head. "Come, have a dram, forget your wife!"

It was ample inducement. Charbonneau went. In the end, Heney invited the surly Frenchman to move forward with his wares, but, when Charbonneau moved, Heney slashed his prices. Charbonneau complained louder. Heney laughed lightly and assumed a condescending smile. "Mister Charbonneau, we are both businessmen. We offer what the traffic will bear. Meet the competition, like me, like Mister Bunch, and they will come to you to trade."

Charbonneau blasted an answer through teeth that clenched his pipe. "You give them twice what you gave me when I brought you supple skins with hairs smooth as silk, better than any the natives supply." His thumbs pressed against his paunch as he pulled deeply on his pipe. He exhaled smoke through mouth and nose, but could not expel the anger within.

Heney shrugged. A self-righteous smirk coated his puffy face like icing on a birthday cake and crinkles of mockery smudged his eyes. "You were late, Mister Charbonneau. A pelt that was worth three knives yesterday is worth only one today. Take your business to the Americans. See if they will pay you more." Heney lay a quieting hand on the Frenchman's arm.

Charbonneau thrust it away. "*Cochon, va-t'en!*" The insult snapped like a barbed whip.

"I am not a pig or a thief, Mister Charbonneau. I sell my wares honestly, and I understand your dithering French." Heney's eyes receded and his voice assumed an infuriating calm as he added pointedly: "You do have one item of currency that is always valuable. You could sell one of your wives."

Charbonneau threw down his pipe and leaped for Heney's throat, but the Englishman ducked agilely and withdrew behind his henchmen and his crates.

Purple with rage, Charbonneau kicked dirt, drew his lips back, and hissed: "To you, *m'sieur*, I sell never!"

But Heney had already turned away, happy to be rid of the obstinate Frenchman. Charbonneau had become too independent, too closely allied with the natives and derisive of accepted British business practice.

Charbonneau shrieked in vain at the departing Englishman: "I will live to see the Americans humble and impoverish you!" He bent to retrieve his pipe, stumbled, and fell to his knees. He pushed the muddied stem back into his mouth, pulled it out again, and spat mud. Finally, when he heaved himself up, a coin slipped from the folds of his sash. On the slick ground, it gleamed like a full moon in a black sky. He stared at it blankly for a moment until his heated brain recorded what had happened. Then he snatched it up and rubbed it carefully between thick fingers. It was hard and round and smooth to the touch like a religious medal or the soothing, miraculous relic of a saint. He wiped it reverently with the end of his sash and whispered to himself: "See what blind anger will do, Toussaint. You must not sacrifice one penny to a fit of blind rage."

He packed his wares on his scruffy horse, herded his wives together, and left the village. With another willow switch, he prodded wives and horses the few miles to Fort Mandan and to *Patron* Deschamps who knew a supple, well-cured pelt from a hard, dry, smoke-cured pelt and would deal fairly with a fellow Frenchman.

He found Deschamps loading the keelboat for the trip downriver. His timing was excellent. Meriwether Lewis had just paid the *patron* for services, and Deschamps had not yet distributed wages to his boatmen. Deschamps greeted him warmly, ushered him aboard, and examined his furs. It was a fine sunny day and he poured the gleaming guineas out from a leather purse onto the hardwood deck. They *clinked* against the boards like a lively dance. Charbonneau weighed each in his hand. There was more here than Heney or the North West Company had ever contracted to pay him, more gold than he had ever seen in his life. Charbonneau blinked and accepted on the spot. He unloaded his pelts, and Deschamps handed over the guineas in a purse tied with a thong. Satisfied, Charbonneau took a long slow pull on his pipe. "How can you afford to pay me so handsomely?"

"Consider, *monsieur*. If I pay my men now, they will bicker and gamble all the way home. So I pay you. I buy furs. I will not sell them in Saint Louis to the greedy Spaniards. I will take them to Kaskaskia . . . to the Americans . . . where Pierre and Auguste Choteau do not monopolize the trade, and I will demand a high price."

Charbonneau understood what Deschamps left unspoken — that the boatmen would not be paid until after the furs were sold.

Deschamps volunteered: "My men will thank me when I am able to increase the meager stipend Captain Lewis has promised." He added a caution: "Keep your purse hidden from the captains until I am well away."

The transaction was complete. Smiling broadly, Charbonneau grabbed Deschamps by the shoulders, slapped his back, and planted a dry kiss on each hairy cheek in grand French fashion. Deschamps reciprocated, and added with a wink: "And now I give you wise counsel, my friend. The guineas will be of no use to you in the mountains. Cache them here in the village. Bury them until you return."

"And have you come to dig them up. My good friend, I am not a fool." He untied his sash, tucked the purse into a wide fold, and knotted it tightly.

"Sew them in. You travel far. The gold can drown you."

Charbonneau laughed. "And I cannot swim. You think me foolish." It was the bitter truth although he said it blithely. Smiling, he held out his hand. "Next year, we meet again."

In the privacy of his hut outside the stockade at Fort Mandan, he recounted his guineas three times. He polished each one and placed it carefully in the purse. With sturdy twine, he sewed the purse tightly into his sash. It was heavy and lumpy and weighted down, but he cushioned it with a layer of grass so that it looked like an extra layer of gut.

Finally he settled his two wives in the humble dwelling. There he sat like lord of the manor with his musket across his knees, guarding his treasure, chewing the lip of his eternal pipe. The second wife, the mother, ministered to him. She carried her baby in his cradleboard on her back, chopped wood, cooked, scraped flesh from hides, and repaired clothing. But there was no peace in the household. The first wife, soured by Heney's rejection, tramped about the fort like a bitch in heat.

Deschamps came to warn him: "Friend, the tall one will bring you grief. Denounce her. Sell her. Send her back to her people."

Charbonneau nodded agreeably, but he did not heed the warning and grief descended like an avenging angel. Tomahawk in hand and blood in her demented eye, the first wife charged after the mother, knocking over pots and upsetting the fire. The mother grabbed her baby and ran. But she was short and not a good runner and she carried the baby. The first wife followed fast on her heels. The sight of two women threatening to fight drew virile, male spectators like gnats to a flame. They dropped tools, dice, mess bowls full of food, and leaped to the ramparts for a front row view.

The short wife raced for Shields's forge and grabbed his red-hot tongs. Turning, she waved the sizzling irons before her. Her pursuer leaped back but too late. They caught her greased braid, whipped her head around, pulling her down and igniting her hair. She dropped the tomahawk and rolled frantically in the cold mud, clawing and screeching like a harpy. Charbonneau ran to her with knife in hand. He seized the braid in his vise grip, sliced it free, and heaved the tongs like a javelin into the river. Then he slapped her hard across the face and bent to place his burned hand in the cold, wet slush. Finally he smeared melting snow on her burns and dragged her by one arm back to the hovel.

The mother had run with her baby for the gates of the fort. Bug-eyed, young Shannon cracked them open to admit her. She rested now in a circle of men who brought her water and food and cooed like old grandmothers at the tiny baby. Old one-eyed Cruzatte announced the result of the contest from his pulpit atop the stockade. "The fires of hell have chastised the sinner. Might make an honest woman of her." No one was placing bets. Cruzatte smiled benevolently down at the mother.

The next day, Toussaint Charbonneau asked for an audience with Meriwether Lewis. Sergeant Pryor ushered him into the dim cubicle where the two captains sat at their rough table. A single candle illuminated the space between them. Lewis did the talking with an occasional nod from Clark. He motioned to a stool. "Sit, Mister Charbonneau."

The Frenchman sat and placed his hands palms down, flat, upon the table. He did not remove his pipe, which protruded like a sprouting fungus from his tangle of black beard.

Lewis spoke in accented French: "Mister Charbonneau, how can we help you?"

"What shall be the wages and conditions of my service if I agree to come with you?"

"We will pay you as we pay our scout, Mister Drouillard, no more and no less."

Lewis lowered his head, raised his brows, and spoke decisively. "We will permit your short wife, the mother of your child to accompany us. She is industrious and may be of help when we reach the mountains where she was born. But she will be responsible for the care of her infant, and you must guard her well from the advances of our lustful young men. The other one, the tall one, is not welcome. She would only cause jealousy and division."

Charbonneau stared for a moment at the candle flame. He inhaled the smoke of his pipe and blew out the thick stream.

"That is our final offer," William Clark added cautiously.

The Frenchman removed the clay pipe and made his pronouncement. "*D'accord. F'accepte.*" Beads of saliva spattered the table. He replaced the pipe and held out his broad palm. Lewis shook it, followed by Clark. The agreement was sealed.

Captain Clark introduced the new member to the Corps of Discovery at muster the following day. The announcement caused laughter for some, speculation for others, and anger for John Collins. When Sergeant Pryor shouted dismissal, Collins stood with two feet rooted to his square of ground, behind Bratton in front of John Colter. Bratton, the stocky blacksmith, older by ten years than Collins, sensed his distress and stayed by him until Pryor assigned Collins to a wood detail where Georges Drouillard could keep an eye on him.

Collins sent splinters flying.

Drouillard finally scolded: "You'll hurt someone. Go, sleep with your wife in the village. Calm down."

Collins stiffened and answered stubbornly: "I can't."

"Is it your pride or your heart that speaks?" Drouillard asked. "No matter. Tend your duties like a man, Johnny. You have signed your mark. You're a soldier and you're already a topic for gossip in

Matootonha because you did not share your woman. Do you want to become a laughingstock here, too?"

Collins set a hard, stubborn jaw. He swung the axe into a fat burl of wood that split with an audible crack. "I'm not sure I'm still welcome in the village." He said nothing more but redoubled his efforts, attacking the heavy logs like a bloodthirsty executioner.

The keelboat was loaded for the trip downriver. The boatmen had gathered their gear. In a short time, the expedition would depart from Fort Mandan. Collins took his dinner bowl into a dark corner beneath the walls where the moonlight did not penetrate. He wasn't hungry.

Sergeant Pryor called him back. "Before we leave, settle your affairs with your wife. Be back in time for muster."

Because he was ordered, Collins went to the lodge of Laughing Water. His welcome was not cheerful; his bed was not warm. He had no sooner come through the entry when he caught a glimpse of Laughing Water in the far recesses of the lodge. She was so still that at first he did not distinguish her from a supporting post. The old woman was waiting to intercept him. Her skeletal form hovered like a witch before the orange flames. She held up a bony finger and shrieked a curse like a flood released when the ice lets go. Collins drew back. He comprehended only snatches of the tirade. How dare he desecrate the sacred ceremonies! How dare he deny Laughing Water the blessings of the brave ones of the tribe! How dare he jeopardize the return of the buffalo and threaten the future of this family!

Collins fled from the onslaught. He lunged for the exit, knocking his head on a low beam. Stunned, he looked back. The old woman came after him, screeching like a harpy and poking at his back with the sharp end of a digging stick. He felt the jabs like points of a dagger. He tripped, clambered up, and ran. She was cursing his seed, condemning every child he would father and every child of Laughing Water. The pursuit did not stop when he reached the edge of the village. The old woman had sicked the dogs on him. They chased him through a maze of willows to the river's edge. Other dogs joined them. He lost his way, ran out on the ice to foil the hounds, skidded and tottered as fast as his long legs could carry. The hounds pursued him onto the ice. When he could run no farther, he drew his knife and turned to face the snarling beasts. They circled and stopped.

But the ice awakened. He heard a *crack* and shuddered in panic. The lead dog drew away, and the rest followed. Collins's hands were shaking, his breath coming in gasps. His leggings that Laughing Water had sewed with care were caked with mud and ice. Worse, they were wet inside and his body was shedding heat like a dead dog sheds fleas. The ice beneath his feet was melting, loosening its hold on the river. Water was flooding in over it. He fell to his knees to distribute his weight and clawed his way toward land like a drunken man. His hands floundered and stiffened with wet cold. When the surface shifted under him, he panicked and backed up farther out onto the quaking ice again. His heart racing, he espied a log, one of the deadly sawyers that had threatened to puncture the boats on the way upriver. He inched his way toward the log that proved to be slippery but firm, and then he wormed his way along its length to solid footing.

He found the trail. The still moon shed an eerie light through clouds that had gathered and formed a smoky halo around it. It was a cold retreat. His leggings, the arms and front of his shirt, froze board-stiff. The cold crept over his skin, into his bones, lungs, and workings of his bowels. A worse cold gripped his heart. Numbed and shivering, he arrived at the fort. His bunkmates rushed him inside to the fire, stripped his icy clothing, and wrapped him in a warm robe.

He did not return again to the village the next night or the night after. The flight on the ice had sickened and weakened him. He slept on the hard wooden bunk in his cramped quarters near the reassuring heat of the fire. With his messmates, Labiche, Whitehouse, Bratton, Cruzatte, and Shannon, he inhaled the sweet smell of wood smoke, tobacco, and the pungent sweat of men. He had been cruelly rebuffed. The violence in the old woman had shocked and repelled him, but the denial of Laughing Water had broken his heart. To his thinking, he had committed no wrong. He had tried only to guard his wife from the advances of lecherous men. But according to the logic of the Mandans, he had erred grievously and embarrassed his wife irreparably before the elders of her tribe. For this, the old woman exiled him. For this, his young heart bled.

His fellows at Fort Mandan offered sympathy and useless explanations: different culture, heathen religion, ignorant superstition. "They'll be other tribes and other maids." "Be grateful the old hag didn't take a knife to your hair." Their looks cut deep. Their laughter forced open the wound. But Labiche's sad comment hurt most. "Maybe her heart has changed. Maybe she doesn't love you any more." Collins would have liked to ask a member of the Mandan tribe where he had transgressed, but his command of the language, which sufficed in everyday situations, could not handle complex questions of ethics, commitment, and deep emotion.

Then there was no more time. All at once, the ice broke in the river, a great flood of water crashed down, and the captains ordered an immediate departure.

On April 7, 1805, Corporal Richard Warfington, his troop, *Patron* Deschamps and his boatmen, with specimens, notes, and packs of Charbonneau's furs, set sail with the flood in the keelboat for St. Louis. The same day, the two captains and the Corps of Discovery pushed off into the oncoming current with thirty men, Charbonneau's second wife, a baby, one slave, and one dog. The wind blew in their favor. They took two *pirogues*, six dugout canoes, maps, and supplies for a six-month journey to the western ocean. And Charbonneau took his gold.

CHAPTER
SIX

Thirty eager men hooted and waved their good byes as they shoved off. They looked forward to a short pole and paddle upriver, a gentle climb over the Continental Divide, and a happy sleigh ride down to the western ocean. And they expected to return within the year to a hero's welcome.

Their leaders had the accounts of Alexander Mackenzie who had crossed the continent from Canada ten years before. They had the reports of ship's captain, Robert Gray, who had entered the estuary of the river he named Columbia in 1792, and the accounts of Mackay and Evans who had explored the territory for Spain. Meriwether Lewis had consulted Benjamin Rush and others whose wise counsel President Jefferson had enlisted. Jefferson had signed a letter of credit that promised payment for any supplies issued to the corps, and had dispatched a ship to meet the corps with reinforcements on the other side of the continent. That ship and other traders — Chinese traders that plied the northwest coast — would honor the new President's credit.

But already the river had exceeded the narrow confines of their knowledge. The Indians described a river with giant waterfalls and mountains whose snow-covered teeth scratched the clouds. But no one believed an Indian. The corps dismissed the accounts as tall tales and boastful exaggeration. Neither did they believe the breadth of the arid, wind-swept plains, the ferocity of storms, and the numbers of predatory animals. They did not know the pathway through the mountains and what peoples, friends or foes, lived there. And they were unaware of the critical shortcomings of Toussaint Charbonneau.

From Collins's perch behind Labiche in the rear canoe, he couldn't see the Frenchman. He watched the water as he rowed. Men and women, children and old ones followed along the banks and tossed tokens of good luck to the departing men who accepted graciously with nods and promises to return with riches from where the western waters began. But Collins was silent. He had searched the shore in vain and finally gave up. Laughing Water was not there.

The red *pirogue* caught in an eddy and swept back past the canoes while the crew struggled to steer the heavier boat. Charbonneau sat like lord of the manor in the bow. His young wife sat cross-legged at his feet on the rough deck. A surge of indignation smothered Collins, and he lifted his paddle. His pilot Labiche shouted: "Johnny, set to!" Collins plunged the paddle back into the water with terrifying force, and the canoe pushed ahead. But the vision of Charbonneau stayed with Collins for the rest of the day, like a splinter that festers, if it is not removed, and works itself deeper with every tiny motion.

Later, when they were beaching the canoes, Collins spotted Charbonneau again, sitting, doing nothing. Labiche followed the line of his vision. The pirate recognized the feeling. A hideous scar marred his own face, and, when Collins had asked how it had happened, he replied: "I repaid him well." The suggestion lay pregnant in Collins's fertile brain.

The red *pirogue* drifted quietly now in the shallows. The water was flat. John Shields fumbled with the anchor to prevent downstream slippage while Cruzatte and Ordway paddled and poled to pull the boat into the main channel. When the order sounded to beach and make camp, every man pulled and tugged and heaved and carried. They unloaded and set up camp, but not Charbonneau. He sat idle while his wife worked side-by-side with the men.

Labiche commented: "Thinks he's a sainted prince. Not a man accustomed to rivers. Cruzatte's assigned to teach him." He thrust a sack of corn at Collins. "Lay this out to dry and don't let the birds get at it."

Collins narrowed his eyes and shouldered the sack. "Does he paddle or tow or pull guard duty?"

Labiche half nodded. "He has a wife do it for him."

Collins questioned: "Not guard duty."

"She cooks."

"So do I, and I don't want a woman tagging after me." Collins was bitter. William Clark had appointed him superintendent of his mess, a responsible position charged with apportioning and preparing food and drink. Interference from a woman was degrading. "Why'd they let him bring a baby?"

"The mother speaks Shoshone. She can help with the Indians." Labiche added cynically: "They hope."

On a sudden impulse, John Collins set down his sack of grain, swept off his hat, and bowed to Charbonneau. "All hail, your highness." Labiche burst out laughing, and the laughter blew like a brisk wind across the camp. Collins basked in the attention, grinned, and said: "I have a wife, too. I had to leave her behind."

"Maybe he'll share 'is woman, Johnny. Ask 'im." The comment came from Hugh Hall, an instigator.

But Drouillard had splashed ashore in time to witness the exchange. "Stop it, both of you. Take up your sack, Johnny. Bluster is the stuff of clowns."

Sergeant Pryor's voice clapped loudly: "Collins, get that sack to dry ground!"

Collins hoisted the sack and moved inshore but not before he caught Charbonneau's icy stare. The Frenchman had understood, if not the words, the universal language of mockery. Collins carried the corn above the high watermark and set it down as Sergeant Pryor approached.

"Clear a dry place for the grain. Get a fire going. Collins, a word with you." He drew the young private aside. "You bait him, Johnny. When he strikes, you'll bleed and others will bleed with you. And you'll draw the captains' ire. As your sergeant, I cannot allow it."

Collins shrugged. He was beyond caring what the Frenchman or his sergeant thought. He only cared what Drouillard would say.

Nathaniel Pryor's mouth turned hard. "You're on wood detail, Collins. Kindling and dry fuel . . . go find it and stay away from Charbonneau."

Collins went. When he returned, a group had gathered. Joe Whitehouse had started the fire, and Labiche was rolling dice, quoting odds, taking bets. The length of the river, the height of the mountains, the number of tribes, when and where Collins and Charbonneau would come to blows, were all the subjects of wager and wild speculation. Collins placed a small bet — that they would reach the mountains in one month.

"You're dreamin', Johnny!" Labiche shouted. "You want to lose?"

But there was too much pain in his heart to know what he wanted. He let the bet stand. As for fighting Charbonneau, he didn't bet. Maybe days, maybe weeks, maybe Charbonneau would get lost, disappear, down.

Sergeant Pryor interrupted the bargaining: "That you, Labiche, stirring up fights? You do, you'll reap the same punishment as Collins."

Collins sat down next to gentle Joe Whitehouse, who took a stick and began to draw letters in the sand. Collins knew eight letters that Whitehouse had taught him. The next was easy, the letter i, a straight line and a dot. But John Collins wasn't listening. He was watching the woman set up Charbonneau's tent, build Charbonneau's fire, cook Charbonneau's meal. Laughing Water had never worked as hard for him. In frustration, he threw the writing stick into the fire.

Next morning, ice covered the water in the buckets. Before they launched the boats, two Indians wrapped in thick buffalo robes walked into camp. One was Black Cat, a powerful chief. The other was Stands In The River, father of Laughing Water. Collins was sitting next to Drouillard, across from Labiche, in the circle around the fire. He started to rise, but Drouillard grabbed his shirt and pulled him down. "They come for the captains, not you." Drouillard had recommended Collins to Captain Clark and taken a special interest in the young man. Since the incident with Charbonneau, he watched Collins closely.

The two Indians came and went without ever seeking out John Collins, but William Clark summoned him shortly after they left. Clark held out his hand. "Stands In The River gave me this for you, Private Collins." He opened his fingers on a tiny black stone, tied on a thong.

Collins gripped both hands stiffly against his thighs and stared.

"Take it, Private. Would you refuse a freely offered gift?" Clark's voice was smooth as butter on bread. "You try our patience, Private. You are a soldier, not a fractious schoolboy." The rebuke stung. Reluctantly Collins took the proffered gift. Clark continued: "You're pining and you're jealous, Private. But you have talent and intelligence. The many gifts with which you are endowed are more than most men here can claim. Look on Labiche in his ugliness, or old Cruzatte who lost an eye and lives bound by fears of hellfire." He stopped. Collins hung his head. "I know your story. It is

69

all over the camp and I'm sorry. But if you let your misfortune provoke your anger and if you let your jealousy fester, I will put you in a canoe and send you back downriver. We have not come so far along that it is impossible." It sounded like a lecture, and ended on a threat. Clark's cheek throbbed with each beat of his heart. He dropped his gaze. When he raised it again, his blue eyes pleaded: "I don't want to lose a good man, Private."

Collins stared glassily back and muttered coldly: "Yes, sir."

"One last thing, Private, Stands In The River said the little stone would heal your soul and protect you from the curse. What curse, Private?"

Collins's lips worked nervously. He closed his eyes and bit down hard in an effort to stop the involuntary movement.

"Stand easy, Private, if it will loosen your tongue."

Collins looked at the sky, at the earth, at the waiting boats, anywhere but into the steely eyes of Captain William Clark. He began haltingly to relate all that had passed between him and the old woman.

Clark listened incredulously, shaking his head. "You believed her, Collins? You who have faced down wild bison and braved the mighty rapids of the Missouri, you believed a besotted old woman?"

"She was possessed, sir."

"Is that what Heney and the shaman told you?" Clark was tired. He pinched the bridge of his nose. It was a characteristic gesture when his eyes ached, his cheek ticked, and he struggled to maintain his calm.

"Private Collins, you are a good hunter, a good cook, an excellent swimmer and scout. Do not credit some heathen superstition. Believe in me and in Captain Lewis and our worthy enterprise. Believe in the destiny of your great country. Treat all men equitably as we try to treat you." He repeated: "*All* men, Private Collins. Even Toussaint Charbonneau."

The stone glowed with an oily sheen against the pale pink skin of John Collins's palm. It was carved in the shape of an owl.

Clark's deep voice echoed eerily. "Stands in The River thought you brave and honorable. He wished you well. He did not belittle you, Private. That amulet is as much a symbol of their good faith as this curse you speak of. It is cold stone, incapable of deciding your future. Tie it around your neck if you need, but let it lay lightly. When you feel its coldness, let your heart warm. Let it inspire good will toward me, toward your fellows, toward this man Charbonneau. Forgive him if you can. As for the amulet, in time, I hope you will shed the need of it, trade it, sell it, give it to Captain Lewis for his collection."

Woodenly Collins slipped the thong over his head and let the owl fall against his breast.

Finally Clark sighed and murmured: "Now come, Private, take a dram with me." He scrounged a moment in the belly of a battered trunk, winked, unscrewed the cap from a flask, and poured out two full cups. "My special reserve, medicine for the soul. Today, Collins, your soul."

Collins drained his cup dry, but words still stuck like cotton in his mouth. But he managed to mumble — "Thank you, sir." — and forced a smile. But he was not sorry for confronting Charbonneau.

In a daze, he walked back to the mess fire where Drouillard intercepted him, sat him down, and spoke frankly. "In one week, we'll have proceeded too far to send you back. Charbonneau is proud and lazy, but not a bad man. If he's the pit you chew, *mon ami*, spit it up, or pass it through. One rash act has caused you pain enough."

The fire sputtered. John Collins listened to Georges Drouillard.

Days passed, and the river flowed on. Collins joined his fellows, reluctantly at first, then obediently. Together, they uncoiled the tow rope, put their shoulders to the weight, and heaved the boat forward until their shoulders blistered. The shore was slick with clay and studded with hidden rocks. They camped in pleasant, wooded bottoms, under clay-colored bluffs that threatened to collapse over them, on sandy islands that flooded when the river rose, and on hard, rock-strewn beaches. At the week's end, Collins felt better. He was drinking his gill with Shields and Shannon, Whitehouse and Labiche, and singing along when old Cruzatte played his fiddle. Most of all he was laughing a little in the fellowship of men. But when it rained, when he sat damp and cold under the tarp, or when he lay awake waiting for sleep, his heart ached.

CHAPTER
SEVEN

Alexander Heney and Rupert Bunch had walked out on Matootonha's high bluff to watch the Americans depart. Bunch grinned giddily at his compatriot. "Good riddance to fools and paupers. I wash my hands of them."

Heney agreed heartily. "They'll run out of food and half will desert. The rest will bicker or drown or prey on each other. Lewis is the only half intelligent one among them. Clark can hardly write the King's English. He surely cannot spell it." He took out a folded paper from his coat pocket and held it up. "Correspondence from Captain William Clark." He tore the paper in half, cast the pieces over the edge of the cliff, and watched them flutter like snow into the depths of the river. "To the Americans! May they sink like the common stone!"

The two Englishmen pivoted as a unit and started back to the village. Heney pulled a silver flask from under his coat and offered it to Bunch. "Here's brandy. Drink to their demise." He added as an afterthought: "You spoke with the natives?"

"Of course, Horned Weasel understands perfectly. He knows who keeps his powder dry. The Hidatsa, too."

"And the Sioux?"

"Those rogues charge exorbitant tolls to anyone who wants to descend the river, like Deschamps and his battery of blackguards. They have nothing to trade."

"He has Charbonneau's furs."

Bunch's head wobbled like a ball on a string. "Does he? Then we must inform the Sioux. But Warfington is trivial, a tiny pea in a sea of pods. It's those pompous captains who must not succeed. The rebellious colonies must not fatten on lands that rightfully belong to the British crown." His mouth slammed shut.

"They won't. Charbonneau will see to that . . . Charbonneau and the Blackfeet."

They mounted and jogged away from Matootonha, toward Awatixa, the Hidatsa village on the Knife River where Heney kept his permanent lodge. Bunch squinted at the horizon as they rode. "Have you ever seen such emptiness? Wasteland except for the beaver in the rivers, but beaver enough to enrich you and me." He added: "That's why we don't want Americans on the river. They are competitive rogues. They'll deplete the beaver and pay no heed to royal charters."

In the early evening, they reached Awatixa. The village basked sleepily in the pink light of sunset, like a reptile on a rock. The residents had just returned to the main village on the bluff after the long winter sojourn in the protected bottomlands and Awatixa hummed with life. Women were sweeping out the winter's dust from their lodges, airing buffalo robes, and sharpening tools for the spring planting. Children and dogs ran about shouting and yipping. But the men were absent.

74

They had gone to the prairie to burn the grass to attract the buffalo.

The two Englishmen dismounted at Heney's lodge. It was large by Indian standards, a full thirty feet in diameter with ample storage space for trade goods. Heney kept a wine cellar. He funded his little luxuries by skimming off the proceeds due the Hudson's Bay Company and inflating the prices he charged the unsuspecting Indians. Bunch did the same in the Assiniboin village. They had an understanding. Neither informed on the other.

Bunch ducked through the low entry and collapsed into a cushioned chair. "Civilized seating is a decided pleasure. You've prospered, Alex, since I saw you last."

Heney grinned. He knew the ritual. "Which do you prefer, Rupert, port, rum or brandy?"

Bunch licked his red lips. "Rum, if I may?" He liked the sugary taste. "Jamaican or Barbadian?"

"Barbadian. I keep my wife happy, and her sister. They prefer Barbadian." Heney filled matching silver goblets: rum for Bunch, port for himself. He winked, kicked back into a chair, and held his glass high. "To the luscious liquor as John Milton says, and sweet compensation for us both, living as we do so far from the comforts of Mother England."

"And to the demise of rebellious Americans. May hell and damnation be their just reward," Bunch said by way of a toast, downed his rum, licked his thin lips, stretched his long legs, and kicked his feet up on the table. "Have you called the council of chiefs?"

"Yes," responded Heney, "and I invited the Blackfeet to send a delegation."

"Are they coming?" The Blackfeet had never come so far east at the request of a white man.

Heney took a hefty swallow, filled his pipe, and tamped it down. He inhaled, expanding the width of his barrel chest. "I've offered them ample inducement. The Assiniboins are diminished in their usefulness to us. The pox took its toll two years ago. They will never fully recover. The Blackfeet are more than an adequate replacement and an easy mark when the prize is whiskey and horses. See that their delegation returns rich in horses, and England will gain influence and status."

"Will they intercept the Americans?" Bunch asked.

Heney prodded: "I thought your Assiniboins would accomplish that."

Bunch smiled confidently. "They may. But the epidemic was a rude shock. If they fail, the Blackfeet can serve as reserve."

Heney nodded and took a long swig of port and smacked his lips. "The Americans will destroy themselves. Mark my words." A buttery grin spread over his ruddy face and he muttered: "Charbonneau is with them."

Bunch narrowed his steely eyes. He did not follow the train of thought. "Why Charbonneau?"

"He's an ass and a blowhard. He has the discretion of a stag in rut and the vanity of a peacock and he has never been west of the Yellowstone or seen the falls. He will not speak at all, or, when he does, he will issue decrees of dogma like the Roman Pope, in French. He cannot bear affronts to his pride, and he will insist on error. Believe me. When the river forks, when rapids threaten, he will confuse and retard. He takes a woman and baby with him who cannot help but cause jealousy and slow their progress. I've watched him on the water. He's afraid of it. He cannot swim. He cannot even paddle a bullboat with confidence." Heney's face crinkled in mirth. "He's terrified of the smallest ripple." He poured more port for himself, and emptied the bottle of rum into Bunch's goblet.

Bunch drank to the dregs. His thin face flushed. His lips froze in a pasty grin and he set his empty cup down with a thud. "Another toast, my friend, to the Americans' nemesis, our unsuspecting servant, Toussaint Charbonneau."

"And to the fur trade that has made you a connoisseur of demon rum and both of us wealthy as Croesus." Heney refilled the cups, sipped, and let the sweet liquid glide lovingly over his palate. They drank together until they fell like dead men into their robes, slept soundly, and awakened sober and alert before sunrise. Heney signaled his woman, who prepared food and lay out robes in readiness for the council of chiefs, where the two Englishmen would preside in honored positions around the central fire.

One hour later, the delegations of chiefs with their retinues arrived. They rode sleek horses meticulously groomed and rigged with colorful paint and feathers. Dressed in the finest robes, they were handsome, tall, stately men. Beads, shells, feathers, and quills in bright colors adorned their rich costumes.

Eagle's Claw of the Blackfeet nation led the parade. He was a strikingly handsome man, tall with the tough muscle and scar of a warrior. His smooth, copper skin stretched over the bones of his face without a crease. His hair was rich ebony black and he wore it in two long braids wrapped in white ermine that hung down below his waist. His leggings and shirt were of supple, brain-cured buckskin, ornamented with blue and red beads. He rode a horse black as coal and carried a shield painted white with the red insignia of his totem. To the Englishmen, he seemed some predatory bird like the animal emblems of the noble houses of Europe. His bow, a quiver of arrows, and a polished trade gun were strapped to his back. His tomahawk hung on a thong at his belt. He held a lance in his right hand and guided the horse with his left. Light seemed to radiate from his torso like reflections on the metallic armor of a crusading knight.

Horned Weasel of the Assiniboins followed. He was as tall as the Blackfoot but hump-shouldered and seemed older. His face was wan, pitted, and thin. His shoulders slumped and his hollow cheeks and cavernous eyes revealed that he had lost strength to sickness and loved ones to the great beyond. He sat his horse loosely as if maintaining his balance drained every ounce of his energy. He, too, carried weapons, but the muscles of his arms sagged. His grip was weak. His delegation was small, only himself and one other youth.

A Cheyenne followed with a face like a hawk and a bonnet of fine eagle feathers. He rode straight as a lodge pole on a magnificent paint stud and held the animal in check with only a thin rawhide bit. It pranced majestically, and his lithe body flowed easily with the proud motions of the horse. His shirt bore the scalps of many enemies he had killed, and the high tilt of his chin proclaimed superiority and courage.

They dismounted at the council lodge. Grooms, like squires to their lords, took charge of their mounts as they walked like feudal sovereigns into the lodge. Bunch and Heney sat at the head of the circle and greeted each one as they entered. Women passed around a filled, steaming bowl, and all ate until satisfied. Then Heney presented gifts: knives, guns, small clay horses, replicas of living animals they would receive. He lit a red stone pipe, invoked the east, south, west, and north, the sky above and the earth below. He inhaled the precious smoke three times, and passed the pipe around the circle. Finally he spoke in sign and in English, stopping only at a gesture from Horned Weasel for greater clarification.

It was an oration calculated to compliment and inflate. Heney's soft tenor voice washed like warm oil over the ears of his listeners. He began slowly: "I bid you welcome and I thank you. You have traveled far to hear my humble words." A dog barked in the distance, but no head turned and Heney continued: "Mister Bunch and I and your friends at Hudson's Bay . . ." — he stopped and nodded to each man around the circle and repeated — "your good English friends from the

Hudson's Bay, have called you together today to tell you about a new threat to your prosperity, an American threat."

Horned Weasel squinted ominously and interrupted: "You say they are a threat, yet we have just seen them depart."

"Then you have witnessed their poverty and weakness. They are fractious and deceitful. Do not underestimate them." Heney stopped to let the knowledge simmer. He began again, speaking specifically to Horned Weasel. He was an important man. All trade goods destined for tribes to the south had to pass through Assiniboin lands. Heney continued: "The Americans promise you rich trade. They say they will bring you gifts. They ask you to make peace with your sworn enemies, to reject Mother England, and swear allegiance to a distant father in a far-off place called Washington. They say they have established a new nation, the United States, not one state but many, a strange conglomeration. You represent your own nations. You know what a nation should be. Look how the Americans bicker and fight. They have among them all manner of humanity . . . whites, Indians, French, a black man . . . and they call themselves united! You send your delegates to a council arrayed in the finest robes, mounted on swift horses. They come groveling upriver, wet and dirty. Is this a good father who cares so little for his children that they dress in rags and cast-offs? Is this a great nation? What can they do for you that your Mother England and her Hudson's Bay Company have not already done better?"

80

Heney's light tenor increased in volume and depth as he warmed to his subject. "The Americans come upriver from the south, through the lands of your enemies. How will they keep open the waters of the wide Missouri past the powerful Omahas and the Sioux? There are two ways, my brothers, only two. They can befriend your enemies or they can control them by arms and war. They are too weak to make war. So they will pay, and the Omahas and Sioux will reap a rich harvest of American guns and turn them against you. You will lose your power to defend your villages. The Americans will steal from you the respect that comes with victory. They will strip you of your honor and your pride." Heney held the rapt attention of every chief. Now he paused before the final question. "The Americans carry evil spirits and disease. The Sioux did not stop them. They sent them past quickly because they breathe sickness and death. Your enemies have saved themselves so as to destroy you. They want to see you die with rotten faces."

An anxious glance flashed from Bunch to Heney. White man's disease was a dangerous subject.

Rupert Bunch raised his voice: "The Americans ask you to forsake your loyal British friends of the Hudson's Bay Company. They ask you to betray Mister Heney and to deny me. You have heard the promises of the Americans. They are soft and moist with decay." He eyed his listeners keenly, and waited. Every head nodded.

Eagle's Claw, the Blackfoot, raised his voice for the first time. "These Americans, they have no horses, not enough guns, very little whiskey. There is no need to contest them. Let them die of their own poverty and ignorance. The grass is greening. The buffalo are returning to the northern plains. It is time for us to hunt." He did not reveal what else he was thinking: that it was a good time to steal a horse. Theft of Assiniboin horses would be easy.

Heney did not contradict the Blackfoot, but he added: "And it is time to make war." The suggestion was pointed. He would have preferred a more decisive conclusion. He would have liked to count American bodies.

Eagle's Claw resumed: "There is no glory in fighting the poor and the weak. I will not commit Blackfoot warriors to such a battle. But I will promise to shun the bearers of disease. They come here without sustenance for themselves, without payment for our game or the sweet waters of our rivers. Thirty men trample our trails like the hoofs of a thousand horses. Let the land and the Great Spirit demand restitution." He nodded toward Horned Weasel of the Assiniboins, who concurred. Cheyenne, Hidatsa, and other heads agreed. Only Sheheke, chief of Matootonha, remained silent.

Heney and Bunch were no longer smiling. The final consensus was only partially to their liking. Heney tried one last time. "These dirty Americans bring their pestilence among you. Kill them and you kill the disease they bring."

Horned Weasel stared back coldly. He had survived an epidemic and bore the scars on his face. But there were no scars on his agile mind, and he drew his thin body straight and inhaled to add breadth and weight to his words. "The disease that has ravaged my people was borne on their skin and the air they breathed. We must not touch the Americans. We must not inhale their breath. The disease is a weapon that will act on us even after they are dead. Their bodies will decay and plant the pestilence in our soil and in the animals that graze on the grass that grows at our feet. I have seen it. I have suffered. My scars bear witness." Horned Weasel's dark eyes locked on Alexander Heney. He lifted an arm and extended a bony finger. "But friend, Heney, it was your company, your traders, and your trappers who brought the sickness among us. It was you English, and the French before you. You are the white skins. It is your curse we suffer."

Heney retreated in shocked silence. Rupert Bunch was scowling like a gargoyle. He could not let the remark stand. He reacted in shrill falsetto. "Not so! Our men died, too. We helped to relieve the suffering of your people."

Horned Weasel rose up. His voice rumbled like a distant war drum. "It does not matter that your company lost men. You have replaced the men you lost. You brought more from across the sea. Here, there are wives without husbands, children without mothers, brothers without sisters. Whole villages are no more. When our old ones, our fathers, our mothers, and our children are gone, the land will lie empty. Look at the Mandans, our friends. They were nine villages. Now they are two. It is a terrible way to die." He sat down again, breathless and exhausted.

Bunch drew in his lips. He had to break the train of thought. He paused and began again. "You are wrong, Horned Weasel. Do you see holes in my face? Why would we kill our good friends with whom we trade? Think again. Go about your hunting. Feed your women and children and your old men. Gather in the plenty that these fertile plains provide. But avoid the Americans. Do not approach them. Do not point out the well-trodden trails. Do not lead them to the springs of clear water. Do not show them where the great herds gather. Let their mouths cry out in hunger. Let their gums shrink from thirst. Let the rivers and the tall mountains erase them and wash the pestilence you fear from the face of the land." Bunch was smiling at his own eloquence. His length of neck amplified his words like the chambers of a horn. "I leave you now to consider the truth of my words." He signaled to the women to pass around a plate of meat, then to Heney to depart. He pulled his robe about him like a mantle of divine right and exited the lodge.

The chiefs mumbled softly among themselves, while the woman circulated the platter of boiled meats.

Rupert Bunch drew Alexander Heney away from the lodge to a quiet clearing at the edge of the village. He lifted a hand as if ready to strike, but the attack came verbally. "Have you no tact? Have you no sense of diplomacy? You can thank me for salvaging the wreckage of your council."

But Alexander Heney was not intimidated. "Calm yourself, Rupert. I have insured other means of obstructing the Americans. They tried to buy trade goods from me . . . with a letter of credit drawn on the treasury of their new republic. I told them that I could not honor a worthless slip of paper, signed by a president of a rebellious union of petty states that I, that England, should not recognize." He laughed. "I told them that after the winter and the recent trading, I had precious little left and awaited a shipment of goods all the way from Montreal." Heney smacked his lips together and crinkled his eyes with glee. "The Americans are the enemy, Rupert. I don't trade with the enemy." He laughed out loud. "And I told Sheheke to keep that woman in camp."

"What woman?"

"Pretty wench named Laughing Water. She married one of the Americans and wanted to go along. The Indians are superstitious folk. They think the gods frowned on the husband because he would not share his wife at the buffalo calling." Heney shook his head in amazement. "The incident has devolved to our advantage. Then there is the whiskey. Their whiskey is terrible stuff, some country brew fit for convicts and debtors made from fermented corn. Bourbon they call it. A Frenchman must have invented it and named it after a dead king. They have only about a two months' supply. When they run out, men will desert in droves. And they hired Charbonneau with his woman. The worm is in the fruit. I ask you of what use is a woman to thirty young and virile men?"

Bunch laughed. His beady eyes flashed derision. "They will fight each other for her favors."

Smiling, the two men resumed their seats at the council with true British aplomb. The Blackfoot, Eagle's Claw, spoke loudly and clearly for all the chiefs present. "It is not difficult to avoid the Americans and hinder their progress. This we will do willingly." He did not add *because it requires no risk.* He nodded graciously and said: "We thank you for the many fine horses."

He left the council a richer man in horses. On the way to his homeland he raided the hapless Assiniboins of still more horses and drove them to his village. There he claimed a wife and led warriors to intercept the Americans. But he found the Americans struggling deep in the brakes of the river. It was a difficult descent and little would have been gained that he had not already gained from the British. Eagle's Claw observed from the heights and led his warriors away to hunt the buffalo. He would have understood Toussaint Charbonneau. He did not labor when there was no need, and he was a covetous man, but he counted his wealth in horses, not in coins of gold.

CHAPTER
EIGHT

Charbonneau and his little family traveled like honored guests in the red *pirogue*, far from the canoes of the enlisted men, under the careful watch of the officers. Charbonneau kept to himself, except for sailing lessons from the half-blind boatman, Cruzatte. He set up his own camp near the captains, and carefully guarded his wife and child from the advances of lustful men. He spoke always in French, only to Meriwether Lewis, Pierre Cruzatte, and, occasionally, Drouillard. His wife set his fires and cooked his meals. He brought his own supplies: muskets, knives, blankets and buffalo robes, baskets of hulled corn, tobacco for his eternal pipe, a collection of iron beaver traps, and a teepee in which he invited the two captains to sleep for a small monetary consideration.

Freed from the tyranny of his first wife, the second wife settled happily to caring for her baby and husband, and without the brazen, flirtatious first wife, Charbonneau's jealousy diminished. His second wife was dumpy and short, but she tended his physical needs very well. He basked contentedly in her attentions. He was beginning to take mild interest in his son, but his primary interest was the gold that he had sewn tightly in the red sash wrapped around his middle. He had a habit of inserting his thumbs in the sash when he wasn't cradling his pipe. Then he would spread his wide palms over his mid-section and feel the hidden cache of gold. It gave him a sense of security and comfort.

On a sunny afternoon, a steady breeze rose from the east, directly downriver. Charbonneau sat in the stern of the *pirogue* with his wife and Cruzatte, puffing impassively on his pipe. Cruzatte steered the boat by sound and feel. He listened closely to the whispering flow and sensed every lap of wave and change of pressure. The river was flat as a dinner plate when he handed the tiller to Charbonneau and hoisted the sail. He settled himself snugly against the mast, dropped a fishing line over the side, leaned back, and fell asleep.

The Frenchman steered smoothly, but, as the day wore on, he grew bored and eased his grip. The sail luffed. Charbonneau didn't notice the sudden puff that jangled the rigging. A second puff was stronger. More puffs converged and strengthened into a brisk wind that intensified quickly. Its touch cooled and refreshed in the hot dry air, and wavelets appeared on the surface of the water until a sudden hard gust jerked the tiller from Charbonneau's beefy hands. He lurched for the unruly rod and held it grimly, like a statue carved in stone. He was a stubborn, proud man. He clenched his teeth harder on the stoneware pipe and did not ask for help. Sergeant Ordway, the look-out, was watching the shore. Captain Lewis was absorbed in his journals. The little wife sat faithfully by her husband, humming to her baby and sewing moccasins. Pierre Cruzatte slept on.

The lighter canoes reacted quickly when the current swelled and the wind strengthened from out of the north. A black thunderhead was bearing down. The lashing rain was already in sight, a dank, gray curtain pulled tightly across the western prairie. Labiche had stopped paddling. Collins had lifted his oar and let the canoe fall back. When he looked up, the red *pirogue*, with Charbonneau at the helm, was bracing the flow. Charbonneau crouched over the tiller, pulling with both hands, straining every fiber of neck and back, fighting the relentless push of the river.

Labiche waved his paddle like a flag. He screamed at the struggling Frenchman. A chorus of shouts welled up from other canoes. But Charbonneau did not listen to English speakers, especially frantic shouts of lesser men, and the wind howled and drowned out their cries and the current tossed the hapless *pirogue*. Ordway turned, but too late. The black water came alive like a serpent from its winter sleep. It uncoiled gradually, warmed to the movement, hissed and roiled and tossed the *pirogue* in its jaws. A brutal gust tore the tiller from Charbonneau's grasp. With a *crack*, the heavy boom swept over the deck and the *pirogue* swung broadside to the current. Now it swept downriver like a bobbing cork toward the flotilla of floundering canoes.

Collins, Howard, Pryor, Drouillard, every man in every canoe, battled the waves. They rowed fiercely toward shore to save themselves, out of the path of the careening *pirogue* that heeled to larboard and started to fill and swept down on them like an avalanche.

Barrels and crates rolled across the deck. Captain Lewis wrapped his precious papers in oilcloth and prepared to jump. Water gushed in. Medicines, trade goods, equipment, barrels of whiskey and flour sloshed and floated free. The sail flapped like a flag in the wind. The rudder rose helplessly above the stream, crashing against the planking of the stern as slowly, irrevocably, the *pirogue* nosed down into the river and irreplaceable supplies began to float away.

The *crash* of the rudder finally awakened old Cruzatte who skidded over the deck, grabbed his rifle, and screeched: "Charbonneau, grab that tiller, steer this boat, or I shoot!"

Charbonneau had clambered to the starboard gunwale high above the water where he clung, red-sashed belly to planking, like a tick on a dog. Cruzatte pointed the gun. Terrified, Charbonneau looked up. His hands held his middle as if he'd been shot. Cruzatte cocked the gun. He pulled the trigger, and the flint snapped on wet powder. Comprehension dawned slowly.

Charbonneau threw up a hand. "*Ne tirez pas! F'irai!*" He waded to the tiller, locked his iron fists around it, leaned his weight against it, and the boat came around graceful as a swan into the wind. But it was barely afloat.

"Take to the shallows!" The high-pitched peal came from Lewis himself as he manned an oar and began to paddle while Ordway bailed frantically and all eyes centered on the swamped boat. As if dispatched by God, the diminutive mother, Charbonneau's tiny second wife, with baby strapped securely to her back, leaned out of the boat, reached into the flow, and picked out books, maps, vials of medicines, and carrots of tobacco that had fallen overboard and floated past. A loud cheer went up as she grabbed a gaff and hooked a barrel of whiskey that would have floated briskly downstream.

Gently, carefully, Cruzatte maneuvered the *pirogue* into the shallows. Men grabbed the *pirogue*, pushed it up the beach, and pulled the plug to let it drain. The wind died as rapidly as it had risen. The circle of men — wet, bruised, shaking from the strain — stood on shore. Their black looks condemned Toussaint Charbonneau.

Charbonneau paid no heed. He slinked away to the edge of camp, behind a curtain of brush, shoved his pipe in his mouth, lit it, and fumbled with the wet knot that held his sash. It would not give.

"The point of your knife will loosen it faster." The voice was oily sweet.

"*Merde*, Labiche." Charbonneau swore like a teamster, but he was shaking so he nearly dropped his pipe.

"I've watched you. Yes, I speak good French, and I suspect you speak good English." With a crooked leer, Labiche reached for the sash. "I show you how to untie it. Your fingers play you tricks." He inserted the point of his blade into the knot and gently pried apart the fibers.

Weighted by the gold, the sash sagged and started to fall. Labiche caught it, tested its weight, and grinned. Charbonneau snatched at it like a hungry wolf, but

Labiche held it beyond his reach. Their eyes met and held. Finally Charbonneau blundered: "You know."

Labiche nodded. "I only suspected until now. You are a rich man, Toussaint. I am a gambler. I can smell an easy mark. I have waited for you to betray your hand." He undid the thong that held the purse, and shiny guineas fell to the earth.

Charbonneau had black, calculating eyes. "How much do you want to keep my secret?"

Labiche's squinty eyes narrowed. The scar on his cheek contracted to a thin purple line as he rubbed the stubble on his chin. "Count them first. Then I tell you."

Charbonneau unfolded the sash, and silently lifted out each coin. When he finished, Labiche picked up the sash, shook it. Twelve more guineas fell to earth. "Sixty. I need sixty guineas. Forty guineas to insure my silence and twenty more to save you from the wrath of other men." He smiled at Charbonneau's glazed shock, nodded cynically, and walked away.

Charbonneau puffed his pipe like an angry dragon until the smoke made him cough. Then he re-tied his sash and returned to the camp. He went immediately to the tent that his wife had set up and did not come out.

John Collins and Tom Howard volunteered to dive to retrieve the sunken goods. But Howard was drunk, and Captain Clark refused the offer. "We have not come for beaver. We're mercifully relieved of his heavy traps. The water is murky and the current too swift. Let them rest in peace." They built a blazing fire and lay out dripping items to dry as Clark tapped the whiskey barrel and issued each man a gill.

In the morning, François Labiche went to look for Toussaint Charbonneau. Their eyes locked on first glance.

"What do you want?" Charbonneau asked.

"My payment in full." Labiche paused and squinted. "Or do I tell the captains?"

Charbonneau pulled his pipe from his mouth and cleared his throat. His toady eyes bulged. The hairs of his black beard trembled with the workings of his lips. "I have a wife, a family."

"So did I, once. I did not appreciate their value. You call me pirate. I have lived my life with water. I can swim, and you cannot, yet you tie weights to your waist. I will see to it that you do not drown. To you, I have great value."

Loud voices and laughter rose from the camp. Charbonneau's eyes flicked. "They don't know I carry it. They will question."

"I'll say I won it from Heney in a game of dice, or from Bunch when he was drunk. They'll never know." He lied. The captains knew. Labiche knew that they knew. They'd seen Deschamps pack the furs, like Labiche, like Drouillard, like others. And everyone had seen Deschamps's boats floating too low in the water.

"I give you forty."

"Your life, their life" — he pointed toward the baby — "is cheap. Sixty."

In the end, Charbonneau agreed. He had no choice. He began to accompany Labiche and to take on chores around the camp and enter games of chance that Labiche always won. But no one befriended him. No one understood why the captains had hired him or why he was allowed privileges that were denied everyone else: a work-free ride, a private tent, a woman to set up his camp, gather wood, care for his child, warm his bed. When addressed in English, he did not answer. He communicated only with his wife, Cruzatte, Labiche, Captain Lewis, and, occasionally, Georges Drouillard. He used more than his share of tobacco in his infernal pipe. Rumor spread that he had brought his own whiskey because, when he wasn't smoking, he was always drinking from a smelly jug. He was alien, not to be trusted, an object of suspicion and envy.

The second wife, on the other hand, had earned the confidence and admiration of the rough men of the corps. She collected herbs to flavor meat. She mended clothing. She removed thorns from feet and splinters from hands. She gathered currants and turnips and the wild fennel that cured stomach cramps. Her womanly hands soothed more than the gentlest touch of any gruff male. Gradually men began to respect, even idolize her. Some learned her name, Sacagawea. Some, like Captain Clark, nicknamed her Janey. Cruzatte even called her *Sainte*, and, when Captain Lewis thanked her publicly at muster for saving his precious records from the river, the whole party hooted and cheered. They were especially grateful for the barrel of whiskey. But the abundant supply did not last.

One rainy day, the captains reduced the whiskey ration. Captain Lewis enumerated the reasons at muster in the pouring rain. "Our supply is dwindling. No one's to blame except Captain Clark and myself. We did not accurately estimate the capacity of the natives for strong drink or the need to regale them with gifts. We did not fully comprehend the length of this journey." As usual, he did not transfer blame, but ignorant, resentful men did.

"It's all 'cause of Charbonneau an' 'is guzzlin'." Hugh Hall said it, and the rumor percolated down the muster line. No one admitted where it began.

Captain Lewis heard only a meaningless slur and continued: "It's July. We thought by now we should have reached the mountains." He hung his rain-soaked head. "I am truly sorry."

At the order to dismiss, grumblings multiplied like fleas. "The Frenchman sucks liquor like his babe sucks milk." Others taunted and goaded. "Smart little woman. Too bad she didn't let 'im drown."

Cruzatte no longer trusted him to steer. Men refused to work beside him on the towline, lest he let go and the heavy cord pull a man under. They set him aside, quarantined him like a victim of the deadly pox while others manned the poling and the paddling. His inertia only increased their aversion.

Around the mess fires, when the officers were absent, thinly veiled jabs fed John Collins's simmering resentment. Finally Hugh Hall's needling pushed him over the edge. "Collins an' me, we got fifty lashes fer drinkin' an' we didn't do no harm. Never swamped a boat. You ain't forgot the whippin' Johnny? A man feels the lash, and the stripes itch fer life. You got twice as many as me. You go after the Frenchie, I'm yer second, right behind ye, boy."

But Joe Whitehouse cautioned: "Johnny can't fight. Captain threatened to send 'im back."

Hall was insistent. "We've come too far fer that. We stage a little contest far enough away in the woods, captains'll never know."

"What woods? Ain't seen a tree fer a week."

"We find a buffler wallow, that'll do, out of sight of camp."

"What about Pryor and Ordway and Gass?"

"The sergeants? Gass is Irish. They love a good fight. An' look at 'is face. He's fought a time or two. As fer Ordway, the boys can sink a canoe, find 'im a woman, lose a box o' Lewis's precious specimens, give 'im somethin' to hold 'is mind. Won't take Collins ten minutes to lay the Frenchie flat."

"Pryor'll sniff us out."

"Not if we do it at night when we's supposed to be asleep."

"What about Drouillard?"

"He goes huntin'. He won't even be here. You with us, Johnny?"

The sniff of contest sparked fire in Collins's young blood. Secretly he couldn't wait to get his hands on Charbonneau. But Labiche whispered a warning in the Frenchman's ear, and Charbonneau could not be pried away from the captains' side.

They paddled on, past vast herds of buffalo and elk, antelope that had just calved, beaver dams, and coveys of grouse, but no Indians. The grass glowed greener than emerald fire under the hot prairie sun and the mighty river swelled with spring rain and distant mountain thaw.

Then, suddenly, the river forked and the expedition came to an abrupt halt. Speculation buzzed like gnats around the fires while the captains huddled in conference. "Injuns didn't tell us there were two."

"Ain't two, only one right one. We got to choose."

The choice was crucial, and the captains elicited every man's counsel. Meriwether Lewis even asked Charbonneau's advice. "We've been gone two months. What of this fork in the river? Where are the waterfalls the Mandans described?"

Charbonneau clamped his teeth on his pipe. "*Fe n'en sais rien.* I've never come this far."

Lewis gaped a moment in disbelief. "We hired you for your knowledge of the western waters." He held his patience in tight check, like a tempest in a bottle. "It would have gone easier for you, Mister Charbonneau, if you had told us your limitations. You cannot swim. You're afraid of water." He sputtered in sharp, serrated syllables. "You profess none of the knowledge we so desperately need, and the corps detests you to a man."

Charbonneau removed his pipe from his lips and blew out thick smoke. It was as close as he would come to admitting fault. "I drink water. I am not to blame."

They took a vote. Most men chose to go north up the starboard stream, but, in the end, Meriwether Lewis overturned the decision and the expedition turned south. The larboard fork ran clear and pure like water running from a mountain spring. Lewis decreed it so, but doubts persisted. Days later, he climbed an outcrop with his looking glass and finally spied mountains. But only when they heard the roar of water crashing on rocks, did men believe him right. It was June 13th, over two months since they had left the Mandan villages. Here were the thunderous falls that the Mandans described. They tumbled from great heights and spewed a thin fabric of shimmering mist into the sun-bright air.

Charbonneau didn't see the beauty. His wife was sick. He rigged a travois to transport her and hoisted the infant on his own back. And he cried — the men thought it unmanly and derided him for it.

But the woman grew worse and concern deepened. Her arms and legs twitched like dry leaves in a summer breeze, not unlike Sergeant Floyd in his last days. They had buried him, one year ago, in the land of the Omahas. Her skin grew cold to the touch or burned with fever. Clark bled her. Lewis dosed her with opium and barks. The hungry infant fretted when he could not suckle. His cries grew insistent and loud, and the frantic father fashioned a nipple from an antelope tit and filled it with water to quiet him. They killed a buffalo cow and offered milk, but the baby spit it out.

Some who had wives and had fathered children, like blacksmiths Bratton and Shields, old Cruzatte, Labiche, recognized the Frenchman's pain and extended a thin strand of friendship. Cruzatte carved a wooden cross and placed it around the woman's neck to effect a cure. Shields brought a pillow. Labiche wiped the feverish sweat from her brow. Each day men carried her carefully from campsite to boat and back again. Collins took the Mandan amulet from around his neck and lay it next to Cruzatte's cross on her breast.

At a Sunday muster, Captain Lewis conducted prayers. "Direct us through her to her mountain people, oh, Lord. Grant us horses to ease our burdens and bless us with swift and easy passage over the mountains. Show us an easy path around these magnificent falls, the work of your mighty hands, and restore our Janey to good health. For this we pray and place our trust in your benevolent care." Every man in the corps whispered: "Amen."

But when Charbonneau returned to his wife's side, Cruzatte's cross had slipped from her throat. The black amulet rested at her breast. He recognized instantly that it belonged to Collins and his face purpled with rage. Ripping the little owl from her neck, he swung back his arm and threw it with explosive force into the river. Collins did not witness the act, but Drouillard was there and protested vehemently: "He offered it in kindness for her health and good fortune."

Charbonneau screamed: "It's the seducer's, the devil's! I saw him wearing it. You think I do not forget how he dishonors and insults me? It is an owl and black as faces painted for war, black as the night of the Christian hell."

Drouillard objected: "Stands In The River who brought it, offered it in peace." But Charbonneau had closed his ears. Drouillard went for Collins, and together they plumbed the river bottom. But the current was swift, the waters deep, and the mud of the riverbed filled with stones. They didn't find the shiny black owl. Drouillard commiserated: "You knew one day you must part with it."

Collins nodded but his lips were white as dry salt, and the look on his face could have sliced hard stone.

"Come, Johnny, get your gun. We hunt."

As Collins went for the weapon, Nathaniel Pryor whispered in Drouillard's keen ear. "You are wise to put the river between him and Charbonneau."

Drouillard launched a canoe, and they left with night fast approaching. They bedded near a giant spring and slept soundly to the lullaby of its waters. When Collins awakened, the sun shone brightly. The waters smelled like the bowels of the earth and glowed yellow as cured hay. "It's a sign. These are the sun's waters. Drink and it will heal your bitterness." Drouillard so declared, drank, and filled a flask. Collins did the same. They carried the water to Sacagawea who also drank. That night, the fever broke, and in the morning she was sitting up and asking for her son. But Charbonneau resented the cure because it came from the hands of John Collins.

The expedition moved on. There were five falls to portage on twelve miles of river, and sixteen miles to march over dry hills. They felled huge cottonwoods and hacked out axles, wheels, and couplings for wagons and lifted the heavy dugouts on the makeshift carriages. They butchered meat enough to sustain thirty hungry, active men during a long, laborious portage. Cacti, insects, hail tormented the hapless men worse than the hammering of the river's swift current. They yanked thorns from their feet, slapped away biting insects, pulled thirty tons of supplies on crude, wobbly wagons, and collapsed each night like dead men into their robes. Collins and Charbonneau, the captains and sergeants, no one was exempt from the labor. Collins shouldered the effort as willingly as the rest, but the effort strained. And he resented the loss of his amulet. "He had no right. It was charmed."

Drouillard didn't want to hear complaining, and grumbled: "For me, I would have traded it for a horse."

CHAPTER
NINE

As they neared the mountains, the great herds thinned and the air grew dry. The river narrowed. A buffalo bull charged the camp in the black of night, scattering bits of flame and setting fire to blankets and robes. Hail the size of a man's fist rained down. Captain Lewis's iron boat sank. Worst of all, on July 4th, they drank the last of the whiskey. There was nothing left to kill pain, inspire a song, lull a tired man to sleep.

They sailed on through deep cañons and past white cliffs, rock formations that rose like cathedral spires and giant portals, to a wide prairie where the river divided in three. Fire had ravaged the land. Irish Sergeant Patrick Gass described the scene with sadness. "Should be green as shamrocks and clover and 'tis black as devils' turds." Black again — the color that troubled Charbonneau and haunted Collins. Black as the owl, black as the burned-over grass, black as the powder that blasts death from the barrel of a rifle, black as York, the slave, black as Charbonneau's tangled beard and the smoke that belches from his infernal pipe. Black, the color of war.

Game had fled the blackened earth. Collins cooked fish and fowl, thin fare for active men used to

102

devouring pounds of meat each day. He breathed the powdery ash that caked in nostrils and ears, parched throats sore, and stuck in moist eyeballs when it rained. The earth smelled of decay and death. Men ached and sickened in body and soul.

Clouds rolled into the valley and the rain turned the black ash to lather. Moisture masked the distant mountains in an envelope of fog. Pryor, Drouillard, Collins, Labiche, Shields, Whitehouse, and Shannon huddled under a tarp, nursing a smoking fire. They stamped feet and clapped hands and crowded together to warm and dry themselves. A pot of soup simmered.

Shields sniffed angrily. "Soup again. They gi' thicker fare to prisoners an' galley slaves." His eyes were bloodshot, his skin gray, his mind wandering like a lost child.

An anxious glance flicked from Collins to Whitehouse to young Georgie Shannon — around the circle of men — and finally to Sergeant Pryor. Shields ranted on. "Can't work a forge if I don't eat." Shields was a burly blacksmith from Kentucky, wide as he was tall, older than most, prudent and steady, skilled in his craft, a valued member of the corps. To the Indians, he crafted strong metal that absorbed the miraculous power of smoke and flame. The Indian woman brought him gifts of squash, beans, dried berries, and roots, but Shields demanded red meat. Some of his comments were cruel. "She gives the brown brat sweet mother's milk an' me dry roots and leaves." His messmates let the comment pass. His mind was ailing. It had been three long months since they'd rested in a village, seen another mother, heard another woman sing, or another baby cry. For many men, Sacagawea and the baby were their only reminders of a gentler, warmer existence.

Joe Whitehouse stated what they were all thinking. He was bouncing the chubby infant on his knee, contorting his face into clownish expressions. The baby grinned back and giggled. "If I ever see home again, gonna find me a pretty woman, make me a little feller just like him."

Labiche laughed. "What you want pretty for? Pretty brings heartbreak and loneliness. Ask Johnny."

Collins threw up his hands in denial. They turned as one. Shields had resumed his complaint. "Fine bunch o' hunters, comin' in always empty. Need me own commissary like that there baby, like friend Johnny had with his pretty Mandan."

It was a crude comment and silenced the friendly banter. Collins felt the insult keenly. Labiche saw his jaw tense and laid a restraining hand on his arm. "You got to learn how to hold it in, Johnny, like Whitehouse, here." Joe Whitehouse, a mild-mannered, discreet young man, nodded agreeably.

Shields ranted on: "You an' Warner an' Thompson, you're stashin' the meat . . . Collins, savin' the best for yer favorites. You want to make a hungry man pay, let him eat salt pork an' dried soup, let him mop up yer lickings like Clark's blackie slave, like Captain Lewis's dog."

Collins turned his empty bowl toward Shields. "We eat same as you and not much of that." But he knew rations were diminishing quickly.

104

"Show me yer bowl when it's full at the start of a meal." Shields turned on Labiche. "He likes you. He gives you somethin' to stuff yer skinny cheeks?" Labiche's eyes narrowed while Shields's bulged like shiny marbles. "I ain't eatin' this mush. I ain't lappin' my dinner like a dog. Gimme a plate an' a knife an fork." He got up and staggered away. They heard his voice rise to a wail and watched as he set his bowl upon the ground for Seaman, Lewis's Chesapeake retriever, to lick. He patted the animal's head and scratched its ears. "Good dog. Catch a squirrel and I'll see these bastards don't let you starve." He and the dog walked out through the willows that bordered the river.

"He's sick. Got a demon inside, eatin' what he swallows, suckin' at his soul." As a group they looked to Sergeant Nathaniel Pryor who shook his head. "We may have to leash him."

Labiche murmured grimly: "On the ships, we squeezed lemon juice into the rum. Good for the brain. Good for the teeth. Cleans out the rust from the stomach."

"Lemons? Out here? But a lick o' rum would set him right."

"That an' some greens. The Indian woman and Charbonneau went out diggin' roots."

Labiche laughed derisively. "She's diggin'. Charbonneau's singin' and smokin' and pattin' his paunch." The syllables slipped out. Pryor's head turned and Shannon blinked. Collins had averted his eyes, but he, too, had marked the errant words. A fire was rising in his chest. It stayed with him and ravaged his soul like the blaze that blackened the land. It stuck just below his rib cage, destroyed his appetite and his sleep, and flared every time he heard the name Charbonneau. His memories were too vivid, his wife too dear, the amulet too precious. Conversation swirled around him, but he held his tongue. Resentment bubbled into his throat. Charbonneau was out alone with only the woman. He could take him on, relieve him of his riches, eke the revenge he was due. He asked: "What kinda roots they diggin'?"

"How should I know? Roots is the only thing the fire didn't touch. She boils 'em to mush. Tries to make Shields eat. Woman deserves better. So does the kid."

Thoughts of Charbonneau preoccupied Collins. He began to falter on the tow. His axe slipped dangerously when he chopped wood. He hacked the meat he butchered. Early one morning, at muster, he had not cleaned his rifle, and Sergeant Pryor rebuked him soundly. "Clean that gun, Private. Captain issued you a brand new Harpers. Treat it like your mother, like your wife. Swab it. Polish it. If Charbonneau's still creasin' your pride after these three months, smooth it out, burn it, bury it."

"Yes, sir," Collins answered coldly, but the rebuke clawed like a cat caged inside him. Burn, bury, Charbonneau — the words melted into his brain like rain on dry desert. Like John Shields, he stared without blinking, and Charbonneau's hairy face loomed everywhere before him.

Days passed. Charbonneau and his wife did not return. Again, dinner was boiled fowl and not very palatable. Labiche cooked because Collins was sick, and Collins only ate because Labiche was his friend. Drouillard took him out to hunt to clear his addled brain. Dry ash flaked away like scales beneath their feet. Vultures pecked at carcasses whose roasted ribs lay exposed like beckoning arms held wide. Once he chased the birds away, bent, and sliced off a cut of putrid meat. His lips puckered and he spat it out. "Lays on my tongue like his cursed name." He rinsed his mouth with river water and walked on.

Drouillard pointed to impressions in the ash — elk, an antelope, game enough to restock the larder. "Follow the antelope and I'll track the elk. The game is returning."

Collins stomach lurched as he set out. The tracks wandered across the blackened plain and crossed the river. He swam the icy stream. The cold cleared his head and he rested to collect his thoughts on the sandy shore. The cloven prints were there, engraved like half moons in the wet sand. And there were other prints, human prints. One set towed out like duck's feet. The second were tiny, arched, and straight. Toussaint Charbonneau and his second wife had passed this way.

Collins could see the mountains clearly now. His imagination stamped the face of the surly Frenchman on every peak. Light lingered late in the mountains but night overtook him like the blackness that darkened his mind. It came suddenly — he had not minded the weeks or the months since he left Laughing Water. He had not minded the time of day. He was here, far away, with strangeness all around him. The sky turned purple, then ghostly gray, and finally faded to ebony black. There were no stars, no moon. Collins moved on, one tentative step at a time. It started to rain big splatting drops that washed the prints and the soil they inscribed into deep gullies. He lost the track, looked for shelter, tripped, and fell. He could not see the hand he held at arm's length. Shivering, he reached for his firebox and its small wad of lint to strike a flame. The wool ignited but there was no dry fuel to feed the fire and it died. He gave himself up to the blackness, slumped to the ground, and tried to sleep. Dry, numbing cold seeped through the burned earth into his limbs and collided in his bones with the wet cold of the night. He slapped his arms against himself and listened to the shriek of the night hawk and the dirge of a great horned owl. A goose honked. A pack of wolves howled. He wondered if they, too, tracked the lonely antelope, if they had smelled his human scent, if they, too, longed for a mate. When a glimmer of light pierced the eastern sky, a cold haze enveloped the plain, but the rain had stopped. He slapped himself again to see if he was still alive, took his bearings, and headed south.

Georges Drouillard found him miles from camp. "Johnny, hurry. You'll miss the muster." Drouillard had to lead him by the hand.

Collins took his place in the line, behind Bratton, in front of lanky John Colter. His garments were dirty, his moccasins torn, and the barrel of his rifle was black with wet soot.

Captain Clark frowned when he saw him. His voice cracked like splitting wood. "Collins, where have you been?" But he passed on by. When he finished reviewing the ranks, he returned.

John Colter tried to explain. "Sun's touched 'im in the head, sir. Speak up, Johnny, tell him."

But Collins had never perfected the talent of alibi. He bridled.

Clark snapped suspiciously at Colter. "What sun, Private Colter? He's had all night to sleep it off." His anger showed in the steady tick of his cheek and the iron clamp of his jaw. He muttered blandly: "Report to me, Private Collins, for special duty."

For the next week William Clark kept John Collins and John Shields confined to camp, under the strict surveillance of Nathaniel Pryor.

It was another week before Charbonneau returned. He and his wife had ventured past the perimeter of the burning to where the river meandered through reed-choked bogs. A spring spouted hot steam and tall mountains cleaved the rivers. They had found roots, fish, fowl, antelope, and curative herbs, and, when they appeared before the captains, the little woman trembled with excitement. Her gestures flicked quickly. Her speech bubbled like the gushing spring.

Clark looked to Lewis who translated and whose passion rose in the telling. "She's been here before, Will. She recognized the places where they walked, the place where she was captured. We're in Shoshone land!"

Clark jumped up. It was August 8th, nearly four months to the day that they had departed Fort Mandan. He clasped Charbonneau's hand, took the baby from its board, bounced him joyfully on his knee, and clapped the Frenchman hard between the shoulders. He withdrew a small scissors from his pocket and handed it to Charbonneau. "Give her this for her trouble." But the little woman refused the gift, and Lewis spoke up. "Then eat with us and we'll talk of her people."

They dined and discussed the value of pelts, the politics of the British fur trade, the great wealth of beaver in the rivers, and the tug and pull of Indian migration that banished the Shoshone nation from the plains. Charbonneau told of the powerful and fearsome Blackfoot tribe and the Crows whose territory they had entered, how the more powerful tribes had overwhelmed the less fortunate.

Lightning crashed and the heavens opened. The mountain storms were brief and violent and the rain abated quickly, but not Lewis's boundless curiosity. "Where are they now, the Blackfeet and the Crows?"

"North and east with the buffalo herds and the British traders." Charbonneau chuckled that the Americans did not know.

"But the British have not come this far. We've passed the place where your wife was taken."

Charbonneau puckered his lips around the stem of his pipe. "The British have come here. Hidatsa raiders and the French came before them. My wife was taken when they stormed this place. Her people do not linger where there is danger. They are over the divide on the western-facing slopes, where they are safe."

"You mean we will not meet natives until after we cross the mountains?"

"*Absolument oui, mon capitaine.*" Charbonneau showed no visible emotion.

The reality stunned Meriwether Lewis. He waited until Charbonneau and Sacagawea had gone, and cursed louder than a drunken seaman and pounded his fists into the rough bark of a tree. "Damn Charbonneau. Damn the English. Where are the bloody Shoshones? How can we secure their help if we can't find them?"

Clark stared back intently. He remained icily calm and replied: "They are here, in the cañons and behind the high peaks. We've seen their fire rings, lodges, tombs, weapons." His deep monotone insisted: "Charbonneau must be mistaken."

"Saying it does not make it so, Will. Four months we've been gone. Too long."

They followed the western fork and named the river, Jefferson. It narrowed, grew shallow, and forked again and yet again. Days passed. The mountains expanded and loomed all around, near enough to reach out and touch. Water shot down their slopes in torrents and runs. Ropes broke. Men slipped and sprained ankles and knees. Captain Clark dropped his knife, which slashed the skin from his ankle. It swelled to twice its size. He tried to hide the limp, but grew impatient and irritated. No Indians appeared. The land was empty.

Meriwether Lewis was losing sleep. In the privacy of his tent, he lamented: "Not one flat place to stand an inkwell or lay a page to write upon. Scrape bottom one minute, stick like a stump in the clay the next. Spin and crash and bounce and swirl. I'd sell my soul for a horse, a big, sure-footed charger like kings used to ride in battle, strong enough to carry us and all we possess over the bloody mountains and down the other side."

Lewis was not alone in his complaint. The men needed a scapegoat and settled on Charbonneau. They blamed him for the length of the journey, for the height of the mountains, for the absence of friendly natives, for not sharing his tobacco. They blamed him for his ignorance. Hugh Hall, the gossipmonger, started the prickly comment. "Charbonneau says there's Indians with horses." No one believed Charbonneau. Shields grumbled: "Words, not worth the smoke he pumps from his pipe." And Labiche snapped derisively: "If he finds horses like he sails a boat . . ." He didn't finish the sentence. Everyone laughed.

"Cap'n should've let you take him out, Johnny, like I know you wanted. Time we had somethin' worth wagerin', a good fight, a few bloody knuckles." Hugh Hall rubbed his hands together.

Collins narrowed his gaze and licked his lips. "I'm willin'. Always was."

Hall was gloating. "Labiche, name the odds. You don't take 'im, Johnny, I will. Where is the bastard?"

"Huntin' with Drouillard and Shannon."

"Won't bag a damn' thing. I heard he was a lumberman. Best he can do is trap not shoot. But he can fling a tomahawk."

112

Drouillard came in with an elk. Charbonneau arrived shortly after, as expected empty-handed. Shannon did not appear at all, and the vicious murmuring continued unabated.

"Hexed us when he brought that woman along. Women's bad luck. Tell 'im, Labiche. Tell 'im what every sailor knows." Hall said this to Charbonneau's face. "A woman aboard's bad luck, worse than a curse."

Charbonneau barely blinked, but Labiche replied: "Not our little woman." He didn't press the thought.

Hall grunted like a rooting hog, and Charbonneau bowed his head.

Next day, Charbonneau was towing the *pirogue*, silent and malleable as a lump of clay, with Hugh Hall at his side. Sergeant Ordway worked behind them. The riverbed was rocky, the current rapid, the water barely deep enough to float a boat. Charbonneau stumbled suddenly and started to fall, let go the rope, and grabbed the lump in the sash at his waist. The boat stopped instantly in the press of current, ripping the cord from Hall's beefy grasp.

Labiche jumped from his own boat to seize the flapping cord. He was too light. He caught the cord, but the weight of boat and rush of water pulled him down. He let go to save himself and the heavy *pirogue* careened downstream into the path of the oncoming canoes. Men shouted and scrambled to get out of the way.

Joe Whitehouse jumped into the water to turn the bow of his lumbering dugout. He didn't see the *pirogue* swerve. It sped down upon him, felled him like a sapling, and ground him like a millstone against the hard bedrock of the channel. He surfaced face down in the water.

Collins watched in horror as Whitehouse's limp form floated swiftly with the current, away downstream. He beached his own canoe and screeched his panic. Drouillard, hunting on shore, heard the cry, waded in, and pulled Whitehouse from the flow. He laid him flat on his stomach and opened his mouth.

Labiche was in the water, splashing frantically to Drouillard's side. The pirate turned Whitehouse over, shoved back the lolling head, opened the mouth, and thumped the chest. He shouted presumptuously to God above. Whitehouse coughed, vomited, and gasped air.

Then the pirate cursed. "He's a disgrace to his Christian patrimony. Thinks of his gold before a man's life. I'll kill 'im before he kills us, damn him to hell. Where's Collins? We'll take 'im down together."

CHAPTER
TEN

It began to rain. They stopped on the spot to let Whitehouse recover, and bound rawhide strips around his cracked ribs.

"Place him under the canopy out of the rain with the captains." Meriwether Lewis gave his captain's place to the injured man and took a seat under the stormy sky in the circle of disgruntled men. Black anger was written large on angry, vindictive faces but Lewis's voice was soft as down. "I've sent Charbonneau away." He did not mention where, and smiled wanly. The smile smoothed the anxious furrows and transformed his face from concern to friendliness. He held a cup in his hand, catching the raindrops as they fell. "Can't write. Can't read. Can't see the sun's zenith or the phase of the moon." Grim silence met his gentle stare. He sat hatless, hair plastered to his skull, interrupted only by the *ping* of droplets as they hit the tin cup. He rambled on. "Captain's ankle has festered. Shannon hasn't come back. Shouldn't have let him go. It's August already and summer's half gone." He glanced dolefully at his men. "And all you men want to fight each other." It was a spontaneous outburst, directed as much at the smoke and the rain as the circle of men.

His gaunt face, his sad eyes in their hollow sockets focused on the wet ashes of a former fire. He pleaded: "Where did I go wrong?" One by one, intimidated by his doleful glance, men got up to move away. Water dripped from the strands of his red hair into his face and onto his buckskin shirt. He rubbed the wetness from his eyes and continued in a voice that sounded more like a prayer. "Don't go. I want to hear from every one of you. Should we split the party, send the strongest on?" He choked on his next words like hardened pits. "What should we do? I ask each one of you."

Stunned faces glared back mutely. Officers did not consult simple enlisted men. It undermined leadership and threatened confidence. What was the captain thinking? With Clark disabled, was Lewis suffering the burdens of a sole command? Pryor, Collins, Labiche, and old Cruzatte squirmed. Hugh Hall giggled. But sharp glances flicked from one man to the next until, finally, Ordway muttered: "The weak would be defenseless, sir, if you leave, if you take the strong and leave the rest."

"Not all are weak." Lewis closed his eyes and pinched the bridge of his nose. He had pressed the tin cup so tightly between his fingers that it bent to hourglass shape.

When he looked up, Ordway was standing over him. "The Indian woman's asking to speak with you, sir. She brings a native curative."

Lewis nodded and waved him away. "Take her to Captain Clark. She, at least, wants to do some good."

He patted the dog and turned back to his silent listeners. "Think on it, boys. Think hard. Forget your vengeful ways and find us some way across those mountains. I will come back to hear your thoughts." He went to intercept the Indian woman.

Sacagawea was rubbing a smelly paste on the ugly wound on Clark's ankle while he slept. She withdrew when Lewis appeared, and came back again a few minutes later with a steaming kettle. Ordway followed like a fussy orderly. "Tea, for the captain, sir. Says to wake him and make him drink. I'll ask York to do it."

Soon the slave entered and roused his master. Clark sipped drowsily.

The sun began to set and replaced the afternoon colors with its crimson glow. Ordway turned the Indian woman away, but she shook her fist in his face and pushed her way to the captain's side.

Ordway looked to Lewis for vindication. "I told her she must stay away, sir, not interrupt the captain's rest with her heathen ranting. Don't want to force the little mother . . ." Ordway was a tough disciplinarian with men but malleable and uncertain with women.

Lewis muttered: "The captain's awake. Let her stay. Let him see the boy." He lifted the baby from his cradleboard and sat him gently down next to Clark.

The mother planted herself firmly between Captains Lewis and Clark so that neither man could ignore her tiny presence. She chattered like a magpie.

Lewis translated what he understood of the strange admixture of Hidatsa and French. "A rock on our right hand . . . shaped like a beaver's head. We should see it

117

clearly now that the storm has lifted. It's outlined starkly against the light of the setting sun. It marks the meeting place of her people."

"I can't see. Help me up." William Clark forgot his pain and raised himself.

Lewis picked up the chubby baby so that the rays of the setting sun splashed its fiery heat across his face. He spoke to the infant. " 'Tis a wide and beautiful land, my boy, the land of your grandfathers."

They stood for a moment, framed in the light, two tall captains, the tiny Sacagawea, and the baby boy. The rock was unmistakable, a giant extrusion of earth spit out by some ancient upwelling magma, black, in the orange flame of sunset. It was flat on top, snubbed at the nose and rounded in the cheek, as perfect a beaver's head as a master sculptor could carve. But Indians themselves were nowhere to be seen.

Lewis and Clark questioned the woman, and she answered eagerly: "In one moon, my people will pass this way."

Clark groaned. A frown and a silence intervened, and Lewis uttered the dreadful truth. "We cannot wait that long."

Still, news of the sighting restored flagging spirits and replaced bitter talk of Charbonneau with vitality and resolve. Whitehouse sat up. William Clark walked on his swollen foot, and young Georgie Shannon marched into camp like a drummer boy on parade. He pulled a makeshift travois behind him and dropped it with a thump next to the fire pit. The carcasses of two fat

118

bucks rolled off. Shannon was filthy, wet, a little thinner, and he smelled rank as sewer slops. Dirt had plastered his curly blond hair over pointed ears that stuck out like an elf's from beneath a floppy felt hat. He had a clownish grin that framed a row of buckteeth and separated two soot-streaked cheeks. His nose was dripping. He wiped it across his sleeve, wiped his sleeve on his shirt, and explained his absence in two short words. "Got lost."

"Shannon's back!" The news echoed like a rallying cry from the bevy of men. There were back slaps for Shannon, whoops and cheers that pealed like church bells because Shannon had brought red meat. Collins and Warner hacked off chunks and tossed them into the pot while John Thompson spitted steaks to roast.

But Meriwether Lewis sat wringing his hands beside weary William Clark. Deliberately he outlined his plan: "I've spoken with the men, Will. They all agree. Tomorrow I'll take Drouillard and McNeal, two of our strongest, and move ahead quickly to find help." He didn't ask or solicit advice. William Clark understood that he was asserting his superior rank. Clark said nothing. Lewis would determine the fate of the expedition. It had happened before when the river forked and Lewis had been right. Meriwether Lewis continued: "Your ankle's better, but the boil has drained your energy. Rest now. Recover your strength. Shannon has brought meat. I'll take Shields, too . . . he's strong enough in body. I'll watch him, let him air his brain. And I'll take the dog. You can rest. Proceed

119

with the main party at your own pace. I'll send back help and leave word where we will rejoin you."

"Take Charbonneau with you."

"Why? Because he sticks like a splinter in everyone's craw? With a wife and baby, he's too slow."

"Then take Collins and Hall."

"That won't settle it, Will. My patience is at an end. Charbonneau's not a soldier. We cannot threaten court martial. Neither can we dismiss half the corps because they hate him. Our hands are tied. But this expedition cannot be held hostage to the petty whims of a selfish man. Let them fight. Let him defend himself. He must learn, if not at our hands, then at the hands of men whose anger and vindictiveness he has caused."

William Clark nodded at the inevitable. Meriwether Lewis did not want to concern himself with the petty quarrels of subordinates. He had deposited the future of Toussaint Charbonneau squarely in William Clark's lap.

The next morning, while others slept, Lewis, Drouillard, McNeal, Shields, and Lewis's Chesapeake retriever disappeared like smoke in the mist. But Clark was awake and watched them go with a wrinkled brow and the old tick in his cheek. He was worried. He and the three sergeants remained in command. Half the men were injured or sick. Two were sworn enemies. And one was the object of scorn.

Lewis's parting words haunted Clark. What to do with Charbonneau? He spent a day and a sleepless night balancing possible solutions. The next night, when the moon shone low in the west, he arrived at a conclusion. In the early dawn before muster, as the camp began to stir, he summoned Private François Labiche.

The pirate straggled in with sleep still crusting his eyes. William Clark sat hunched on a camp stool, his swollen ankle stretched out before him like a fat stump. He had not shaved or combed his hair, and wisps of red protruded from under his cap like whiskers on a cat. Impulsively he pushed them away and began: "Private Labiche, Captain Lewis has left Charbonneau with us." He leveled his gaze on the unsuspecting pirate. "I have observed you, Private. You have not exhibited the animosity, I should say belligerence, of many members of this corps toward the Frenchman."

Labiche remained silent as Clark probed deeper. "I'm assuming, Private Labiche, that you have an interest in Mister Charbonneau's welfare."

Labiche lowered his chin and drew back his lips, but said nothing.

Clark stared at the ugly face, then at his knuckles. He placed his hands on his knees and straightened his long arms, pushing his broad shoulders wide. The action lent him breadth and authority. "You have your scars, Private Labiche, and I have my bloated leg. The experience of pain has sharpened our perceptions. You and I can perceive the desires and cares of men better than many others." He sucked in air and blew the next words out in a gush. "You know why Charbonneau avoids the company of men. He is concealing something, and you, Private Labiche, and I know what that is." Clark stopped to let the statement simmer.

Labiche's chin rose defensively.

Clark noted the slight movement and continued: "We must convince Mister Charbonneau that he needs to shoulder his share of work. Captain Lewis and I have tried words to no avail. I have devised a way to pressure, to wedge, but I need your help, Private. I need leverage."

Labiche was a survivor. He understood perfectly. He cocked his head, narrowed his eyes, and scratched the purple scar that marred his cheek. "I will not lie to you, sir. He carries the gold Deschamps has paid him, that you have paid Deschamps . . . guineas, one hundred twenty of them. He has paid me a percentage in exchange for . . ." — he chose his words carefully — "my good will and protection."

Clark laughed. "How great a percentage?" He waved away the question before Labiche could answer. "No matter, Private. I saw Deschamps loading the furs. I know Charbonneau carries the monies that I paid, monies that were intended for his boatmen, and I know how much. But I'm glad the gold has come this far, because we may need it. Bring me what guineas you have for safekeeping. I can promise you your share only if this troop does not need stipends for sea captains and native chiefs. Bribes is a better word. You say protection. We may all have need of that before we see the Missouri again. If Charbonneau does not drown with his treasure strapped to his middle, if you have not lost your share on some lonely beach, only if there is

122

something left at the end of our travels which are proving to be long, of much longer duration than any of us anticipated, can I repay you in gold. But I will repay you in land. You have my word."

Labiche licked a lip. "I'm a seaman. I'm not familiar with the value of land. Besides, I'll receive land already as an enrolled member of this corps."

"Three hundred acres would be your due from the War Department of these United States. I will double that."

"The land must be well-watered and fertile."

"You shall have your choice in all Louisiana Territory. You will be a rich man."

It did not take the pirate long to assess his options. He replied: "I've always wanted to know how it would feel to be a farmer. I'm agreeable. But please, sir, guard the gold well."

Clark smiled. He thought of Labiche as pirate, acrobat, knife-thrower, gambler. To imagine him as a gentle, earth-bound farmer seemed unlikely. He stroked the red stubble on his chin and extended a hand. "Thank you, Private. I count on your support."

After Labiche left and the gold was safely stored, William Clark summoned John Collins. The young man rambled up uncertainly, and Clark motioned him to sit. He began slowly in a hushed murmur: "I need your co-operation, Private, in a somewhat risky enterprise. But I think you will approve my proposal. You may even relish it."

Collins nodded curiously. "If you say, sir." He had faced *grizzly* bears and charging buffalo and braved raging rapids, but nothing had surprised him like the captain's present secretiveness. He listened intently.

"It concerns Toussaint Charbonneau. You are not a favorite of his, nor is he a favorite of yours."

Collins was honest. "I detest him, sir."

"And you would fight him, one on one, in fair and equal combat, if the opportunity allowed?"

"I'll crush him like a fat beetle." Collins's anger flared and he blurted belatedly: "Sir."

Clark laughed. "He has a carapace hard as a beetle. You shall have your chance, Private. I am granting you leave from this Army for one day. I ask only that you constrain your anger until then, when I shall set the place and time of reckoning." Clark's lip curled. "I have in mind a duel, if you so choose."

Collins broke into a clownish grin. Was he hearing things? His captain was abetting a fight, sanctioning a kill. He stammered: "With Charbonneau?" Clark gave a single nod, and Collin's blood lust spilled into his speech. He licked his lips. "I'll stuff his stinking pipe down his throat."

The call to muster sounded and Collins ran to report, to spread the news, to bet on his own combativeness. He felt alive, circling for the kill, panting with anticipation. Like the mountains before him, he would stand tall. He would conquer all comers.

Ordway reviewed the ranks while William Clark looked on, shoulders hunched, eyes peering narrowly, contemplating the scheme to humiliate Toussaint Charbonneau once and for all and hopefully point out the error of his ways.

★ ★ ★

The expedition pushed on, a few more days, a few more miles upriver, to a wide plateau opposite the Beaver's Rock. When they set up camp for the night, high peaks loomed in the distance in the purple glow of dusk. Clark hobbled to the shelter of Toussaint Charbonneau. He entered softly, nodded to Sacagawea who promptly took the baby and left the men to their private discussions.

Charbonneau had been eating. He licked his greasy fingers, lit his pipe, and leaned back on a log support. He did not offer food or drink.

Clark remained standing and began: "The men resent you, Mister Charbonneau. They think you evade your share of work and perform the work you accept with carelessness and disdain. They have asked that you defend your honor, and I have decided to let their challenge stand. In fact, I am delivering it. They bid you meet Private Collins at sunrise tomorrow, before muster, at a place to be leveled and marked out by Sergeants Ordway and Gass for fair and equal combat. Sergeant Pryor has volunteered to insure the equity of the match. You may choose a second in the event that you are immobilized, one who will see that all proceedings are conducted honorably."

Charbonneau stared incredulously and spoke through clenched teeth. The words blew out in a heavy puff of smoke. "Dueling is forbidden."

Clark reasoned softly, "In the realm of Britain, yes. Perhaps also in France. This is neither Britain nor France. It is Louisiana, sir. There are no laws in place here. I could invoke the Articles of War, but you are not a soldier, and Private Collins has requested permission to act as a free agent, a civilian. I have granted his request. My own ailments are such that I am too weak and sore to countermand the animosity that has arisen against you. We face treacherous mountains, privation, and exhaustion. Captain Lewis is not here, and I can tolerate dissension no longer." He concluded with a gracious smile. "You do understand my position." This last was conclusive. Clark did not wait for a reply. He turned and left.

Charbonneau withdrew his clay pipe from between his yellow teeth, spat, and threw the pipe straight into the fire. He pulled it out angrily and shouted for Sacagawea. He'd burned his fingers. Like a hound barking and snarling, he stormed up to Sergeant Pryor's mess searching for Labiche, the only member of the troop who might offer support and agree to serve as his second. Finally he returned to his lodge, untied his sash, lay it flat, and ripped open the purse that held his guineas. They poured out in a twinkling mass, and he counted and recounted them long into the night. The touch of gold was smooth and cool and soothing.

In the morning, Captain Clark summoned the contestants. Collins won the toss and choice of weapons — longknives. Labiche had a matching pair. While the sergeants swept clean the ground for the contest, Drouillard sat by Collins, positioning his grip on the knife, directing the thrust of his arm. He loosened the thong that held the flaps of his shirt and exhorted: "Win, boy. His second is Labiche, and he is a

126

demon with a knife. It must not come to that. Repay the lout for your loss and Joe Whitehouse's suffering." He wrapped Collins's forearms in layers of rawhide, enough to lessen a blow but not to hinder movement, and bound his unruly locks against his skull with a tight scarf. "You need your eyes, Johnny, to counter his thrust."

"Labiche would not hurt me."

"Labiche will fight for his own advantage. He will not see that it is you."

Pryor instructed him in the position of his feet. Cruzatte gave his blessing. "I'd drink to yer victory, Johnny, if I had whiskey." Tom Howard leered, and Joe Whitehouse urged: "Strike the soft under parts . . . stomach, throat. You have longer arms, a longer reach."

Collins himself was strangely elated. His height, his youth, his reach and agility gave him the advantage. At the appointed hour, he marched forward, grinning, with a hero's heart. He stood his tallest, neck arched, shoulders pulled back, spine straight as a ramrod. His young body was lean and hard from months of physical toil. His eyes sparkled as he took his place silently at the right hand of William Clark. Death danced like a ghoul on the mountain peaks, but John Collins didn't care. He loathed Charbonneau. As the men lined up in two columns on either side of the dueling ground, cheered and cajoled and wagered and cursed, he calculated exactly where he would thrust the blade.

Charbonneau did not at first appear. When finally he shuffled forward behind the wiry form of Labiche, obscenities and insults flew in his face. His lips were parted, his yellow teeth bared. There was no sign of his pipe or wife or baby. He stepped up to the mark slowly and stood with thumbs tucked under his belt, fingers spread wide over the red sash around his girth.

William Clark stepped between the contestants. He carried the knives on a bright swath of red cloth, on outstretched forearms. They lay, glinting like polished flatware, one handle toward Collins, the other toward Charbonneau. Collins grasped the hilt and dropped his arm to let the blade lay harmlessly against his thigh.

Charbonneau stepped up and placed a flat palm on the hilt. A sudden spasm seized him. There was no pipe to clamp and steady his jaw, and it quivered involuntarily. He centered a black stare on William Clark and croaked: "I am a married man, a father. I am not free to fight. I will not be a part of this barbarity." And he retracted his hand without the knife.

For less than a second, a faint smirk tinged the corners of William Clark's mouth. "You refuse combat, Toussaint Charbonneau, you relinquish all claim against this man?" The bright morning light flashed from the knife across the eyes of Toussaint Charbonneau, and he blinked. Clark continued: "Mister Charbonneau, if you wish to leave us now, you are free to go. Set forth into this wilderness and find your own way. But if you wish to remain with this corps, you must stand guard. You will tow. You will row. You will obey orders in English like all other men here present, from me, from Captain Lewis when he returns, from Sergeants Ordway, Pryor, and Gass. You will not hinder other men in the proper execution of their duties, and you

128

will contribute to the progress of this expedition to the best of your ability. The survival of this troop is paramount. Your labor, your knowledge, and, yes, your gold, sir, must serve the success of our voyage. As for your wife, we will keep her with us or return her safely to her own people, or she may elect to go with you. She shall have her choice. As for the safety of your gold, should you wish to stay, I will lock it safely in my trunk, lest it prove too great a distraction from your responsibilities and too irresistible a temptation to other men. Consider well and decide now. Leave us if you cannot obey or take up the knife and fight."

Charbonneau stood speechless. His eye flicked from the knives to the formidable mountains. He answered in English. "I would die out there alone." A tremor of fear resounded in his voice.

William Clark prompted: "Your reply, sir? We must proceed up the river."

Charbonneau did not rush his decision. Finally he bowed his head and hissed: "*D'accord*. I will work."

Clark nodded agreeably. "Sergeant Ordway and Private Labiche will go with you now to collect this gold that you value so highly. Bring it to me when the muster is dismissed. I remind you that I am the agent who paid *Patron* Deschamps and am well aware of the amount dispersed and the amount you shared with Private Labiche. Sergeant Ordway will acquaint you with your duties. Go now, eat your breakfast with the rest of this company, and serve your wife who meets your every need."

Charbonneau snapped back: "It is for my wife that I save myself." He pivoted on his heel and stomped away.

Captain Clark, Sergeant Pryor, and Collins watched him go in silence. When he was out of earshot, Clark broke out in an enveloping grin. "Thank you, Private. I could see no other way. I was not strong enough to challenge him myself. You were young, able, obstinate, and angry enough. I knew you'd stand, and I surmised he would submit. I was right." He held out his hand. "Give me the knife." Collins placed the hilt in his hand. Clark wrapped the two knives together carefully in the red cloth and handed them to Sergeant Pryor. "Return them to Private Labiche with my compliments." He turned back to Collins. "Now give me your hand." He shook it heartily. "With hope, now, Mister Charbonneau will respect our property and our persons. Go. Serve yourself a double ration. Private Collins, you have won the day." He added under his breath: "We will make him pay and pay well. And we'll make the mountains lie down before us." Clark's bony face expanded as he reminded Collins: "Say nothing of this to Captain Lewis."

CHAPTER
ELEVEN

Captain Lewis was far away. On August 12th, Lewis, Drouillard, Shields, and McNeal, four men, stopped at Lemhi Pass on the sharp backbone of the continent and looked out over the corrugated landscape of deep-cut valleys and snow-covered mountains. They saw no river, no navigable water. A stinging west wind sculpted their buckskin clothing to their ribs and drove granite clouds like crashing waves across a wine-dark sky. Lewis and Drouillard resisted the onslaught: Lewis, fair and delicately boned, reared in the houses of gentlemen, amid silk velvet and polished silver; Drouillard, dark, rugged, suckled at the breast of earth and sky. Privates Shields and McNeal huddled with the dog just below the summit, in the shadowy lee of a rock.

Lewis squinted into the sliver of sunlight that gleamed in the west beneath the cornice of cloud. Drouillard stood beside him, stark and straight. Lewis was laughing lightly. "I'm thirty-one today, Georges. I've led half a life."

Drouillard cast him a sidelong glance. He'd forgotten his own birthday and could only guess his age.

Lewis took two steps down the western slope, turned, and lay the palm of his hand in his own footprint, then scooped up a handful of dust. "No more Spanish, no more British to stop us. Maybe the tribes, maybe the mountains. Maybe we'll stop ourselves by our bickering." He smiled. It was an ethereal expression, and he continued: "If I had whiskey, I'd drink to us, Georges, and to my next thirty years."

Drouillard had drawn in his lips. "Happy birthday, *mon capitaine*, I wish you a happy hundred more."

Lewis wiped his dirty hand on his shirt. He glanced at Private McNeal who stood where the waters divided. A tiny spring spilled both east and west. McNeal placed one foot on either side and cupped his hands to drink.

Drouillard commented: "You drink the water that's closest to God."

But McNeal sputtered. The icy water had chilled his insides. "It's the divide you all speak of. It's so small. Does this mean we've come only halfway?"

"Only." Lewis snorted and laughed at his innocence. He shrugged and motioned the little group forward. "We've come the most difficult half of the way. From here on, we march downhill. We'll move quickly with the river's swift flow. He gazed west at folds upon folds of mountains. "See what manner of lands we will explore and who inhabits them. See if they will befriend us." But he left McNeal without an answer and turned back to Drouillard.

Drouillard was frowning, and Lewis sensed his thoughts. "God willing, I will live those hundred years you wish me, Georges. But if I must die, I would rather die swiftly at the hands of humans than inch by inch at the mercy of the land."

Drouillard muttered under his breath so that Lewis could not hear: "The land, *mon bon capitaine*, will not have mercy."

Lewis pretended not to hear. He shouted to the dog and started swiftly down the mountain. He jumped in leaps and bounds and outdistanced his companions and stopped to wait for them to catch up. When Drouillard came up, he raised his looking glass to look, rubbed the eye, looked again, and passed the glass to Drouillard. "My mind paints imaginary visions. Look, there." He nodded toward the slope opposite, at a large gray protrusion of rock amid green tamarack and fir.

Drouillard took the looking glass, wiped the lens, raised it, and muttered: "A horseman."

Lewis grabbed the glass for a second look. Faint movement, like an insect's flicker of wing, brushed the greenery. It descended gradually to a grassy bottom. The troop of explorers proceeded toward it. As the distance between them diminished, a human figure took shape.

"Shields, McNeal, come, look." Lewis could not contain his excitement. "Sacagawea said we'd find them on this side of the mountains." It was the first native they had seen since they left Fort Mandan four months before. Lewis handed the looking glass back to Drouillard. "How soon before he sees us?"

"A few minutes, maybe seconds." Drouillard looked again, and lowered the glass. "There is water. He

133

drinks." Instinctively his hand gripped the hilt of his knife.

Lewis's lips worked feverishly in and out. He stammered: "The Columbia River? You think? It would be only a trickle at this altitude."

The Indian rode into plain view, and stopped on a gravel bar. He dismounted to let his horse drink, looked up, and stooped to slake his own thirst.

Drouillard held up a hand and cautioned: "He's alone. Walk slowly so he doesn't flee to summon help." The advantage was theirs, four to one. They fanned out, Drouillard on the left, Lewis and McNeal in the center, and Shields to the right. A few slippery steps farther, Meriwether Lewis held up a hand. He lay down his gun, took a blanket from his sack, waved it like a signal flag, and shouted the Shoshone words that Sacagawea had taught him. The horse's head snapped up. The man froze. Had he heard? Had he understood? Or had Lewis's impatient tongue so twisted the soft syllables that comprehension was impossible? He shouted again, then ordered his men to halt, but Shields on his far right did not hear or did not obey.

The horse was backing away now and pulling the Indian after. As suddenly as he had appeared, the Indian jumped astride and galloped up the slope, into the cover of trees, and out of sight.

Meriwether Lewis's mouth hung open. "He didn't hear. There'll be others farther on."

Drouillard's black pools of eyes laced Private Shields. "You heard the order. Why didn't you wait?"

134

Shields glared defiantly back. "I don't wait for Indians. Where I come from, Indians is hostile. It's August. Four months they leave us alone. I like it that way."

They camped on the mountainside that night under a cover of thin skins, and the following day they crossed the creek where the man had drunk. It was the Lemhi River at low water, not the long-sought Columbia, but they found a trail that opened suddenly through a grove of thick willows. Drouillard warned: "There's danger if he's gathered his friends and they lie in wait."

Shields was grumbling: "Just like savages to spring an ambush."

"You never called the Mandans savage, or the Osages, or the Omahas."

"We were forty men when we met the Mandans. Now we're four."

The four marched on. They met two women fishing, who fled in panic. But their dogs stayed behind, and Lewis tossed them chunks of meat. He was shaking his head quizzically. His jaw rotated nervously like a cow chewing cud. "We have lured the dogs. What do we have that can lure their masters?"

"They'll come when their numbers are stronger. They'll come if Shields can obey orders." Drouillard's face pinched with accusation.

Shields muttered again. "When they're stronger and we're sitting like geese on the nest. They'll kill us for our red and yellow scalps."

"My scalp is black." Drouillard nailed John Shields with a glance.

Shields spat a bitter reply. "That's 'cause you're half one of them."

Drouillard led them another mile through a deep washout and over a wide bar. They met more women fishing, who froze like hunted prey at their approach. The white men froze, too. Like statues they waited, then Lewis commanded: "Lay down your arms." He had to repeat it harshly: "Shields, put the gun down!" Then he pulled up his sleeve and waved the white inside of his arm and inched ahead, alone, one short step at a time. He paused, removed strings of beads, vermilion, and a mirror from his pack and held them in his outstretched hands.

The sunlight splashed glittering prisms across the beads and spattered the mirrors with light. The nearest woman barely flicked the pupils of her eyes. Lewis moved a half stride forward to within a few yards of her reach and saw the muscles of her throat contract and her chest rise and fall with the rapid intake of her breath. Her eyes glanced momentarily at his offering. A light breeze rumpled wisps of her hair. The sound of water tumbling over rocks broke the stillness. Lewis risked another half step closer and extended his arm so she could touch the tempting baubles. Her hand moved haltingly, separate from her body, as if testing the heat of a flame. She touched the beads and immediately withdrew her hand.

Lewis nodded, smiled and said: "*Ta-ba-bone.*"

She stared blankly. No flutter of lash betrayed understanding. Minutes passed. A puff of wind ruffled the wisps of her hair. Suddenly her hand shot forward.

136

She snatched up the beads, her black eyes glaring like dark coals into his deep blue. When he continued to smile, she took a mirror and lifted it into her line of vision and blinked as the blinding reflection of the sun sliced across her eyes. She was smiling now. The expression widened her mouth, creased the corners of her eyes, and erased the suspicion that had contracted the lines of her face. She spoke to her companions, then turned and gestured in the graceful language of sign.

Drouillard answered. The women came forward, and Lewis presented more beads and smeared red paint — red the color of friendship — on the smooth copper skin of her face.

Soon the three women were chattering like children on Christmas morn. When they started to move away, into the willows that bordered the creek, they signaled the four white men to follow.

Drouillard muttered: "Their men are over the hill. Keep your guns to hand and palm your knives."

They crossed the creek and started up the trail that curved through dense sage on the side of a low hill. It was an easy jaunt after the steep angle of mountain, but, as they rounded the hillside, Indians came into view. Sixty mounted men, hard and muscular, faces streaked black like devils. They carried bows, lances, and shields of hard buffalo hide and blocked the trail. Their horses pawed the ground impatiently.

Drouillard's voice cracked like a dry twig. "It's a bloody war party."

McNeal and Shields had already grouped defensively, eyes menacing. Shields cocked his gun and grasped it like a lover to his chest. "No bloody savage's gonna get my Nancy without a fight."

Lewis roared at him: "No woman begs a fight, Shields. Hold your fire. They can cut us down like stalks of dry corn." His voice rumbled ominously like a river buried deep in the earth.

Shields hardly heard. "Nancy an' me, we take one with us." He looked down the barrel of his rifle that shook with the trembling of his hands. "Should put Charbonneau out in front. Let 'em take the ornery Frenchie."

Lewis had tightened his grip on his own musket. The enthusiasm had drained from his voice. A gravelly harshness was left. "We have four shots to their sixty arrows. They are as accurate with arrows as we are with guns." He stared like a man transfixed, watching, studying every shadow of Indian movement. Finally, deliberately, he put up his rifle, lay it in the grass, pulled his hat down hard, and croaked: "Georges, come with me. You privates, stay where you are. Cover us but don't shoot. I will personally whip the one who fires."

The two terrified privates watched in disbelief as Georges Drouillard lay down his weapon and walked with Lewis casually and courageously toward sixty milling Indians.

Shields blinked back tears in his eyes and whimpered: "They'll kill us. Never see my Nancy again. August Fourteenth, who's to write the date on my headstone? Who's to tell 'er where my lonely body lies?"

138

McNeal's lips sealed tightly over the emotions that wanted to erupt.

Lewis and Drouillard stopped just short of half the distance to the Indians and stood like lonely targets in the sea of yellow grass.

Minutes passed. A shrill voice echoed amid the crowd of warriors. Other voices, deeper, more doubtful and challenging, interrupted. Suspicious Shoshone eyes appraised the strangers. Who were these shaggy visitors? Where was their home? Could these dirty creatures possibly be Blackfeet seeking slaves and plunder? Voices were animated and loud.

Lewis and Drouillard waited. Horses stamped and blew. A bird twittered, and sounds of argument rose and fell until one man charged out from the covey of nervous warriors. He galloped forward on a swift black horse and came to a sliding halt in front of the two men. He was a powerful man, broadly shouldered and muscular. A quiver of arrows and a small bow were strapped across his back. He held an eight-foot spear in one hand and the reins of the horse in the other. His face was streaked black as the horse he rode, black the color of war and white man's mourning and death. He sat motionless and looked down his hawk's nose at the two men.

The horse neighed. A companion animal answered. The Indian jumped down, quick and agile as an acrobat. He lifted his bow above his head in one hand, his spear in the other, like a challenge to an angry god. But he stooped suddenly and laid them in the grass at his feet.

Lewis exhaled audibly. No scrap of the turmoil in his soul had erupted into action, not a blink, not a shudder. He held his forearms outstretched, palms empty, open to the sky, and stepped to meet the Indian.

They came together. Lewis's lips curved in a smile. The man smiled back, thumped his breast and bellowed: "Cameahwait!" And he threw a strong arm around Lewis shouting: "Âh-hí-e!"

Dumbfounded, Lewis hugged back. Relief flooded over him, and he started to talk to ease the pounding in his chest. "Friend . . . peace . . ." His words were disjointed and quick. He repeated the sounds he heard in the Shoshone language — "Âh-hí-e!" — over and over, like the sweet refrain of a favorite song.

The Indian turned to Drouillard who was flicking his fingers and mimicking the same magic sounds. Lewis motioned the two privates to come forward. They eyed each other. McNeal came first, staggering like a convict to his sentencing. Shields ran a hand down the barrel of his Nancy, slung her across his back, and followed. A seething throng of curious natives engulfed them, crowding, elbowing, combing their fingers through McNeal's blond hair, pinching Shields's sunburned nose to see what manner of paint he used. They stroked knives and guns and strange articles of clothing. They touched black-painted cheek to white and smeared the men joyfully. Shields and McNeal submitted stoically but not without fear.

In sign, the Indians asked Drouillard, who looked like them, what was his tribe. Drouillard answered with agile, expert fingers and asked some questions of his own. He explained what he learned to Meriwether Lewis. "The leader's name is Cameahwait. They have never seen white skin or blond hair." He added with gravity: "They want to know if we come alone. I told them we have friends, just over the mountain."

"Don't show weakness. Tell them we have been looking for them, that we have goods to trade for their horses. Don't mention guns." Drouillard did as he was told. It was Cameahwait who asked for guns, the guns he needed to defeat the Blackfeet and regain the Shoshone homeland on the plains. Lewis answered: "You see our guns. Our friends have more, but only a few, not enough for trade."

"How many friends?"

Drouillard answered ambiguously: "Many."

Cameahwait narrowed his dark eyes. Carefully he scrutinized every wrinkle, every shadow and motion of the ragged white men who stood before him. Finally he questioned again: "Your friends are in the east, over the mountain?" The Indians were headed east to the plains for their annual buffalo hunt.

Drouillard nodded, and Cameahwait acceded. "We're going the same way. Lead us to your friends."

They led the Indians back over the sharp divide to the forks of the Beaverhead River where Clark and the rest of the expedition should have been waiting. But when they arrived, the expedition was not there.

The afternoon waned. So did the hospitality. Doubters among the natives grew restless, and rumblings of discontent seethed beneath the placid surface. Conversation, white and red, rang with suspicion.

"Friends, we see no friends. They lie." The Indian voices filled with accusation.

Meriwether Lewis explained and cajoled. A day passed. Still Clark and the expedition did not come, and the lonely four hovered closely, watchfully.

Drouillard reported what news he could glean from hand signs. "They've been raided recently by the Blackfeet. Yesterday, they believed we were gods. Today, we are enemy spies and some want to kill us."

"Buy time. Give them presents." Lewis contributed his cocked hat and retrieved notes that he had written and left for Clark. He told Cameahwait that they were messages from his friend who apologized for his delay and explained that his men were sick and slow, that the passage upriver was difficult and enervating.

Drouillard volunteered to ride out with an Indian guide to find the expedition and hurry it on. The guide was doubtful and grim. A quiver of arrows and a small bow rested gently across his back. He grunted as he handed the reins of a shaggy pony to Drouillard, kicked his own pony in the ribs, and galloped off before Drouillard could mount.

Lewis held the scout back. "Be on your guard. He will kill you if you fail."

"He may kill me if I succeed. They may kill you and dance on your scalp if I do not find them." Drouillard said it lightly, but Lewis did not smile, and Drouillard added: "I'll need your captain's looking glass." Silently

Lewis handed over the instrument, and Drouillard leaped on the horse and galloped away.

He caught up when the Indian slowed as they reached the banks of the Beaverhead. There was still no sign of the expedition, no sign of human presence. They rode on. The Indian smirked and called him forward, but Drouillard hung back. He drew close enough to hear but not close enough for the man to strike. His rifle was not primed. He rested his hand on his tomahawk.

Like a trail of soldier ants, toiling diligently, the corps snaked into view between yellowed, dry-grass hills. The long stems undulated gently in the wind that stirred white-caps on the river. Water tumbled swiftly over rocks and around the corps. Men towed the heavy canoes, which inched ahead so slowly they seemed almost stationary.

Drouillard lifted the glass to his eagle eye. The men were wet and stooped with exhaustion. Their buckskin clothing was black with sweat. He handed the Indian the glass for a closer look.

The Indian peered once, flung the glass away like a burning brand, and signed: "Blackfeet! You betray me." He put his heels to his horse, whirled the animal on its haunches, and raced away. He had seen only the guns that each man carried.

Drouillard let him go, retrieved the glass, and hailed the troop.

Clark hugged him like a brother. Collins hugged him like a father. But Charbonneau retreated. He had not uttered one word to Collins or Labiche since the duel.

Nor had he spoken to William Clark. Now he ignored Drouillard.

Drouillard did not linger. "I must go back. The Indian who came with me has gone to sound the alarm, and I must stop him." He mounted the horse and galloped away.

CHAPTER
TWELVE

The Shoshone scout rode into the Indian camp shouting news of an attack. Warriors rushed for their bows. The sounds of their war songs welled up like a wail. Some had already mounted their chargers when Meriwether Lewis heard the cries. He ran to reassure Cameahwait that the expedition was peaceful, that the guns they brought were for hunting, and his cohorts for defense. "We will kill only game to feed your people. Help us and we will trade with you and protect you from the Blackfeet who you fear."

Cameahwait took the young scout in hand. "The Blackfeet will not come by boat. The Blackfeet cannot descend upon us without horses. They do not climb mountains or march in small numbers. We will follow these men and see with our own eyes how many they are and why they come." And he led his people to intercept the coming troop.

They stopped in amazement on the crest of the hill where Drouillard had spied the corps. There was the red-headed captain and Charbonneau in his red sash, Labiche, the skinny pirate, and Collins's tall yellow head. There were boats and equipment unknown to the natives. There were many guns, and there was a woman.

Nathaniel Pryor, the steady sergeant who was walking point, spotted the Shoshone scout first and called a halt. Sergeant Gass grouped the canoes. A horde of natives was bearing down upon them, and they prepared to fight. Labiche drew his knife, Collins his powder horn. He began to load.

William Clark hobbled forward to meet two Indians who galloped ahead toward him. His gait was uneven. He used his rifle as a staff. The Indians stopped and called him by name. He straightened suddenly, cupped his hands to his mouth, and bellowed so the wide width of valley could hear: "Captain Lewis and Georges Drouillard!"

The Shoshones rode down upon him, dismounted, clapped backs, and clasped hands. Every muscle eased and every heart lifted. Pryor issued the call. "At ease, men. Breathe and smile. They're friendly." Collins laughed. Labiche swore. Gentle Joe Whitehouse spat, and Cruzatte crossed himself and spouted: "Thanks be to God." But Charbonneau frowned and shoved his wife and child away.

Sacagawea drew back from her husband's bulky form. She looked and listened and childhood memories came flooding back. All at once she broke from Charbonneau and ran toward the massed Indians. Charbonneau gave chase, but stopped when he came even with Clark. An Indian woman in a bright-beaded robe rode out from the mass of milling men. Sacagawea raced to her and threw her arms around her horse's neck. The woman jumped down, enveloped mother and child in her embrace, lifted the baby from his board and twirled him high in the air. He squealed with delight as the woman gathered him lovingly to her breast.

The scene subdued the warriors and tweaked the white men's hearts. They put aside their fears and watched the scene with longing. Each man thought back to the soft caresses of womanly hands in the Mandan villages, and further back still to the smell of hearth fires in homes and log cabins, the smell of spring thaw, fresh-baked bread, and roasting mutton. Some pined for a mother's loving kiss, others for a deep-throated lover's. Some eyes cried nostalgic tears. Some whistled and guffawed in lusty admiration. Others withheld their swelling emotion like a secret, treasured gem.

The strange woman was taller by a head than Sacagawea. Her buckskin dress was tightly belted at the waist, revealing a full bust and lithe curve of hip. John Collins could not help himself. He thought of Laughing Water. Without the company of women, he had buried the painful thought in the deep recesses of his psyche, but now desire and loneliness welled up in his throat. He learned later who she was. She had been captured with Sacagawea years ago. This woman had escaped, but Sacagawea, still a small child, could not run fast enough. Now Sacagawea had come home, and this lithe and graceful creature embraced her.

Collins bowed his head at the sight. He prayed; he hoped for such a reunion when he returned to

Laughing Water. Would she be there with open arms for him? And who would embrace Labiche or Drouillard, the iron men who seemed to need no assurance? And what of the captains and young Shannon and Whitehouse? Who would greet them? Who would know that they were still alive?

A cry recalled Collins from his reverie. It was Pryor, assigning him a horse, a curious creature, whose spots concealed a fine slope of shoulder and curve of haunch. Like the woman, the young private had not seen a horse since he had left the Mandans and given his own animal to the Indians. The sight of a horse always lightened his soul, and he accepted eagerly. Time to bury boats, let sore feet heal, and ride like a proud cavalier behind the captain on the way to the Shoshone village.

It was a large and friendly place, but the Shoshones lived simply. Except for their horses, they were poor, but they welcomed each man, and braided glistening white seashells into their hair.

Collins stroked the silky shell, muttering: "A cowrie, a salt-water animal. It's from the ocean."

Labiche recognized it, too. "Feel it. Smell it. Sea salt has worn it smooth and crusted the carapace. Drill a hole and wear it around your neck and you have a new amulet in a sainted color . . . white." He laughed and added: "Wear it for our safe passage and for good luck." A whisper of mockery tinged his voice. "Wear it on a thong around your neck to dispel the resentment of Charbonneau."

148

Collins took the cowrie. "You think me foolish, but I will do it."

"I think we may need your luck and a prayer. Look around you. Look at Charbonneau's woman, busy for the last week, making pemmican. What do you see that a hungry man can eat?"

"They're on their way to kill the buffalo."

Labiche skewed his ugly face. "If they can avoid the Blackfeet."

They watched the two captains, together again, remove their moccasins and take their places under an arbor with Charbonneau and Sacagawea and the elders of the tribe. They paid little attention to the proceedings. Women meandered among the group, tall, young, beautiful creatures, but the food they offered was scanty and the barriers of language and culture high.

The tall chief, who had ridden the black horse and led the warriors in, arrived with his retinue. He, too, removed his moccasins and took a place between Lewis and Clark. His garments were heavily quilled in orange and blue with a bold stripe of red and decorated with ornaments that resembled seashells. The chief waved food away and explained that, until they killed buffalo, the Shoshone hunters would go hungry and reserve whatever meat they killed for the women, children, and old ones. His eyes settled on Sacagawea, and he questioned Lewis. "Who is that?"

"She comes from your tribe and speaks your language. She will translate my words."

Sacagawea sat humbly with head bowed. She was studying Cameahwait's striped moccasins as Cameahwait was studying her.

"Look up, woman. Look at me." He lifted her chin.

Her lips parted and moved slightly in the suggestion of a smile. She had recognized the bright moccasins. Hesitantly she placed her hand over his. She stammered: "I have been long gone." She spoke Shoshone, and the captains did not understand.

Cameahwait clasped her hand reverently. Suddenly they were talking in torrents, oblivious to all around.

Daughter, mistress, lover, the possibilities danced like sparks before the captains' eyes. Finally Sacagawea turned toward them, drew back her shoulders, brought her right hand to her mouth, swept it forward, and raised her index finger. Lewis knew the gesture and gaped in amazement. She repeated the sign several times to each person in the council circle. Charbonneau translated to French as Lewis, wide-eyed with disbelief, stammered loudly: "He's her brother."

Cameahwait enveloped his sister in his huge bear hug, then released her gently. He brought her with her husband to sit by him, took a shell from his hair, and gently wove it into hers. He lifted a string of bear's claws from around his neck and placed it around her neck. In thanksgiving, he lifted the sacred pipe to the four directions and the earth and sky. He passed it first to Sacagawea, then to Charbonneau, and finally to Lewis. Thus was established the order of translation, Shoshone to Hidatsa to French to English. And thus Charbonneau was thrust squarely into the sequence.

He swelled his barrel chest and basked in his newfound prestige.

Cameahwait protested the poverty of his people and lamented their fall from dominance on the plains, their retreat to the safety of the mountains, their weakness in the face of invaders. That weakness had caused the theft of his sister. This was why the Shoshones needed firearms to fight off the powerful Blackfeet and any others who came to plunder. This was why they needed to match their opponents, weapon for weapon, man for man, to hunt buffalo without fear, and live as they had previously on warmer, gentler, game-filled plains. Cameahwait made an impassioned plea. "The Spanish in the south will not trade guns to us. The English in the north will trade, but only with the Blackfeet who prey upon our people. Here we have only antelope and wolf. Once each year we go east to the plains to harvest the buffalo. Once a year we must risk our lives to feed our women and children. The rest of the year, we place the mountains between us and them, and we eat only the small game that the mountains provide and pray that the goat and the antelope, the beaver and the wolf may wander among us. We do not live in fine lodges. We do not dress in fine robes. You can count the ribs of every Shoshone. But our warriors are brave. More than the mirrors and beads and metal knives that you offer, we need fire sticks, guns to hunt and defend ourselves and take back what is ours."

Captain Lewis understood very well, but he had no solution. "We, too, are poor. Our journey is long and arduous. We cannot part with the guns we carry, but, if you can wait a year or two, if you trade us horses now, I will send friends with a gun for every Shoshone. This and some corn to feed your women and children are all I can offer. Take the guns you see from us and you will see us no more because my men are few and will not survive in these cruel mountains unarmed. Leave us our guns and lend us some of your many horses and we will go west quickly where a great ship awaits us. We will procure guns for you. Act now and you act rashly. You will gain few guns. Wait and you shall have plenty. You have my word."

Sacagawea finished translating into Shoshone and silence fell. Cameahwait lowered his eyes. The interval seemed endless. Then Sacagawea leaned toward him. She whispered: "I go with them. These are good men."

The great chief's smile radiated. "Ask them what they need."

Lewis did not mince words. "We need horses." The Shoshones had hundreds. He added softly: "And a reliable guide."

The men of the expedition had gathered now and watched with interest as Lewis queried the Shoshone chief about rivers and mountains. With sticks, stones, and diagrams in the sand, Cameahwait conveyed what he knew. He dribbled handfuls of soil in a dozen tiny cones. His meaning was clear: there were high mountains between this place and the ocean, and many more peaks, which masked the setting sun. There was a river, but it was walled with jagged rock. It twisted, eddied, whirled, and sucked men down into its watery chasms.

When he ended, the men dispersed slowly.

Collins murmured to Labiche: "What do you think?"

The pirate's eyes narrowed shrewdly. "I think this Charbonneau has just assumed great influence." That was all.

The comment worried Collins who sought out Drouillard for reassurance. He found him standing by an open keg of black powder, filling his powder horn. Drouillard thrust a tongue in his cheek. "I think this man Charbonneau will not be kind to you or to Labiche who betrayed his trust. And he will not heed carefully the orders of Captain Clark." He gazed out over the panorama of mountains and added: "Watch your back, Johnny. I go to scout the trail. I'll tell you what I find when I come back tomorrow."

The white men dismissed the hazards the Indians described. Meriwether Lewis assumed the river Cameahwait described was the Columbia. He announced his conclusions the following day, at muster, and the entire corps broke out in hoots and cheers. Discipline collapsed, and the captains were too tired to enforce it. Men stomped and clapped to the *screech* of Cruzatte's fiddle. For the first time Charbonneau joined them in an old French drinking song. The Indians came; music and song echoed far into the night. When at last their voices stilled, it was early dawn.

Collins threw a log on the fire and whispered: "They're like us. They love a good time."

Labiche was awake and answered ominously: "They marvel at our canoes, the color of our skin, at the

153

captain's dog, but they know nothing of the navigation of rivers. And they say the route is long and hard. But it is Charbonneau who interprets. I don't believe him, Johnny. I don't want to believe him." He yawned. "We'll see what Drouillard has to say when he comes back."

Collins was more confident. "If the little woman can find her brother, we thirty strong men can find an ocean. And now we have horses. From here on, we ride." Collins loved the sight of good horseflesh and the motion of a horse between his long legs swelled his heart with power and pride. "We'll all ride, François. We'll gallop away like cavalry, fly like eagles." He rolled over on his back. "Look at the stars. I've never seen so many."

Labiche dampened his ardor. "You dream. A horse cannot fly. Shut up and let me sleep."

The Indians nodded politely and ate the hulled corn that the corps brought and shared the meat that the white men killed. But the guns that the Shoshones desired most, the captains could only promise. And the dangers that the Indians described, the white men stubbornly refused to believe.

CHAPTER
THIRTEEN

Drouillard did not return the following day. The officers convened to determine what to do. For the first time, Lewis included Charbonneau and his wife in the discussion. Sergeant Gass questioned the addition: "The Frenchman cannot speak to the rest of us, only to Captain Lewis."

William Clark explained: "He knows the Shoshones better than the rest of us. Through his wife, he is party to their councils."

Gass drew his craggy brows together and turned the conversation to Drouillard. "Georgie Shannon was lost. Sure that wee lad found the bloody way. So will the scout."

Sergeant Pryor declared firmly — "Drouillard does not get lost, sir." — as if by his avowal he could will Drouillard home. "But he may be hurt or disabled."

Ordway asked glibly: "Did he take a horse?"

The meeting produced nothing definitive, and finally Clark ended it.

Pryor had the last word. "Send a rider to find him, to bring him back. Bribe an Indian. Buy a horse. But send a good horseman on a fast horse."

At Pryor's suggestion, they decided on Collins. "He loves to ride, he's like kin to Drouillard, and may bag us a deer in his travels."

Night had fallen and Collins was already in bed when Pryor went to alert him. He had to shake him awake. "Captain says you're to go after Drouillard in the morning. He's missing. Take that spotted horse you rode in on. Go fast. Start before muster."

It was easy duty, free from camp regulation and routine. Collins should have been pleased, but he was worried. This was mountain country with thick forests, upthrusts of rock, deep cañons, gullies, and fissures where danger lurked. A man could fall, break a bone. So could a horse. Wild cats, grizzly bears, and wolves stalked. Storms were fast and furious with crashing thunder and bolts of sizzling lightning. As for a speedy trip, running a horse like the sergeant suggested, he would be lucky to move at a steady trot. He slept fitfully until morning and arose before the sun, pulled on shirt and leggings, gulped down breakfast, and cut the spotted horse from the herd. He grabbed a morsel of dried meat and a bladder of water, jumped on the horse's back, and headed west, the direction Drouillard had gone.

There were horse droppings and hoof prints on the soft earth where Drouillard had deliberately guided his animal, blazes on trees, broken branches, and a bit of fabric snagged on a limb. But it was not an easy trail, not one the expedition with all its baggage might readily follow. It wound up steep rocky slopes, strewn with the naked carcasses of pine and fir, and coiled dangerously around a massive peak. The trees thinned as he rode, and the wind increased and rattled their limbs like hollow bones.

It was an eerie climb, the only sounds the moan of empty wind and the *clop* of the horse's hard hoofs on rock. The animal wearied. Collins took turns alternately riding and walking to rest the flagging horse. The air was cool and he slapped his arms for warmth. He grew thirsty, and he drank from an icy spring and refilled his water bag. Higher up, the way flattened above a slide of rocks that littered the slope like the droppings of a monster bird. It squeezed between rock outcrops, then narrowed again and led along the rim of a steep palisade. Collins's lungs pumped in the thin air and his ears hummed. He looked over the edge at a green valley two thousand feet below, and the blood drained from his heart. But the horse plodded steadily on. Finally the trail wound away from the precipice to the last narrow bench below the summit.

He found Drouillard's horse cropping the scant brown grass. A water bag lay empty on a rock nearby. Shivering, he dismounted. He heard the scout before he saw him. Drouillard was sitting above him, on an overhanging rock, feet dangling over a thousand-foot drop, warming his hands at a small fire whose heat and smoke were swept away with the force of wind. Collins pulled out hobbles for the horses, but Drouillard shook his dark head and called: "Leave them free! They'll not test the cliff!"

Drouillard's tomahawk was bloody and resting on a wolf's hide at his side. He had partially scraped off the flesh. He was smiling. Collins had never seen him smile. No one had. Drouillard had never smiled as long as Collins had known him — until now. The smile erased the furrows in his brow and lent a fullness to his mouth. It ignited the dark luminosity of his eyes so that they exuded a magnetic glow. He was handsome when he smiled, and his gaze drew in Collins's questioning stare.

"You found me! I knew they'd send you." The voice was sure and deep.

How did he know? Collins grinned back dumbly and stated the obvious. "You left a marked trail."

"Did they miss me? I thought they would. Did they offer the Shoshones Charbonneau's foolish gold?"

"They offered corn and meat, whatever they could shoot and a man could eat." Collins took in the vastness of the view for the first time. There were peaks in every direction, jagged vertebrae on the spine of a continent and valleys that cut deep, gaping wounds. He gulped in air, laid a hand on a rock to steady himself, and continued: "No gold. Captain Lewis gave Cameahwait a cocked hat."

Drouillard burst out laughing. "White men trade horses for gold . . . twenty guineas buys a fast runner. The Shoshones would not trade horses for gold. They have no need or knowledge of gold. They know the value of a good horse, but they crave what they do not have . . . our pots, knives, guns. Only Indians would trade a horse for a knife." Drouillard shook his head and paused. He studied Collins closely, then rambled on blithely. "Are you afraid?" He swept an arm over the mountains and valleys. It was a familiar gesture.

Two years ago, on a high bluff overlooking the Mississippi and the trading post of St. Louis, Drouillard had lifted the same arm over the river toward the western plains and inspired Collins to join the expedition. Write your footprints in history was the way he had put it. Now those same plains were behind them, and Collins doubted the rightness of his decision.

Ebullient, Drouillard continued: "Beautiful, isn't it? The world as only God could make it." He looked around, and his eyes settled on the flayed carcass of the wolf. "Elk . . . I saw them yesterday, in the meadow on the other side. The wolf was feeding on one when I shot him. I left the meat for the remainder of his pack."

Something in his tone, in the personification of the animal, rang false. Drouillard had always brought in meat. The corps was hungry; the Shoshones were thin and emaciated. A responsible hunter did not leave good meat for wolves and buzzards. A responsible hunter hung his kill out of reach, dried it, packed it, preserved it. A responsible hunter brought in meat to feed his people, hobbled and watered his horse.

Collins glanced back at the tired animals. They stood forlornly, tails to the wind. "No water for them here," he said.

Now Drouillard was beckoning. "Climb up here beside me. See what I see."

Collins felt the prick of fear and smothered the impulse. He took a step and a pebble rolled. One misstep here could send him hurtling into the depths, flapping like a wounded bird into the darkness below. Unconsciously he drew away from the rim and muttered: "Captain sent me to bring you back. Come. Get your horse."

Drouillard laughed and stood up, waving Collins forward. "Follow me and I'll show you what I found." He began to climb higher, leaping like a goat from one flat surface to the next to the topmost pinnacle where the vault of sky began. There he drew himself to his tallest on the highest point of rock. Long strands of dark hair swept away from his proud head like streamers on a kite.

Collins's breath came in gasps as he followed on all fours. At the top he, too, stood, but only for a moment, then his head began to spin and his balance falter. He dared to look down and fell again to his hands and knees. He looked out and away. For hundreds of miles north, east, south, and west, the earth had vomited heaps of toothed mountains. Deep, dark valleys dimpled their rutted face. Brutal wind slammed his body like a battering ram. Collins's mouth went dry as dust. He gripped the rasping surface of rock until his fingers bled. "Why bring me here? You risk my life and yours." The words hung in suspension for a moment and blew away with the roar of wind. He was not sure Drouillard had heard.

Drouillard was breathing in the cold wind, inhaling the wild reality, his chest rising and falling, pumping like a bellows. "It's an ancient place, filled with spirit and power. Look there." He pointed.

Collins looked. He saw only the intimidating jumble of rock.

"Look again, *mon ami*, more closely, lest your eyes deceive you, not out over the abyss, but, here, at your feet."

Collins redirected his eyes. He squinted at the sun's blinding reflection off the polished facets of stones. Gradually the outline of a cairn took shape. Nearby, what seemed like an illusion carefully sculpted in the rock, was a chair. It faced the east and the warm rising sun, but it was not built for comfort. To sit for any length of time, exposed to wind and weather, with granite points of stone gouging flesh and bone, would be penance no saint could endure.

Drouillard explained: "It's a vision seat. Natives contemplate the sun when it rises. They commune with their gods." He caressed the rough edges reverently. "Sit."

Dry fear was congealing in Collins's throat, and he swallowed hard. He stroked the smooth white cowrie shell that hung at his neck.

Drouillard remarked on the gesture. "This is stronger medicine than the amulet you lost or the lifeless ocean shell you wear, stronger than the love of a woman or your white man's gold. If you cannot sit, go now. Leave me until morning to witness the rising sun and absorb its power."

Collins shook his head, but Drouillard waved him away with a casual motion of hand and head. "The

161

horses need water. Go. Take your bearing from the slit in the mountains. Follow the trail to the tree that grows from rock. You'll see a spring. It will lead you to a high meadow where there's good grass and water. Rest the horses there and they will see you back safely to camp tomorrow."

Collins nodded. He set his full water bag next to Drouillard, mumbling — "Take this. You'll need it." — and backed away. He thought of tackling his friend, forcing him to come, to comply with the captains' wishes, but one false step could topple them both from the precarious peak. He started down slowly, at first, then with increasing alarm, and fled to the waiting animals. They had not wandered. The touch of their velvet muzzles, their even breathing, the quiet luster of their brown, liquid eyes, eased his thumping heart. He picked up the leads and started down. He descended quickly across the face of the cliff to the forest of fir, and marched until the last slant pink glow of day sliced each branch and needle. A deep-cut valley cleaved the horizon. The sun was setting. It glowed brilliant red between two dark peaks like a crack in the wall of hell, and he headed that way.

His mouth was dry as smoke and his mind wandered for lack of fluid. The horses, too, began to weave and stumble. He imagined water in every crevice and depression. In the twilight, he almost passed the tree growing in rock. It was a twisted pine, not small, not large, clinging to life by a tenuous root and pushing, straight and strong, out of a narrow fissure in a block of granite. He stopped abruptly, muttering to the horses and to himself. "Getting dark. Can't go on. Miss muster." His mind was wandering. Drouillard's words flashed in his head like so many cards in a deck. He tried to reshuffle the events in his mind. Charbonneau's lust for gold. Drouillard's mysterious refusal to follow. His own lost love and stiff prejudice and fears tumbled together and bumped, one against the other. He needed a long slake of cold, refreshing water. He imagined wetness in his throat, rain in his face, the rush of river against his legs, the damp smell of an approaching storm. Now his thoughts condensed to a burning singularity — one shiny drop of water — a salty tear dripping from an eye, a wet bead on the feather of a duck. He whipped the horses ahead of him and pinned his sights on their rumps.

The spring was there, as Drouillard had predicted, in a grassy draw behind the rock. The horses smelled the dampness and broke into a jarring trot. He ran after and flung himself down on the muddy bank and drank until bursting. He splashed his face until his foggy head cleared, dunked his head, and shook the water from his hair, then rolled on his back and watched the sky darken, violet, purple, deep blue.

Later he summoned the strength to hobble the horses before they wandered too far. He lit a fire and cut fir branches to construct a crude shelter and boiled the meat that he had shoved in his pocket that morning. As blackness fell, he set a snare and sat down to think. Drouillard did not have food. Would he survive the night? Would starvation or lack of sleep craze him? Kill him? Would his tortured body have

163

stamina enough to climb down without tumbling into the abyss? Drouillard had wanted and waited for him to come, had known he would come. How? Why?

There was a hollow in Collins's heart that wouldn't fill. Never had he spent a night alone in such a place with only wind and the low breathing of companion animals. He should not have left Drouillard, or any man, even Charbonneau, without food, without shelter, at the mercy of beasts and wind and weather and lightless night. He castigated himself and shook with remorse. Loss of Drouillard, his mentor and defender, would threaten the very core of the expedition. And it would shatter his own fragile soul.

He mumbled aloud, bland, reassuring words: "He's Drouillard. He has his rifle, a tomahawk, and water. He's the best among us, better than the captains, better than gold." Did the captains know that? Did Charbonneau admit that a man's life was worth more than gold? Like tiny flames, the stars came out and licked the fantastic images that popped up before his eyes. They crammed the black sky like pebbles in a jar. He studied their fantastic patterns and marveled at the depth of the cavern that housed them. He shivered and drew his blanket tightly around him, rocked himself, tried to sleep, and blinked all the while at the cold glory of the night.

He must have slept. In the morning he rose refreshed and went to check the snare. It held a skinny squirrel that he butchered and boiled and forced himself to chew and swallow. He gathered the horses and followed the creek that flowed down from the spring. He recognized the meadow. He had been there before and shot a fat buck, but it was empty now and he pressed on to camp and the company of fellows.

Sergeant Pryor came out to meet him, asking: "Where's Drouillard?"

"He wouldn't come, sir."

"You found him and you didn't bring him back?" There was disbelief.

"Yes, sir. I brought his horse." It was a lame explanation, an unacceptable excuse. Collins shrunk from the sergeant's reproachful stare.

Pryor snapped peevishly: "I'll tend the horses! You tell the captains."

Lewis was sitting on a log, with Sacagawea and Charbonneau, busy with his sextant, taking the measure of the mountains when Collins approached. He waited while Lewis delicately adjusted the instrument.

Once Collins had reported on Drouillard, Lewis did not raise his eyes from the sextant. After he had absorbed the news, he replied: "Two horses and no meat, Private Collins? I take it Mister Drouillard is not injured, or you would have brought him, too. Has he . . . have *you* . . . killed us some game?"

"He killed one wolf, sir. He would not come. He's watching the sun rise." When he sensed disapproval, Collins choked on his own words. "As for me, I killed nothing."

Lewis cocked his head, thrust his chin forward, and gaped. "Did I hear you correctly, Private? I have thirty hungry men. We need meat." Lewis lay away the sextant carefully in its box and handed it to Charbonneau. He restrained his movements like water behind a dam, but his voice jumped an octave and fluttered when he spoke. "I need facts and directions, Private, altitudes and river sightings, temperatures, and estimates of game, and you talk of visions!"

Collins's head snapped up at the rebuke. He stood as still as a slave on the block.

Charbonneau was staring at him, enjoying his discomfort.

William Clark came up behind Lewis and interjected in gentler tones: "Where is Mister Drouillard, Private? How far away?"

"A day's ride, sir."

Lewis paled. The look he flashed to Clark could have shattered bedrock.

Collins toed a pebble and wished with all his heart he were that pebble, as insignificant and as small. He stammered incoherently: "There was no grass, no water for the horses, sir, where he was."

"And where was that?"

"On a high mountain, sir." Collins bridled.

Captain Lewis's hands folded so tightly his fingers pressed the blood from his knuckles. A gruesome frown disfigured his face.

Clark stepped around Lewis, placed a steady hand on Collins's shoulder, and guided the young man away. When they were out of Lewis's earshot, he said: "Does Mister Drouillard have provisions?"

"Wolf meat, sir, and water. I left my bag."

Clark's voice soothed like a father confessor. "You did what you could, Private. Mister Drouillard must deal with his own demons. Perhaps he has killed game and hung it for us to gather?"

Collins shrugged. His voice had left him. He read the nervous tick throbbing steadily in the corner of Clark's cheek. It meant that despite the soothing tone William Clark doubted his word.

News of Drouillard's refusal to return hovered in the brittle air. Tired and tense, Lewis summoned the officers and had them sit around a low fire. He briefed them in clipped, officious spurts. His bloodshot eyes hung like weights in dark sockets that deepened in the fire's soft glow. He sat cross-legged on a dirty blanket spread over the ground, skinny legs folded, knees protruding like raw stumps. His spine curved inwards like a scythe. Charbonneau clung to his side as Sergeants Pryor, Ordway, and Gass assembled and William Clark seated himself beside him. Lewis clasped his hands tightly and began in a voice tenuous and rasping: "Are we sure of Collins, that he didn't offend Drouillard as he offended Charbonneau, that he didn't overwhelm and abandon him?"

Sergeant Pryor defended his man. "Collins would never slight, never willingly abandon Drouillard, sir, never Drouillard." An afterthought remained unspoken: *Maybe Charbonneau, but never Drouillard.* But then most of the corps would have abandoned Charbonneau with no regrets.

Clark seconded Pryor. "I'd vouch for Collins as for any of these men, Meri. They can be insubordinate and short-tempered. They fuss and fight, but they are steadfastly loyal to each other and to this corps." He waved the sergeants abruptly away, explaining: "I would speak with Captain Lewis alone, if you will allow."

The three sergeants rose reluctantly, but Charbonneau pretended not to have understood.

"You, too, Mister Charbonneau."

The Frenchman grunted, took a long pull on his pipe, exhaled a stream of smoke, and arose slowly.

Clark waited, and then spoke quietly because Charbonneau positioned himself nearby. "That one is the outsider, Meri, like Deschamps and his boatmen. Charbonneau's a lone wolf who has not yet earned acceptance from the pack. So far, all he's done is snarl."

Lewis's hands twitched. He scratched up handfuls of earth and drained the grains from one hand to another, then, with a sharp stick, picked the dirt from under his nails. "But that's why I trust Charbonneau, Will, because he is independent, because he will not give in to their whims and their suspicions. We need him more than ever, now. But for him, but for his wife, the Shoshones could well have killed the lot of us."

William Clark bowed his head. He inhaled the dry air and blew it out with force. Meriwether Lewis was not about to change his mind. Better not to confront him now. Better to wait for a more auspicious moment. He stated calmly: "We have more pressing concerns than the whims of a single man. The season is waning . . . the air is cooling. Summer is passing with the

168

month of August. We've lost valuable time, Meri. The ship that President Jefferson has sent to intercept us is anchored at the mouth of the Columbia this very day."

Meriwether Lewis pressed a shiny pebble into the flesh of his palm. When he set it down in a line beside three others, it was pink with blood. Finally he spoke in a hurried, high-pitched stream as if confident words could settle fears of failure. "Yes, Will, the ship! We cannot wait for Drouillard. Cameahwait has graciously assigned us a guide . . . Toby, is his name. Mister Charbonneau will assume Drouillard's duties. He is an able man, Will, no less able because he is French. You, the sergeants, the men will have to try harder to understand him."

They were words, not convictions, and they had no effective power, and Clark did not contradict them. He would choose his moment, but not now, not when Lewis vacillated in his own unsettled mind. "The Shoshones need their men," he said, "every last one, to hunt and lay in meat for winter." It was a simple statement of fact.

"They don't need Toby. He is old but experienced. Cameahwait says the Pierced Nose people, who live on the Columbia and adorn their clothes with the shells of the ocean, are just over the mountains. We are near, Will, very near." Breathless excitement gripped Lewis's voice. He held one pink pebble up to the sunlight, observed his own blood and licked it.

The action unsettled Clark. "I know of Toby," he said. "He's very old." And in his soul, he repeated: *Over the mountains, but what mountains? . . . high dizzying, colossal mountains!* The thought started his cheek pulsating with every beat of his heart.

Lewis leveled him with a knife-edged glare. "Toby has spent his life in these mountains. He must know every turn of trail."

"Then we must leave as soon as Drouillard returns," Clark said in a steady monotone, but he could not soften Lewis's grim stare or the simmering apprehensions that lurked in his own heart.

"And if, God forbid," Lewis responded, "Mister Drouillard does not return, we have Mister Charbonneau and his woman, who are trustworthy and intelligent." Lewis's eyes were blinking, his shaggy head bobbing, his cheeks flushed. "Let Drouillard find *us*. As you say, he's Georges Drouillard. I am tired of waiting. He will see we have scant need of his services."

Clark cut short the interview, rose abruptly, and summoned Sergeant Ordway after him. "He's unwell," he confided. "He needs sleep. Put him to rest."

The two led Meriwether Lewis to his bed where they wrapped him in warm blankets. But one hour later, Lewis was up again, pacing the camp.

CHAPTER
FOURTEEN

Drouillard tramped into camp the following evening, singing and swinging his rifle. He carried the carcass of a large buck draped over his shoulders and flipped it down like a hollow log at the edge of the fire pit. "Where're the captains?" he bellowed.

A circle of men, shoulders hunched, greeted him. Collins, John Colter, John Shields, the two brothers, Joe and Reuben Fields, Joe Whitehouse, and Cruzatte watched as Labiche rolled the dice. They wagered their dinner, their clothing, the number and placement of stars in the sky, the coming weather, and the direction of the changing wind. Laughter and loud banter rang, but they quieted when they heard Drouillard's loud bass and looked to the nearby officers.

The officers had erected a crude scaffold of skins upwind of the blowing smoke from a low fire. The cover broke the wind only partially. It blew in capricious gusts and threatened to tear the scaffold from its anchors. They sat in a semicircle, in the lee of the scaffold, with Lewis at their center. At his right elbow, Clark hunched, pressing open the pages of a small leather-bound book and drawing his fingernail carefully across the page. Charbonneau sat on Lewis's left, then

Sacagawea and the sergeants. Meriwether Lewis traced a line on the ground with the point of an espontoon. It was an ancient weapon, a murderous, elongated dagger.

Drouillard thrust himself into their presence. "*Mes capitaines*, time now for us to make haste. I've seen how and where we must cross the mountains."

Pale and red-eyed, Lewis looked up. The point of the espontoon wandered as he replied: "You were not here. Cameahwait has assigned another to guide us." His words were ponderous, his displeasure evident. "Toby is his name."

Drouillard broke out laughing. The sound echoed eerily over the crackling fire, and the enlisted men stopped their game. Drouillard stepped between Lewis and the fire, forcing his tall silhouette into Lewis's reluctant consciousness. He did not mince words. "Has Toby told you we will venture beyond the lands of his people, beyond landmarks he can recall? He comes with us because his people have long assigned him lowly stature. He expects you to treat him as third captain and heed his words like pearls of prophesy although his brain is stiff with age."

It was true. Everyone had seen Toby hobbling past the fire, eyeing the roasting meat, waiting furtively until allowed to approach and snatch a few scraps to feed himself. He hovered near the enlisted men like an orphan pup waiting, hoping for permission to eat. The men noted the swollen fingers, crimped with gout, the skin draped like fine gauze over blue, protruding joints. Age had shriveled Toby in body and mind, rounded his shoulders, turned his black hair gray and his sharp eyes cloudy. The contrast with the tall, dark, virile Drouillard, who stood before them now, was stark. Toby was a weasel of a man, scurrying after rodents and birds to feed himself, clinging to crumbs of past dignity. Nomadic peoples left his kind behind when too weak to keep up with the march. And so the Shoshones had left Toby now to an uncertain future with the struggling Americans.

Meriwether Lewis was not used to contradiction. He arched his neck and snapped his spine straight. "Toby has lived here all his life. His age further illustrates his wise experience. He says the headwaters of the Columbia are one day's journey, west. He says there is a generous tribe of men who wear ornaments of bone through the cartilage of their noses, who will help us, if we need, on the other side."

Drouillard did not anticipate resistance. He turned to the dice players and called: "Cast one for the captain, Labiche, and cast a lucky one for Toby! He'll need it." The ring of sarcasm was obvious but not malicious.

Lewis's patience was wearing thin. "I trust, Mister Drouillard, that your news is of greater certainty than a game of chance."

Drouillard whirled effortlessly on his heel. "It is, sir. I've seen the eagle fly on the high drafts of air. I've witnessed a worm tunneling in the caverns of the earth. The river has led us too far south. The passage we seek is north. We must go north to correct our error. We play more than a child's game." He lifted his eyes to Lewis's direct line of vision. Lewis could not evade his

173

meaning. Drouillard repeated: "North, sir, then west to find the passage we seek. Beware, *mon capitaine et Monsieur* Toussaint Charbonneau, of strangers who profess knowledge they have not acquired, who flatter those who reward them with sweet words and promises." He named no one. Everyone understood.

Lewis blanched and his jaw froze. The sinews of his neck drew taut as bowstrings, and he blustered angry words through clenched teeth. "Show me what you saw, Mister Drouillard?"

"I cannot. It's too far and too high. Ask Collins. He's my witness. He was there." An interval of static silence intervened. Drouillard threw back his head, waited, and nodded. "I leave you now to your own ignorant demons. Mark my words, sir. You will rue the day you trust this Indian." He bowed like a prince, turned on his heel, and stalked away.

Lewis held the espontoon point down in two cramped fists. His fingers tensed around the hilt so that the veins stood out blue and swollen in the backs of his hands. He wrinkled his nose. "Ask Collins, he says, as if Collins were a reliable witness." He spat the name, clamped his teeth shut, and glared at the fire. A flame shot high on a gust of wind, and he shouted at the dice players: "Bring more fuel! Private Collins, what have you to say for yourself?" The tip of the espontoon flipped up like a divining rod, pointing in the direction of Drouillard's passing. "Trifles, games, dice, cards, your silly nutshells. You conspire to undermine the righteous authority of this corps, to interrupt the chain of command. I'm captain here. Do you understand

174

that, Private Collins . . . Private Labiche? You are responsible to your captain and not to an insolent, impetuous, half-breed scout. This expedition shall proceed according to the best knowledge and advice available. It shall not chase baseless visions. I should have replaced Mister Drouillard long ago and dismissed him from this service." He snapped this like an angry dog. "As it is, I should bring him up on charges."

With the flat of his own knife, William Clark guided the point of Lewis's espontoon to the ground. His voice was compliant and soothing. "Meri, Mister Drouillard is a civilian, not a conscript. We pay him a salary for each day he is with us. He is not bound by the Articles of War or U.S. Army discipline. He has served well until now. As for this game, it intends no harm. It's a relief and a balm to tired men." He added summarily: "Meri, Private Collins acted on my orders."

"Your orders?" Lewis stopped in midsentence. His eyes narrowed and his lips thinned as he swallowed his displeasure. "Lucky Collins to have you for a defender, Will. You should be more circumspect about whom you entrust with important missions." Lewis's jaw quivered. He cast his eyes down and resumed scribbling in the sand with the espontoon. The design was branched, the lines convoluted like the entwining pathways of his own brain. He issued his final remark without looking up. "Mister Drouillard has been absent without leave. The privations he has endured have demented his thought. He has corrupted the integrity of this corps." His voice jumped an octave to a high-pitched wail. "The headwaters of the Columbia are here as Toby states!"

He thrust the espontoon with a mighty stab down into the earth. The long blade *twanged*, and he pulled it with a twist to disengage it. It came free, but the point snapped and remained imbedded. Frantically, with bare hands, he dug it out, and then flung the broken stub with all the force of his arm. It flew across the camp, landed with a *clatter* on a rock, and deflected into the dice game.

Men leaped out of range of the flying razor-sharp blade, the tiny game cubes scattering. Finally the blade came to rest at Labiche's moccasined feet. He reached down, picked it up, and tested its sharpness. His keen eyes retracted and his scarred face reddened, but he said nothing.

All men looked on in shock. Lewis seemed not to realize the danger of his action. Silence fell as he flashed his eyes righteously from man to man, each of whom avoided the sanctimonious stare.

Finally Clark instructed: "Private Labiche, take the broken pieces to Private Shields for repair." He added with a nod: "Best to keep it safely, Private. With such a weapon, if the captain ails again, he could cut himself." Left unspoken was the certain knowledge that the blind toss could have sliced a man's foot.

All eyes turned to Meriwether Lewis whose attention diverted again to Labiche. "Gather up your dice and take your foolish game elsewhere . . . and butcher the meat Mister Drouillard has brought."

Labiche moved slowly, with a defiant eye. He retrieved the dice, then lined up the two pieces of knife. "Broken beyond repair, sir. Even rejoined, the blade will never regain its former strength." He addressed Clark, positioning himself to shield Collins from Lewis's self-righteous glare.

"Go, Private, and remove your game elsewhere."

Clark tried to dismiss the incident as a regretful slight, but Lewis would not let him. He looked for justification to the one man he knew would support him unconditionally. "Mister Charbonneau, what think you? You've lived with natives. Does this Toby state the truth?"

The Frenchman narrowed his eyes, took a hefty pull on his pipe, exhaled the smoke, and lowered his bull's head. "*Comme vous le dites, mon capitaine.*"

"Amen. Yes, as I say . . ." It was not a judgment. It was fawning agreement, and Lewis restated what he had construed in the tortured passageways of his brain. He had drawn his plans with care and precision just as he had planned the entire expedition with Jefferson and Dr. Rush and the savants of Philadelphia. He had not solicited the advice of any he considered subordinate, and he would not allow a lesser man to interrupt his execution now. He declared: "Toby will lead us to the Columbia and we will pay him well, in gold."

He stood up. The sun was declining in the evening sky. "Come Toussaint," he said. "And you, Will, come closer to the fire, where we can better see . . . where we'll enjoy the company of saner men and plot tomorrow's course. And bring Toby."

Labiche wrapped the broken espontoon in a flap of hide, shoved it under his belt, and moved off to Sergeant Gass's mess on the opposite side of the campsite. He tossed the dice casually from hand to hand to see if interest in play would rekindle. It would not.

John Colter summed up the reason: "It's Lewis and the Frenchman who ignore Drouillard, trust the Indians. They don't care how much smoke blows in our faces." He coughed once and turned his face away.

The thought settled like cold rain on the hearts of the men. Lewis's denials, his false positioning, and blind adherence to a contrived reality nibbled away motivation and eroded confidence. Lewis was a dedicated, determined leader, but there was a righteous obstinacy in him that had led to false accusations and harsh punishments for Warner, Hall, and Collins when at first they started upriver. Those old wounds had healed. But now it was not fear of discipline or physical pain that worried the men. It was the knowledge that reason and justice had relinquished command of the corps. Ignorance, prejudice, and obstinacy held sway at this most dangerous juncture, the mountain crossing. They could lose friends, countrymen, a hand, a foot, their lives.

Collins stood exposed before the remaining officers as Labiche walked away. His reserve crashed suddenly like a wave on a beach. "Trustin' a Frenchman an' a crazy Indian's like serving them our scalps on a platter." His voice was insulting and loud and the syllables scattered like buckshot. William Clark and the three sergeants could not help hearing.

Sergeant Pryor took him by the shoulders and turned him away. "The men are waiting for their supper, Private. You're the cook. They're hungry, and so am I."

Stew bubbled in the cauldron. Collins ladled it into the waiting bowls, but the usual mealtime banter did not develop.

As was his habit, William Clark came to sit and offer his encouragement. He sought out Collins. "Eat, Private. I have not charged you with wrongdoing. It was a mistake. We are all overwrought."

Collins filled his own bowl, but he had no sooner started to eat, when Charbonneau sidled up and broke into an obsequious smile. Pipe clamped in his teeth, belching smoke, he muttered: "*Grâce à Dieu, demain, ils partent.*" The sounds slipped like liquid through the crack where the pipe stem emerged.

Clark blinked. He understood only partially, and demanded: "Speak English, man!" Then he called Labiche over to translate.

Labiche listened, and with barely a pause, he blurted: "Who's leaving?"

"*Cameahwait et les indiens.*"

The news took hold like a garrote at the throat. It cut off breath. Clark choked. His bowl clattered to the ground, the contents spilled, and the dog ran over to lap it up.

Labiche seized Charbonneau by the shoulders, shook him hard. "They can't go. What of the horses they promised us?"

Charbonneau shrugged him off and reverted to an excited rush of argot that made comprehension nearly impossible.

Labiche stammered the shocking translation. "Cameahwait's entire band intends to hunt buffalo on the eastern plains. They're packing now, sir. Tomorrow, at first light, they're leaving." He looked in desperation toward William Clark. "We've just found them, sir."

The wind had changed and smoke was writhing along the ground. Clark blinked at Labiche, then his eyes widened slightly and his lips parted. "Get Captain Lewis. Wake him, if you must. He must face the folly of his assumptions." Charbonneau was moving away. "Stay here, Mister Charbonneau," Clark ordered. "You, too, must face your error. You should have spoken sooner." The words accused Charbonneau squarely. Clark clamped his jaw shut to stop his cheek from pulsing and castigated himself. "I should have known. I should have suspected. They're nomads. They move when and where they please." Finally he closed his eyes and heaved a sigh. "The weight of our duties saps poor Lewis of his strength and his wits. It robs me of certainty and judgment. God help me. God help us."

Lewis had already bedded for the night, but he returned reluctantly at Clark's bidding. He sat down, cross-legged, opposite the sergeants, and folded his hands tightly in his lap as Charbonneau repeated the news in clear, coherent French.

The respite had refreshed Lewis. He was calmer now and more clear-headed. He pressed Charbonneau:

"Where are they going? When do they leave? How long, Mister Charbonneau, have you known?"

"This morning, my woman told me. She heard it from *son frère, le chef*, Cameahwait. The Shoshones must go east for the meat that will nourish them through the mountain winter. I thought you knew. I would have told you, *mon capitaine*, but you troubled yourself with Mister Drouillard. I did not want to worry you further. Tomorrow they leave."

Lewis's face flushed suddenly. He nodded and spoke with decision and clarity. "It's not too late. I will muster all my powers of persuasion, and Captain Clark will marshal his. You, Mister Charbonneau, must tell your wife to intercede. You understand me? Have I spoken too vaguely, too quickly? Tell them we must have horses, now, immediately. Tell them we will pay in gold."

Charbonneau gasped: "They have no use for gold."

"But I do and you do, sir, and so do the Blackfeet and their English sponsors. Tell your wife to convince her brother to give us horses, or I will personally pitch your precious gold from the peak of the highest mountain to depths of the deepest river."

"*Non!*" Charbonneau shouted. The pipe dropped out of the mat of black beard, and he growled: "I tell them. I go now."

Cameahwait agreed to supply the horses, enough to carry the baggage, and no more. He did not want gold; he did not know its value. And he assigned the expedition a second guide, Toby's grandson, a boy of thirteen years.

On September 1ˢᵗ, when the Corps of Discovery awakened, the Shoshones had vanished. The expedition was alone again, left to its own misguided perceptions and those of an old man and an inexperienced boy.

They headed west into the maze of mountains. Toby led them down the Lemhi River to its juncture with the Salmon, a fierce river that roared like a demon rampant, through a narrow, rock-strewn channel. High cañon walls cut the biting wind. No one was riding, but neither were any burdened with heavy gear. They walked two to a pack horse on an established Indian trail. Their feet were dry. The long labor of pulling canoes was over. The sun shone brightly and reflected off the sheer cañon walls and the bright thread of river. But a fresh anxiety clawed like a thorn at the hearts of the corps: Meriwether Lewis was unstable.

Days passed. Difficulties mounted. Drouillard's assessment was proving true. Toby was old, his eyesight fading. Impressed with his new importance, he marched at the head of the column with his grandson by his side. The boy did most of the scouting. He had large, perceptive eyes that bulged from a smooth, oval face and glared suspiciously at all white men from behind a curtain of black, shoulder-length hair. Grandfather and grandson ate with Charbonneau and Sacagawea who alone could speak their language. The Indian boy followed the woman like an orphaned child. He carried water, cooked, and entertained the baby. But his primary capacity was that of servant or orderly

182

to the old man. He pointed out landmarks, cut a staff to help him over rocky terrain, and rubbed his joints with herbal oils when they halted. Charbonneau and Sacagawea followed after the old man and the boy, then Lewis, Clark, and his slave, York, the rest of the corps, and finally Collins and Drouillard, like an old, defiant bull.

The banks of the Salmon were steep, walled with giant spruce whose roots clung to the rocky slope like talons that reached out and snagged men and horses. Here and there, wind and water had snapped the mighty trunks like stalks of dry grass and sent them crashing down. The horses, tough and mountain-bred, could not pass. The corps went around or hacked the trees down, leaving the raw stumps as crude markers, stark testimony to the cruel land.

Progress was slow. It was late summer, but it was cold in the valley. The corps lacked winter clothing and nourishing food. Large game animals did not enter here in the densely forested slopes near the river, but gathered in the warmer, wider valleys on the plains to the east. There were only rodent and bird and bloodless fish to supplement a diet of year-old, dried soup. The meeting with the natives had been fortuitous but all too brief. The men were weak. They needed more horses, more direction, more help. And they needed reassurance that their leaders could not give.

They found human footprints, long, narrow, and widely spaced, unlike Shoshone feet. Toby declared them to be friendly people, but the men from Kentucky looked on with apprehension. They had fought Creeks and Shawnees, contested the English in the north and west, and the Spanish in the south. Their fathers had struggled to Fort Vincennes with William Clark's own brother, George Rogers Clark. The same men had seen Lewis's diplomacy fail at the Sioux villages. Now they watched with slits of eyes and blade-straight lips. There would be other tribes and more threats, more efforts to halt their progress. They did not doubt. They knew.

Others would suffer from strained emotions and devious impulses, similar to those of Lewis. Hugh Hall started it — "Drouillard saw devils on his mountain." Old Cruzatte picked up the refrain — "Old Toby's the devil with us, all horns, tail, and pitchfork." Around the campfire, whispers flew like insidious darts, aimed first at one, then at another. Shields, the hefty blacksmith, began to babble unchecked, and men began to listen and agree. He attacked Collins. "Drouillard give you that piece of bone to hang around your skinny neck? Indian luck? Black Mandan magic? The curse of Satan?"

"It's a shell, life from the sea, the western sea, where we're headed," Collins tried to assure.

"An' you think because you wear it, it'll get you there?"

"Better'n that Indian, it will."

Joe Whitehouse carped: "The toady Frenchman don't know where he's going, suckin' up to the captain, infestin' him with his Papist potions, poisonin' his brain. You should've killed 'im, Johnny."

Colter agreed: "Only Clark still has his wits, just about . . . him and the sergeants." He snapped his

184

mouth shut, then flashed a glance at Shields and quipped: "An' how many of us is thinkin' straight?"

Conversation stopped abruptly when Lewis or Clark approached. This night, Lewis came with Charbonneau and Toby. The captain held his cold hands over the fire to warm them. He had rubbed the skin raw from anxiety. Furtive, sidelong glances greeted him. He noticed the unnatural silence and spoke to fill it as if all was right with the world. "Did I interrupt? Be at ease, men, and continue."

But no one dared mention their speculations or the very real apprehensions that triggered them. Their thoughts ran to questions without answers. How close were these Pierced Nose Indians Toby spoke of? What other tribes, friendly or hostile, lay in wait? How far was the great western river? How reliable was Toby? The portents were discouraging. Toby stopped too frequently, cast his watery glance east, west, south, led up narrow animal tracks and over rocky, treacherous talus, and wrapped himself in a cloak of self-importance. The only person who could speak directly to him was Sacagawea. And the only person who could relay Toby's counsel to the captains was the gold lover, the greedy one, Toussaint Charbonneau. But Captain Lewis and his lapses were the greatest concern. The men of the corps slurped their thin stew so that the only sounds were the air sucking between their teeth, loud gulps, and the *clink* of cup and bowl.

On the 4th of September, the third night deep in the valley of the Salmon River, ice formed on the water in

185

the vessels. Drouillard came to the central fire where the corps huddled to keep warm. He sat by Collins and hugged a blanket around his shoulders. He had caught a squirrel and roasted it on a stick and, now, passed it around the hungry circle. It was their only meat.

He addressed only Collins. "We need friends, *mon ami*, better friends than we find in our midst."

CHAPTER
FIFTEEN

Flathead Indians were shadowing the corps's every move. Hidden in crevices and behind deadfall on the ridge, they watched the hungry men eat. They always concealed themselves carefully at the approach of strangers, because they had been raided. Enemy Blackfeet had used the Salmon valley, sneaking past Flathead scouts, to steal horses, capture women, and carry away children.

Now the Flatheads crept down the steep slope, moving like shadows through the brush. Three Eagles, chief of the band, motioned them forward. He sniffed snow in the air, snow that would chill bones but also hide tracks. He tread lightly as a cat and stopped only when he could clearly distinguish one man from another. He looked back for his followers and cursed them for melting into the forest. He knew what had frightened them — the long, shiny, black sticks that shot murderous, orange flame. Every one of these strangers carried one, cradled under his arm or flung in a sling across his back. The Indian touched the row of bear's claws that hung around his neck and pressed the points into the thin skin of his collarbone. They pricked, but he smiled. They were proof of his courage.

No one else in his band had braved the grizzly and lived to tell the tale. His was strong medicine, great enough to foil a Blackfoot fire stick, great enough to face an enemy alone, so great that he dismissed his fear, dug a depression in the lee of a rock, and settled in to watch.

What he saw surprised him. These strangers were not warriors. They were not Blackfeet, not even Indian, although some looked Indian and one was painted black for war. Their horses were too skinny and too few, their clothing too ragged. One tiny form intrigued him: a woman who carried an infant, Indian fashion in a cradleboard on her back. But they lacked essentials any Indian would have carried: arrows, bows, skin shelters, and preserved, nourishing food. September in the mountains brought chill winds and snow. These people wore light summer skins and stopped intermittently to stuff grasses in their moccasins to warm and cushion their feet. Others, without proper moccasins, laced the bare grasses to their feet with strips of bark. Three Eagles cringed at the careless suffering. He concluded they must have been expelled from their tribe, robbed, or lost.

He looked up. Black clouds, heavy with moisture, swept over the great conical evergreens that poked their spires at the darkening sky. The expected snow began to fall. The soft flakes melted on his nose and chin and nestled on the frozen ground. He pulled his robe around him, crept closer, and keened his ears to the tones of their speech and the dull echo of their activity. The voices were deep and trembling, interrupted by hacking coughs. The movements were noisy: the *squeak* of scraping wood, the *rasp* of stone, the *clink* of metal. They carried knives and tomahawks and the deadly fire sticks, but their shoulders slumped and their feet dragged. Cruel weapons did not make them brave.

A tall man with hair the color of red sunset swept an arm in a wide circle to indicate the perimeter of a camp. They stopped at his bidding in an unlikely place, on a slope where there was no level ground and no possible forage for the tired horses. They tugged the hapless beasts into a tight, defensible knot, lined up the packs to form a windbreak, and started a fire.

The snow thickened, washing away Three Eagle's vision. A black dog, a stark silhouette in the sea of white flakes, growled. The huge beast froze suddenly, nostrils flaring, pointing directly at the Flathead chief. Three Eagles hunkered down as a tall, ragged, yellow-hair, with rifle in hand, came after the dog. Three Eagles held his breath to hide his warmth in the icy air. Had the wind shifted? Had the dog sniffed his scent?"

The yellow-hair stopped suddenly. "Nothin' here, Seaman, not even a snake."

A second voice called: "Snakes is smart, Johnny. Bundle together and sleep when it's cold. Seaman's huntin' rabbits. Nothin' but a rabbit's dumb enough to come outta his hole today."

The man with yellow hair collared the dog, drew him away, and announced: "Could use a rabbit for dinner. I'm so hungry I'd eat rat, bones an' all." He led the dog back toward the camp.

The words were strident to Three Eagle's ears. The ring was not Blackfeet, or Shoshone, or Crow. He would have recognized these because the Flatheads traded regularly with Crows and Shoshones. A Blackfoot raider had killed his mother. He could still hear him shouting obscenities, still see him thumping his chest, claiming his coup, a bloody, baseless act, against a weaponless woman.

A cold flake brushed Three Eagles's neck and he wiped it away. The voices quieted and died. The men were cold, too cold to let precious warmth escape in words. In a short while, without food and better clothing, they would turn numb and faint. How long? Two days, maybe three. If the temperature dropped further, maybe not even one. They coiled together now like wintering snakes.

Finally activity stopped and there was only the soft padding of falling snow, only the hazy vision of enveloping whiteness. The bear's claw necklace lay cold upon Three Eagle's skin as he moved away. Dusk was falling. He retraced his steps swiftly back up the familiar trail, over the high ridge, and down again to his village in the wider, warmer hole of a valley where herds of elk and mule deer passed their winters and Indian horses fattened on the tall, sheltered, flatland grasses. He hurried home before the air and the sky turned a uniform, sightless black and the land an unmitigated, implacable white.

News of the strangers had preceded him. The tribal elders had gathered in the shadowy interior of the

190

council lodge and were passing a glowing pipe when he entered. He took his place, waited for the pipe to come to him, inhaled deeply and slowly, and began to relate what he had seen. "They carry fire sticks like Blackfeet, but they lead Shoshone horses, and bring a woman. The horses are skinny, and they rest them in a place where grass is thin. The animals wither and weaken. So do the men. There is a chief, muscular and black-faced, painted for war, and another with hair colored red who waves his arms and shouts like one possessed. Others have colored their hair yellow as the sunflowers that dot the watercourses. All are thinner than this finger I raise before you."

The elders were silent, but a younger, impatient man protested. "They are Blackfeet. The Blackfeet come disguised."

Three Eagles's denial was firm. "You were not there, Red Elk. You did not see. You did not hear. I watched as long as light painted the land. They are weak. Weak men cannot scale mountains or make war."

"They'll rob the game from our forests. Their horses will fatten on our grasses." Red points of light, reflections of flames of the fire, shone in the pupils of the young brave's eyes. "You elders have killed your enemies, seized your captives, amassed your herds. You've snatched your victory from the jaws of conflict, but you're loathe to allow younger men to surpass you. You hobble us like servile animals so we cannot run . . . cage us so we cannot fight."

Three Eagles let the young man's temper flare and simmer. He didn't scold. He didn't blame. He waited for silence, then countered softly. "Where were you when the bear raised his claw, when the snow began to fall? You left with the storm's first howl. You let discomfort drive you from your purpose. Perhaps these hapless strangers were worthy opponents once, but not now. Privation and isolation have depleted them. They suffer. They are afraid. They know an enemy will not pursue into the valley of no return where they can lick their wounds and restore their strength. But they were not anticipating snow, and it has confounded them. They have lost the way. For us, there is no honor in attacking them. There is no reason to provoke them to use fire sticks against us. Let the storm gnash its teeth. They will perish, or they will come to us as friends in their need and exchange guns for the food and forage they need. They will trade away their fire sticks." He touched the huge grizzly's claws that hung about his neck. "I have fought the bear. You cannot run from the grizzly and you will enrage him if you attack. You must stare him down. Patience is the father of wisdom. Patience has won many battles."

Grudgingly the young brave withdrew.

The storm cleared overnight, and in the morning, in the bright, cold light of day, the Indians herded their ponies into the cover of trees and hid their old people and children in the forest. They mounted their horses, strung their bows, fanned out in a defensive crescent behind their chief and waited while the Corps of Discovery climbed over the high divide and marched down through the gap between the mountains. The tall grass waved gently and blowing snow changed to gentle rain.

The expedition snaked slowly into view. Meriwether Lewis, leading, halted when he saw mounted Indians about fifty yards away. Charbonneau stumbled up behind him, cursed in vulgar French, and unplugged his powder horn. But Sacagawea elbowed around the leaders and into the open. Charbonneau called her back, waving his long gun high, jumping like a goat on stubby legs while Toby, with a sheepish grin, followed her. As she ran, the baby bounced hard in the straps of the cradleboard.

She ran to within two strides of Three Eagles, drew back her shoulders, stood her tallest, and broke into a stream of animated speech. The chief looked past her, toward William Clark. She cackled words like an excited hen. He raised an arm, and a lone Indian rode forward from the band. He wore a plain buckskin shirt adorned only with fringes. His hair hung in two black braids that reached to his waist and flipped with the motion of his horse. He was Shoshone, married to a Flathead woman and come to live with her people, and he answered the tiny woman in her own tongue, whirled his horse on its hocks, and spewed a string of cackling syllables at the chief. Suddenly the line of warriors peeled in perfect ranks to each side of the hapless corps.

At the end of the column, John Collins clutched his rifle to his chest. He was aware only of faceless forms — men and horses, black heads, manes, tails, scalps dangling from coup sticks and shields — streaming back and forth in front of his face. He dismounted and knelt to steady his aim.

As he sighted down the barrel, Drouillard slapped it down with a cry: "They're friendly! What are you doing, man? They're our salvation." And he wrenched the rifle from Collins's desperate grasp. Powder from the pan sprinkled over wet grass.

The sound of cocking rifles still splintered the air. From the head of the column, William Clark screeched: "Hold your fire!"

Drouillard repeated the plea at the rear. "It's an escort," he explained, "not a trap. Don't shoot." His tall form jumped from man to man, knocking guns, powder horns, bullet pouches from the hands of frightened men who blinked unbelievingly at the stunned sergeants.

John Collins wanted to run for the forest or melt like rain water into the ground. He pulled the spotted horse after him, out of the line. "Won't give them my horse or my scalp," he stated. Labiche bumped his shoulder as he tried again to load. Beads of moisture had invaded the powder horn. The powder had congealed, caked, and would not pour.

"Didn't I tell you a knife is the surest weapon?" Labiche spit. "You waste good powder on a wet and fouled gun. They mean no harm."

Labiche was a pirate, Collins thought. *How could he know?* Then Collins heard William Clark, calling for calm. He put up his rifle.

The march into the village was anxious and short. The Flatheads conducted the captains, Sacagawea, Toby,

194

and Charbonneau to a tall painted lodge and sat them with the elders on an elk-skin carpet near a blazing fire. But they left the enlisted men hollow-eyed, hungry, stamping their feet, blowing on cold, chapped hands, waiting, grumbling and milling, outside.

"Treatin' Charbonneau like 'is heir apparent an' that old Injun like a lord." Colter said it.

Hugh Hall agreed. "Licks the captain's boots an' strokes his fur ever' time he wags his tail."

Sergeant Pryor assumed careful charge of his men. "Unload the packs. Let the animals rest."

They stacked the supplies in a single pile, tied the horses to it, and listened for familiar voices emanating from the lodge. They could hear easily through its thin skin and fell silent so as to glean any crumb of fact that could bear on their situation.

Lewis was repeating his outworn promises, the same ones he had recited to the Osages, Omahas, Arikaras, Sioux, and Mandans. Hall observed: "We know it by heart. He regurgitates the same tasteless fare, spongy as a rotted log. Thinks they love Tom Jefferson like he loves his Christian God. They never heard of Tommy Jeff."

Labiche expanded: "He thinks he can bribe them with promises. They want guns, not promises." He added with a flick of knife: "The Frenchman carves the words, shapes them like a sculptor to his own design, and Lewis bends to the knife. Drouillard isn't even there." Drouillard had moved off by himself, nearer the horses and the reassuring breath of the animals, beyond the noise of competing voices.

Inside the tent, Lewis's statements rambled. They passed from English to French to Shoshone to Flathead; from Charbonneau to Sacagawea to the Shoshone man to Three Eagles. Voices were muddied; thought was hard to follow. Each version suffered distortions, some cultural and inevitable, others deliberate. Gentle words — trade, friendship, peace, prosperity — twisted and transformed with every flap of Charbonneau's tongue. The Indian jabbered the Flathead version. Did the words even exist in the Flathead language? Or were the Flatheads limited to immediate, physical meanings? Was Lewis's good intent slanted, diminished, or lost completely in a span of syllables?

Like most, Collins did not speak. He tried to decipher intonation. It appalled him. Drouillard's influence was eroding with each passing minute. Charbonneau was taking control not only of the captains' thought processes and expressions but, by extension, of the conduct of the corps. A chasm between officers and enlisted men was widening hourly while Drouillard was talking aimlessly to the horses, allowing it to happen.

There was no more gaming. Labiche sat idle and complaining: "No one will play, Johnny. None will laugh and sing. I feel mutiny in the wind. Do you know what mutiny is? It drips like drops of cold water on your spine, little by little, chilling loyalties and dampening friendships. It always starts with a captain who is deaf to the cries of his men. It can divert a ship's course and a man's life, forever." A horse stomped. An

Indian woman brought fodder for the horses but offered nothing to the men. Labiche's criticisms grew bolder and more derisive. He raised his voice and addressed the entire collection of enlisted men. "Does Lewis know we wait cold and hungry and wet? Does he know what he's asking of these innocents . . . that they submit to capture and plunder?"

No one answered. A dreadful silence hovered. Then Hugh Hall responded: "He stumbles on about friendship and peace and a father in Washington while they hold us hostage. He should give them guns and black powder in exchange for horses. It's what the Flatheads wait to hear. Then they'll feed us and give us shelter."

Labiche added: "We are the bargaining chips, and Charbonneau is the player."

They moved closer to the lodge, keening their ears for any sound of argument or agreement that would bring food and warmth and an end to immediate, physical pain. Flathead women came and beckoned finally. They led the men to a second lodge where a meal waited. But they let no one enter who had not first put down his gun.

One by one, according to the muster roll, the men of the corps entered. Collins trudged after Bratton, before John Colter. They fell on the food, a rich meat stew, devoured every drop and sucked the marrow from the bones. Drouillard was not part of the muster and lingered to the last with the animals, hobbling them and staking them securely where the grass was tallest. Finally he, too, came to eat.

Lewis bargained as best he could, as best Charbonneau's interpretation would allow. He had twelve horses. The Flatheads owned over four hundred tough, muscular animals with deep hearts and powerful quarters. The corps needed about twenty. It needed food and robes to keep warm on the high mountain crossing. Meriwether Lewis sacrificed powder, ball, and rifles, but not too many. He bought buckskin shirts and horses. But he could not buy food. The Indians carried only enough to feed their own.

Three Eagles was pleased with the bargain. His band did not linger long with the strangers. He had new and powerful weapons with which to pursue the buffalo and fend off enemies. With arms raised and fingers peaked, he described the tall spires and deep cañons that the corps would cross. He warned of dangers. He traced the route in the wet soil, with the point of an arrow, and piled pebble upon pebble to indicate mountains. There were many high piles for the many saw-toothed summits. He sent riders to cut the desired number of horses from the Flathead herds, and presented them to the captains who assigned the spotted horse to Collins, a bay to Labiche, a gentle gray to Shields, to each man one horse.

Darkness fell. Men drowsed and slept in the warm lodge and the hours skipped away. Collins was sleeping soundly for the first time in days when Labiche ripped off his blanket. "They're driving them off."

Collins heard, rolled, and snatched the cover back to keep out the cold. Dawn was breaking. He could see the faint light through the smoke hole. He lay back.

Vibrations rattled his skull. Through the narrow entry, he saw dark shapes fleeting like phantom streaks in the dawn mist. Horses were trotting, loping, galloping past. Mounted Indians hooted and whipped after them. The pounding soon shook the hefty poles that held up the lodge. The entire Flathead herd was streaming past.

Labiche was screaming: "Get your animal! Hold him tight before he breaks his tether and gallops away!"

Collins didn't bother to dress. He pulled on moccasins, leaped up, and ran out half naked. Men were bounding from their beds, screaming, flinging arms and blankets to divert the excited herd, pulling valuable gear out of harm's way, charging through moving animals, securing picket pins and lead shanks. A few horses had already broken loose. Collins grabbed the lead of Shields's fat gray as he passed. His spotted horse was still tied, but snorting, pawing the ground, and straining at the end of his rope. He pulled loose the lead. The horse reared and drew back, dragging him and the little gray toward the thundering mass. He braced his legs, jerked both reins hard. Both horses turned and slowed. He looped the leads over the animals' muzzles and tugged them back to the center of the camp.

Other men saved their horses, but Labiche's bay was gone and Whitehouse's roan. They took a count — thirty horses, one per man, a few sickly spares, and two nursing foals that had followed their dams. It would have to be enough because the Indians — horses, dogs, lodges, and all their belongings — had disappeared.

"Toby could've told us. He knew. Charbonneau's to blame. He's the one was doin' the talkin'. Not doin' much listenin'." Colter's red face flushed angrily. He held a wild-eyed black and hissed: "Bruised his cannon bone from all the damn' runnin'. But that's why he slowed and I caught 'im." The horse was lame in the right fore, and Colter stooped to examine its legs. The move took him out of the line of vision, let him conceal his swelling anger.

Labiche slogged up with a blue-eyed, knock-kneed paint and an ugly colt that tagged after her.

Collins laughed. "Ugly as you and lamer. Trust a pirate to pick a lame horse and one with a useless mouth to feed."

Labiche shrugged off the derision. "I never had a blue-eyed woman. She was easy to catch. And she's not so old that she does not produce. If ride I must, she'll carry me carefully as any mother tends her baby." For the pirate, riding was a necessary evil and every horse was stupid and stubborn. The foal nipped suddenly at Labiche's shirt and came away with a patch in his teeth.

Collins laughed and smacked the soft muzzle. He quipped: "Teething like all babies. Watch it's not a piece of your shoulder next time." He picked up the injured hoof and with the point of his knife popped out a pebble that had wedged in the mare's heel. He went to dress and collect his gear, but he was worried. Labiche's horse was too fine-boned, a bad choice. So was Colter's. The foal was a liability. The weak, the distracted, could slip and fall. So could weak and disheartened men.

Shannon came up behind him, leading a sturdy bay. At least he had chosen well. But Shannon's eyes darted suspiciously. "Indians, captains, Charbonneau, that crazy Shoshone an' his gran'kid. I don't trust 'em. Can't find it in my heart to think they care a fig if the rest of us live or die." He sniffled and ran a dirty finger under his dripping nose. "I trust this horse more'n Toby. No tellin' what that old Indian will do. No tellin' what Captain Lewis will do with that Frenchie blathering in his ear. Wish I could fly like the eagles. I'd scoot back to the plains an' the buffler an' the pretty Mandan girls. Should 'a' gone east with the Flat-heads." Shannon was shaking his head. "Where is this damn' ocean, Johnny? Who says we're headed the right way? Ain't we supposed to be there by now? What's Drouillard say?"

Collins had notched the same thoughts. He said: "Captain doesn't believe Drouillard any more."

But Shannon would not be put off. "I do. Cap'n says be friends. Took months before I could call a Mandan buddy. Cap'n says we'll meet a ship. I ain't seen a ship. All I see is mountains, like waves on an endless sea. Maybe that's what they mean by the western ocean. Maybe old Noah left his ark on a peak somewheres. Maybe we can sail away on thin air. Maybe God drank the ocean up like when Moses crossed the Red Sea. I saw a palm reader once at Lexington . . . a woman, but she had those black fiery eyes like Drouillard. He sees things others don't. So did she. Told me I'd live long an' happy on the bounty of waters. What's that mean? I think she lied."

Collins nodded. "What if Drouillard tells us we'll all die?"

"He wouldn't."

"He would." The words escaped, and Collins regretted uttering them. He studied the anguish in young Shannon's eyes and read his own worry there. They were both scared, but not so scared they had lost courage. They were scared of poor leadership, lost possibilities, and bad advice, and so was every thinking man on the expedition.

At noon, all was ready. Collins cinched the pack tight on the speckled horse, picked up the lead, and pulled the animal into line. Shannon was already there, head bowed, lips sealed tightly over gritted teeth and a rigid jaw.

Drouillard appeared leading the black horse Colter had caught. The horse tracked square and sound as a soldier, and Drouillard took his place at the end of the line.

Collins followed. He couched his own fear in other men's questions. "Shannon wants to know if we'll see the ocean."

Drouillard cast a quizzical glance his way. "Only a fool would answer no. Tell him yes, but tell him we have a long way to go."

CHAPTER
SIXTEEN

Shannon smiled when Collins told him Drouillard had answered yes. But the answer didn't satisfy. Drouillard's was not an unqualified yes. It was a nod to what he thought would please and console. Still, it gave cause for hope for the next days.

The horses eased the men's physical burdens. There was no more meandering up streams, weaving haplessly north and south, down dead-end trails, up tall mountains, and down blind valleys, at Toby's capricious behest. Now they headed straight as an arrow west toward the setting sun and the far-off ocean. The scuff of hoofs, the pungent steam that rose from the horse's warm droppings, the swish of tail, and ripple of muscle calmed their hearts and minds.

They plodded on to a hot spring, sat and inhaled the warmth, bathed and basked in the bright afternoon sun. Collins lay down next to Labiche and fell asleep. A few feet away, Drouillard propped himself against a rock. He gazed at the dark wall of spruce and fir, as if with his eyes he could burn through their shield and penetrate their mystery. Toby curled like a mouse on his nest, head resting in the lap of the boy.

In the morning, they pushed higher into the forest. The air grew colder. The days grew shorter. There was no warm bed ground, only hard, pitted, frozen, earth. "We're still climbin'." It was young Shannon who expressed it best. "No grass, no deer, no birds, no fairy ships, and phantom oceans. Can't fill my lungs when I breathe. Can't fill my stomach on water. Can't sleep on ice-hard ground."

The captains eliminated first the noon meal, then breakfast. Empty stomachs caused dizziness and despondency until finally men gnawed candles, sucked rocks, and chewed the leather fringes of their clothing to quiet their hunger. Through it all, Drouillard was silent.

John Collins, Billy Warner, and John Thompson, commissaries and cooks, allotted the remaining stores. It was a thankless chore. The only available necessity was the water that ran in icy torrents from the high peaks, and they used it with abandon to dilute cubes of year-old, dried soup. The result was an unsavory mixture that stuck to the tongue like thinned clay and hardened like chalk in the stomach. More than one man heaved it up. Lips cracked and shrank. Eyes sank deep into their sockets. Feet dragged like limp rags over the ground.

Collins turned away rather than watch the straggling line that came to the fire for dinner. They held out their empty bowls like street beggars. He filled them only half way and watched their pink tongues lick the bowls clean. Once he threw down his ladle and wandered to the fringe of forest, where he knelt, searching for signs of anything alive, a sparrow, a rat, anything to add nourishment to the boil. He picked up a handful of dirt and threw it down and cried: "The devil don't care if I fill their bowls with mud and tell them it's soup."

Drouillard had come up behind him. "They also watch you . . . You won't catch enough to feed one man, but you'll keep hope alive. Set a snare, Johnny."

Collins bit his lip. "They should send out hunters, send you." He kicked futilely at the dirt with a worn moccasin. It hardly scuffed the surface. "This is no good. We should make our case before the captains. Make the captains listen."

"They do listen . . . to the Frenchman."

"Who parrots everything old Toby pronounces and licks their boots like a panting dog."

Drouillard almost smiled. "The Frenchman is greedy, not stupid. He has a son. He does not want to die. Tomorrow, we go to Pryor. He is intelligent. He is discreet and he is brave. He has helped before. He'll find a way."

They set snares and walked back to camp empty-handed.

In the morning they took Sergeant Pryor to check them. Drouillard explained: "Not a quill, not a claw, and men stumbling and weaving on their feet."

Pryor settled his gaze on the circular trace of the empty snare. "Go quietly, both of you. Take Labiche, take reliable rifles . . . the new Harpers . . . and hunt. Johnny, stay with Drouillard to make sure he comes back. Truss him like chicken for roasting if you have to, but bring him back. I'll think what to tell the captains." He pivoted on his heel and stalked away.

Collins, Drouillard, and Labiche filled their powder horns and their ball pouches and crept from the camp. They marched away in the early mountain mist, before the sun broke the horizon, and set out east under a gray and threatening sky. The captains never saw them go.

It started to rain. Drouillard waved Labiche forward. They walked through a thick forest of lodgepole pine, into a narrow cañon watered by an icy creek. It was dark where the tall trees bordered the creek and the smell of moisture suspended in the air. The trees filtered the rain that dripped from the length of every needle and cone. They crossed the creek, mounted a slope, then skidded down a steep incline where the wind had felled every tree in sight and eerie light penetrated the land. Huge, eighty-foot trunks stretched like corpses laid out for burial. Drouillard remarked: "A blow-down, the wind's cruel whipping." Rain ran in torrents between the trunks and carved deep gouges in the flesh of the mountain.

Lightning cracked and a bolt of raw flame knifed the land. It sizzled from the crackling heat. "We should seek shelter," Collins said, and looked around for cover just as Drouillard lifted his rifle and fired. He shot a skinny wolf the color of rain and rock, crazed by the storm, that Collins and Labiche had not seen.

Labiche whispered to Collins: "He sees the invisible and he keeps his powder dry. I could not and neither can you, my friend."

While the two men cowered, Drouillard ran to his kill. He shouted: "Come quickly! There will be more that the storm has flushed."

Labiche waved at Drouillard, but warned Collins: "Only one rifle that will shoot. Watch your feet. The rain sucks sinkholes in the mountain."

The two had started down to Drouillard when the earth's soft muscle gave way. Pebbles rolled and smacked on larger stones that crashed down, tearing out swaths of saturated mud like great bloody gouges and exposing the ligaments that laced together the structure of the mountain. An ugly fissure widened.

The gaping hole caught Georges Drouillard. He felt the break coming and lunged for a branch where he held himself, hanging like a cat by its claws, until the branch weakened and descended slowly, sinking, like a breached ship into the implacable sea.

Gradually the vibrations of earth quieted and the pelt of rain alone broke the stillness. A sizzling wetness settled on the surface of a man's skin. Collins tasted tingling particles upon his tongue. Every hair of his head twitched. He waited, expecting Labiche to speak before the ground beneath their feet gave way. Miraculously it held.

The old pirate's voice flapped finally: "A corpse will surface in an ocean but not here."

Collins choked out: "Drouillard . . . where's Drouillard?" His eyes misted. He slapped his arms against his body and jumped and landed hard on his feet and started to scramble down.

Labiche tackled him, felled him like a tree. "Stay still, the earth has not settled."

Collins hardly heard. His mind screamed at the sight before his eyes, the upturned earth, exposed roots and rocks, and nowhere Drouillard. In the watery stillness, he cried the name until the echo screeched back from the face of the cañon and Labiche clamped a hand on his mouth to signal enough.

"He'll answer if he's alive," he assured Collins. A belated pebble tapped its way down the mutilated slope and a response came like a bubble rising from a spring. "Clear the drops from your eyes and the clouds from your brain. You clatter so loudly you make her rumble more." Then the barrel of a rifle waved back and forth behind the lightning-struck tree like a signal flag on a mountaintop, and the deep, familiar bass scolded: "Let the earth resume her slumbers, Johnny, before you rouse her again and press your feet in her wounds."

But Collins paid no attention. He slithered down.

Drouillard lay on his back, legs pinned tightly under a root the width of a man's thigh. Drouillard had a hand on the root. "Shackled like a prisoner in irons," he hissed, and tried to twist free. Pain wrenched the stoic features of his face.

Labiche scrambled down. "Lay a hand with me, Johnny." They pulled. The root held and would not give.

"I'll go for a horse," Collins said.

"No horse. Hoofs will only jar the soil. Bring a shovel and an axe." Labiche pointed. "Go that way where the land is firm. I'll stay with him."

208

Collins wormed his way over root and rock to solid ground. He stood then and took off at a run over the deadfall, through the brush-choked way they had come. He kept running.

He was nearing the camp when he stopped short. Someone was singing. He continued on.

Toussaint Charbonneau knelt on a flat stone in the center of the trail, kindling a flame. The wet carcass of a lynx that he had skinned lay by him. His pipe poked from between yellow teeth and smoke rose from the bowl. And he sang with abandon. He had a surprisingly pleasing voice, and the notes of his Gallic melody were slow and sweet.

Collins mind raced. This man was best avoided. But Charbonneau had heard him coming and had stopped singing.

John Collins approached with caution.

"*Que veux-tu?*" The harsh tone belied the plaintive song. The black head, bearded and matted with hair, bobbed. Charbonneau leered and blew smoke through his nose. His rifle lay beyond reach, propped in the crook of a rock, and his powder horn hung from the barrel.

Collins grinned when he spotted the useless gun. "Let me pass. I need no grief from you."

Charbonneau wiped bloody fingers on the front of his shirt. He cupped the stem of his pipe in his massive palm, removed it, and licked his lips. He spoke good English. "The fire would not light. Kill me and know you will leave a wife without a husband, a son without a father."

"She's not your wife. She's your slave."

"She is my wife according to their custom, and the babe is my son." With his free hand, he pulled his tomahawk from his belt. "This is my weapon. I was a lumberman." He laughed and with an easy swipe sliced off a wad of beard. "I keep her sharp. You would not have lived if we had fought with this."

Charbonneau's laughter was challenging, and Collins matched it to show he was not afraid. But it produced a static curdling in his throat, and he let it die. Silence hovered. A gurgle arose from Charbonneau's barrel chest, crimped his eyes, and rippled every strand in his beard. He rose, stepped to the lynx he had killed, and started to slice up the carcass. He threw a scrap of bloody meat to Collins and laughed. "A predator. Eat. It will make you brave."

Collins let the meat lay at his feet. "A man is down. I come for help." He did not name Drouillard.

Charbonneau smiled and answered: "There are better, stronger men than I who are hungry. I will not leave good meat." His eyes narrowed in spite. He added: "I know who you would help. I could kill you. I could throw this tomahawk."

Collins's back straightened at the challenge and his mouth spread in a clownish grin. "Strike me, coward, strike me in my back."

They laughed again cautiously like evenly-matched and circling enemies, until Charbonneau put up the tomahawk and confessed: "It's a mortal sin to kill a man and carries terrible punishment."

210

Another silence. Collins swallowed hard and declared: "I never touched your wife."

"No? Then who did?" He projected a long stream of saliva toward Collins's feet. "Theft of a wife is a grave sin, also, cause for restitution."

Collins licked his lips. "The man waits. I cannot waste more time with you." He turned his back to Charbonneau, waited a moment for the blow of the tomahawk he thought would come, and walked away. When no strike came, he broke into a run.

Patrick Gass, the sergeant/carpenter, was on guard when Collins arrived. Born on the far Emerald Isle, Gass favored men like Collins, with fair hair, rosy cheeks, clear blue eyes, and obvious Celtic blood. But he accosted Collins now. "Be ye out of breath, Private? Absent without a leave? Where's Drouillard? Where's Labiche? Or did ye sneak away for meat to feed your own pink cheeks?"

Collins stammered. "Sergeant Pryor gave us leave, sir, myself, Labiche, and Mister Drouillard. Drouillard is trapped, sir. An earth slide caught him. Labiche is with him." He added: "We have killed meat . . . a wolf . . . and will bring it in. And Charbonneau has a cat."

Gass narrowed his eyes. "A wolf ye say and Charby has a cat . . . bless him. Grab some soup and a blanket. I'll ne'er condemn a man for feedin' himself when he's starvin' if he shares with his God-fearin' neighbor. I'll get my tools."

The rain had stopped and a brisk wind had arisen. Billy Warner was stirring the soup when Collins filled his bowl. "Captain was askin' for you, Johnny. Pryor told him you an' Labiche and Drouillard had already eaten. Where you been?"

Before Collins could respond, Gass appeared with shovel, broad axe, and saw. He cut short the chatter. "Pryor will cover for us, but you, my good Private Warner, must mind they don't suspect or we'll all be sweatin' like Gaelic rebels in a Brit's cold jail. We be bringin' in meat." Warner nodded and Gass resumed: "'Tis a fair wind blows out the rain, dries and quiets the sod." He led off swiftly through the forest.

Labiche was singing as they approached, a whaler's tune of a tropical paradise. Drouillard had turned his body so that his back rested against the rough surface of the stump. He wasn't listening. He was wet and shivering and his face was frozen in its passive mold.

Collins wrapped the blanket around Drouillard's shoulders while Gass assessed the situation, laying a massive hand on the root. He handed Labiche the shovel, took one end of the saw, and grunted: "Gently as a maiden's breath, lightly as she sleeps, pirate. Collins, grab th' other end."

They took one swipe with the saw and stopped. Labiche began to scrape away one thin layer at a time. "Rest a mite so as not to waken her." They waited to see if the earth would shudder. "Now once again. Johnny Collins, gimme your tomahawk." Collins put a hand to his belt. It was not there. "Lost it, did ye? Here's mine." Gass pulled the weapon from his belt.

212

"As I move the saw, wedge the 'hawk in the crease, so's she doesn't pinch."

The three men toiled patiently, waiting, watching, after each singular motion for the soil to quiver and heave. They wedged the cut wider with every slice of saw. Shavings and earth flaked away slowly, the root separated, cracked, split, and Drouillard's leg turned. They pulled him free and crawled away lest another sudden jar would send the slope sliding.

When they reached standing trees, they stood up slowly. Drouillard's leggings were torn and an ugly gash streaked his thigh with blood. But he tested the leg, and it bore his weight.

They carried on in silence, stopping to collect the precious meat. They arrived back at camp as dusk was falling. They brought one wolf, with Charbonneau's lynx — starvation rations for thirty hungry men.

News of the kills percolated down the mess line. When the call sounded, there were only a few bites per man, but red meat evoked grudging thanks and marked new loyalties born of shared privation, not purchased by bribery and gold, or forced by the exigency of command.

The corps bedded down that night under worn, thin hides. The wind died and the clouds lifted from the towering spruce, exposing a moon that smiled benevolently and a brilliant panoply of stars. The tired, the injured, the demented, and the hungry slept soundly. But in the early hours of dawn, clouds descended again and an unwelcome presence slipped like a silent ghost into the camp and lay white and cold over men and beasts.

The snow was pure and soft as a virgin, untouched and unwarmed by the hands of men. The fires had died during the night, and there was nothing more to eat. Grimly, as the cold sun rose, as its dazzling rays glinted off the shimmering whiteness, men squinted and rubbed their sore eyes. They stuffed their moccasins with moss and cut bark to patch their clothing and cover themselves. They brushed the snow from the shaggy horses' backs, lashed down the packs, and moved out.

The snow covered all traces of any trail. Toby had come this way only once before and only in summer. Now he stopped often for his young grandson to sweep aside the snow. He bent down, touched the cold, hard earth, and stared intently at the patch of ground below. He studied it, tasted it, sniffed his fingers, then raised his right arm, and pointed the way. It led down a steep, treacherous slope, slick with ice, deeper into the valley. The true trail hovered on the ridge high above.

Drouillard caught the mistake and told Pryor who carried the information to William Clark and Meriwether Lewis.

For a full day, Lewis ignored it. Toby and Charbonneau, resplendent in his skin of lynx, stood by his side. Charbonneau wore the wet skin with the head propped over his brow like a crown, the forepaws draped over his meaty shoulders. With smoke rising from his perennial pipe, he seemed a dragon of a man. He looked down his craggy nose at all who had a hand in his disgrace, especially Collins, who had challenged him, and Labiche who was his dubious second. But he blamed Drouillard who alone had the power to replace him in the captains' good graces.

Drouillard had lost blood in the landslide. He clung desperately to the mane of the black horse that pulled him along in an effort to keep up with the herd.

Collins worried: "He cannot walk much farther."

Labiche muttered: "I'll talk with Pryor."

Pryor agreed. "Redistribute the packs. Place him on your horse." He didn't consult the captains. "And keep the mare well back, hidden from view, behind a tree, a rock, a turn in the trail." He smacked his lips. Nathaniel Pryor, sergeant, had stepped beyond the ordinary chain of command and exposed himself to rebuke and punishment. He added: "If you're caught, don't look to me."

"Aye, sir. Thank you, sir. You'll not regret it, sir."

The trail switched back and weaved through evergreens where sunshine shimmered on the glaring white and splattered the sparkling needles with silver. The scent of pine perfumed the crisp air. The earth warmed and the snow melted. Toward evening, the trail curved north into the shadow of the mountain and the temperature dropped perceptibly. Mud from the morning melt congealed and hardened into icy patches, but Lewis did not call a halt.

The press of feet and the scuff of hoofs exposed root and rock and carved a slippery furrow in the trail. For the last in line, the furrow was deeper and the rocks naked and sharp. Labiche's blue-eyed paint stumbled and scrambled nimbly to her feet many times. Finally she fell to her knees, and Drouillard slid like a limp rag doll onto the ground. Collins rushed to him. Echoes of man overboard reverberated up the line, and both William Clark and Meriwether Lewis rushed to the rear.

Lewis spied the pesky foal first, then the paint mare. "Why does this horse not carry her load?" His icy stare swept over the ranks and came to rest on Drouillard who lay on his back at the side of the trail. "Get this man up so he can walk." He fired the salvo at Labiche and raised his hand as if to strike. Both Labiche and Collins shied back. Lewis stood, arm raised, jaw clenched.

Clark came up behind him, grasped the poised arm, and held it in place. "Stop, Meri, leave him be. You carry the weight of the long struggle on your shoulders." Lewis whirled suddenly to strike the hand that held him, but he caught himself and lowered the arm. Clark murmured: "Today, you drive too hard, Meri. You, me, this man, the men, the horses . . . we're all exhausted."

Embarrassed, Lewis seemed to shrink. Realization slowly came into focus, and he inquired: "Who permitted Drouillard to ride?"

Clark did not answer but held his eye riveted.

Sergeant Pryor stepped forward. "I did, sir." He did not explain.

Collins lifted Drouillard, who stood straight and walked unaided back into line. Collins looked to the animal that was standing, trembling slightly. He bent and picked up a hoof. "A stone bruise, sir. The horse was lame. The load was too great. Drouillard is thin, lighter."

"You?" Anger colored Lewis's face again as his eyes fell on Collins, then Pryor. "A careless sergeant, a disobedient soldier, a stupid, unruly beast." The foal trotted up. Lewis threw up his arm, and the animal whirled and kicked. Lewis jumped back to avoid the flashing hoofs, raised a fist, and shouted at the horse: "Fall again, I shoot you! I shoot your unruly foal and roast him for dinner!"

John Collins's frustration had been growing for weeks, filling the cavity of his chest and burgeoning upward into his throat. He jumped to the defense of Drouillard. "Shoot the horse, sir, or shoot Sergeant Pryor because he defended a man who cannot walk? Perhaps we should have shot Whitehouse when the dugout crushed him, or Shields because he talks. Captain you are, but privates and sergeants and stupid beasts know better than you how to conduct this corps!"

"Silence, Private!" William Clark bellowed.

Meriwether Lewis blanched in shock. Never had anyone defied his authority.

However, once started, Collins could not stop. Days and weeks of compressed frustration welled up in his throat and spouted out like vomit. He was screaming, pleading: "Mister Drouillard is our hope . . . not this Toby, not Charbonneau who flatters you and calls you sir because you hold his purse strings, because you are the keeper of his gold!"

The outburst echoed down the line of march. There was a pause, and little by little other men started to speak, nodding and approving the young private's statements.

William Clark lay a hand on Lewis's arm and murmured softly: "Meri, he has reason. You hear how many men agree. Go with Sergeant Pryor, rest." He made no apology. He issued no rebuke. He spoke firmly but softly over his shoulder as Pryor led Meriwether Lewis away: "We'll pretend this exchange never happened, Privates. Now get that horse back in line . . . Mister Drouillard, are you able to keep up?"

"I can walk. The cold helped stanch the flow of blood." Drouillard gave an impassive nod.

"Then we will stop as soon as we find level bed ground."

The incident left a gravelly churning in Collins's belly. He had defied an officer, his captain and chief. He could have been, would have surely been, brought before a court at any other time, in any other place. He waited daily for the punishment that did not come and harbored a gut-wrenching fear in his heart that his leaders were losing control, that mutiny, not leadership, might be the salvation of the corps. The captains had allowed his blatant breach of discipline to go unpunished. Last year, closer to the settlements, closer to procedure and planning and protocols of Army discipline, he would have been hauled before a court martial for a lesser offense. But now Meriwether Lewis and William Clark had lost status in his eyes and in the eyes of the men. The captains seemed not to know where to go or who to follow. The old Indian was walking blindly. Collins knew it. Drouillard knew it. Every man in the corps knew it and each harbored his own apprehensions. But Collins alone had let his demons escape. He was not sorry. He would take his punishment when meted out. He gravitated to the rear of the march, even behind Drouillard. He didn't want to walk in the footsteps of contentious captains, of Charbonneau and Toby. He didn't want to hear the ring of argument that echoed faintly from the head of the column, because argument concealed too many doubts. He didn't like to watch Toby and his grandson hesitate and guess the trail. John Collins preferred to contemplate only the wind that whipped the tail of the horse in front of him, the twitch of the animal's hocks, the tread of its hoofs, and the uneven footprints of Georges Drouillard. It was frightening to think of miscalculation and madness, terrifying to think too far ahead. The worst time was night, after the lone meal of rock chuck or polecat that Labiche or another had snared. Divided by thirty, the meat was not even a small puddle in the pit of his stomach.

The captains ordered a horse killed for food — the paint mare's mischievous foal. Collins didn't fill his plate and Labiche brought a portion to him. "Eat before they cut the ration further." So Collins ate, repressing his revulsion at the impish little life cut short, thinking only of how he would have to rise up and march on in the morning. He was tired, more tired than ever before on this fateful trip, and more afraid. To evince even minor dissatisfaction was to evoke the possibility of failure, and after failure . . . death. To admit his fear was to provoke that same dread in the souls of his fellows, and John Collins had already said enough.

A week dragged by, seven lonely, enervating days since the Flatheads had left, since the corps had entered the cold mountain fortress. The scant horsemeat only increased the longing for meat. Labiche rose before dawn and checked his snares. The small supplement helped. Drouillard's wound healed. The trail was descending now and the air warming. But cold and privation had taken its toll, had dulled the ambitions, and honed the frustrations of impetuous men.

Toby and his grandson paraded on. Meriwether Lewis had not spoken since the day Pryor had led him away. He did not attend muster, take scientific readings, or write an account in his journal. One morning he fainted. Clark caught him as he fell. The collapse forced a decision. That night, William Clark addressed the gathering of the corps. Cold firelight flashed across his haggard face, ignited the surfaces, and shaded the hollows that hid his bright eyes. Clark was thinner now, the facial furrows cut deeper, the tic in his cheek had become more pronounced.

He bowed his head and began: "Tomorrow, at daybreak, I will go ahead with our strongest men. We will return with help. Captain Lewis did as much for you when we found the Shoshones. Now our need, his need, is greater." The entire corps listened mutely.

220

William Clark was taking charge of their destiny. They welcomed his resolution that rebuilt, if only partially, the crumbling edifice of their own resolve.

In the morning, Clark assigned duties. "Privates Reuben and Joseph Fields, Shields, Collins, Colter, and Mister Drouillard, collect your gear. Saddle your horses. Meet at the lodgepole near the creek, in one half hour. We ride to lower altitudes, greener pastures, and game." He stopped. He didn't mention Toby. He was taking the most contentious and outspoken: Drouillard, Collins, Shields. He continued: "Captain Lewis will remain with the rest of you. Obey your sergeants, and care well for your captain and your fellows. Move ahead as your strength permits. We will hunt and leave meat for you." He inhaled, smiled, and let his breath out slowly. "I'll see you all again in a few days."

There was no good bye. He sniffed, cast his eyes over the men, nodded once, dropped his eyes, and walked away.

John Collins waited until Labiche pulled his arm. "Johnny, go! Get your horse."

Collins glanced at his pirate friend. "You were not chosen."

"And neither was Charbonneau. He wants you. He wants Drouillard and Shields because he cannot trust either of you with Lewis . . . or Lewis with you." Labiche held out a hand. "Good bye, Johnny. Good luck." With the other, he punched his partner affectionately in the hollow of his shoulder.

CHAPTER
SEVENTEEN

Collins was waiting at the lodgepole at the appointed time. Colter, Shields, and the Field brothers waited with him. It was not the enlisted men who lagged when it was time to leave, or the scout, Georges Drouillard. It was William Clark. He had retreated behind a rawhide windbreak that shielded Meriwether Lewis and he shuffled nervously about while throwing items into his pack. When he finished, he settled on a rock at creekside to wait out the minutes until departure.

Meriwether Lewis stood over him. He gripped a staff firmly to maintain his balance. His knuckles were white. Bones protruded from thin sticks of fingers that kneaded the soft wood of the staff. His face was drawn. With the loss of flesh, the skin had receded from nose, chin, and cheek bones, exposing sharp, skeletal angles. His head was wrapped in a green rag, and its loose threads combined with his limp red hair casting a sickly hue over his face. He had topped the rag with a beaver hat that perched like a fish hawk on its scraggly nest. "I'll miss you, Will," he said. "God go with you. My hopes rest on your shoulders."

Clark's cheek ticked. "Not *my* shoulders, Meri, the backs and brawn of these fine men. They have earned their just rewards." Lewis nodded, and Clark added: "Don't accuse them unjustly."

"I could never, Will." Lewis frowned. "I did not credit the height and breadth of these mountains, or the width of the continent. What of the tribes? What will you do when you meet them? We've not much left to buy their friendship except the shirts on our backs." He turned his head to avoid Clark's direct gaze. "I think you should take gold, Will, a few pieces, and take Toby."

Clark smiled. "We have powder and lead, muskets, rifles. That's what they want, Meri. They'll trade a horse for a musket, but not for gold." He dangled a stick in the creek and watched it create a tiny wake. The rushing current erased its imprint long before the creek became a river, and the river an endless sea. Clark looked up at Lewis's cavernous eyes, rounded shoulders, and knees that would not straighten. He lifted the stick from the stream. "Sit, Meri. Rest a minute with me. Lord knows when we'll meet again."

But Lewis did not sit. His head bobbed like a doddering grandfather. Greasy hairs hung in his face and the look in his eyes was mercurial and distant. Clark's words bounced off him without effect. He'd lost much of the power of abstract thought, but his lips moved and sounds emerged. "Offer them gold. They'll take gold, Will. They trade for skins and beads and guns and whiskey. They trade the attentions of their women. They'll trade for gold."

"Did you hear, Meri?" Clark gazed into the demented eyes and lowered the stick again into the stream. "Gold doesn't count. Charbonneau can keep his treasure. It's no good to him, or us. This place is not inhabited. We haven't found a single human soul on this side of the Divide. And Indians, when we find them, if we find them, will throw it away." He placed his hand in the water and tried to grab the liquid in his palm. It splashed between his fingers and turned them red with cold. He withdrew his hand and held it up and spread the wet fingers as if his gesture would illustrate his thought. "Empty every time, empty as the counsel of Toby and the price of Charbonneau's gold. A twig creates a greater ripple on the surface of this river than thirty men on the face of a continent." He threw the stick into the creek, let it float away, and followed it with his eyes so as not to look at Lewis. "I'm taking Drouillard with me, Meri, and Collins and Shields, so you will have peace in the camp. Controversy seems to cling to them like dirty fringe. And I'll take Toby because he will be of no help to you here. Labiche will stay. He's a good shot . . . if you find something to shoot. And the sergeants will be with you." He knit his brows together and closed his eyes. Did Meriwether Lewis comprehend? Clark's left cheek hammered. He gritted his teeth and sucked in his lips to hide the motion. "We'll leave sign. Follow as slowly or quickly as you must. We'll find meat, Meri, I promise. We'll hang it where you will find it. And Meri, let the sergeants share your burden."

A flash of lucidity struck Lewis and he blurted: "The stick floats, Will, like us. God will cradle us and bear us up like Noah on the waters." Enthusiasm burst from his voice. "We saw lodges and burial sites. Someone

224

constructed them. Someone cared for them. People are here, behind trees, under rocks. Have you looked? They have eyes in places we cannot imagine."

Clark let the vision wash over his friend. Should he destroy the crazed glimmer of hope? Should he tell Meriwether Lewis the truth? What had become of the secretary to President Jefferson, soldier, scout, and scholar? He said: "Chimeras, shadows." And he thought: *Like you, Meri, only a breath of your former self*. But he bit back the words, forced a wan smile while his mind painted a starker image of prairie burials, corpses elevated on scaffolds, abandoned to the elements and the vultures. He had not seen any burials since they entered the mountains. Meriwether Lewis had confused the time and the place.

Lewis's thought reversed abruptly: "Suppose they attack. Suppose the tribes are hostile." He shook his head as if to dispel the possibility.

"Hostile?" Clark rose to his full height and inhaled. The rising sun flashed red across his eyes and he looked away. "They will see we are too weak to fight. The men are waiting. I'll leave news for you of our whereabouts. You have my word."

Still Lewis grabbed his arm and would not let go. "A scrap of paper impaled on a limb for the wind to seize and blow, a scratch on the surface of the soil, a single stick in a mighty river. Leave something permanent, Will. I'll alert the sergeants to watch for the sign."

"Yes, do." William Clark had run out of patience. He held out his hand, but Lewis's watery eyes missed the motion.

Meriwether Lewis flung both arms around William Clark and fell against him. Clark took hold of the emaciated shoulders, felt the soft bend of spine, stood him straight, and wondered if his fellow captain would live to see the promised ship and the expanse of western ocean. "Come, Meri," he said, "back to the fire."

Clark's send-off was not silent. The enlisted men deliberately cheered and hooted. It was a sunny day. The snow was melting on the north-facing slopes. Cruzatte struck up a lively hornpipe on his fiddle. Its strings were stretched thin and its box damp. The instrument squeaked like scratched slate, but the tune inspired song and laughter. Men slapped shoulders and danced. Labiche flipped heels over head, and Collins fingered the silken surface of the cowrie shell that hung about his neck. Even Hugh Hall, whose voice was flat as the prairie horizon, sang out loudly, and Joe Whitehouse skipped a caper.

When the time finally came to leave, Collins tried to swallow but his throat was desert dry. He lined up, at once glad to move on and sorry to part with friends.

At the last moment, Labiche offered him a knife. "You'll need it if you find meat. I took it off a Moroccan sailor, and it has brought me good fortune. It wants a younger hand than mine. And I have the espontoon."

Collins laughed. "I already have a knife." But he let it lay in his palm because it had a silver hilt with an inlaid blue stone and to decline would have offended. Labiche was somber as a gravedigger when he closed Collins's fingers around the hilt.

Collins mounted his speckled horse, took his place in line after John Colter, and glanced once at the gathering of men. When he lifted a hand to signal good bye, they had resumed their singing. The song was mournful now, "Barbara Allen", about love long lost. Collins turned the horse west, down the narrow trail.

It was barely a trace cut nearly level into the mountain's face. William Clark pushed his animal to a swift trot so as to escape more quickly from the sight and sound of the corps. Collins pressed his horse to keep up. Pain racked his soul, and fear, not of the unknown, but of losing friends and colleagues forever. Still, there was a new resolve that beat down his fears: William Clark rode at their head under the wise and all-seeing direction of Georges Drouillard. It was easy to follow Georges Drouillard and heartening to know Toby and his fawning boy tagged in the rear.

When the camp was out of sight, they slowed to a walk and moved steadily along a gravel creek. Clark led with Drouillard, while the other five, Toby, and the boy followed in single file. Gradually they descended to a wide, sandy bar where the sun glinted obliquely off the water and tall cottonwoods shaded the opening of a gulch. A bald eagle perched in the high arms of an ancient tree. Shields lifted his rifle to shoot, but Drouillard screeched: "A predator means there are fish in the river. Cast a line. Set a snare."

"Beaver maybe, an' trout." John Colter pointed to the telltale stumps. "They're here. Their lodge is close."

They had come ten miles, far enough. Lewis would be lucky to travel three. They set up camp. Drouillard stripped cottonwood bark to feed the horses. Shields and the two Fields set out traps. Collins and Colter gathered driftwood for a fire. They sauntered across the bar to where a beaver dam blocked the flood and flotsam collected. The river had changed course recently and scoured out a crevice under the bank. The pink light of sunset struck this depression now and reflected off the exposed rock face.

Colter laughed. "Rocks is winkin' at me pink as a flirty girl's tit." He picked up a pebble, wiped it on his sleeve, bit into it with his teeth. "If girls is this hard, I'll never pinch another one." He handed the pebble to Collins with a wink.

Collins didn't know Colter well. Their proximity in the muster line had never blossomed to friendship, but not because they did not like each other. In fact, they were much alike: both were young and headstrong; both had a fondness for whiskey and women; both were excellent woodsmen and dead shots. Collins was the handsome one, Colter more craggy and roughshod. Both had been disciplined for turning hunting forays into visits to the grog shop, and both had taken Mandan women. Still, the work assigned them was always separate, according to mess. Colter was in Sergeant Ordway's mess while Collins answered to Sergeant Pryor.

Collins took the pebble, rubbed it between his fingers. He unsheathed the knife Labiche had given him and scraped the pebble lightly.

228

Colter watched. "That yours? I never seen a knife like that. Like a pretty blue eye winking up at you . . . pretty but dangerous. Where'd you get it?"

"Labiche gave it to me before we left. Says it's a good luck jewel. He took it in a fight with a Barbary sailor." Collins rinsed the pebble in the river. When he brought it back up to the light, a pinkish-yellow streak sparkled like a candle flame.

Colter continued to talk, but his eyes had narrowed. "Pirate treasure. Like to have seen Labiche fight. I see 'im with a dagger like Cap'n Lewie's. Espontoon . . . that what he called it? Labiche could be a rich man." He was staring at the pebble. "Pink like the sunset, like red gold. There's yellow an' white an' red gold. My mother had a ring made with strands of all three, set with a green bezel stone like your blue one, an' she wore it on a chain around her neck." He knelt at the lip of the creek, scooped up a handful of mud, and let water run through the soft folds of his palm. "There's more flakes."

Collins stared as Colter opened his hand. Tiny bits of grit glittered in every crease. He fell to his knees and sank his two hands in the mud. Together they scooped the shiny stones from the bottom mud and picked the shiny bits from the folds of their skin. John Colter cut a patch of buckskin from his shirt. In it, they deposited the gold, then folded and tied the patch with a strip of bark. "I'll keep it careful as you keep that shell around your neck." Colter shoved the package under his shirt. "Can you write? Make us a map?"

"I can only write my mark. Captain'll fix us a map."

"An' pray this whore of a river's still sleepin' in the same bed next year." Colter pointed. "Beaver, sandbar, tall trees . . . they pines or spruces? I'm rememberin'. I'm comin' back."

"Spruces. I'm comin' with you."

They laughed and shook hands.

Colter said: "Wisht I could write like the captain, I'd make me my own map and keep our little find secret."

"With this bunch. You'd keep a secret the way Charbonneau keeps wives. You'd forget duty and friendship, like we're forgettin' we're supposed to find wood."

Colter didn't answer. They gathered wood, but not much.

Drouillard met them at the edge of the camp. He'd already kindled a fire, caught, skinned, and spitted three trout. "I went for my own wood. Shields thinks you found a whiskey spring, lay down, and drank yourselves numb."

Colter drew out the patch and spread the folds. "We found gold, Georges." His eyes gloated, wide as marbles.

Drouillard glanced casually. "Clap your hands in a light wind, it'll blow away."

Labiche and Shields heard the exchange and came to look. Colter moved to the fire where the light was brighter. He opened the patch. The tiny stones flickered like near stars. Others came and marveled at the sight, but William Clark sniffed when he saw, raised a brow, and pronounced: "We're explorers, not fortune seekers. You can't eat it, shoot it, or drink it. Fresh water, red meat, and dry fuel are worth more." He didn't draw a map, but he recorded the longitude and the latitude of the place.

Night fell. Clark, Drouillard, Toby, and the boy slept, but other men lingered at the fire. Collins wove a necklace of horsehair for Colter to tie the bundle safely around his neck. Colter drew his own crude map by the light of the fire on a square of stripped bark. They fingered the pebbles — some looked more like flakes — rolled them in their palms, rubbed them like a lover against their cheeks. When they fell into their robes beside the creek, they talked of fine clothes, fast horses, whiskey, and women with long tresses in soft beds with mattresses of thick feathers.

Colter lay back, cradling his head in his hands. "I'll hire me some rivermen, head my own expedition. Gold's layin' there like eggs in a hen's nest, gold an' beaver."

Joe Fields added: "Beaver's worth as much, maybe more. Lotsa beaver swimmin' in the rivers. We'll all be rich, richer 'n Frenchie, richer 'n Croesus."

Through it all, John Collins was quiet. What he wished for, a desire he had repressed these last long months, neither gold nor beaver pelts could buy.

"What'd you do, Johnny, if you were a rich man?" Colter's query drew attention to Collins's silence. "Speak up, Johnny, you never been shy. You want that long-legged Mandan girl, but she don't want you, not for gold or nothin' else."

The comment stung. John Collins pitched a stone at the fire, saying: "*She* wanted me. Her old mother didn't. No amount of gold or beaver can buy her back. I lost that gamble." He rolled over, mumbling: "We go back that way, I'll try to set things right." He fell asleep on the flickering hope.

In the morning, they rose early, before sunrise. Sleep still crusted their eyes when they mounted the horses, but their step was lighter, their pace quicker. The creek roared past giant pines that stood shoulder to shoulder along its banks. The horses clopped over bare-faced rock or trudged through sticky, wet sand. They rode, eyes down, studying every depression for the glint of gold, except for Collins who swayed to the motion of the horse. He closed his eyes and beat back prickly memories.

CHAPTER
EIGHTEEN

Four days after they left Lewis, the little troop began the descent. Drouillard rode at the head. Collins felt his horse's hoofs slip slightly on the carpet of needles as weight shifted from haunch to fore. He leaned back and braced his feet against the stirrups for balance. The scent of evergreen drugged his senses. He was very tired. His eyes closed, his head lolled as the spotted horse padded evenly forward. A buck bounded away. Colter called: "Wake up, everybody! We're passin' good meat by!" Collins just glimpsed the tips of the antlers as they disappeared into the brush.

Suddenly, as a unit, the horses stopped and pricked their ears. There was an end to the forest; Drouillard shaded his eyes from the sun's strong glare. The trail opened on a wide plain where sunlight spread glittering fingers over a sea of yellow grass that undulated like waves on an ocean. The wind was warm.

Collins rubbed his eyes. It was like a dream, like a tidewater pasture, or the tall grass prairie, like Maryland or Virginia or the gentle blue grass of Kentucky. It was no illusion.

Drouillard squinted hard across the expanse, and lifted an arm. The others pushed their horses forward

233

to see. "Look there . . . and there!" He was speaking to Clark, but he intended all to hear. At the far western edge of the plain, tucked against a backdrop of low hills, a trail of smoke rose. About a mile away, obscured by the waving grass and their own peculiar freckling, a herd of horses grazed. Clark raised a spyglass to his eye.

"They look like your beast, Johnny," Shields said, "like somebody splattered his paint."

"Quiet boys. Come ahead slowly." Clark leaned forward slowly, warily, and his horse moved into the naked grass. Drouillard, Toby, and the rest followed.

Three human forms broke like quail from a covey and fled through the tall grass. Shields grabbed his powder horn and began to measure out grains, but his hands shook and the grains spilled.

Clark bellowed and raised a staying hand. "Don't shoot! They're children!"

But Shields started to pour another charge. "They have fathers and uncles and brothers who'll swat us down like flies." His face was pinched and pale.

"Private Shields, put away the powder horn. Put your gun in its sling. They have no weapons!" Clark's deep voice bellowed, but Shields seemed not to have heard. He was trying to ram a charge home and control the gray horse that weaved frantically from side to side. Shields jerked the reins, but only panicked the animal more.

Drouillard whirled his horse and slammed it into Shields's light mare. The mare staggered from the impact, and Shields lurched. Drouillard twisted the gun from his grasp and dropped it in the grass. "Shoot children. Go on. See who'll befriend you then."

"Gimme my Betsy. She goes where I go, my Betsy." Shields had named his gun for his woman and swung down to retrieve it. He shoved the stock into his shoulder, lifted the barrel, and aimed it at Drouillard. "Betsy don' like you throwin' her off like an empty jug. You're redder 'n the devil himself. You're a red Injun yourself!"

Instinctively Collins drove his horse between the two contenders as Shields pulled the trigger. The flint *clinked* on the empty pan.

Shields turned the gun on Collins. "Outta the way, Collins, or I'll blast you, too."

"Private Shields," Clark ordered, "the guns stay here."

At the sound of his captain's voice, Shields's head snapped around. Eyes like round moons, he stared at William Clark who stretched his broad shoulders skyward, lifted his gun above his head, lowered it slowly, and dropped it deliberately to the ground.

"Do as I do, John Shields."

Shields shook his head wildly. The horse was prancing, lunging, matching its rider's frenzy. Drouillard advanced and dropped his rifle, and Collins followed, then the two Fields and John Colter.

Colter glared at Shields, needling: "What's the matter? You swallow a yellow snake?"

In response, John Shields screamed: "We're soldiers! Soldiers carry arms!" He glared unbelievingly at the stacked guns that lay in a bed of grass — black, gleaming, useless.

"A soldier follows orders, Private Shields. He doesn't bait an enemy. Fire that gun and you'll face dismissal from this troop."

"But I'll have my Betsy."

"Until you have to reload and you spill your powder or ram in a double charge and your gun explodes in your face. Then you'll wish their arrows brought you down." Clark waited, adding: "You'll discover how very friendly these Indians are, alone, wounded, without a gun."

Shields didn't hear. His broad smithy's shoulders trembled. The gun rattled in his hands.

Clark dismounted and walked back to face the frightened man. As he grabbed the reins to steady the horse, he took his knife, cut Shields's powder horn from its thong, and emptied the contents onto the ground. "Give me the gun," he said. "Your flint is loose. You have no powder. Your gun is useless. Gather your wits and marshal your courage, Private, and ride, here, at my side." He remounted and turned his horse toward the village. To the rest, he stated: "He's tired, battle weary. He means no harm."

They overtook the frightened children who cowered like nestlings. Clark addressed them mildly, directing his words to the oldest, a boy of about ten years. He fished a red satin ribbon from his pack, and held it out.

The boy's eyes darted impulsively to the flash of color. He stood with arms held wide, shielding the two smaller boys, one of whom had begun to sob uncontrollably. The third boy had collapsed, face to the earth. He covered the back of his neck with folded hands, waiting for a strike, while the oldest began to babble in yet another Indian language the white men had never heard.

Collins watched. Fear gnawed at his soul, but it was insignificant compared to the dry-mouthed terror of the child. The boy's eyes were white and round as saucers. He glared at this red-bearded giant of a leader with his filthy henchmen. Blackfeet. It was the only answer the Indian boy could fathom, the same Blackfeet who swarmed out of the eastern mountains to plunder and enslave.

Clark tried to sign. The boy either did not know the hand positions or was too scared to notice. Clark stood calmly, his hand outstretched, the red ribbon shimmering in the sunlight, shiny and smooth. He dropped it in the grass. It fluttered like a bird.

The child's eyes darted to the tempting crimson strip and back to the smiling face of William Clark. He licked his lips as fear yielded to desire. Moments ticked away. He reached out suddenly like a snake striking, snatched the ribbon, spun around, and ran headlong for the village. The smaller children ran after.

"Let them go," Clark's voice resounded.

"They'll alert the village," Shields warned, having caught up to the troop.

"Your infernal screaming will alert the village. We're here to ask for help. However we act, they'll repay us in kind. Patience and prudence are our only allies."

Repressed anger filled Clark's smoldering eyes, his jaw was tense and the ticking bulged his cheek. With his eyes, he followed the boys' retreat, then turned a scathing glance at Shields. When he had calmed himself enough to speak softly, he addressed Drouillard: "Collect the rifles. We'll carry them forward in their slings."

Drouillard gathered the weapons, and Clark took his place at the center of a battle line. "Ride tall. Present a formidable front. We are eight. There are surely more of them." He inhaled audibly, and spoke on the exhale: "Advance . . . slowly, gently."

They began the march at a steady walk. Collins gripped reins in one hand, Labiche's knife in the other. His palms were slippery with sweat. His index finger lay gently against the cold stone in the hilt. As Labiche had predicted, the knife was the only reliable weapon, not dependent on dry powder or heated lead, accurate as the strength and direction of an arm's thrust. He had laughed at the ugly pirate and his overweening concern, but he had listened. The horse veered toward the distant herd. Collins tightened his grip on the reins and braced his leg against the bulge. He glued his eyes to the circle of lodges. No living soul was in sight.

"They know we're here," Drouillard warned. "Watch the grass. Watch our flank."

Like a turtle, John Colter tucked his head deeply into the crease of his shoulders, so that Collins could see only the torso of a man and the round turret of his beaver hat. Lips taut, eyes intent, his rifle laced uselessly in the sling in the small of his back, Collins rode forward.

"Shields was one of 'em," John Colter grumbled, "when they met the Shoshones, one of four men facin' sixty warriors." He rubbed his chin. "An' listen to 'im now, singin' like a twitty sparrow?"

Joe Fields shook his shaggy head. "No sleep. No food. Got one wheel stuck in the sand. The other's still turnin' in his head, diggin the hole deeper, same as the cap'n."

They rode on, eight men and a boy, against all the fighting men in the village — eight, if they could trust Toby and Shields to fight. Six was the more certain number.

Collins clenched his teeth and sucked back his tongue. He didn't think. He didn't pray. He didn't listen to Shields or Colter or Fields. He locked the calves of his legs around the barrel of the horse, moved with its stride, and wrenched his mind from thought and volition. Salvation or damnation lay in that distant village. He chose to think of neither.

"There's diggin' sticks!" Shield's high-pitched wail screeched like the call of a scavenger bird. "They's farmers. Someone's been workin' the field." The earth was trampled and muddied. Tools had been hastily abandoned. A crop? There were no neatly plowed rows, only gaping muddy holes interspersed haphazardly about.

They reached the pony herd. Animals raised their heads and nickered; others flattened their ears and bared their teeth, like their masters, like the natives who worked the land, some friendly, some hostile.

Collins heard his own voice counting lodges: "Double lodges . . . twenty-eight, 'nine, maybe thirty warriors." He swallowed air and it parched his dry throat more.

They were about a half mile away when a lone figure emerged from the circle of lodges. The form seemed small in the distance, but he walked in a stout-hearted manner that indicated authority. He carried a shield and a lance, which he leaned on for support.

"An old chief, proud, infirm, no longer fit for battle," Drouillard commented.

The man's shape and the details of his person defined themselves more vividly as they drew closer. The corps' members stopped about ten feet away.

He was square-built, not tall. His hair was streaked with gray, his face, coppery and wrinkled from age. His eyes were black as Drouillard's, and they peered with fiery intensity over a predatory nose. His dress resembled the shirts and leggings of the plains tribes. One salient item drew immediate attention. He had inserted a piece of bone through the cartilage of his nose. It protruded sideways from each nostril, twitched slightly when he breathed.

"He got puke hangin' from his nose?" Colter's crassness made Collins giggle.

Toby dismounted and began frantically to sign.

Colter fired another remark: "The fool has to sign . . . can't speak the language."

Shields wheeled his horse around, ready to bolt.

The Indian appraised the strangers with a haughty air and no hint of fear. He held his right index finger under the bone in his nose and thrust it left.

Drouillard stated: "Nez Percés . . . pierced noses. He says there are only old men, women, and children in the camp. They are as afraid of us as we are of them. It's not a permanent village. They come here to dig roots, and this man's been left in charge."

"We cannot be sure," Clark said. The Indian beckoned them to follow, and began walking toward the lodges. Clark hesitated, then spoke: "Toby and I will go. The rest stay here with Mister Drouillard until we're certain they don't wait in ambush. When I know this man speaks without threat, I'll signal . . . and the rest come forward." He paused, then insisted: "Unarmed, Private Shields, you hear? Rifle in your sling. I order you to come forward unarmed." The sinews of Clark's neck bulged, his cheek throbbed, and he repeated: "Under no circumstance should any of you enter the camp without my signal. They must not sniff any challenge."

Then William Clark kicked his horse to a steady lope. The timid guide and the boy followed. Collins watched them go. Clark's shaggy head was thrust forward like a charging bull. The horses tramped a narrow track through the grass that closed in behind them and left no trace of their passing. They met the Indian and disappeared behind a lodge.

Minutes stretched like a long thread unwinding. Collins chewed his tongue until he tasted blood and stroked the blue stone with his soft thumb until it bled.

John Colter rapped his fingers nervously on the stock of his gun. Reuben Fields cracked his knuckles, a numbing sound like the splitting of nutshells. A horse stamped. A hawk pealed its shrill *ki-ye* and circled on the updrafts.

Shields's high pitch mimicked the bird. "Damn that buzzard . . . like Injuns cryin' war!" He wrinkled his nose. "Smells funny. That buzzard knows. Devil's bird he is. Somethin' in that village is rank. Somethin's dead."

Talk relieved tension. Collins blurted back: "Shove your rantin' back down your gullet, Shields, before I pull your tongue out by its roots."

"That's a hawk not a buzzard," Joe Fields corrected, "but Shields is right. Smells like low tide in a swamp, dead fish . . . like when my Uncle Eb got drunk an' left 'is whole catch rottin' in the noonday sun. Rube wouldn't touch fish fer a year."

Collins grinned. His respect for Joe and Reuben Fields was growing. As with Colter, he hadn't known them well. They were close-knit, quiet, and competent. Like John Colter, they came from Kentucky, but they did not drink or use tobacco. They were never rowdy like Colter or Collins, or gamesters like Labiche, nor did they readily associate with the French speakers like Drouillard and Cruzatte. They ate with Sergeant Ordway's mess, kept their own counsel, and stuck together like flies in a honey pot.

Suddenly Clark appeared and waved them in. The men formed a line: Drouillard on the left, then Joe and

Reuben Fields, Colter, and Collins, and Shields on the far right.

"Walkin' to the gallows!" Shields screamed, reining back his mare. "Noose gets tighter ever' step I take!" He sawed the reins brutally as the animal fought the bit. Then he felt his body sway and pulled harder to balance himself. The mare reared to free her mouth, then lunged toward the other horses. Shields's body snapped like a twig in a storm. He flipped forward, cracked his chin on the bony crest of the horse's neck, and flipped back again as the horse landed. The mare humped her back, whirled left, and kicked her heels to the sky. Shields flew off, graceful as a bird. His gun landed hard, like a knife, and snapped in half. Having wrapped the rein around his right hand, the mare dragged Shields away.

"Cut the rein before it takes his fingers off!" Drouillard bellowed frantically.

Shields screeched in rage or pain. "You're not my captain! You're a half-breed Injun."

Next to Shields in line, Collins raised the silver knife. The blue stone flashed and the blade glinted in the noonday light.

Shields yelped like a wounded pup as the knife came down, the rein snapped and flapped free, and the mare leaped forward to freedom. Whimpering in the soft grass, Shields crouched, stroking his pinched and swelling hand.

Irritated with Shields's behavior, the little troop moved on at a swift jog, five horsemen and a riderless horse. Shields groped for his gun, then padded after, desperately, breathlessly, on foot. Grim faces stared straight ahead and thoughts skipped ominously to the waiting village. Who was there? How many? How strong? Although Toby had disappeared, the unmistakable red head of William Clark shone like a beacon between two brush lodges.

Clark stood tall, proud, towering over the shorter Indians around him and hailing the troop. Figures walked casually about, carrying baskets and sticks. There were several speckled horses hitched to posts, stacks of woven containers, and scaffolds of drying meat. As they grew closer, the figures took shape. Most were female. And the meat was fish, long, pink, slippery slices of oily salmon.

Collins wrinkled his nose at the pungent smell. He'd counted fourteen lodges, each with a wide drying rack. Any one lodge was large enough to hide ten men.

Riding alongside Collins, Joe Fields slouched over his horse's neck, saying: "Scared, Johnny? Duck down on his neck, make a smaller target. Some days, wish I were Shields, trumpeting my woes like one of them swans, loud as a foghorn for ever'one to hear, settin' what ails me on the back of another man." He asked dolefully: "You ever feel like that, Johnny?"

"There's times I'd love to jump in the nearest hole," Collins admitted. "When I feel that way, I grit my teeth and follow Drouillard." He forced a grin. "An' right now, my stomach's cryin' to be filled." He smacked his horse with the end of the rein. He chose not to think of danger. Fanciful images of food loomed up before his

244

eyes. He let his imagination run and blundered incoherently: "That bread I smell baking?"

Joe Fields yelled: "An' I smell whiskey brewing! Maybe we's all crazy as Shields."

"Or merry Captain Lewie!" Collins shouted back, adding: "Crazy hungry . . . so crazy my stomach rules my brain." The syrupy sweetness of molasses, the moist texture of his mother's spoonbread, river mussels that he dug from soft mud and plucked out and ate raw or boiled or fried in sweet butter — the images made Collins's mouth water and his stomach growl.

They rode between the outer lodges into the camp. The horses slowed to a walk, shook their heads, resisted restraint — they, too, smelled fodder. They finally halted in an open space in the center of the encampment where Clark, Toby, and three wrinkled old men stood waiting.

At first, the Indians greeted the little group with reserve. Their women stared. Children peered from behind their mothers' tunics. But curiosity took hold quickly, and they swarmed forward in a solid mass. The children were active and noisy. The women were attractive; some were very young. They had adorned their silken hair with white shells and bits of copper and brass, and they flirted openly.

Collins laughed when two young scamps tugged at his shirt until one fingered the barrel of his rifle. He raised it up out of the eager child's reach as the mother came to pull him away. She used the incident to run a hand the length of his thigh and finger the blue stone in the hilt of his knife. It had been a long time since John

Collins had felt the touch of a woman's hand and it tingled his nerves and curdled the blood in his veins. Then her hand smoothed his tangled beard and came to rest on his chest.

He hardly heard William Clark warn: "Hand me your guns and your gear."

Then came a loud clap, and the voice of the old Indian echoed clearly. The women crowded back toward a smoldering fire where skin pots hung suspended. They added hot rocks to the stew, which steeped like thick chowder. The smell was still of fish, but refined and sweetened with pungent herbs. Collins, Colter, the two Fields, and Toby moved forward. They plunged in their bowls, slopped the stew greedily into their mouths, burning their fingers and tongues.

John Colter wiped his mouth on his sleeve. "Fish," he said. "Pink, scaly fish, bones like needles. Looks like meat. Doesn't taste like meat, but it ain't all that bad. Where's Shields? Make room for Shields."

John Shields stood alone, to one side. His tongue protruded from the corner of cracked lips. He held his cup in a shaking hand. He dipped his bowl, took a few tentative swallows, then ate and drank like a beggar at a feast.

"Poor bloke," Collins commented, "an' to think he was hammerin' steel last winter. A good meal should ease his mind."

Shields fell asleep on a full stomach and slept soundly in warm robes.

"At least he's stopped jammerin'," was Colter's assessment.

CHAPTER
NINETEEN

There was little conversation at breakfast. Shields drank the hot liquid in his bowl, picked out the tender chunks, and sucked them like candy. It had been a long time since he'd filled his stomach. His thick muscles sagged and hung like wet linen over his bones. His skin had shrunk with his muscles. He appeared stick-like with a stiff neck and glassy eyes that never rested long on anyone or anything. The strong man who had hammered and forged iron at Fort Mandan was thin and wan. And with the loss of weight and tone, he had lost sound judgment. Now he sat by Collins and Drouillard, across from Colter and Joe Fields, muttering: "Indian fish. Could be poison."

The others nodded to placate him; the food was tasty and filling.

"Toby's gone with the boy," Colter announced. "I saw them go."

Shields's head snapped up. His food spat out with his words from between decaying teeth. "Better rid o' the damn' Injuns."

Drouillard locked John Shields in an implacable glare through glowing black eyes he had inherited from his Shawnee mother. "Without Indians," he responded, "you'd be frozen in ice somewhere up on that mountain."

"Toby went ahead to the main village," Collins informed Colter. "They'll put on a pot to boil and prepare a lodge for us. We'll follow shortly." He read the apprehension that still lingered in Shields's glassy stare and added: "We're over the Divide. No more British selling guns or Blackfeet lifting hair."

A silence ensued until Drouillard declared: "These people have welcomed us. We owe them our gratitude and respect."

Shields rose and stalked off to fetch more wood for the fire. When he returned and threw it on to burn, sparks flew. "Spit and burn, all of you," he admonished, "throw gunpowder on hot coals. You'll learn an' you'll remember I warned you. There's more Injuns out there, an' they're hostile."

Drouillard pushed to his feet, and Collins felt the scout's strong fingers press into his shoulder. "Get the horses, Johnny. They're with the Indian herd. And saddle Shields's mare. Or maybe Shields would rather walk than ride an Indian horse."

The horses were easy to cut out from the Indian herd. They were skinny. Collins never realized how skinny until he saw them grazing with the round-rumped Indian ponies. He cut the hobbles from his spotted gelding and from Shields's docile mare, then saddled and bridled both. They balked when he pulled them off the waist-high grass to lead them back to camp.

248

Drouillard and Clark were already mounted and stood waiting with the Nez Percé guide.

Shields ran a nervous hand over the mare's soft neck. He was an ironworker, a fashioner of hinges and nails, tomahawks and gun barrels. He'd never shoed a horse. He'd hardly ever ridden one and was not at ease in the company of large animals. The mare was quiet, but Shields's movements were awkward and quick. Instinctively the animal drew away.

Finally Clark barked: "Mount up, Private, or stay with the women."

Shields jerked the reins tightly and grabbed a handful of mane. He shoved his foot into the left stirrup, and the mare swung her haunches away.

"Mount an Injun horse from the right side!" Collins shouted.

Shields jabbed his toe through the stirrup into the horse's ribs. The mare jumped a few paces. Shields fell backwards with his foot wedged in the stirrup. The docile mare stopped and turned her head to stare at the weight of human cargo that hung at her side.

"Thinks she's trailin' a foal," Colter observed. "Can't understand why he don't get up." He burst out laughing.

Collins joined in the fun, and Drouillard's dark eyes crinkled with mirth. John Shields extricated his foot and surged up red-faced and yelling: "Tryin' to tear me apart. Somebody hold the god-damned horse."

Clark's cheek had started its hammering. "Collins, get that man in the saddle," he advised, and Collins took hold of the mare.

Shields got up, brushed himself off, and hauled himself aboard. He sat crimped over the neck, legs wrapped like barrel rims around the horse, one hand locked in a clump of tough mane, the other steadying himself on the rein.

"Shields," Clark said, taking charge, "sit up like a soldier and see that you maintain the pace."

They lined out across the plain after the Nez Percé guide: Clark followed by Collins and Colter, the two Fields and Drouillard, and finally John Shields.

The Indian guide looked more the leader of men than William Clark. He had an unusual name, Twisted Hair. He wore braids wrapped in white ermine, but his hair was bone straight, not twisted. The long plaits reached below his waist to the horse's backbone. He rode a pale gray horse with wild blue eyes, sat erect as a lodgepole, and looked more like a stately Mandan than the stocky members of his tribe.

Collins grinned at Colter. "Should've left Shields with the Mandans to hammer on his pots all summer. Give him another week, his hair'll turn white. In a fight, I'd bet on the Injun." He turned and shouted: "Shields, catch up! If you let that mare waddle like a donkey, they'll curl your hair an' twist it off your scalp."

In response, Shields whacked the mare in the rump with the end of the rein. The horse leaped ahead, and Shields flapped like a flour sack.

They were all laughing now. "Whoever heard of a man from Kentucky that can't ride?" Colter asked, shaking his head. "Shields is a fightin' name, but you hide behind it like a turkey what's all feathers and no fight. You're scared, John Shields. You're scared to fan your tail, scared o' Injuns. If I gave out a whoop, you'd be scared o' me."

"I ain't scared," Shields shouted back. "I'm careful. You wanna die? You want us prayin' over you, dead, like we did Charlie Floyd?" They had buried Sergeant Charles Floyd one year ago in the land of the Omahas, on a high bluff overlooking the Missouri River.

"You talk of Floyd with respect, soldier." The reference to Floyd and his suffering infuriated Joe Fields. Face red, temples throbbing, he reined his horse around, raised his knife, ready to strike Shields with the flat of the blade.

Hastily Drouillard thrust his horse between the two. "Let it cool, Joe. F is for friend and fellow."

It was a long ride, made longer by contention and resentment, down the switchback trail to the valley of the Clearwater River where the Indian village nestled snugly in a bend of the river. Tall cottonwoods rimmed the banks with a smattering of willows in the brakes. Rock walls converged on the ribbon of water. The valley opened at its western end, on a wide, flat grassland where another herd of spotted horses grazed. Far beyond, tall mountains loomed.

The horses were tiring. So were the men. Collins had knotted the reins and dropped them over his horse's neck. He was almost asleep, slumped in the saddle when his horse nipped at the tail of the mare in front. The horse threw up his head to avoid the flicking hocks, and Collins came awake with a jolt. The scent of salmon that hung heavily in the valley's creases pricked his nostrils and started the saliva flowing over his tongue. He blinked and focused. John Colter and the Fields had stopped. Twisted Hair was trotting swiftly away toward a phalanx of mounted warriors who blocked the trail. Collins sucked back and swallowed. A coldness came over him and the face of Laughing Water flashed in his brain beside the elongated and agonized face of dead Charles Floyd. Collins pulled up. The Indians held lances ready, points to the ground.

"Stay here!" The words of Clark came more as exclamation than command as the captain trotted after Twisted Hair, toward the wall of waiting lances.

Collins reached for the smooth silver hilt of the knife. The blue stone was cool to touch. He heard a *click*. Colter had primed his gun. It resounded with a clap over the scuffle of hoofs.

A voice intoned like a casual spectator: "And now, gentlemen, hand your weapons . . . mark off the paces. On the count of five . . ." It was Reuben Fields, the quiet brother, who was now laughing. He spoke so little, Collins hadn't recognized his voice.

Drouillard sat silently, eyes narrowed, his dark gaze following Clark's path, lips chewing some imaginary pit, engrossed, purposeful. "I'm a Jonah," he said. "I'm goin' after him. Come with me whoever wants." He kicked his horse hard and the startled animal broke from a standstill to a gallop.

Collins charged after him. The two Fields brothers could not hold their horses and rode up next. Finally Colter whirled behind Shields, slapping the frantic mare and shouting: "Let 'er rip, soldier!" The mare lunged; Shields hung on screaming like a blaring trumpet.

The battle was never joined. The warriors filed in a flanking motion, smooth as the drilled maneuver of seasoned cavalry. Clark, Drouillard, Collins, Colter, Joe and Reuben Fields, and John Shields rode straight into the gauntlet. But the Indians did not fight or raise a hand. They escorted their guests into the village where a lodge had been prepared and a council fire blazing.

Toby was there to greet them. He ushered Clark and Drouillard inside while the others remained, in a close huddle, with the horses, guarding their sparse supplies under the intense scrutiny of the curious inhabitants.

An hour passed. They unsaddled and unpacked the horses and led them to the river to drink. Women brought fodder for the animals but nothing for the men.

Collins drummed his fingernails on his knees as he sat on the ground. "Treat the horses better than us. Don't they know we're hungry?"

"What good are we to 'em," Shields answered, "except for makin' war an' supplyin' scalps." He was close to the truth. No one answered.

Growing more anxious, Collins stood up, sat down, walked in place, slapped his sides.

"Johnny," Colter grumbled. "Sit down and stay down. You make my skin prickle. Could skin ten buffalo for all the time we're wastin'. But they're watchin'."

Joe Fields braced his shoulders and announced: "They'll think we're a bunch o' cowards. I'm hungry. I'm goin' in."

"That's disobeyin' orders," Shields countered.

"What orders?" Joe Fields asked. "Sounded more like he was invitin' to me."

"If we all go, what can Clark do?" Colter posed, a devilish leer stretched across his face.

"I'll go. No callin' me pansy," Joe Fields stated. "What's that Labiche talks about . . . mutiny? . . . takin' over the ship when things go wrong?" He shouted over his shoulder: "Hey, Shields, watch the horses!"

"Watch 'em yourself, Joe Fields, I ain't stayin' here."

So the five men entered the lodge, armed like seasoned bandits. Through the hazy, smoke-filled air that stung his eyes, Collins saw Clark and Drouillard sitting cross-legged opposite a white-haired chief, popping food into their mouths from a large communal basket. Twisted Hair sat between them. Women toiled over a large skin bag suspended over a central fire.

William Clark frowned when he saw his men. With an effort, he took a deep breath, exhaled, and nodded. "Gentlemen, put the guns down. You have not been summoned." There was a cold edge to his voice.

Drouillard leaned to whisper in Clark's ear: "Sir, I think they thought you were held against your will."

It was a lie and Clark knew it, but he didn't chastise. Instead, he nodded, opened his arms wide, and said: "Then I thank you all for your kind concern. These fine people have welcomed us. Stack the guns. Sit, all of you, and their women will feed you."

254

Collins gripped the silver knife more tightly. The chief and Twisted Hair rose abruptly, nodded to Clark, and turned to leave. Clark rose as the two left, then approached John Shields. He was especially gentle. "Private Shields, sit and eat. Mister Drouillard will fetch your gear." And to the rest: "Bring in your gear. Turn the horses out with the pony herd. We are to have the use of this lodge to sleep and eat and regain our strength. Be grateful to our hosts. Show them your appreciation." But he did not abandon all caution. "I'll take first watch. Then follow by alphabet . . . Collins, Colter, Drouillard, Joe Fields, and you, Shields. Reuben Fields, you go immediately with provisions to rescue Captain Lewis. The Indians are collecting fresh horses and loading them with food for you now. The guides will lead the way." It was a dangerous, nighttime mission, but Reuben Fields did not flinch. Clark continued: "The rest of you eat, sleep, rotate the watch every hour."

Collins ate and took his first turn at watch, after Clark. When Colter came to replace him, he went inside the lodge but couldn't sleep because Shields was talking in his sleep.

"Why'd he send Rube?" Joe Fields asked of no one in particular. "Shields could've jabbered his way back. I'd like to gag 'im, but it'd wake him up."

Collins closed his eyes and slept briefly until he was roused as Colter was shaking Drouillard who came next in the rotation of the watch. Shields was still talking in his sleep. Collins drifted back to fitful sleep until he was awakened again for his second watch. It was the middle of the night, ebony black, blowing with the first hints of winter on September 22nd.

Collins took his robe with him, wrapping it around his shoulders. In the intense darkness, he stumbled into Drouillard who was sitting at the lodge entry with his rifle across his knees. "Gonna rain," said the half-breed. "I smell it." Then Drouillard's arm thrust forward in the blackness. "Drink, Johnny?" It was a question.

Collins felt the cold wet bag against his arm. "Where's Clark?" he asked, surprised to have found Drouillard on watch since, alphabetically, he should have been relieving the captain.

"Clark's tending Fields. He's sick."

Having taken the water bag as Drouillard left, Collins now drank, sat down, wedged his back against the hard pole that held up the lodge, and settled his rifle across his knees. He stared at the scattered, dark conical lodges, black against the blacker background of night. Beyond, like a grim stockade, trees rimmed the horse pasture. Banks of clouds rolled overhead like ocean waves across the sky, blotting out the moon. His mind wandered in directions he did not want to go. He was no longer a carefree youth. He was a man with disappointments and worries and fears. He'd promised Laughing Water he would return in the Moon of Falling Leaves. That was now. He couldn't keep the promise, but how would she know that? Here, west of the Divide, in the high country, the aspen was fading from green to gold. Only the stately evergreens still held their needles. He wondered if it was the same autumn on the plains where she lived, if somehow he had miscalculated the passage of time in the deep, persistent stirring of his heart. He pictured her standing atop a round earth lodge and peering at the trail that led west from Matootonha village. Two furrows marred the smooth space between her brows over the straight ridge of her nose. Her eyes were downcast. She held one hand over her heart, the other flat against her middle while her old grandmother cackled in the background. He willed her to smile. Winter was a time made warm by the arms of the woman he loved. That was last winter. He wished he could relive it. The image pinched its lips and closed its eyes. He clenched his teeth and drove his knuckles into the corners of his eyes to snuff back the tears that had welled up. Unmanly wetness, they dripped down his cheeks in cold streaks. No one saw, not the captain or any of his fellows, especially not an Indian.

John Colter crawled out to relieve him. "Damn' fish they fed us. Stomach's grindin' like a millstone. Mouth's dry as cotton."

Collins turned from his thoughts toward the dim outline of his friend. He thrust out the water bag. "Have a drink. Settle what ails you."

"A lick o' whiskey might," Colter amended, and belched. He took the bag, although he didn't drink. "Can't see yer face, Johnny, but I hear splinters in your voice. Somethin's bad wrong. Go on in. There's women inside. A good lay'll set you right."

"Or make me belch like you. You been sleepin' with one?"

"Two. One too many, I admit, but that ain't what ails me." Colter belched again and put an arm around his friend. "My gut's jawin' like a fibbin' child, tellin' me all's well when I know it ain't." Colter heaved suddenly, put a hand to his mouth, and darted toward the darkness.

William Clark stepped out in time to glimpse his fleeting form. "Follow him so he won't get lost," he ordered.

Collins rushed after Colter. When they came back to the lodge, Colter leaning on his shoulder for support, he reported: "He's purged, sir, of every last drop he ate."

Clark nodded. "I'll bed him. Stay with the watch."

When Clark came back to relieve Collins, the robe had fallen from his shoulders and his hands, clutching his rifle, ached with cold. He'd fallen asleep on guard duty, a grievous offense, but Clark sympathized and gently urged: "Get what rest you can, Private. Shields is quiet now, and, God knows, tonight you've earned your peace."

Collins groped his way inside, stretched out, and let sweet sleep consume him. But he awakened early with fire in his gut, only to find Colter and Joe Fields supporting him on both sides and propelling him, shivering, from the lodge. At the edge of the village, they let him fall to his knees and vomit until clear liquid dripped from the corners of his mouth.

"Couldn't let you foul the lodge," Colter commented. "First decent home we've had in months."

"Hope Rube made it back to Lewis and the rest," Fields added, "before the cramps felled 'im."

Collins must have passed out. Now he felt cool drops, like gentle fingers, stroking the back of his neck. He rolled over so the cold rain could wash his lips and face. People were standing over him, talking. Drouillard was smoothing back his hair, cradling his head. "Drink, Johnny." He drank until the bag was empty because it was Drouillard who held it. With Drouillard to lean on, he stood, then walked. Indians were watching, their eyes hovering like large brown moons everywhere he looked. Didn't they sleep? Had they been spying all night? Had they seen the sickness overcome him? He stared at Drouillard and muttered: "Poison . . . Shields said it was poison."

"It was fever," Drouillard answered, "and now it's broken. The sun is up."

Sleep overcame him. It was nearly noon, the rain had stopped and sunlight was pouring in through the open flap when he awakened. His head was clear. His bowels were cleansed. People were shouting and scurrying past, running toward the opposite end of the village.

Joe Fields stuck his head in the entry. "It's Captain Lewis," he announced. "Rube's bringing him in."

Collins pushed up. He had to see, had to be there to welcome the rest of the corps.

Lewis and the main party inched forward, as grimy and frayed a tatter of humanity as ever marched. Skin and bone projected through shredded garments. Eyes bulged over craggy cheek bones; skin sagged like old drapery. Guns, shovels, muskets, and gear were strapped carelessly onto spindly animals. The long Kentucky rifles so carefully polished and oiled, they used as staffs. Horses struggled, too. There were fewer now and their coats had grown long and matted, their hoofs cracked and dry. Like the men, their heads sagged on gangling necks. The twenty-five helpless men were no match for warriors, no match even for an angry woman, but they formed a column of twos and tried to walk in step as they came, lending a pathetic dignity to their entry into the village.

The appearance of his suffering fellows revived John Collins. Stalwart Sergeant Pryor led the procession, then Labiche sitting straight and thin, white teeth gleaming, grinning like a grotesque clown on his blue-eyed paint. Old Cruzatte, clutching his precious fiddle, leaned against Shannon's shoulder. Charbonneau carried the baby in the cradleboard and his little wife came behind.

Labiche stopped when he saw Collins, and the whole procession bunched behind him. He was needle thin, a page torn from a dream, but he grinned. "You still have the knife, Johnny. Good."

John Collins touched the silver hilt. "Where's Lewis?"

"Back there . . . bay horse . . . Ordway leading . . ." Labiche hardly had breath enough to finish the sentence. "We ate . . . too quickly. Didn't stay with us."

Collins eyes traveled down the line. Then he saw Lewis's flaccid body, drooped loosely over the horse's neck, about ten paces back. Ordway stood at the animal's head. York, the slave, stood by Lewis on the near side. The trio approached Clark.

"The black man holds him on, sir," Ordway explained. "He kept sliding off, sir, like Drouillard. He remembered how it had been with Drouillard, sir. And he's sorry." He stopped and reverted to proper protocol. "All present and accounted for, sir. Food you sent . . . Men snorted it like pigs. But captain wouldn't eat, sir, till the rest of us had our fill." He shook his head. "Fishy powder it was. Mushroomed like a fungus in the gut."

Collins watched the scene play out as Clark asked — "Meri, how did this happen?" — and took the reins of Lewis's horse in one hand and, with the other, reached and cupped his fellow captain's haggard cheek in the broad palm of his hand.

Lewis croaked: "Good men, Will . . . They had to eat." He had an ethereal smile. "Your black man pulled me through."

Collins stood in awe, an uncertain witness to private and sacred emotions. It was a defining moment, pregnant with power, like Moses on the Mount or Christ in the Garden.

"Help him down," Clark exhorted the men around him. "Prepare a bed for Captain Lewis. Colter, go with them. Show them to the lodge. Fields, strike a fire. Shields, tell the women to prepare a meal." Collins turned away, but Clark called him back. "Collins, find Drouillard. Where's Georges Drouillard?"

"There, sir" — he pointed — "with Cruzatte and Shannon. Permission, sir, to go to help Labiche."

But William Clark did not hear. He began frantically to bellow: "Sergeant, rouse the chief, call the shaman . . . See what remedies they can provide." To his fellow captain, he whispered: "Meri, for God's sake, Meri, what have we done?"

"I've asked the same question." The voice, at Collins's elbow, was John Colter's. "Too much of our fair captain's life has wasted." Colter shook his shaggy head. "And a good portion of our own." Then he laughed. Collins laughed, too. It was the only relief.

The Indian women added chunks of fish to the stew. As the oil rose to the top, they skimmed it off and gave it warm to the men to drink. Some sipped slowly. Most gulped it ravenously and swallowed the fish raw. Collins, Colter, Drouillard, Joe Fields, and John Shields warned of poisoning. It did no good. They watched in silence as their fellow corps members doubled over in pain.

The Nez Percés took pity on the starving men, delegated two more lodges for their use, brought food and clothing, nursed the travelers, and fed their horses. They were especially kind to the woman, her baby and husband, and Captain Meriwether Lewis. A special lodge was allotted for them. The shaman came with his herbal remedies. But too many men lay on pallets, cramped with spasms that Clark treated with calomel and jalap — emetics that cancelled the shaman's cures, purged, dehydrated, and demented. The expedition recovered slowly.

Drouillard predicted: "The Nez Percés are kind, but they will expect payment for their help."

CHAPTER
TWENTY

Georges Drouillard was the first to recover. He threw Clark's emetics into the fire, strapped his rifle to his back, and went hunting.

"Devil made him well, that, an' his red skin." Shields was droning again and he'd chosen Drouillard for a target. But Drouillard returned with a fat beaver. He roasted it over a hot fire, and passed out the chunks of sizzling meat to the sick. From that day they started to improve.

Sacagawea, another who did not subscribe to purges and bleedings, rallied next. She'd suffered only mildly and had never stopped nursing the child. Now she spoon-fed the sick men. Labiche set out his snares and caught rock chuck and rat and force-fed those who refused Charbonneau's little wife. He accused them openly of baser motives. "If we fed you buffalo on a china plate, you wouldn't eat, because it's Indian food. Frenchmen eat snails. Sailors eat rat and eel and shark. You forget you sucked bones and chewed the laces of your moccasins in the mountains."

That Lewis's medicine was the cause of suffering, most men gradually came to understand, but Meriwether Lewis insisted on his cures and continued to weaken. Sergeant Ordway fussed over him like a nun, attentive to the smallest drop on his cheek.

Collins counted six days until his own strength returned and he could work for short periods. On the seventh, he awakened alert and rested, cleaned his rifle, and shouldered an axe. On the eighth, his strength rebounding, he was helping Joe Fields walk when a frenzy of shouts echoed from the edge of the village. The earth shook as a herd of galloping horses bore down upon them. He rushed Joe Fields into the nearest lodge.

The animals crashed headlong through the village, tearing up lodge pins and upsetting scaffolds and pots. Dogs barked. Women grabbed children out of harm's way. Warriors chased after, brandishing their coup sticks. Dark tufts waved like bobtails from the revered sticks. The riders displayed booty that they had wrested from the enemy. Animals bore heavy sacks of meat tied in the hides of buffalo. The clamor was happy; the hunt had been good. The warriors had battled and won, acquired horses, counted coups, and obtained coveted guns.

Drouillard squinted at the new arrivals, observing: "Scalps black as raven's wings, Blackfoot horses, and North West trade guns . . . the kind the English trade. They've met the Blackfeet. Now they have guns, they won't want ours. We can repay them for their kindness with powder and ball, and that we have in plenty."

"Do they know how to load and shoot?" Collins asked.

Labiche flashed a happy smile. "I start a little game. They love to play. We teach them the use of guns in exchange for meat."

"Might give us dog meat. Captain Lewis won't like it."

"Says who? Lewis is sick."

"Clark's on his feet. He'll give a nod."

Drouillard had been silent throughout the exchange. Now he smiled, saying: "Clark cures bedsores and watery eyes, trades away his doctoring talents. Why shouldn't we trade what we know? Clark's a practical man. He'll approve any bargain we strike for dog, horse, snake, manna from heaven . . . and Lewis need never know."

"What of the sergeants?"

"They want to eat, they'll help."

The sergeants concurred unanimously.

Pryor informed Clark that very night. Clark bit down on his cheek to stop the tick, then he nodded. "Do whatever you must. Let the games begin. But I shall forever deny I condoned them."

The games were long and varied. Horse and foot races, shooting matches with bow and arrow or gun, contests of strength, shell games and craps filled the days as long as there was light enough to see. Labiche won consistently but not enough to discourage his opponents. He earned native cures, foods, and the ministrations of shamans and women. The corps loved the presence of women in the lodges in the early morning, if only to watch and dream. Labiche observed: "Without their women, without the meat of their dogs, we would have been months recovering."

One fine morning, when the first fingers of morning light crept over the horizon and the conical lodges cast long, triangular shadows, Collins threw back the lodge flap to watch the women shake out the sleeping robes. The sun rose and cast a rosy light on the copper skin of their faces. They were happy, laughing and chattering like songbirds. He muttered to himself: "If we go back by ship, I'll never see her again."

"You let an old woman scare you to running, Johnny." It was Labiche who'd been on watch, standing at his elbow. "Yes, Johnny, I heard."

Then a voice came from the dark interior of the lodge. "Water, fresh water . . . cold from the river . . . and some good buffalo to eat and tell Sergeant Ordway to shave my beard." Surprised, the two men followed the sound of the voice.

"It's Lewis," Collins announced. "He's better and he's thirsty. I'll go for water. You wake the captain." He grabbed a bucket and set off at a loping run. When he returned, William Clark, Ordway, Sacagawea, and Charbonneau had gathered around the ailing captain.

Lewis sat propped against Labiche's arm. His two-week growth of beard was matted and stained and his red hair fell over his eyes, but the blue eyes were clear and free from pain.

Clark did not bother with formality. "Help him on with his shirt. Heat some water for shaving." Charbonneau went for the shirt. Collins built up the fire and put the water on.

Lewis began to speak, haltingly at first, and then rattled off a litany of past events: Wood River Camp, the snags of the river, the cold of Fort Mandan, and the negotiations with Charbonneau. They were all present time to him. Meriwether Lewis did not know the day or the year. His listeners stood in silent shock as he focused on Collins: "How's your wife, Private? Handsome woman . . . mindful, smart, smarter than that woman of Charbonneau's. We'll hire the husband and take Sheheke, too." Sheheke was chief of the Mandans.

"Meri, these are not Mandans," Clark corrected gently. "We've left the Mandans far behind." He dipped a cloth in the water and began to sponge Lewis's face.

Lewis put a hand to his face. "Bring a razor, Will. Why haven't they shaved me?" He closed his eyes, reopened them, and flashed a brilliant smile that erased the deep-carved furrows in his brow. "I know where we are, Will. I've been recording the distances and latitudes, the depth of the river, and the vagaries of the weather every day since we left Saint Louis." But he had erased all consciousness of pain and struggle. Only happier memories surfaced.

Clark closed his eyes and pulled at his ear. "Take him outside, where he can see what are our circumstances." Ordway jumped to lift his captain.

Disgruntled, Lewis waved Ordway away. "Fetch me Sheheke, Sergeant. Prepare us a pipe."

They took Captain Lewis outside and sat him on a clean robe. Men came to congratulate him on his recovery, but his derangement was evident, especially

268

when he spoke, which he did often, trying to validate his own aberrant vision.

"He's mad," Labiche explained. "Our lives, this effort, have become like a roll of the dice. He has studied, prepared, measured, recorded, all to insure the brightest outcome of his expedition. Now, when its issue is in doubt, he falters. He resists submitting to chance, and, now that he must, it frightens him. Perhaps now he will allow Drouillard to guide. Perhaps now Clark will decide whether we go or stay, and throw his weight behind Drouillard."

They watched William Clark walk woodenly out beyond the village. Drouillard fell into step behind him. Clark did not stop until he reached the pony herd. The animals grazed comfortably as the morning sun warmed the earth and wiped the fresh dew from the grass. Indian boys came and drove the horses in groups to water. Drouillard sat himself in the tall grass nearby, but Clark stood straight and silent as if consumed in reverent prayer. He did not rush. He turned in his own time and stated: "Call in the men, all of them. I would speak to them without regard to rank . . . Then thank our hosts. Tell them we'll leave promptly. I must make the announcement. Tell Ordway to sound the call and muster the men."

The news spread like wind-whipped flame among the men, from Collins to Colter to Fields and around the mess. Spines snapped straight and shoulders squared. They had full stomachs, shirts on their backs, and moccasins on their feet. Their hair was queued, their beards were combed, their faces scrubbed, and their good health restored. There was no marching or saluting, no military drill and decorum. They came together as friends and brothers linked by tight strands of hardship. They counted off in a row to assure all were present and listened attentively to William Clark.

A faint smile creased Clark's lips. "The month of October is upon us," he began, unable to disguise his eagerness. "Boys . . . excuse me, you are men . . . you are crucible hard, tempered by struggle. The canoes are ready. Sergeant Gass has assured me they are finished, burned out the Indian way. Twisted Hair and another of this tribe are ready to guide us. The horses are branded and grazing on sweet grass. The Nez Percés will mind them for us. Clean your rifles . . . pack your bedding . . . mend your clothing . . . say your good byes. We've rested long enough. Tomorrow we sail."

That was all. No word of Meriwether Lewis. It was October 6th.

The men needed a moment to digest his words. Then they broke out in wild hurrahs, clapping, shouting, slapping backs, before they settled down to prepare. No one shirked. No one complained. Survival was too important. Tomorrow they'd be floating downriver and glad of it. But tomorrow they would be without the guidance of one captain. Fortunately they had two.

John Collins stood by Drouillard who alone did not cheer, but mused: "There's an ugly blot on the flood plain, on the south fork of this river, an extrusion of clay and rock, earth turned inside out by the hand of their god. It grows a few clumps of yellowed grass soft

270

as the whiskers on young man's chin. An Indian showed it to me when we were hunting, near a grove of cottonwoods. They say it's a monster's heart, wrested from the bosom of the earth." Drouillard's dark eyes twinkled as he read the puzzlement in Collins's face. "I knew you'd believe me. The others would not."

Collins's face pinched. "I try. You've never lied to me."

Drouillard smiled and began again. "It's a curious legend. They say that before men walked the earth, the monster devoured the animals that inhabited this land. Only Coyote escaped. He tried to kill the beast. He lashed himself with mighty sinews to the tall mountains surrounding, armed himself with sharp knives, and jumped into the monster's jaws. The monster's sharp teeth cut the sinews that held him. The beast swallowed him whole and he tumbled down the terrible throat and into the dark belly. There he cut away the creature's heart. With its last gasp, the beast opened its mouth and the animals escaped. But not without mishaps. Coyote stepped on the beaver's tail and flattened it. 'Possum was slow . . . his tail caught between the teeth when the great jaws snapped shut, which stripped it of its hair. But Coyote killed the beast, butchered him, cast the parts to the four corners of the earth, and wiped the blood from his hands. Droplets fell to earth and softened the hard mountain shale, and the Nez Percé people sprang up, like weeds from seeds of monster blood." He stopped and shrugged. "It's as true as your seven days of creation, as Adam rising from the clay of the earth and the woman from his rib."

Collins nodded obediently to please Drouillard. He looked up. A bald eagle flapped its massive wings, rose higher, and coasted on the updraft directly overhead.

Drouillard took off his hat and waved at the shining white head. "God go with you, my friend." He replaced his hat and turned to Collins. "He leaves us with his blessing. Thank him, *mon ami*, and pray we will meet no monsters."

"The land holds us in its jaws tightly as any monster," Collins replied.

CHAPTER
TWENTY-ONE

That night, Collins dreamed of the beast. It had no eyes or nose, just a giant jaw that opened wide with rows of teeth like a shark's and hot, acrid breath. The tongue, the color of flame, forked and licked out like a snake's, but the throat was deep and dark and Collins could not see the end of it. He imagined the animals sucked in, tumbling against one another, snapping, kicking, snarling. He heard their squeals of pain and groans of despair as they landed in the pit of the creature's stomach. It was dark there, blacker than he could ever imagine without even a flicker of dim light and he groped like a blind man.

He awakened in a feverish sweat and threw off his robes. The fire was hot but cold air had penetrated the lodge. It was close to the hour of rising. He wondered why Drouillard had told him such a frightening tale. Drouillard never spoke without a reason. Where was the truth couched? What was symbol and what was fact? The monster, the mountain, the land, his own hunger and loneliness . . . where was the meaning? In the eerie grayness before the dawn, Collins's mind worked the riddle.

Morning came. He shivered from cold and moved to the fire. Someone had added fuel during the night. He jumped suddenly at Pryor's voice.

"Good, Collins, you're up. Wake the others. Captain's up and packing to leave." It was an unpopular task, waking the sleeping men, one Sergeant Pryor liked to leave to a subordinate.

Collins began the task by shuffling noisily and ended rapping a pot with the flat of his tomahawk. At the banging, Shannon, Bratton, and Cruzatte sat up. Labiche rolled over and stuck thumbs in his ears. Pryor stepped forward and snatched off his covering. "Say your farewell . . . kiss your girl, pirate. 'Tis the seventh day of the tenth month, and the boats are loaded. Muster call in ten minutes."

Muster was short, a simple roll call, checking that weapons were in order, assignment to canoes, and then they launched the boats into the Clearwater River.

The launching was a happy ceremony, a christening and new beginning. Cruzatte fiddled and men sang. There were five boats, one small Indian canoe, and four large dugouts. The smaller Indian canoe they christened the *Judith*. Clark chose the name and splashed a bucket of water over her bow.

"Judy ain't his sister," Gass said, and winked. "Cap'n has a lady love, light and fair and seaworthy as the skiff."

The *Judith* would lead the flotilla under the guidance of Tom Howard, whose keen eyesight would pick out shoals and snags and steer the expedition safely by.

274

Sacagawea and the child sat behind Howard. William Clark and the slave, York, paddled in the stern.

The first, heavier dugout they named the *Lucy* for Lewis's mother. This was a respectable boat, carved from an elegant straight tree. She was Lewis's boat, with Sergeant Ordway as skipper. The *Sally*, stouter, named for Shannon's sister, followed, with Sergeant Gass commanding a crew of four. Then came Sergeant Pryor's *Fannie*, named for a popular innkeeper's daughter in St. Charles who had caused several detours to the tavern where she worked. The last was the *Annie*, a heavy, lumbering craft, carved from the canting trunk of a pine, which gave her a peculiar starboard list. Annie was a buxom, half-Osage whore who roamed the barracks at Fort Massac and had a similar right-side tilt because her right leg was shorter than her left. Piloting the *Annie* would be tricky. The seasoned watermen, François Labiche and Pierre Cruzatte, took on the effort with Collins, Drouillard, Shannon, and Shields at the paddles.

They were about to cast off when Ordway shouted: "Where's Charbonneau?" The stocky Frenchman was not anywhere on board. He had not reported to muster because he was a civilian and so had not been missed.

No more were the words out, than he appeared, bouncing on his stubby legs, duck feet flapping, bent under a weighty pack. He waded into the shallows to Ordway's dugout, pitched in the pack, climbed aboard, and grunted: "*Il serait parti sans l'or.*"

Lewis braced him with an ethereal smile. "Gold? What gold?" he teased.

The captain's earlier ailments were absent from men's minds, and song and merriment were loud. The good wishes of the Nez Percé echoed from the bank. The canoes moved slowly into the channel, the water seized them and swept them on their way.

The current was swifter than it appeared from the shore. The men were eager and rowed with gusto. They followed carefully in the wake of the leader so as to stay in the deep channel and avoid snags and eddies.

Serving as an escort, Twisted Hair rode overland, rather than in a boat. His pale horse appeared intermittently like a small white dot on the tawny October hills. He alerted the downriver tribes to the coming of men white like the horse was white — the god-like color. There were many tribes, many people, and he was a convincing advocate. He was tall and broad-shouldered, bore the regal carriage and keen intelligence of a seasoned diplomat. His jaw was square and framed a determined mouth. His eyes were dark umber brown and penetrating. Like Drouillard's, they detected small shades of expression that most men ignored. Most important, he was admired for speaking the truth.

Every evening, he rode into camp and reported to the captains. There were animated meetings. In sign, he instructed them as best he could of the hazards they would meet and the territories they would enter. Still, his communication was limited. The innuendo that colors human voice remained forever unspoken, the expressions that illumine a human face were forever invisible. The details that Clark needed for his record and for the direction of the expedition, he could not convey.

The Indians were equally mystified. The only white men they had known were greedy sailors who spewed in swarms from the dank holds of tall-masted ships that anchored in the Columbia estuary every spring. They were rowdy, dirty, ungodly males, their energy compressed by months in a ship's tight quarters. They traded for the fur of the otter, sought easy pleasures with Indian women on the beaches, did not venture inland, and by late summer had sailed away with their furs and their desires. But here was a new, gentler breed of whites that came down the rivers from the eastern mountains. They came with a man as black as the night sky, a sickly one who they carried at times in a litter, an Indian woman with a baby, and a huge, black dog.

Twisted Hair met with blank disbelief when he described them. The natives elbowed each other and scratched their heads and wrinkled their heavy brows. Some glared in amazement, but others drew away in doubt and disgust. Who were these strangers that sprouted like a new spring from the cracks of mountains, from the home of their gods? No one among them could explain. Nor could any of the corps help, not Drouillard, not Charbonneau or the Shoshone woman. No one spoke their language.

Still Captain Clark invited each chief to parley. He muttered the same promises Lewis had recited in healthier days on the distant plains, the message of peace and trade and friendship. He told them of the new father, Thomas Jefferson, in Washington. The chiefs nodded, gushed the prescribed syllables, and treated Clark as they would a pretty child. Their meaning blew away with the smoke of their pipes.

Drouillard was present at these encounters and described what he witnessed to Collins. "They're like two dogs sniffing one another. One wags. The other reciprocates. Neither listens. Neither is sure." He added with a shrug: "At least Charbonneau is quiet."

"We hardly see or hear him any more," Collins affirmed.

"He sticks like filth on a collar around Lewis's scrawny neck," Drouillard concluded. "Lewis is sick. He needs the help."

"So does Clark," Labiche put in. "He makes a valiant effort. He cannot trust Lewis. He takes all readings, figures the miles, the depths, the hazards and dangers. Look in their eyes. One is mad . . . the other is overburdened. The gold, remember the gold? They've forgotten, but Charbonneau has not."

The Corps of Discovery traveled fast and far. Clark drove them on as if Drouillard's Indian monster breathed fire in their wake. In three days, on October 10th, they reached the mouth of the Clearwater, where it empties into the Snake. Here they halted. Twisted Hair came at dusk, spent an hour with the captains, and disappeared again among the shadows between the creases in the yellow hills that hovered over the river. They watched him go.

"He travels more swiftly by horse," Collins commented, envious.

278

Labiche mused: "We could never move like he does with thirty men and baggage. The tribes would challenge us."

"But we could use a horse to hunt, range farther, find meat." It was true. The hunting had been dreadful, game non-existent. The surrounding high plains were barren of trees. They scoured every crack of earth for firewood and built grass fires to cook fish and fowl and unsavory roots. Labiche bargained hard for dog, the only red meat.

Suddenly the fish began to die. Drouillard shrugged, remarking: "The monster is spitting them out." The dying fish writhed in their death throes, floated belly-up in the water, littering the shore.

One dark day, they stopped earlier than usual because wind and heavy rain whipped the frenzied river. But inactivity, hunger, and the smell of death threatened worse than the weather. Men chided and contested each other. Fear showed its hideous face. Collins could feel his muscles tense and his temper unravel. He was not alone. His old drinking buddy, Hugh Hall, and the whiskey-lover, Tom Howard, argued over food, blankets, a stick of driftwood, or a handful of grass for a fire. And John Shields was blabbing again, hurtful comments meant to inflame. "It's a graveyard. God don't want us here. Don't believe me? Breathe it in, damned blackguards!" He threw the curse, like a glove, in their faces.

Collins countered: "It's the belly of the monster, Shields. Scratch it. See if it'll cough."

"Ain't no monster. The whole river's throwin' its insides at us." Shields picked up a fishy skeleton and flipped it in Collins's face.

Instantly Collins's restraint broke. He flew at Shields. But Drouillard tripped him halfway. He held him down and shoved his face hard into the sandy beach. "The madness mustn't spread to you, *mon ami*. Cobble it, nail it down." When he let go, Collins spit the grit from his teeth and went for Drouillard, but, this time, he stopped himself.

William Clark and the sergeants resolved differences where they could. They worked men harder, kept them occupied at menial tasks, decamped early, and traveled late. Clark pushed hard, twenty-five, thirty miles a day, two hundred miles in six days, a furious pace. But it limited the potential hours of friction between men, and between the corps and the ubiquitous, nosy natives. Every morning and every night the natives came with their insatiable curiosity, their wares, and their help, for sale at a high price.

On October 16th, after only six days on the Snake, the expedition sailed into the mighty Columbia. The furious pace continued. Collins felt his mind wander, his hold on his emotions fray. They let him sleep at his oars on mirror-flat stretches of blue water. Fatigue was the monster now. Cruzatte snored intermittently, Labiche's head lolled, and Shannon slumped like a wet hide more than once. Even Shields's nervous glare relaxed. They were on the Columbia, nearing the Pacific, almost there, almost at the end, almost . . . The

Annie floated quietly with only an occasional pull to starboard.

Labiche didn't notice the divergence of ripples that should have revealed the rock. It lurked just beneath the dark wake of the preceding boat. *Annie* rose on the wave, dropped, and struck. Collins came awake with a jolt as *Annie*'s hull cracked. She rested suspended an instant, careened to starboard, and sent cargo catapulting into the river. Labiche's head snapped up like a ball on a string. He threw his whole weight against his oar to fend off the rock and started to fall overboard into the raging stream. Without thinking, Collins dropped his paddle and threw himself across his legs. *Annie* veered sharply toward the starboard rocks.

"Keep her afloat! Ease her downriver! Take her to shore!" Cruzatte screamed and cursed. His words flew over their heads on the gusting wind and bounced off a wall of solid granite. There was no shore. A gash, two feet long, had opened in *Annie*'s starboard hull. The force of water flung the heavy boat sideways out of the main channel into untested waters. Other boats, conscious only of their own headway, sped ahead on the racing current, out of sight, beyond the range of human voices.

Collins clung desperately to Labiche, who pushed himself back into the boat. Water was spilling through the crack, steadily filling the hull. "Johnny, let go. Pick up your paddle." Labiche twirled his paddle in a blur of motion. Cruzatte, Shields, Shannon, Drouillard, all were fighting frantically to align the boat with the racing current. Labiche ripped off his shirt and stuffed it in the hole. Collins groped for his paddle. It floated freely on the watery fill. "Cast out ballast." He heard the shout. He lay hold of lead canisters, heavy flints, and pitched them over the side. An iron pot bounced on the watery fill. He picked it up and started to bail, handed it to Shannon, took up his oar.

The boat came about suddenly, but water spewed through the breach, slamming skinny Labiche again into the hard hull. Collins pulled him off. The cold water was rising. It numbed his feet and the calves of his legs. He heaved it, smacked it, shoveled it like loose soil, away from the widening breach. Like loose sand, it poured back in. His lungs pumped. Sweat poured from his shoulders as the water rose up the soft skin of his thighs. He heard Shields scream — "We're goin' down!" — and Drouillard shout back: "Hold your oar to your chin and keep your head up!"

Then the boat lurched suddenly and plunged between jagged rocks on a giant wave toward a tiny hidden cove where the water flattened like the skin on heavy cream. They came to rest on the detritus of the river, on thousands of dead fish tossed into a common grave.

Collins felt the hull scrape bottom. He listened as the rush of the current and the lap of waves gave way to sounds of human endurance: Labiche's teeth chattering like a ticking clock; Shannon, the youngest, sobbing lightly; Cruzatte praying. Drouillard cursed the bloody monster of the river. Collins wiped his face with the back of a hand and counted limbs and digits. His ten fingers clung to the gunwales like talons gripping prey. Shields jumped out of the boat. Without his weight, the canoe slipped dangerously back toward the river.

"Stay in the boat or the river will snatch us back like a jealous lover!" Cruzatte called to the others, and threw out a line to Shields. "Wrap it around your waist, John. Dig in. Hold your ground."

Shields threw his shoulder against the line and his old smithy's strength revived. Labiche tied a second line around his own waist and handed a third to Drouillard. They scrambled out. Collins strapped a line around his chest before he, too, leaped out and fell to his knees in the water. The rope grabbed, pressed flesh to bone. The heavy dugout resisted. He straightened, saw Labiche stagger, but Shields and stubborn Drouillard held. Cruzatte and Shannon climbed out, took hold with the others, and the boat came to rest. It was brimful of water. Packs were soaked. Men were wet to the armpits, exhausted, stranded on a wild shore hemmed by a wall of stone, far from the rest of the party and without a worthy boat. Worse, the air was heavy with the stink of death. Monster's breath, Drouillard described it.

Collins bit his lip and tasted blood on his tongue. He fell back, sitting suddenly on the littered ground, legs straight as sticks before him. With the palms of his hands, he gripped his arms and rocked to and fro. "They're gone," he lamented. "Clark an' Lewis an' Pryor, an' all the trade goods an' the gold." Tears were streaming down his face.

Labiche ran to him. The ugly pirate spoke softly: "Nobody's leaving us, Johnny. They'll wait. Indians saw. They'll tell them. Twisted Hair will ride back." Labiche held him like a mother holds her injured child, the small man rocking the larger, a full head taller and twice as thick.

A giggle from John Shields revived John Collins. Shields dropped his hands, compressed his lips to a bloodless stripe in an angry face, walked up to John Collins, bent down, and punched him squarely in the mouth, shouting: "Stop yer bloody bawlin', coward!" The blow drew blood. Shields raised his arm to strike again, but Labiche blocked the blow. Collins wiped his mouth, rolled away, and jumped to his feet. Shields whirled, striking out at whoever was within arm's reach, but old Cruzatte rushed in and twisted his arm helplessly behind his back. Drouillard lay hold of his legs, pleading: "Nobody's fault, nobody who's with us."

Collins tasted salty blood flowing from his quivering lip. He felt pressure behind his eyes, a thumping in his chest, and a consuming urge to hit and smash. Shields stood exposed before him, held in the iron grip of Pierre Cruzatte and Georges Drouillard. He stared at his white knuckles, balled them into fists, closed his eyes, breathed, then spread his fingers wide, counted them, flexed them, and shoved them down against his thighs.

"Wash your face in the river, Johnny," Drouillard recommended. "The cold will stanch the blood." He still held Shields, and he advised Cruzatte: "Watch him, gag him, if you must, and bind his hands. And see he does no harm to the Indians when they come."

Drouillard propelled John Collins away from the beach, through a narrow fissure up a narrow creek, which widened gradually as the rock wall diminished. The steep slope leveled to a gentle hill that rose invitingly to a grassy plateau. Drouillard chose a patch of soft earth and sat. "You've changed, Johnny. Last year, you would have retaliated, brawled, and bruised."

But Collins was embarrassed. "He called me coward. I ran. What kind of man cries tears and runs from a fight?"

"A honest man who admits his fears and does not strike when struck, although I know you wanted to. Courage demands restraint. Shields spills his fears, lets his feelings crack his patience like poor *Annie's* hull. But not you, *mon ami*. You are hardened iron."

Collins blushed. It was high praise.

Drouillard was not finished. He cut a lock of his hair, braided it, and bound it to the thong that held the cowrie shell that Collins wore around his neck. "Today, you are my brother." He took a slice of dried dog meat from his pouch, cut it in half, and handed one of the halves to Collins. When they had consumed the strip, he smiled. "Now drink. Then we see what we can do about Charbonneau. On the Missouri, he knew the buffalo and beaver and elk and antelope. He knew the residents of the warm earth lodges. The Missouri was gentle and its bounty plentiful. Here, where the river is savage and game scarce, Charbonneau is no longer of use. He would prefer you, I, and others who contest him disappear, stay behind."

Drouillard's voice soothed. Collins lay back and dozed. His mind was a blank when Drouillard poked him awake. He sat up and followed the direction of Drouillard's keen gaze. A hazy figure took shape in the cold light of the sun. He led a horse piled high with driftwood and picked his way toward them between the stones along the creek. As he drew closer, he waved a hand and explained in sign that he brought fuel for the men trapped in the cove. Others were coming after him with food. He was friendly and courteous, from a strange new tribe whose name Drouillard mimicked: "Oo-ma-teel-ah." The word was later corrupted — "Umatilla".

It was near dusk when Collins and Drouillard arrived back in the cove. The contents of the boat had been set out to dry. The Indian had taken dry grass from his pouch and hair from his horse's tail and kindled a small fire. He had added precious driftwood to build the flame, selected fish that lay about, and boiled them to mush. The dugout lay propped on its side to let the water drain. Men sat in its shadow, close to a low fire. No one spoke. They ate and slept.

Collins awakened to Cruzatte's fiddling a lively "St. Anne's Reel" in honor of *Annie*, the unsaintly canoe. Men were dancing. A horse whinnied. The little beach was alive with activity. Indians had arrived with William Clark and a rescue party. Women were killing fish — catching them with their bare hands and smacking them against rocks — skinning them, splitting them, roasting them, and hanging them on scaffolds to dry. Men packed them in baskets, lifted the baskets onto the horses, and led them away up the creek. Dogs barked. Shannon and Drouillard were loading boats. Whitehouse and Howard were cleaning fouled rifles.

Over the din, Clark's deep voice steered the effort. "We let you sleep to refresh your soul, Johnny, you and Shields," Labiche explained. "They're here. They didn't abandon us as Charbonneau would have. And we have our whore back, our very own *Annie*. Gass has stitched up the gash in her belly. They're waiting for us, Captain Lewis and the rest, downriver."

John Collins rose refreshed and took his place in the dugout. They left the little cove with a flotilla of Indians in their wake.

CHAPTER
TWENTY-TWO

The Indians disappeared on October 19th as the rescue party and crew of the *Annie* approached the island where Lewis and the main party waited. Lewis himself hobbled to the beach to welcome them. It was a lonely, unpopulated place. Twisted Hair appeared briefly on the beach opposite but did not cross to the island, and no other Indian approached.

Collins, Drouillard, and Labiche spotted the frail captain first from the boat. He leaned on an oar that he used for a staff. Charbonneau stood like a servant beside him. Lewis looked up at the boats' approach and waved.

Drouillard turned his face away. He pointed to a black, snaking neck that protruded above the water. "A cormorant, he suits this place, slippery as a snake, greedy as a wolf." The cormorant arched his long neck and dove, caught his fish, popped up again, and swallowed the fish in one gulp. Collins could see the long neck expand and contract as the fish glided down the deep throat.

As they beached the boat, John Colter appeared running toward the camp. He'd been shooting waterfowl and had discovered a native building, a wooden house. He'd pried off a few boards and now displayed them proudly to all, then announced to Captain Lewis: "For the fire, sir. We'll build it hot tonight."

Lewis was outraged by what Colter had done. These were cut boards, like shingles. He marveled how the natives had cut them precisely with tools of stone and bone. "No burning. Pack them safely away. A stunning example of native craft, I must go and see it with my own eyes. It will stir my interest." As Clark approached, Lewis continued: "Let me go, Will, to anchor my restless mind."

Clark frowned. "Then take a reliable escort. Take Drouillard."

But Lewis seemed not to hear. "Gass is a carpenter. He'll tell us how they were made, and John Colter will lead us there, and I'll need Charbonneau to lean on."

Silently Clark watched them leave.

Lewis returned in less than an hour, glassy-eyed and trembling, with Charbonneau leading him by the hand. Asked what they had seen, Lewis raised his eyes to the sky. "Death. I saw death, Will. First the fish, now human bones . . . skulls, legs, rib cages, young, old. It's a burial house. That's why the natives stay away. Who they are, I cannot say. When and how did they die?" He shrugged. His voice wavered. "It's a fearful place. How I pray for a ship, you cannot know, Will, how fervently I pray a ship that will send civilized folk to meet us. I don't want to come back this way."

Clark avoided Lewis's glassy stare, feeling sorry for his fellow captain. "Where is Sergeant Gass?" he inquired. "He didn't return with you."

"He and Fields stayed behind to measure the house. I could not. They dismiss my fears as madness, but tell me, Will, do you think that I am mad?"

William Clark evaded. "Madness to one man is genius to another. Death is never a pretty sight, Meri. We can fetch Gass and Fields tomorrow, when we pass that way."

But Gass and Fields returned late in the evening. Gass described the house in minute detail. "On the north lip of the island, sir, as long a house as the Iroquois build, made of boards, very large, sixty feet long and twelve wide. The roof is low, so they are not tall people. It's amazing how they cut the wood . . . must have used stones and sharp bones, I guess . . . and transported the wood from the far mountains. 'Tis a crypt where the heathen store the bones of their dead."

"And you were not afraid?"

"I've seen enough men die in my time and our holy Lord restores all faithful men to life. 'Twas the Frenchman filled the captain's head with fancy. The Frenchman's lived too long in sin with the savages, listenin' to his wives and their heathen tales. Surprised me that the good captain listened. But now he's visited Hades and returned." He added with a grin: "Maybe he's come back to his senses, too."

In the morning, they stopped at the house. It lay silent, and solitary, on a barren knuckle of land. Clark and Drouillard entered, counted the corpses, emerged, unfazed, and the expedition moved on.

At the noon stop, a dozen sturdy canoes from a new tribe, the Walla Wallas, met them. The captains held a parley on the beach with their soft-spoken chief, Yellept. Charbonneau, puffing his pipe, presided as interpreter. Labiche gave a running translation and complained of Charbonneau's racing French. "He speaks fast with the damnable pipe always clenched and distorting his speech, and that disgusting beard concealing the shape of his lips. The ideas mingle, and I have no time to sort them. But I don't like what I hear, sir. Yellept asks that we leave our sick ones here to rest with these Walla Walla so we can proceed more quickly to the ocean before the storms of winter rage. He promises to feed them well, sir."

William Clark blanched in shock. "On whose authority does he ask?"

Labiche shrugged. "I presume Captain Lewis's, sir." He added warily: "But Charbonneau plants his own ominous seeds."

"Who would he have us leave?"

Another shrug. "Certainly Collins who he despises ever since the duel, sir, and Drouillard whose position he has assumed. Whoever's sick? Whoever's a burden? Shields, Whitehouse . . . anyone who is unhealthy or unpopular."

"Captain Lewis himself falls in that category."

"He does, sir, but Charbonneau would never suggest the captain. Lewis gives him credence and prestige."

Yellept was nodding agreeably. Charbonneau and Lewis were smiling. William Clark pushed forward to interrupt, but it was too late. The chief of the Walla Wallas arose, threw his robe like a mark of kingship over his shoulders, and with his delegation paraded regally from the camp.

Labiche fled to warn his friends. They gathered in a secret huddle at the edge of camp after nightfall. Labiche shook his dice so that they rattled in his hand as he began to speak. "Clark did not act swiftly enough. He leaves our fortune to a roll of the dice. We may lose Johnny and Shields and Drouillard, more if the Frenchman has his way. This is not a game of chance, not even a duel of equals. It is a cruel and vital contest to the death. We must take whatever measures are necessary. We cannot leave our lives to the whim of an unbalanced captain and his scheming aide."

Shields was trembling visibly. He held a rawhide strip and drew it across the palm of his hand. "Kill the bloody Frenchman. Bury him in the bone house. We could seize him as he sleeps."

"That's murder."

"That's self-defense."

"Clark will condemn the man who kills," Collins said, and then admitted: "I killed a man once. It was a dirty business . . . Does Clark have any influence? Does he speak to Lewis?"

"He speaks to Ordway who speaks with Lewis, but, I fear, the Frenchman turns the words to his own design."

292

"Let me speak. Let me go to Clark." Collins's voice was firm, deep as the river. Silence. Heads turned. The offer was not characteristic of Collins who had never been adept with words, never eager to demand favors.

Labiche was incredulous. "You an advocate, Johnny? You didn't defend yourself against your own mother-in-law. You let Louise Bourgeron and her lies prevail. You submitted to whipping before you raised your voice to defend yourself."

"That was then," Collins stated. "There were conspirators among us who muddied the truth. Now I'll speak not only for me, but for all of you. Have you forgotten? I faced down Charbonneau when Clark could not. Captain Clark will listen to me."

They considered, and agreed. "Then we'll all go with you."

Before he went, Drouillard drew Collins aside. "You confessed to killing. Say no more about it, *mon ami*. The man is dead and deserved his death. And tell Sergeant Pryor of your intent. You will bear more weight if you have an officer by your side."

Sergeant Pryor agreed to go with him. Collins's heart pounded as he rehearsed what he would say, locked it in his brain, repeated it in front of Labiche and Drouillard. He was sweating, his heart hammering, as he went to find Clark. Every man of the mess went with him.

They approached Clark when he was alone — Sergeant Gass, having gone to inspect the boats. The speech was short. Pryor opened the exchange. "My man Collins, sir, has a right grievance. I think you should hear him."

Clark whirled on his heel. "You're out of order, Sergeant." His sparkling blue eyes appraised Collins as if he were a sale horse or a slave on the block, then passed over the grim stares of the seven men with him.

Collins moved forward, squared his shoulders, and locked his knees. He began haltingly: "The crew of the *Annie*, sir, and the rest of Sergeant Pryor's mess, myself and Privates Labiche, Shannon, Cruzatte, Bratton, Whitehouse and Shields" — his voice leveled and increased in volume — "we have heard that Charbonneau and Captain Lewis want to leave men in the Walla Walla village and we are here to object, to tell you that if you leave one, sir, you must leave all, every member of this mess. We will not be separated. We will not abandon one of ours, a few of ours, any of ours."

Silence. Clark drew in his lips. The cormorant, the same black omen that had followed, surfaced from the depths of the river. Clark watched it dive. Slowly he turned back to the men and said: "I was hoping, Private, that the issue would not raise its ugly head. Be assured Captain Lewis means no harm. But he is a reader of books and the elements, not the minds of men. It has fallen to me to manage you men. You are an unruly group, sometimes recalcitrant, sometimes selfish, sometimes magnanimous and heroic." He stopped and put a hand to his brow. "You have a legitimate concern, Private. I will speak to him. I will speak forcefully on behalf of all of you, and I will demand the re-instatement of Mister Drouillard. If

294

Captain Lewis, if anyone, attempts to leave any one of you . . ." He stopped, blinked. Collins watched the vein pulsate in the side of his face as he flashed a fiery stare. "I will stay with you," Clark continued. "Captain Lewis must leave me, also." He added: "I hope, Private Collins, that mine is a satisfactory response."

The black bird dove and resurfaced, paddling smoothly over the water, then dove again and disappeared.

William Clark confronted Meriwether Lewis that very night. He did not mention Collins or Drouillard. He began softly. "Meri, no man will agree to stay with the Indians. That was not a condition of their enlistment." His voice grew more determined as he continued. "You can order. They will disobey. I will disobey. You fear we cannot feed and clothe them, that we cannot find shelter. They also fear. They fear separation." He paused to let the notion settle, then resumed: "A yoke of pessimism weighs inordinately on your soul. The ocean is close. If ships ply these shores, if the Indians trade with sailors, we will buy what we need. We have gold, Meri, and these Indians know its value as well as you and I and Mister Charbonneau. And these men we bring rely the one on the other."

Lewis blinked. "But we are the guardians, not the owners, of the gold."

"Did Charbonneau tell you that? Would you sacrifice a man's life to save a guinea? A horse is worth twenty. My York cost fifty." William Clark flung the rebuke at his friend.

"I am not a thief, Will."

"Are you a murderer? Would you jeopardize the success of this entire expedition or will you face the urgency of our circumstances and the solution to our troubles?" William Clark pivoted on his heel and walked away. Blood rose to his temples and hammered at his brain like a beating drum.

It was late. Eyes like dim lanterns hovered, and whispers circled like smoke over the sleepless camp. But Lewis was silent.

Late in the night Clark woke Labiche from a deep sleep. "Take Drouillard. Go now and find Yellept. Thank him for his trouble and tell him we will gladly pay him a visit on our return. Make him believe that we will return. Whatever you do, make him understand that we will leave no one behind." He stopped to see if any other men were awake and listening, then added: "One more question, pirate. Lewis insists there will be a ship, that supplies will be forthcoming, that there is no need to spend the gold. You have sailed. What do you say? Is it at all possible that a ship awaits us?"

Labiche confirmed what he already knew. "There will be no ship. In these latitudes, ice will have choked the harbors."

"Could a ship have sailed away and left supplies?"

"Supplies that the natives will pilfer faster than they harvest fish."

Yellept had not been hard to find. Labiche and Drouillard returned by morning, their mission complete.

Sunrise did not improve tensions. It was raining. The wind was blowing and driving the drops like stinging pellets against the skin. The expedition shoved off with all hands. The wind howled at their backs and clouds streaked like banners of combat, across an ironclad sky. By mid-morning the clouds had vanished, and the Columbia unfolded like a long, flat lake licking the feet of the barren hills.

For three days, there was no further mention of Yellept, and they sailed smoothly. On the third evening, October 24th, before the sky turned dark, Clark came to the fire and sat among the men. His brow and cheek bones protruded where flesh had once smoothed the angles; concern had etched deep furrows at the edges of his eyes. His broad shoulders curved inward and his shaggy head hung forward like an aged buffalo. He blinked and motioned his men to gather round.

Gently, as the evening mist, he began: "It's the twenty-fourth day of the tenth month, in the year of our Lord, Eighteen Hundred Five . . . one half year since we departed the Mandan nation. We were to have returned to the kind Mandans this very month, but we've not completed half of the year's intended journey." He stopped, inhaled, and blew out a breath. "I cannot promise you rest and plenty when we reach the western sea. You see the width of the river. The year wanes. The weather cools. I can only assure you that the threat of separation is past. And whatever ship might have met us has surely given us up for lost." He stopped to survey the grizzled faces.

Sergeant Pryor squared his hefty shoulders. "Sir, we are far from lost. We're on the Columbia, the river we sought."

A tremor shook William Clark's round shoulders. "The river, yes, we are on the River Columbia, thanks to the foresight of a man named Twisted Hair, a native . . . no thanks to any intelligence of our own. Some would call him savage, but he has guided far more wisely than Captain Lewis, or I, or the feckless Shoshone, Toby."

A deep silence hovered. William Clark let it lay like sunlight on flat water. He studied the sea of faces before him. They were round and square, wrinkled and smooth, white, red, and black. They were restless and worried. They stared at their feet, at the fire, at the darkening sky above, anywhere to avoid the reality, the truth, that Clark was confessing.

Clark dropped his eyes, rose to his full height, and folded his arms solemnly across his chest. "I came here to tell you that our staying together will require sacrifice. We do not know the inhabitants of these shores, but they are many. Captain Lewis tells me the ships do come here in the warmer season from Britain, Spain, and Russia. None desires us here. I expect all of you to stand with me as I have stood with you, and all of us to stand together if we meet foreigners or threats." He turned to walk away, stopped, and added: "Mister Drouillard, come. You are sorely needed."

Sounds of relief echoed around him. Men laughed and joked, but Collins felt an elbow in the ribs. He shrugged off Labiche. He was sick of rivers, sick of senseless chatter, sick of Labiche and Shannon and Cruzatte and Shields and Whitehouse and Sergeant Pryor, sick of fruitless plans and vain hopes. He'd spent the last two years of his life hip-deep in water, mired in alluvial mud, stumbling on submerged rocks, starving, freezing, and he'd made his speech, done all he could. He picked up a stone and slammed it into the dry ground at his feet. It hardly dented the surface although it had rained and he had projected it with all the force of his long arm. The hard earth repelled moisture, rejected anything soft or comforting. It had been a long journey. There were times when he felt tears rim his eyes, other times when a knot of despair tightened around his heart and his eyes were dry and cold and nobody cared, like now.

He lay down in the grass, ground his spine into the earth, cupped his head in his hands, and watched the stars appear one at a time, so distant, so bright, so implacably the same, night after night. He roused only when he heard footsteps. His head ached. He was sweating and breathing in short, erratic gasps. He expected Drouillard to come for him, but the forms that hovered over him seemed hardly human, the profiles flat and elongated, the eyes set at the sides of the head like a horse's, small and beady as a pig's. He must have screamed, because he was running suddenly toward the blazing light of the fire and the company of familiar men, and they, mere shadows, were coming to meet him. They made him eat and rest, but his mind churned up images of deformities and monsters. He couldn't sleep.

All the next day, Drouillard did not leave his side. They sailed on. The river widened, then narrowed and widened again. The current slowed and gathered like a cat ready to spring, and the noise of the water grew steadily louder. Indians crowded the beach in ever-growing numbers, squat, alien people, with the same glaring, widespread eyes, pointed heads, and straight, profiles unbroken from the tip of the crown to the point of the nose. They rushed out from rectangular lodges, and they shouted and waved.

Collins remembered the hideous stares. On his back, in the grass, he thought he'd been dreaming. By any standard he knew, they were ugly. Most were fully one head shorter than Drouillard or himself. Black, straight-cut bangs cut a stark line across backward sloping foreheads. The arrangement accentuated the width of their eyes that were almond in shape. They bulged from shallow sockets and assumed a glassiness that Collins found expressionless and cold. They had met white men before. One sported a tricorn hat. Another had strapped a cutlass to his waist, and a third carried a British rifle in a sling. Otherwise, their dress was scant. The men wore simple breechcloths. The women dressed in flimsy capes of woven reeds that hung no lower than the waist and left breasts and buttocks in full view, even now with the winds of winter beginning to blow. Their language was an incomprehensible succession of clucks that seemed more fowl than human. Their effect on the corps was sexless and repulsive.

300

On one of his short visits, Twisted Hair explained how each tribe controlled its stretch of river, here, where the waters collected, then fell. The falls resembled those on the Missouri, majestic and powerful, but they were crowded with natives who clambered over rocks like an army of ants. They haggled and bartered for advantage on the river. They pilfered and extorted. Personal property was unknown to them. But they did not make war. Each family held its allotted station, a platform or precarious perch, from which to catch fish, the same their ancestors had held from time immemorial. With gigs and nets and lines, they had fished for generations. The men bent over their task with energy and dedication, and the women collected and packed the catch. The gatherings of tribes far outnumbered the corps.

The expedition could not ignore them. Their dress, their habits, their foods, their appearance were to the simple hunters and rivermen of the expedition totally foreign. Comments were not kind and flew like darts.

"They's buck naked, more like fish than men."

"Wet as ducks, scratchin' like mangy dogs."

"They can throw spears," Pryor warned, "hit a swimming fish at ten paces. They could gig us while we sleep like they gig their fish."

But Lewis's strident voice blasted: "Befriend them! Do not insult them until we know their intent."

"Who says? Charbonneau?" The cynical protest would have been in character from Shields, but it echoed from Labiche. "Guard that knife I gave you, Johnny. Guard the blue stone." The natives seemed drawn to the color blue and had bilked Sacagawea out of a stunning blue-beaded belt.

Collins retreated to a suspicious huddle with Cruzatte, John Shields, and Nathaniel Pryor. His breath grew short, his tendons tight as bowstrings. He thought of Clark and the vein that throbbed in his cheek. He thought of his own reaction to these peculiar, human creatures. Where had carefree laughter gone and the reckless propulsion to fight? Finally he asked Drouillard, who smiled and answered: "Gone the way of your youth. When you spoke for us, you took some of the responsibility for the success of this exploration upon yourself. You worry more, not less."

"Watch the guns!" Clark shouted. "Guard your knives and valuables. Keep the powder dry." The alarm died as quickly as it sounded. There was no need. The Indians were too busy fishing.

On a fateful day in the last week of October, Twisted Hair, the Nez Percé guide, rode down to the boats. He did not dismount but raised his right fist and brought it down like a club across the bone of his left forearm. The gesture, like the swipe of a war club, spoke for itself.

Clark's voice cracked like a dry branch. "The Indians downriver will kill him. He's going home. He can go no farther."

Twisted Hair held out a hand to shake in friendship, according to white man's custom. Clark grabbed it eagerly. "Thank you, my friend. We will pay you handsomely."

"Pay him? With what?" Lewis asked, his lips quivering even after the words were spoken.

"Gold . . . pay him in gold."

But Twisted Hair did not wait for gold and, instead, accepted three fish hooks and a handkerchief for his services, meager items that Clark pulled from his pack on the spot. A swift nod of acknowledgment, a smile, and he turned his horse away, east, upriver. His square form retreated until the white shining horse disappeared into the enveloping mist.

It was not a happy departure. The men in their ranks followed the Indian guide with longing eyes and continued to stare, long after he had gone, in the direction of his passing.

Clark passed a cursory inspection. Then he slouched cross-legged with Lewis, Charbonneau, and Sacagawea who sat with the child by a small, sputtering fire. The little fellow crawled to him, tugged happily on the fringes of his shirt, and William Clark smiled. He liked children. Of all in the expedition, only the child did not worry, did not fear, did not react with the constraints of the familiar to the newness of people and place. William Clark took the child in his lap and bounced him on his knee. The baby giggled. The sound was contagious.

That night, the wind began to spit and blow. The river turned to a dangerous choppiness and cold rain poured down. The corps waited for the weather to clear, but the Indians ignored the rain and meandered brazenly among them. Items of value began to disappear. Collins pulled his shirt over the knife with the blue stone. Gass kept an eye on the paddles.

Drouillard stood guard over the guns. Ordway took an inventory. Collins and Warner tried to light a fire. A line of men stood waiting for supper, but the wet wood would not burn.

Collins could feel his patience crumble, and he smacked Shannon's fingers when they tried to invade the cold stew out of turn. Anxiously he fingered the cowrie hanging around his neck and felt the twist of Drouillard's coarse hair.

Even Captain Lewis grew agitated in the Indian presence. He sat only yards away from his men, under a crude skin tarp, and balanced a lap desk on his knees, sheltered it with a blanket, and scratched with thin ink and a dull quill on a damp scrap of paper. An Indian, intrigued by his effort, touched his wet hand to the curious marks. The ink smeared. Lewis flipped the lid closed on the intrusive fingers, and the Indian squealed and fled like a whipped puppy.

"Will, give the order," Lewis snapped. "Forbid these scavengers entry into the camp. These people are thick as fleas and greedy as Shylocks, inveterate thieves and spies. If they do not kill us, they'll rob us blind."

"Speak softly, Meri. Men are listening."

"And that fiddle's playing. Stop the gaiety. I will not have our good men cavorting with the likes of these. They tell me my brain has deceived me. What kind of crazed aberrations must their misshapen brains convey? I'd hoped the natives would at least be generous, would give us clothing and food, but they'd rather pilfer and steal."

"They have not killed, Meri. They have not impeded our progress." Clark let the significance of his statements sink in.

Ordway interrupted to report the results of his inventory. "Absent two kegs of powder, a sheet of lead, sirs. Ten shirts, five kettles, and six knives. But Labiche has some hidden, I'm sure."

Sergeant Pryor turned from his mess and called: "More's missing if you ask the men. Tell him, Collins."

"A hat, two blankets, some flints, an axe . . . Shannon lost his Harpers rifle and powder horn, sir."

"If I may speak, sir?" This request came uncertainly from beyond the little gathering, where Charbonneau stood with his wife and child. The Frenchman stumbled over words, choppy English sprinkled and accented with French, blowing out the words with the smoke of his pipe. "We have *de l'or*. We can buy clothes and food, retake *ce que l'on a volé*."

"*L'or* . . . that's gold." Labiche sneered. "I'll not give a penny for what they've stolen. It is ours by right."

"But we can buy what we need, food and fuel," Drouillard proposed. "They'll trade for gold. I saw a guinea dangling from a woman's ear? Labiche was there, and others. Collins, Whitehouse, Colter also saw. They are not so savage that they have no desire for gold."

Gass grinned. The smile filled his ruddy Irish face. "They're blond an' red-haired natives, bluer eyes than the king of England poppin' out from their flat faces. My sainted mother called them angels' children." He nodded. "Sure they're bastards, sir, sired by seamen.

The natives not only sell their goods, they share their women. A gold piece for a bawdy's bed, better bargain than a second wife, eh, Charbonneau?" Gass's voice prickled with sarcasm. "We be grateful to ye, Mister Charbonneau, for your Christian generosity." He bowed like a courtier, and a chuckle passed through the crowd of men.

Charbonneau's nostrils flared. Puffs of smoke burst in rapid succession from his nose. Before he could speak, Clark intervened. "Would you give the gold, Mister Charbonneau, for the well-being of these men, for the safety and survival of your wife and babe?"

Charbonneau's black eyes danced. He inhaled, filled his lungs, and blew out smoke between his teeth. Slowly he removed the pipe. "They must not mock me. I paid *dix pièces d'or* for my wife. My *enfant* grows from my own seed. I do not know the price of a white man but for *Monsieur* Collins, I give you zero. Him I would have left on the island of bones."

CHAPTER
TWENTY-THREE

They sailed on that fateful week, the last of October, twenty, thirty miles each day, until darkness made progress impossible. They portaged falls and slept on swampy shores, walled the camp with a stockade of canoes, and posted a ready guard each night to keep the Indians at bay. But still equipment, tools, any item left unattended, disappeared. It began to rain relentlessly, and in the brief moments, when the rain stopped, a heavy mist weighted the air. Wetness settled on skin. Decay penetrated the bedding and gray mildew powdered clothing. But lush green abounded on the mountains that hemmed the river tightly on both sides. Huge trees sprouted from every crack of soil, thrived and threaded their massive talons between the crags. Vines and mosses hung from the branches, and waterfalls poured from the heights. Animals grew to incredible sizes. Giant fish with plates of bony armor swam in the clear depths of the river. A vulture, whose wings spanned wider than a man's height, roosted on the heights. But the beauty remained unseen because heavy fog choked the valley and clouds hung low. The sun came out only once for a few hours, at dawn, when the corps awakened to a hot and welcome sunrise. They drank in the sunlight like sweet elixir, rose, and shoved off with a song.

Drouillard ranged ahead as had Twisted Hair, and returned each noon. Men gathered on muddy ground, close by the officers, to hear him tell what lay in store. On October 31st, his report was ominous. "High bluffs confine the river. It pools, then gushes in a swift torrent through narrow defiles where rocks dot the channel and waves smash its clean-shaven face. In some places, the cañon rises hundreds of feet directly from deep water. There's not a strip of sand, no landing, and not one Indian canoe the length of it."

Lewis was writing as Drouillard recited the news. His fingers twisted the soft stem of his quill until it broke. He lay aside his journal and stared blankly at the scout. His soft voice was steady. "When you kill a goose, pluck me a new quill, please, Mister Drouillard."

A dozen men witnessed the exchange. A dozen men looked on, mystified. Had Lewis heard? Was he retreating again from the struggle, content to live in his own gentler mind's space?

Clark raised his eyes in alarm to meet Drouillard's. "What of the land around? Can we portage?"

"Barely." Drouillard waited, hoped Lewis would react, then added: "We can carry the *Judith*, because she is light, but to carry the dugouts overland would be impossible. The land is mountainous and pitted, heavily treed, snarled with vines, slippery with mosses. Lightly burdened, a man could walk, but the girls, our boats, will have to brave the rapids."

308

There was a faint nod and smile from Lewis. He was slow to respond, so Clark intervened. "Take Labiche, Howard, and Cruzatte. Show them the river and they will tell us how to proceed." Of the men of the corps, the three were the most able boatmen. "How much farther until we meet these hazards?"

"Three, four miles."

Lewis seemed to drift away, and Clark anchored the task at hand. "Gass, check the boats, especially the *Annie*. See that there are no leaks. Pryor, bring me our strongest men and our ablest boatmen. Ordway, load the girls. Prepare to run the course. We will make honest women of them." He sat, elbows on knees, head cradled in his hands, on a rough rock at the edge of the water, because it was the only protuberance above the muddy ground.

He remained lost in his own thoughts until Nathaniel Pryor came back with Bratton, York, Shannon, Warner, Colter, Collins, the two Fields, and McNeal. The three boatmen — Labiche, Cruzatte and Howard — followed. It began to rain. They stood wet, silent, and grim as Clark rose to address them. "You men are our best hope. You know the paucity of our supplies. We have endured the native pilfering long enough. Our patience wears and our anger mounts. We are all repelled by these ungainly natives. Now nature herself throws obstacles in our path." He took a breath, expanded his chest, and let the air out slowly. "The great mouth of the monster yawns. There are rapids and a defile before us. The land surrounding is too pitted and steep to portage with the dugouts." He wiped the moisture from his brow, heaved back his shoulders, and let his eyes wash over each man in turn. "Here is what I propose . . . the less able among us, Mister Charbonneau and his family, will proceed overland with the light baggage, the *Judith*, and the journals. The bulk of our baggage must travel in the *Lucy*, the *Sally*, the *Fannie*, and the *Annie*, safe from thieving fingers . . . Privates Howard, Labiche, and Cruzatte, you will conduct the boats through the rapids." Clark smiled. He kept his voice animated and firm, the better to convey confidence, and he teased lightly. "Four boats, three of you. One of you will have the honor of escorting two fair ladies. I would submit Private Labiche should have the honor." He let a ripple of laughter intervene. "He will not be without help. Private Whitehouse at this moment is fashioning lines that we will attach to each canoe. You others here will lay hold of the lines from the shore, as you did on the cordelle when you hauled the keelboat up the Missouri. Now you will lower the boats down. Our girls are fragile. Let the lines out slowly. Coax them sweetly around obstacles in the river. Compared to the keelboat, they are light, but the current is strong and the shore jagged. Move as quickly or as slowly as the current warrants. The river will seduce them. Watch where you place your feet. You are all competent men, experienced in the ways of rivers. Myself and Captain Lewis, all available who are not engaged in portaging, will be there to help. By your efforts, by our co-operation and purpose, we shall proceed promptly to the ocean and to our goal." He added with a smile:

"And if a ship is there, I promise you each three gills of rum."

As Clark intended, the smooth confidence of his voice, the hint of humor, relieved and inspired. Laughter erupted with gusto. Men cheered and clapped.

William Clark had to shout for silence. He was not finished. "Privates Labiche, Cruzatte, and Howard go quickly now and reconnoiter the river. Explain what you require on your return." To the rest, he nodded. "That's all, boys. Good luck." He walked away to join Captain Lewis, who sat under a leaky skin shelter, took a smooth-tanned hide, and traced the route of the mighty river.

When the laughter died, the coming effort, like an approaching battle, spread silence over the camp. Apprehension resurfaced and stalked like the persistent rain. John Shields was first to betray it.

"My anvil's in that boat." He didn't need to say more. The heavy weight could slow or sink a boat or cause it to career out of control. And Cruzatte was a pilot with only one eye.

Even solid Sergeant Pryor was visibly nervous, and he said: "No one can estimate the force of the river or the speed of her current. The river changes from one hour to the next."

"Cruzatte's prayin' to Saint Peter to keep the river calm," Joe Whitehouse teased. "Thinks he's Moses at the Red Sea. Only river I heard of in the hereafter takes us all to hell."

Collins was more hopeful. He grinned back and held up thumb and index finger with only a tiny space between them. "We're that close to the western sea. We'll find that ocean tomorrow, or the next." But close to death or heaven or the mouth of hell, he didn't know.

Still the comment brightened John Shields, who quipped: "Tomorrow? . . . you know, Collins, I hope you're right. Cap'n says we've come almost four thousand miles." He was proud of that. It was a distance that only Labiche, who had sailed the seas, could imagine.

Drouillard returned with the three boatmen. They marched straight to the captains, and again the group assembled. This time, Lewis stood before them in the rainy mist. He held his hands clenched behind his back and his head bowed. He waited for silence. His voice was clear, strong, and as cold as the north wind on the Mandan prairie. "Sergeants, privates, scouts, my fellow captain," he began, "I have been sick, but I am not unaware of your struggle. I owe you my deepest gratitude. You have borne with my lapses, and I thank you. We have only a few miles more to travel. They will be difficult miles and there are men here present who are more able than I to confront them, who are more tutored in the ways of waters." He seemed to fade back. "Let them take command today, as brevetted leaders with battlefield commissions, not because Captain Clark and I are unable, but because Privates Labiche,

Howard, and Cruzatte are better able. Pay them your obedience and respect."

All was silent for several moments but for one man who shouted: "Aye, aye!" Then another cheered, and then a chorus of hurrahs echoed over the water.

The voices died as Lewis stepped back and Labiche came forward. He did not mince words. "The danger is mercifully short. The current swirls to larboard, toward the southern shore. With men walking on the starboard, the north shore, and pulling mightily, the rapids can be run. Cruzatte, Howard, and I will try to steer where we can, but our future and yours will rest in the strength of your grip and the muscles of your back." He glanced at the boats that rested on a sandy bar. "Four boats. One of us will have to run her twice. That will be me." He backed away.

A hushed silence was the only response until Clark cleared his throat and said: "Ordway, take the walkers and plot their path. Pryor instruct your men to position the lines. Sergeant Gass is all baggage secured?"

"Aye, sir, like a babe in his mother's womb."

"Then we sail now to the head of the rapids."

As the meeting broke up, Labiche gripped Collins's arm. "Eat something, Johnny, so your strength doesn't fail you, and hone the silver knife." Cruzatte had dropped to his knees and folded his hands in prayer. "And if you pray, pray now. Pray to Saint Elmo, the patron of sailors, and Saint Jude who overcomes impossible odds. Pray like Cruzatte that we may all grow as old."

★　★　★

By ten o'clock they reached the head of the rapids where the river collected in a quiet pool. They beached and started the walkers on their way. Labiche sat quietly in the stern of the *Lucy*, pushed out, and let her drift across the black satin sheen of water. The movement was measured, even lazy, until the line played out and snapped taut. Collins felt the jerk. So did every other except York, who stood like a pillar grounded. The current seized the boat. *Lucy* was off, hurtling down into the maëlstrom. Men stumbled, tottered, and threw their weight against the straining line. It chafed and burned and pulled relentlessly toward the larboard rocks. Clark bellowed: "Lift 'er! Don't let 'er snag!" "Watch the outcrop!" "Shoal there, pull! All together, heave!" They raised the line on their shoulders. They ran with it when the current gushed faster. They slowed when it lagged. The cold wind spat rain at their backs. They lost sight of Labiche who disappeared in sheets of foaming spray and jumbles of rocks. He always appeared again, water boiling around him. The *Lucy* bore down, then lifted like a soaring bird and plunged headlong at incredible speed toward the watery oblivion. The descent seemed endless. Collins's ears rang and muscles strained. And as suddenly as they had twanged taut, the lines went slack. Collins collapsed. Colter dropped to his knees and emptied his stomach. Shannon and Warner fell face first onto the hard dirt, and York sat down. Labiche was paddling mechanically toward the sandy beach, grinning gleefully and shouting: "Go back! Take the next!"

Charbonneau and his little wife arrived with food, water, and fish oil for sore muscles. They came first to the hero of the hour, François Labiche, then to each lineman in turn. But old animosities died hard, and Charbonneau passed by Collins as if he did not exist.

Thomas Howard piloted the *Sally*. He tied a separate rope around his waist and handed the end to Collins. "I lose it, you pull me in. And if I drown, place a round piece of gold over each o' my eyes. Bury me on a hill where the wind can dry my bones far away from this accursed river. Bury me near my *Sally*. Shannon swears she's buxom and beautiful."

"Bury him with a full jug," Colter suggested sarcastically.

But Howard was sober and deadly serious. The rain had stopped and a heavy mist had settled over the river. He held out a hand, and Collins took it and patted his shoulder as he stepped into the waiting canoe.

It was the same quiet drift, then mad seizure as the *Sally* bucked like a whore on a pallet. Howard bounced hard, crumpled, and folded. But the linemen guided more confidently now. They knew what to expect and where to expect it and set a steady rhythm. They were jogging evenly, the *Sally* planing smoothly and John Colter calling a steady beat, when Collins felt his knees buckle. He fell and the line raced through his hands. Dazed, he picked himself up and struggled to catch up.

The safety line that Howard had tied to his waist flapped like a loose sail. The *Sally* was still afloat but had taken on water. Howard had lost his paddle and was gesturing wildly and reaching for his knife. A horrible flash of gold pieces on a dead man's eyes, and Howard sinking the knife into his heart flashed before John Collins's eyes. But Howard reached down, cut the flying rope, and the contest between man and river resumed.

Collins retrieved the line. Warner, Colter, Shannon, and Clark himself lay on a hand. The *Sally* skipped around a sharp-toothed boulder and plunged to larboard toward the sheer cliff face. They hauled her back. Collins blinked through his own salty sweat. He had a good hold now, could not let go, even to wipe his stinging eyes. He didn't hear the cry: "Ease up!" It was York who shouted, and York who finally uncramped his fingers from their grip. They were bloody and blue. Collins looked up at the hulking black man and said: "Thank you."

York tipped his head in recognition and whispered: "Gonna rain." He rarely spoke to a white and only with impassive observations of the obvious. He started to coil the line; fatigue did not seem to touch him. The only man of the expedition who would receive no recompense for his colossal effort did not even possess the free choice of colleague and friend.

Natives appeared on the banks as Cruzatte began his run. They were an inquisitive tribe of the lower river. They wore odd conical hats whose angular shapes popped sporadically from behind rocks and trees, then vanished as quickly. It started to rain again as the linemen struggled to aid Cruzatte in the *Fannie*, then Labiche again in crooked *Annie*. But *Annie*'s list pulled with the tow and she skipped down without a fault. As he floated into the shallows, Labiche jumped out, clapping, shrieking, and kicking his heels. He was soaking wet. His lips were blue. He shook with cold, but he kissed the little boat like a long-lost lover. "She can deal my cards and roll my dice every time. She's quite a lady, no more a whore."

Collins went for a blanket and handed it to Labiche.

As Labiche wrapped it around himself, he observed of Collins: "You were praying . . . I heard you. Me . . . I was courting my lady, Johnny, begging her not to rock my bed. She has served me well. Today I am alive and richer. *Monsieur* Charbonneau must pay me ten guineas." Collins gave him a questioning look. "Yes, I wagered high. I risked my life."

They rested two days at the foot of the rapids, then proceeded on. They passed villages with whole fleets of canoes littering the beaches. They awakened to thick fog almost daily. Collins longed to see the sun, to see more than twenty feet in front of him. He longed for dry clothing and hot, blazing fires.

On November 6th, he lay out his bed and was about to stoke the fire when Drouillard returned from scouting. Drouillard had climbed a high knob. He was exhausted and soaking wet, and collapsed in Collins's bed. "They chased me, Johnny, a nasty bunch of Skilloots." His voice fluttered like the trilling of a flute. It was not like Drouillard to be scared. He forced out a deep stoic breath before he continued. "I'm half Shawnee, *mon ami*, friend of Mandans, Shoshones,

Nez Percés, even Sioux, but I have never encountered such as the slippery Skilloots. They waited in ambush high on a rock, used their fishing gear for weapons, tried to snare me in their nets, stab me with their gigs. One of them called like the loon. I heard the signal and stopped before the place where they would have waylaid me. They gave chase and would have overtaken me in their boats. I ran inland to escape. They're not runners, but they are formidable boatmen." He stopped and his whole body trembled. "I must tell the captains. We'll have to prepare well for the morrow's trek. Help me up. Take me to the captains."

The officers listened attentively to Drouillard's account. His report was factual and complete, his fears couched in stoic reserve, his voice calm. "The mountains are as high and snowy as any we've seen. A deep gorge slices them like the single swipe of an axe, steeper than the valley of the Salmon. The river gushes through a funnel of rock. It spits out waterfalls and islands and shoals and sharp crags. I could not walk level on the land. With every step, I could reach out and touch bare earth without bending over, and for every mile I walked forward, I climbed three up or down. The slope is treed with fir and hardwood, dense forests thicker than the thickest we've seen, thicker than Ohio or Kentucky." He coughed and the vibration rattled his lungs. They gave him water, and he began again. "I saw the faces of their gods, carved into the rocky heights, staring. They guard the passage. Such a fierce wind blew, it tore the shirt from my back. Nor could I build a fire." He coughed again and spit out heavy phlegm and waited for the spasm to quiet. "The wind whips the river to vicious chop and there are rapids in every quarter." He closed his eyes and put a hand to his brow. "It pounds like a relentless hammer."

"His head or the river?" Ordway asked innocently.

"No matter. He's sick. The gods don't want us there," Clark said as he took Drouillard by the elbow and eased him to a seat.

Lewis put a hand to his cheek. "Fever. He's burning up. Give him more water."

Collins stepped forward, knelt by Drouillard, and gently propped him up. "He's not finished, sir."

Drouillard's voice was faint as a distant echo this time as he spoke. "They ride the crests in their canoes and glory in the surf like playful geese. They laugh at the rain. They pole, they paddle, they fish. They wait by every outcrop for a boat to flounder." Drouillard closed his eyes and whispered: "They are waiting for us, sir."

"When did you last eat and sleep?" Clark interrupted.

Drouillard waved him off. The effort of talking had drained him.

It rained continuously. Meriwether Lewis stood by Drouillard's sleeping form for a long time. His head was bowed, shoulders bent, arms folded for warmth across his chest. Finally he turned to Collins. "Care for him. Keep him dry if you can. Let him sleep. Tell him I've been remiss. I've wronged him and I'm sorry. Tell him we'll decide our course in the morning."

John Collins placed Drouillard in his own bed. He did not notice Lewis following, lingering, and watching until darkness descended and he could no longer see.

CHAPTER
TWENTY-FOUR

In the morning, it was still raining. A large group had gathered to watch as Meriwether Lewis laid out ten pieces of gold, one by one, side by side, upon the smooth, wet surface of his lap desk. Even in the rain, they glittered like the sun and inspired jealous comment.

"Could've bought whiskey enough to last the trip," Colter observed, adding as Labiche laughed: "An' tobacco, an' bacon, an' wood to burn, an' women, an' wine."

Clark raised a hand in admonition. "Boys, boys, we must thank Mister Charbonneau. Without his foresight, we would be paupers today. Now we must decide. How much do we spend? How much do we keep?"

Feet shuffled. Heads bowed. Glances passed furtively from man to man, but no one answered. Finally Labiche came forward. "Sir, if you will chance it, I can earn us a profit."

"Gambling, again, pirate?" Clark asked. "I should not permit it. Captain Lewis would not approve." But Lewis pretended not to hear, and walked out of earshot.

"Games and trade," Labiche assured amidst the silence, "will stretch the little wealth we have."

"You don't speak their language," Clark reminded.

"The language of commerce is universal, sir."

Clark snickered, adding: "And so is the language of wager." He consented, but only partially. "Go to the village. Choose five men. They will guard your safety. I give you ten guineas . . . ten talents, like the Gospel parable . . . to increase and multiply or to bury forever. Buy us fat dogs, a canoe. And take nothing with you that you cannot afford to lose. No guns, no knives."

"A knife, at least, sir . . . you heard Drouillard. They'll kill us." Labiche never parted with his knives — two at his belt and one strapped to the calf of his leg. He trusted them more than his right hand.

"Then take the espontoon," Clark advised. "Its appearance alone is threat enough. They did not kill Mister Drouillard. They have not threatened life, only property. You have your wits and your inestimable pirate's luck. You have stealth. You have gold and permission to pursue trade or caprice. And you have my blessing. You may choose your men now or not choose, go or stay, as you wish."

Streaks of red veined the whites of Labiche's eyes. He glanced in to Clark's eyes, swept the guineas from the captain's hand, and said: "I choose Collins and Drouillard, Colter, Shannon, and McNeal."

The five agreed to go with Labiche and swore allegiance to each other. At noon, they met at the edge of the camp, marched off in tight formation, and stumbled into a disturbing new world.

The village spread like tar at the base of a cliff. It consisted not of round lodges that paralleled the circle of creation, but of stiff, rectangular dwellings built of poles and mats, lined up in straight rows. Smoke curled from slits in flat roofs. Racks of split fish were everywhere, as were boats. And everything about the village reeked of fish and crawled with fleas.

Men and women were busy about the village; some, the boldest, came forward as the white men approached. The natives stared as the small group of white men walked into the village. No one spoke.

Shannon stopped to study a woman carrying a baby. "Head's locked in a box," he observed. Two boards encased the infant's head, flattening the profile, pressing back the forehead so that the skull rose and spread above the ears, forcing the head into a peculiar knob. The child could barely move his head or see in front of him. The white men to a man found the custom barbaric.

Women, bare breasts bobbing, began attaching themselves to the troop. Shannon and McNeal pranced after them like stags in rut.

"Stop, fools!" Drouillard shouted, grabbing Shannon by the collar of his shirt. "Stay with us. We move as a unit." But McNeal disappeared around the corner of a lodge. Collins started after him, but Drouillard yanked him back. "Let him go," he said. "He will pay. They'll infest him with fleas and whatever other filth they carry. They send their women deliberately to distract us."

They walked on among the strange collection of flattened faces, beady eyes, and lips that whispered as they passed. Soon the Indians gathered in a knot, bringing together pelts and dogs to trade. The pelts were thick and soft with hairs that shed water like duck's feathers. The dogs were fat and healthy.

Collins let his hungry eyes travel over the offerings, saliva flooding to the tip of his tongue. He bit back his lip to stifle the flow. Labiche had a hand in his pouch, fingering a guinea.

Drouillard caught his wrist. "Pretty furs are empty bait. Wait." His hawk eyes framed a muscular, bull-necked man. "There" — he pointed — "that is the one we want."

The man had four knives thrust into his belt and a defiant smirk on his face as he brazenly offered to sell knives he'd surely stolen.

"Pay him now and we'll never see McNeal again," Drouillard warned.

"The braggart flaunts in our faces what is ours," Colter said, moving forward. Collins and Shannon advanced with him. "Take his right, Johnny," he instructed. "I have his left."

In one swift grab, John Colter lifted a knife from the man's belt and swung it wide. The Indian jumped to avoid the strike, drew a second knife, and collided with Collins who slammed the Indian's arm hard against his femur. The knife fell to the ground. Shannon snatched it up, threw it to Labiche. Colter thumped his chest and reached out a hand for the third knife. The Indian threw back his head, palmed the fourth blade, and shouted for help. He swiped at John Cotler's hand. Colter jumped back and swore, blood dripping from his fingers.

Faces began appearing in doorways and from around the corners of lodges. Squat men began stepping forward with fish gigs and snares. The advantage shifted in the blink of an eye. Collins, Colter, Shannon, and Drouillard drew back, but Labiche jumped to the fray. His mouth drew into a hideous grin and his eyes to knife-wide slits. The tip of his tongue poked like a pink fang from the right corner of his mouth, and he brandished the vicious espontoon. Collins grabbed the rag that was his shirt in an effort to pull him back. The fibers, rotted from dampness, came away in his hand.

Drouillard's hand gripped Collins's shoulder, as the scout whispered: "Not now, *mon ami*, he plays the odds and he gambles high, but I wager he'll survive."

"He needs help," Collins contradicted. "He plays with our lives." Collins struggled to break Drouillard's iron grasp, but it was useless.

"We wait and see," advised Drouillard.

In silence, the four white men watched as Labiche, inviting contest with his left hand, held the espontoon in his right. His nostrils flared. His eyes darted over the sea of deformed faces. He swept the blade in a semicircle before him, then lifted it like a sacred pipe and lowered it slowly, gently into the flesh of his forearm. It was razor sharp. Blood oozed in a thin red line. With his empty hand, he reached around and pulled the tattered ends of his shirt tails from his belt. With a sweep of his arm, he lifted his shirt and turned his back to display his scars. The gray light of early afternoon illuminated the crests and shaded the hollows of his whip-torn flesh.

The natives recoiled from the horrific scars, the murderous weapon, and the wild-eyed audacity of the man. What kind of man had endured such punishment? What kind of man would draw his own blood? What fiend confronted them now? Surely one empowered by the goddess of the river or possessed by the devil of the white man. And what ungodly weapon would inflict such pain? They knew only one, the nine coiled strips whose barbed tips ripped the flesh from a man's spine. They had heard the screams and rescued the wretches, who had suffered under its lash, from tall-masted ships that anchored in the estuary. A few had lived. Most had died. The natives had watched them all suffer.

Labiche inched forward, his hands extended, gripping a more terrible instrument of torture. The Indians cringed. For each step he took forward, they took one back. The threat was not of death, but of pain and dismemberment. This was not the time honored back and forth of endless bargaining. This was a dangerous challenge, and they drew back.

The knife thief sensed his tribe withdrawing. He reached for his belt and untied it with trembling hands. The last knife and his tomahawk thumped to the ground, and he turned and fled.

Stepping forward, Labiche picked up the abandoned weapons. He turned to his companions, bowed low like an actor to a theater of accolades, and handed them the weapons. "Bluff," he explained, "it's why I'm a good gambler. Now you know how I always win." With an impish grin, he declared: "They will respect us now when we come to buy."

"What about McNeal?" Shannon asked. "What must we pay for his freedom?"

"Freedom?" Labiche scoffed. "He chose his path. He was free to pursue his pleasure. He is free as you to slip his hobbles and come running back."

They purchased six dogs, baskets of black thistle and camas, and the services of a young woman — a cook, Labiche explained. In silence, they marched back to their own encampment.

Dusk was falling as they approached the camp. The rain had stopped. The clouds parted and pink streaks of sunlight painted the evening sky. Presence of a young woman elicited lewd gossip and hungry stares. She cowered and retreated to the protection of Sacagawea.

In the privacy of the shelter the Charbonneau family shared with the captains, she motioned with an index finger, like a blade, across the soft tissue of her throat. Sacagawea comprehended instantly and sent her husband to inform the captains.

"*Ils ont tué* . . . killed one of ours," Charbonneau reported.

"You're sure the deed is done?" Lewis snapped. "Ordway, sound the alarm. Count heads. Call the roll. Gass, make ready the boats to depart immediately downriver that we may flee this place. Find Labiche. Find McNeal."

Labiche came forward with a cynical sneer, followed by Drouillard. "McNeal is dottering after a slouch-hipped whore, sir," the pirate explained. "It was his choice. We warned him."

"I'll go for him," Drouillard volunteered.

Lewis did not stop to think. "Then go and take this heathen woman with you."

"Give her a guinea, sir, as an inducement, to insure her friendship." The suggestion was presumptuous, coming as it did from the scout. But Lewis slapped a guinea impatiently into Drouillard's outstretched hand.

The corps waited. Gass called from the boats: "The girls be cribbed and ready, sir, rocking like babies in the cradle of river!"

"Rotate the guard. Sleep when you can. We leave as soon as Drouillard returns."

Drouillard returned late, but without McNeal.

The next morning, the men of the corps were taking their places in the boats when McNeal appeared, running like a rabbit for his hole. He was barefoot and breathless, scrambling over the rocky shore. His feet were bloody, but he beamed a scarecrow smile and blurted as if to excuse his errant ways: "They came for me, three men with tomahawks. I should have died with a blade in my skull but for an honest woman. I will love her forever with all my heart." He broke into a satisfied grin. "I've earned us a musket, sir." He held it up like a coveted trophy. Then he threw it to Shields in the nearest boat, shouting: "Take that for *Annie*! Take that for your wooden, lifeless whore!"

328

They hauled him aboard by the hair of his head and made their way quickly downstream.

En route, Shields grumbled: "It's a worthless trade gun . . . British made . . . all for a brazen bawdy, not worth a penny in gold."

CHAPTER
TWENTY-FIVE

The expedition proceeded on. On a dismal Monday, November 9th, they stopped in near darkness. They could not see to make a camp. Men collapsed from exhaustion, tripped, sank to their knees, struggled up again. The earth was soft, swampy, and covered with reeds. Waterfalls pitched down from the lofty heights to the river below. The round shape and wide eyes of the face of a goddess stared back down at the men from a slab of black basalt. Drouillard saluted the face. Collins felt the eyes like the raindrops that prickled every pore of his skin.

There was no dry bed ground that was not littered with rocks. They piled bundles of stalks to raise their beds out of the mud. After a cold meal of pounded fish, they lay down. John Collins awakened to screams and curses. Men were jumping up from their slumbers, running to secure the boats that pitched about like corks. The whole camp was awash. Bedding, clothing, guns, knives, anything not safely stored in a boat, was wet. They had reached the tidewater, had stopped on a west-facing shore, and made their camp when the tide had ebbed. During the night, the tide had risen and reclaimed the ground. The Pacific winds blew hard down the funnel of gorge and whipped up waves, driving them headlong into the bed ground. Now water engulfed baggage and bedding.

Collins leaped up. With one swipe, he ripped up the bedding and swore. Why, when they were so close to their goal, must the river obstruct and delay? The river was a contrary spirit. The natives were right to think it alive, right to worship it like a god, to placate it like a greedy devil. He stood ankle-deep in mud, angry, frustrated. He wrung out his bedding and watched the water pour from the folds. He shook water from his hair. All around him men were slogging in deep mud. Some coughed and wheezed. He screeched into the darkness: "A swamp, it's a bloody tidal swamp." It was an unhealthy place, empty of natives. They knew and they stayed away.

Morning light was seeping through the dampness. The wind still blew. Ironclad clouds skipped across the sky.

"Gather your gear!" Pryor ordered, trying to rally his men. "Salvage what you can. Move inland!"

Collins grabbed his gun. It was wet but free of mud; however, the silver-hilted knife had slipped from his belt. Scrambling in the mud, he found it by feel. Grit had crusted in the setting. Next he clutched for the cowrie talisman and Drouillard's lock of hair. It had lodged in a crease of his shirt. It was still clean and white. He gathered his few belongings and started to walk. Others were moving in a slow train, away from the river, and he joined the silent procession, pushing through the tough reeds, listening to the mud suck the balls of his feet, breaking its grip with every step. Which way was high ground? He could not see ahead. Daylight was increasing, but the stalks were high. When he looked back, he realized he could not see the line of shore behind him.

"Judge your direction by the fleeting of the clouds, *mon ami*."

Collins welcomed the sound of Drouillard's even bass. A poignant consciousness of the world around him was taking hold, a definition of gray on black. He felt cold and wet on his left. His right side, the east, was warmer. The reeds bent away from the rainy west wind like the *Annie* with her starboard list or prisoners under the lash. Collins wiped his eyes. His gun weighed heavier on his shoulder with every stride and his knife pulled hard at his belt. He was very tired.

"Pray for sun, *mon ami*, pray hard. There are trees and shelter ahead. See." Drouillard pointed.

The vision beckoned. Huge spruces with trunks wider than five men's width loomed. Collins bit down on his tongue to see if he were dreaming. It pinched. He tasted blood just as he stubbed a toe, hard, on a dry rock. He hadn't realized that he was walking on solid ground. The trees were real. Their roots had drained dry the land and the wind hummed through the needles.

The corps gathered slowly. They hunkered down, ghosts of their former selves. Collins took his place among his fellows seated on a fallen sapling. Sleep pursued him. He closed his eyes and opened them again only when he smelled smoke. Pryor had kept a coal in his firebox and placed it under a pile of dry needles. It was only the beginning of a fire, but it drew men like moths. The rain had ceased.

"Johnny, get up!" Drouillard urged, prodding him. "Come, gather fuel. Sit idle and you'll sicken. Move and you stay warm."

He rose and followed a short way into the forest. They scratched under deadfall, beneath branches where the canopy had kept the wood dry, finally stumbled back with an armload. Now men sat by newly started fires, laying out clothing and bedding to dry, and Pryor's small flame had grown to a steady blaze. Collins took a brand and started his own fire, sat, stripped his buckskin shirt, and propped it on sticks to dry. Nothing to do but wait and shiver as the trials of the last days pressed in. He slept, in spite of the cold and wet, sitting up.

He awakened suddenly. About him, voices droned.

"A day to dry and another to rest. It was a cruel passage."

"No crueler camp, even in the mountains."

A cry above the rest. "Sick man here, Labiche, breathing fluid and cold to touch! Help get him up!"

Labiche? Sick? Collins wrestled with the thought. He grabbed for his shirt. It had dried, but the water had sucked out the oil, and it was stiff and snug. Still, it had absorbed the fire's heat, and he pulled it on because it lay warmly upon his skin. Thoughts of Labiche nettled. Labiche shouldn't sicken, not now that he had earned the respect and admiration of the entire corps. Labiche had gambled with death and won. Collins ground his teeth, ripped the cowrie shell from his neck, and slammed it into the mud. "Luck you're supposed to bring. Where's your ocean? What kind of curse is this?" Alarmed by his own fury, he picked it up again, wiped it clean, and hid it in his pack.

"Make way . . . make space for him near the fire!" came a shout.

Collins looked up. Pryor and Shannon were heading toward him, carrying François Labiche like slaughtered meat in a rude hammock. Meriwether Lewis trotted closely behind. They lay the sick man at Collins's fire.

Labiche smiled up at him. "Johnny, find my knives. Bring them to me. Lay them at my side." He wheezed with every breath. He shivered uncontrollably and lapsed into unconsciousness or sleep — Collins didn't know which.

Lewis examined the sick man and rose silently. He conferred with Sergeant Pryor and pinched the bridge of his nose. "He's full of fluid. He should be bled. I'll get the instruments."

They built the fire higher and moved Labiche closer. He awakened briefly. His eyes pleaded as he whispered: "Johnny, the knives. Get them. Bring them to me here. Bring the espontoon."

Collins tromped back through the marsh. The waters had ebbed enough to reveal the earth beneath. It was matted with débris and a thick carpet of flattened reeds. Collins saw one knife stabbing the muck, point down, as if thrown. Carefully he inched toward it, feeling with his toes for a hidden blade. He found one more and drew it out. The espontoon was lying a few yards away in full view. Before going back, he cleaned them and honed them and carefully oiled the blades.

When he returned to Labiche, Drouillard was at the sick man's side.

"Did they bleed him?" Collins asked.

"He was asleep. I wouldn't let them wake him."

Secretly Collins was glad. He slumped down beside Drouillard.

"Give me the knives," Drouillard said, reaching out. He took them, placed them between two slabs of wood, and wrapped them in strips of hide. "This way he can roll on his mistress without coming to harm." He placed the packet at the sleeping man's right side. "The espontoon we will keep for him. It is too dangerous."

Labiche slept, and the day wore on. His breath came in gasps and wheezes. To hasten the hours, the captains gave permission for hunters to go out. Colter and the Fields brothers went. One-eyed Cruzatte, the worst marksman in the corps, assumed the sick watch, and Collins and Drouillard stayed by Labiche.

"Don't wear down your own power, Johnny," Drouillard advised. "Let him be, let his spirit decide . . ." He did not finish the sentence.

Tears dripped down Collins's cheek. He did not try to hide his pain. He licked his lips and tasted salt. "So close, so near the ocean . . . he said a ship will not be there. You think he gave up? You think he could not face the winter on these stormy shores?"

"I cannot fathom another man's soul. I cannot tell you what I do not know. He is alive and you . . . you invent shadows."

"I wish the sun were bright enough to show me a shadow. The mountains are higher. The river is wilder. The trees, the birds, the journey gets harder with each passing day. We think we have conquered the most treacherous obstacles, and another, worse, looms. What kind of terrible ocean waits for us?"

"Your shadows are in your own mind. You do not know, so you imagine. Labiche is tired. Come, be useful. Hunt." Drouillard handed him a rifle. "Perhaps we will find meat that will make him well."

Collins put a hand to his neck, searching for the cowrie. The thong and cowrie with Drouillard's twist of hair were not there. A panic began to rise.

"Remember, Johnny?" Drouillard smiled. "You placed it in your pack. When the reality is with us, we have no need of the symbol."

They walked without a sound on the soft mold of the forest floor. Collins' eyes pierced the spaces between the trees. He attuned his senses to any quiver of motion. He spotted the buck before Drouillard, the head and six-point rack as if carved in stone, just above the brush. Drouillard waved him forward. Collins took his time, checked his powder and flint to make sure they were dry, lifted the barrel, primed, sighted, and squeezed. It was a good shot. The buck leaped up and crashed down. He was the first red meat they had killed since they had left the Nez Percés. They hung the carcass by its feet from a pole and carried it back to

336

camp. There they butchered it and placed a haunch on the fire to roast. And they sang and laughed at the promised feast.

At the smell of the roasting meat, Indians arrived like flies. They came from downriver with otter pelts, dogs, and conical hats to trade. The hats were tightly woven and waterproof. Collins traded an elk bone for a hat to keep the rain from Labiche's face. But over the months too many Indians, pilfering and poking, had tried the men's patience, and now they held the natives at bay. Lewis and Clark declared the camp off limits and ordered the sergeants to post a heavy guard. The guards were not gentle. Gass slammed an Indian in the stomach with his rifle stock. Ordway fired warning shots while overseeing the boats. But the boats were not in danger, only their contents. The Indians let the heavy dugouts alone. Their own boats were shallow drafted, light and sleek, with bowsprits carved in the likenesses of fanciful animals, far more suited to the wild vagaries of the tidewater river than the expedition's heavy dugouts. Collins counted fifty-two of the strange craft on the beach, and Gass begged for gold enough to purchase one.

Delirious, Labiche tossed and talked incoherently. Sacagawea brought a poultice of sweet herbs to place upon his chest. Billy Warner brought food, but Labiche would not eat. Drouillard brought clear water. Labiche coughed it up. Collins summoned old Cruzatte to pray over him.

"And if you know a hymn, pluck it on your fiddle to ease his heart."

They went again to hunt when Drouillard said: "Where there is a buck, there is his mate." They ascended a high promontory where they could see far to the west. The dark forest was behind them. Before them was a great cavern of space. Black waves, their tops iced white with foam, crashed on a sandy shore hundreds of feet below. Their crests riddled the surface like small mountaintops.

The sun came out and Collins grinned, saying: "Another vision . . . is that why you bring me here?"

Drouillard shook his head. As they watched, the heavens turned to flame and the black waters reflected the crimson fire. Collins lifted a hand to shade his eyes. The blinding light seared his pupils and he blurted: "I can't see. There's no more land."

Drouillard repeated: "No more land. What you see is what we've come for, *mon ami*. You're looking at the Pacific Ocean. Pacific means peaceful. It's not peaceful. The ocean is on fire."

They stood, like the giant trees, bearing witness as a small white speck appeared on the horizon. Drouillard pointed it out. "A ship. Labiche was wrong. The waters are safe and ice-free even at this season."

Collins's heart leaped in his chest. "Rum, medicines, a ship's doctor." The words betrayed his hopes. But as they watched, the speck diminished. The vision faded into the glare, gradually disappearing on the blaze of horizon.

Before they returned, Collins stopped Drouillard. "What do we tell the captains? What do we say to Labiche?"

"Nothing. The ocean is the goal, not the ship. Let them take heart from the success of their mission. Let Labiche enjoy the accuracy of his prediction that there would be no ship."

"And the ship?"

"Did we see a ship, *mon ami?* Or was it a reflection of the sun upon the waters? Was it there, burned into our brains, because we desired it so?"

"It was no dream. I saw a ship."

"Who will believe us?" He looked back at the empty ocean. The sun was sinking, the fire dying. "We'll tell them we couldn't find game, that the hunting was poor."

Darkness was falling. Drouillard had to pull Collins away. They trudged wearily back to camp through the darkening forest. Glimmers of moonlight flickered through the heavy needles and defined the way.

When they arrived, they learned that Labiche had finally eaten. He was sleeping now as old Cruzatte still sat cross-legged by his pallet. He held his fiddle and drew his bow slowly across the strings. When Collins and Drouillard approached, he stopped strumming and stood up. "He likes the music. I prayed over him and forced him to drink, like you did the Indian woman. The fever broke. Captain didn't have to bleed him. Colter and Fields come in with three more deer, an' Lewie threw a feast like he was king and emperor. Saved some for you two." Cruzatte pursed his lips and blinked his good eye. He shuffled uncertainly from one foot to the other. "Don't know if he'd want me to tell you, but Charbonneau come with his little miss. He gave me this to buy him food." He raised and opened his palm. A single guinea glittered in the firelight.

"Give it back!" Collins ordered, resentment still surging through his veins.

Drouillard intervened, closing Cruzatte's fingers over the gold. "Do as he told you."

Collins turned on his heel and marched away.

Rain resumed during the night and in the morning, when the tide moved out, the expedition moved on with the river flowing swiftly to the sea. November was melting quickly away.

CHAPTER
TWENTY-SIX

More natives awaited around a wide point of land. Their village lay on the eastern side of the point, protected from the storms that surged off the ocean by a rocky cornice of land, and screened from the river by the layer of impenetrable mist and sheets of heavy rain. Sixty canoes, sleek and narrow, carved from trunks of giant trees rested above the high watermark on a sandy beach.

The natives were indifferent to the rain and undismayed by the wind. They had the same spreading faces, flat profiles, and wide-set eyes as their neighbors upriver. Chinook was the name of their tribe, and they pronounced the word with a *click* of tongue that the whites found impossible to repeat. The chief wore a cape of sea otter skins tied around his square shoulders. It was a beautiful garment, the sure mark of kingship. Drops of water skimmed from the soft hairs and kept the British officer's coat, that he wore underneath, completely dry.

The Chinooks brought roots and thick otter pelts to trade and fanned out across the beach when the expedition came ashore. Over two hundred men stood waiting. They were cordial, although not overtly friendly. They spoke a jargon interspersed with English and told of other white men with whom they'd traded only a short while ago. The news rekindled Lewis's hope of an ocean passage home while the furs excited the cupidity of men.

Labiche still suffered from the effects of illness, frequently dozed, and talked little. But his trader's sense roused when he eyed the pelts; his seaman's sense awakened when he spied the canoes. "Look at them, Johnny, fleeter than fish that swim the river, long enough for a dozen in crew. By the shape of their hulls, they will outrun us every time. If they come after us, we cannot escape on the water. And their furs are silkier than any I have seen anywhere."

"They're armed," Drouillard injected, having spotted the glint of metal despite the rain. "There's a sword and a musket."

The comment nipped enthusiasm.

"What good's a musket in this weather? They'll wait for rain to join battle and fight with knives and clubs."

"And fists and feet," Collins added, and shuddered at the thought. He watched the two captains jump out to meet the chief who stood in the center of the beach, surrounded by his guard of honor. John Ordway followed, and Charbonneau after.

"What's he doin' there?" Shannon questioned at sight of the Frenchman. "He can't speak the language." His indignation spread like a contagion.

"Charbonneau's a trader," Labiche answered. "He sees furs . . . he comes sniffin' for profit."

342

The silence that followed was tacit confirmation. Profit was exactly what motivated the Frenchman, what had always motivated him, from the day John Collins had first challenged him on the switchback trail above Fort Mandan, to the rocky shores of the Pacific Ocean. Same goose, same feathers. Charbonneau didn't molt with the change of seasons. His greed was a common human failing, one the captains had manipulated once, as they would again. Besides, other men were not immune to the temptation.

Labiche licked his lips, saying: "With such a cape as that chief wears, I could buy a wife like yours, Johnny. I would not trade it for ten horses."

"Sea otter . . . better fur than beaver," offered the Godfearing Cruzatte, wrapping his arms around his old body and rubbing the slick, wet leather of his shirt. "Keep us dry and warm, eh, Labiche?"

Charbonneau had lowered his bull's head, removed his pipe, and was whispering in Lewis's ear. Lewis cocked his head as if he had not heard correctly, glared at the Frenchman with astonishment, and repeated loudly for all to hear: "They're finer than any furs Mister Charbonneau has seen or known. They will be worth much in Saint Louis, more in New Orleans." He waited to let the implication settle, then hawked as if a fishbone blocked the passages of his throat, choking out: "He has offered his whole cache of gold for the lot. He promises to make us all wealthy men."

Everyone heard. Silence fell.

Meriwether Lewis did not anger often. But now purple rage crept from the nape of his neck to the peak of his brow. He balled a fist and spat. When he had controlled himself enough to resume, he blurted a string of vituperative French, then turned toward the corps and declared: "I have told him that if he were a soldier, I should have him whipped according to the Articles of War. I have told him we are not here to wade in filthy lucre." He inhaled to calm his mounting fury. "I have explained to him what the French word corps means . . . a body, a sum of parts. He has chosen to interpret it to suit himself. None should presume to place his goals above the welfare of every man here. He would cut off a leg, an arm, chop a head. Like the murderers of the French Terror, he would decapitate this corps." He turned his face away to remove the stubby Frenchman from his sight.

Clark glared at the self-righteous Frenchman. "You heard? You understood?"

Charbonneau bit down on his pipe, inhaled, and blew out smoke like a discharging cannon. "*Oui.* But that is what I know . . . trading. It is how I provide for my family. It is the future for my son." The words, the phrasing, were perfect English. The only thing that smacked French was the pronunciation. His little family was a convenient excuse. Everyone knew he had bedded other women in the villages, not to mention his other wives at Fort Mandan. But Charbonneau persisted: "I give you . . . how you say . . . a percentage. You write it down. I sign my name."

Clark's jaw dropped in blank disbelief. He turned his face away, glared out over the river, and declared: "Mister Charbonneau, we're not traders. We're searchers and discoverers. We came to map rivers and mountains, to measure the extent of the land, to note what tribes, what flora and fauna, inhabit her. We searched for a Northwest Passage. It does not exist. We have arrived on the Pacific Rim. Your schemes of riches have no countenance here. They are not only self-indulgent, they are dangerous, divisive, and obstructive. They have caused accidents and loss. They have alienated you from Mister Drouillard and every other member of this corps." He stopped, closed his eyes to control the anger that distorted the muscles of his face. "Your gold, Mister Charbonneau, has no place on this expedition. Your gold colors all your dealings with these other men. Captain Lewis and I carried it to Fort Mandan for payment to the rivermen who conducted us so expertly up the Missouri. To this day, I don't know if they ever received their pay. You acquired it, stowed it away, without our knowledge. Think, sir, for a moment of the condition of every man here. We are a lonely band on an alien shore. We possess only the clothes on our backs, no food, five boats that are inferior to any the natives produce, some guns, powder, and ball, and no hope of rescue. Your wife and child share our desperate state. So do you. Your gold is not yours to trade. At this moment it is keeping these kind Indians waiting. Your gold will buy food and shelter and curry favor with the natives. It will buy us survival." Clark narrowed his steely eyes, before continuing. "I cannot imagine that you expect to watch these men die while you sit and amass your riches. And I hope this altercation has not jeopardized our dealings with these gracious and patient people." He motioned to the waiting Indians. "They have been very accommodating."

Charbonneau's black beard twitched to conceal a bitter frown. He chewed the end of his pipe, having nothing to say.

Clark whirled and sounded the order: "Ordway, escort Mister Charbonneau back to the boats before I spit in his face. And tell Sergeant Gass to requisition all remaining guineas from the captain's lap desk . . . from Private Labiche . . . wherever you find them . . . and store them safely. We will dispense them by the vote of every man for the benefit, not of one, but of all."

Clark composed himself and turned back to the chief of the Chinook tribe. With postures and jargon, he made his friendly intentions known. But the Indians read the discord on the faces of the leaders. They were quick to sense vulnerability and seek advantage. They would not trade meat of any sort and only small quantities of fish. The price of their furs was exorbitant. The expedition could afford only inferior roots. The contact suffered from differences difficult to surmount. Language, custom, appearance were all to blame, as was the acquisitive nature of the natives themselves. In this they paralleled Toussaint Charbonneau.

Lewis still hoped for a ship and pushed the corps on through wind and rain to a bay where the weather cleared, although they remained in the Chinooks' land. On November 15th, the two captains gazed over the

346

waters. "The weather is warm, Will. The water has not frozen."

Clark shook his head. "Meri, daily you see your hopes dashed. The Chinooks saw sailors but we cannot in truth know when. Their sense of time's passage diverges from our own. Labiche says any ship that remains in these waters, if we can find it, will be scuttled or wrecked. No captain remains in untested waters for the winter."

But Lewis refused to give up the hope. "I must know for certain, Will. Let me take a party, witness for myself," he implored. "You wait here. Start preparations for winter. This is a protected bay, not a bad place."

He took the two Fields, Drouillard, Hall, McNeal, and Ordway and left the next morning.

For all who stayed behind, the first necessity was food. The second was fuel. Again the hunting was poor. Clark sent Labiche to buy food from the local Chinooks. He returned with four baskets of roots — no dog meat, no dried strips of fish, no fish powder. The Chinooks had out-smarted even wily François Labiche.

"I've been sick," Labiche apologized. "I've lost my touch." Still, his old sense of gamesmanship had revived and he was angry. "They're cheats. I hold up five fingers, they count four. I say meat. They bring root. They bluff. They lie. They anticipate my every maneuver."

The baskets he brought crawled with fleas. Clark untied one and pulled out a black tuber the width and length of a finger and exclaimed: "Fodder for animals!"

McNeal recognized the plant from his lone night in the Indian village. "It's thistle, sir. Has a sour taste that lingers disagreeably on the tongue, but they eat it and grow strong. Put the whole sack in the pot and boil it. The bugs will die and rise to the surface and you can skim them off, like cream. I saw them cook it that night."

Hunters went out, shot three deer, but they were blacktail, smaller than the whitetail of the plains and the meat was stringy.

It rained continuously. On Sunday, the 22nd of November, Lewis returned without sighting a ship. The corps came together for Sabbath prayers and implored the Christian God, the Indian creator, and the strange face of the god they had seen carved on the crags of the gorge, for sun. Wind and rain intensified. Breakers crashed, raced up the beach, and drove the corps from their camp inland to the forest. The earth shook. Men hovered under the spreading branches, then ran for the boats when lightning split the sky and the massive limbs cracked.

"We cannot stay here," Captain Clark asserted.

Only Lewis resisted. "The ship," he reminded, "we'll not find it if we leave."

He fell silent when Clark resumed: "Across the bay, Meri . . . it's time to go."

Lewis covered his face with his hands. His body shuddered and stilled. Finally he looked up. "When the storm abates, we'll cross. We'll search for a place to pass the winter."

★ ★ ★

For the second time, on November 25th, they retraced their steps, this time to a rock in the shape of a Roman obelisk. The men called it "the pillar" and made their camp beneath it. It rained all night, but, in the morning, the clouds lifted and the wind diminished. They crossed the wide estuary to the southern shore and fought their way upriver for two more days to a beach of colorful pebbles that they named William for their stalwart captain. Clatsop Indians, a lesser, gentler tribe, welcomed them. Deer abounded. But the country was thick with fallen timber and brush, and they moved again.

In December, they left the wide Columbia behind and chose a lonely backwater on the Netul River amid a grove of giant spruce and fir. There they hunted, felled trees, honed the logs, and quietly purchased help from the friendly Clatsops. Axes thumped and a fort rose in the forest. One piece at a time, they spent Charbonneau's gold.

Collins, Drouillard, Rube and Joe Fields, George Shannon, and Pierre Cruzatte — all who could — went out to hunt. John Colter burst into camp one evening with the haunches of a fat elk. "I butchered the rest of him, hung it high. There's a whole damn' herd of 'em, sixty animals, about eight miles south, enough to feed us all for months!"

Stores of meat increased, bellies filled, and spirits rose. By late December, the tidy fort was complete. The chimneys smoked and the roofs leaked. Christmas came and went. There were no loud celebrations, only a perfunctory exchange of crude home-made gifts, but

Cruzatte struck up the favorite "St. Anne's Reel", and they danced.

And it rained. The spreading branches of Sitka spruce, hemlock, and fir protected the little fort and provided the fuel that warmed the damp huts. The gold sweetened bargains and bought good will. It procured roots and fish and skins to replace rotted clothing.

Labiche explained it best. He held up his dice, stood before Sergeant Pryor's mess, skewed his ugly face into its familiar, asymmetrical grin, and extended his hands to quiet his comrades. "Lady luck smiles, my friends, when I roll the dice. She has smiled the width of this continent, and I trust she will see us safely home. When I return next year, when I am strong and healthy and we arrive at the fair city of Saint Louis . . ." — he stopped to laugh, and they all laughed; the city, Louisiana, the Missouri, the distant United States, and her Virginian president seemed a distant dream — ". . . and if they pay me for my years of strife and labor, I shall buy a kinder, softer whore than *Annie*. I shall make her my wife and rest my head on her soft bosom. No more wooden bunks and frozen ground. Enough of rain, river, and sea." He thumped his skinny breast with a hard fist, coughed, and placed an arm around the shoulders of Toussaint Charbonneau. "And Mister Charbonneau promises never to cheat a man in trade, never to sacrifice life, even my friend Johnny Collins's life, to his quest for riches." Charbonneau puffed on his pipe and blew out a cloud of smoke that wreathed his head.

Drouillard picked up on Labiche's chain of thought. "What're you going to do, pirate, buy a farm, buy a wife? Open a tavern, play your games, house a whore for every man here? Make us pay? You'll end up a richer man than Charbonneau, and we can all come in out of the rain."

Labiche rolled the dice between agile fingers and announced: "I won't make you pay, Georges Drouillard. Lady luck . . . she will make us all pay before this winter comes to an end, before we see home again, if we see home again. She has changed the heart of our friend, Toussaint. May she give us strength to laugh our way home."